Back from Dead

Inside the Subhas Bose Mystery

Back from Dead

Inside the Subhas Bose Mystery

Anuj Dhar
www.missionnetaji.org

Manas Publications
New Delhi - 110 002 (India)

MANAS PUBLICATIONS
(Publishers-Distributors-Importers-Exporters)
4402/5-A, Ansari Road (Opp. HDFC Bank)
Darya Ganj, New Delhi - 110 002 (India)
Phones: Off.: 011-23260783, 23265523,
Res.: 011-23842660
E-mail: manaspublications@gmail.com
manaspub6@gmail.com
www.manaspublications.in

2018

ISBN: 13 Digits - 978-81-7049-237-5
10 Digits - 81-7049-237-8
Rs. 495/-

Designed at
Manas Publications

Printed in India at
HS Offsets, Delhi
and published by Mrs Suman Lata for
Manas Publications, 4402/5-A,
Ansari Road (Opp HDFC Bank),
Darya Ganj, New Delhi - 110002 (INDIA)

Contents

Foreword to the Second Edition

Through 2004 I raced against time to write a book in a bid to clear up the mystery surrounding the fate of Subhas Chandra Bose. My comprehension was that the circumstances negated the official theory of Netaji's death, and I apprehended that our Government was keeping things under wraps. The report of Justice Mukherjee Commission of Inquiry was due, so I thought the book would be of some use when the chips are down.

Well, it's 2006 and the recently released report of the Commission has exposed the story of Netaji's death as a stratagem for his escape towards the Soviet Russia. The Government too has been exposed, what with the Commission indicting it for hushing up the matter and the Government brazenly rejecting its findings. So my charge in the book that the Government is a most unreliable player sticks even harder. After receiving the report of Justice MK Mukherjee, it should have followed the suit of the Swedes, whose dogged perseverance led to the extraction of facts about Raoul Wallenberg from the Soviets. But the Government's conduct has only underlined its unwillingness to seek a solution to the Netaji mystery for fear of political fallout.

Anyhow, the ball is in people's court now. They have to kick it in the right direction. This book, the end result of my journalistic inquiry, can provide the pointers. I am immensely satisfied that the findings of Mukherjee Commission are in agreement with the conclusions I reached in *Back from Dead: Inside the Subhas Bose Mystery*. Of course the book goes deeper and further into the uncharted territory which was out of bounds for the Commission.

Anuj Dhar

Acknowledgement

Mr Chen Shui-bian, the President of Republic of China; Mr Lin Ling-san, the Minister of Transport and Communication; Dr Ying-jeou Ma, the Mayor of Taipei — to them and the Government of ROC, I am indebted.

I express my gratitude to Her Majesty's Stationary Office, London, for their granting me the permission to make use of the documents held by the British Government. Dr Karl J Schmidt, Director of International Programmes and Associate Professor of History at South Dakota State University, Brookings, USA, was most considerate in allowing me to utilize information collected under "Project South Asia." The staff of National Archives in Delhi was pleasant. The National Archives (TNA), London, the National Archives of Australia (Melbourne and Canberra), US National Archives & Records Administration (NARA), Washington, DC, College Park MD, and the Office of Alexander Downer, the Minister for Foreign Affairs, Australia, were most helpful. I must mention a few names: Loreta Tabellione (National Archives of Australia, Melbourne), Dr Jill Geber (Archivist, India Office Records, the British Library, London), Jean M Callihan, (Cornell Law Library, New York), RE Cookson (NARA), Don Wycliff (Public Editor, *Chicago Tribune*) and James Zobel (Archivist, the MacArthur Memorial, Norfolk). Many thanks.

I acknowledgedly recall that I sourced much information from various newspapers and magazines including the *Hindu,*

Hindustan Times, The Times of India, Indian Express, Pioneer, Statesman, Telegraph, Amrita Bazar Patrika, Ananda Bazar Patrika, Hindustan Standard, Nagpur Times, Motherland, National Herald, Patriot, Northern India Patrika, The Nation, The Week, India Today, TIME, Mainstream, Swatantra Bharat, Ganga, Saptahik Sahara, Nai Duniya and *Amar Ujala*. And I rummaged through the books by Leonard Gordon, Samar Guha, Suresh Bose, Sitanshu Das, Satyanarayan Sinha, SA Ayer, AC Chatterji, Marshall Getz, Hugh Toye, Richard Aldrich, Larry Collins and Dominique Lapiere, Gurbaksh Singh Dhillon, Ranjeet Panchalay, Ashok Tandon, Subodh Markandeya, Mohammad Zaman Kiani, Shahnawaz Khan, Louis Allen, Tatsuo Hayashida, Rudolf Hartog, GD Khosla, HV Hodson, Penderel Moon, TN Kaul, SM Goswami, Harin Shah, VL Sundar Rao, Shivprasad Nag, Durlab Singh, CL Dutta and Lowell Thomas Jr.

I owe a big thank to Vir Sanghvi, Editorial Director *Hindustan Times*, whose passion for Netaji mystery was as inspiring as his words of appreciation. The CEO of *HindustanTimes.com*, Sanjay Trehan, and the Editor, Shailesh Shekhar, gave me the opportunity to get into the matter. I am grateful to you, sirs. To Shali Ittaman, the man who conceived the "Netaji probe" for *Hindustan Times*, I am beholden. Sitanshu Das, Bose's biographer, was supportive before and after our association at *Hindustan Times*.

I wouldn't have moved an inch if it wasn't for Dr Purabi Roy, VP Saini, Debabrata Biswas (MP), Dr Alokesh Bagchi, Bijan Ghosh (Advocate, Supreme Court), Ranjeet Panchalay, Rai Singh, Ashok Tandon, Sunil Krishna Gupta, Bijoy Nag, SK Datta (former Director, Central Bureau of Investigation) and my cousin Shunti. Netaji's niece Shiela Sengupta and nephews Pradip Bose and Subrata Bose (MP) helped me throughout. Then there were eminent people whose reflections made me go deeper: Late Anil Mukherjee (former Deputy Speaker of West Bengal Assembly), Subodh Markandeya, (Senior Advocate, Supreme Court), Barun Sengutpa (Editor, *Bartaman*), Pabitra Ghosh (senior editor, *Bartaman*), Inder Malhotra (former Editor, *The Times of India*), VN Datta

(Emeritus Professor of modern history), Ashoke Ghosh (General Secretary, All India Forward Bloc), Jayanta Roy (MP), Marshall Getz (Bose's biographer), Air Vice Marshal (Retd) Surenji Goyal, Major General (Retd) Ashok Mehta, Debasis Bagchi (former Inspector General of Police), Air Vice Marshal (Retd) Kuldeep Bakshi, Colonel AB Singh (INA), Captain D Dasan (INA), Ashok Sahay, Rudra Jyoti Bhattacharjee (Advocate, Calcutta High Court), Atul Rawat, Suresh Padhye, Sreelatha Menon, Santanu Banerjee, Prabha Jagannathan, Jaigopal Sharma, Tsunaaki Shidei (grandson of Lt General Tsunamasa Shidei) and Pradip Mathur.

I wish I could have a detailed talk with late Samar Guha. When I met him in his residence in Kolkata, Professor Guha was very sick. But luckily there were others who opened up with me: Srikant Sharma, Durga Prasad Pandey, Dr Priyabrat Banerjee, Dr RP Mishra, Dr BN Rai, Rajkumar, Ravindra Shukla, Dilip Kumar Mukherjee, Nandalal Chakravarty, Surojit Dasgupta, Dr Madhusudan Pal, Jagatjit Dasgupta, Kaushal Kishore, Ardhendu Sarkar, Gurubasant Singh, Shakti Singh, Vishwa Bandhav Tewari, Dr Indroneel Banerjee, Anupam Mishra, Padma Kant Sharma, Ramji Pandey and Mohammad Mobin.

I remember my colleagues at *Hindustan Times*: Rosy Mishra, Rupesh Kumar, Prakash Pillai, Vijay Soni, Sunil Rajguru, Abhimanyu Talukdar, Nadeem Ahmed, Archana Yadav, Vijaya Sharma, Rajiv Bagchi (Resident Editor *HT* Kolkata), Khalid Mohammad, Pradip Singh, Rahul Ahmad, Dilip Singh, Shantanu Bhattacharya, Sanjay Kumar, Sridhar Kumaraswami, Deshbandhu Singh, Vishal Thapar, Sanjay Sharma, Meenakshi Iyer, Sharmila Banerjee, Nivedita Mishra, Vantika Gupta, Navneeta, Pragya Joshi, Purwa Khandelwal, Kumud Mehta, Siddharth Ghosh, Saurabh Azad, Vinay Dixit, Gaurav Arora, Raja Biswas, Rajeev Kapoor, Sanjay Anchal, Ashish Arora, Vikas Handu, Girish Chadha, Vivek Rastogi, Rajesh Angara, Prashant Sethi and Chandan Nandy.

My parents and kin were with me throughout. Navni, Kaku, Neetu, Sonu, Sunny, Bunti, Manu, Shunti, uncles. Friends were source of encouragement. Raman Sikand, Parimal Nasa, Ravi Shankar, Vishwa Mohan, Monika Singh, Pramod Dubey.

This book wouldn't have been possible if my publisher, hadn't been so supportive and prompt.

Thank you all.

Anuj Dhar

Preface

The Subhas Bose mystery carries the sobriquet of being the most enduring controversy of modern India. Indians have not known any other case that is so emotive, persisting and politically volatile. It has overgrown in last 59 years despite several probes by foreigners and Indians. Right away, a Commission of Inquiry headed by a former judge of the Supreme Court of India is busy with unravelling the mystery.

In essence, there is a debate about what happened to Netaji Subhas Chandra Bose, one of the greatest Indians ever. Some people say he died, others say he disappeared. But what really happened? There are but three plausibilities: One, Netaji was killed in a plane crash in Taipei on 18 August 1945. This is the most commonly heard version and has much to go by it. There were witnesses to the crash and Bose's death. His ashes are enshrined in Tokyo's Renkoji temple. The most well-known INA veterans, researchers and Bose family members vouch for it. The Government of independent India said repeatedly it so happened. Two probes by the Government proved just this. If that be the case, why do people have doubts?

There is deep-rooted suspicion that Netaji actually escaped to the USSR. No, this version did not come up later on. The "escape" theory was born in 1945 itself and got a new lease of life in early 1990s. A section of INA veterans, researchers, bulk of the Bose family and members of various offshoots of Forward Bloc have all believed it. An "international blackmail " is read along with this line of thinking. Netaji, some say, was dispatched to a Siberian gulag. They believe Soviets kept him alive for some time to do business with independent India. Slowly India wriggled out of the Western influence and sided with the Soviet bloc during the Cold War.

The third option should strain anybody's credulity. It is a sort of wild card entry. Bose is believed to have surreptitiously slipped into India as hermit named Bhagwanji and never surfaced. This tale has been vehemently refuted by almost all the researchers, INA veterans and Bose kin. On gut feeling, one would go with them. Some detractors of the Bhagwanji theory level a most serious charge on the Government of India. It is alleged that to divert people's attention from Bose's incarceration, and possible elimination, in the USSR, the Intelligence Bureau under Prime Minister Jawaharlal Nehru, the protégé of Bose's rival Mohandas Gandhi, planted several holy men across the country, beginning with the infamous Shoulmari Baba. People either went gaga about these fake "Netajis" or scoffed at the very controversy. This also helped hushing up the Soviet connection altogether.

So what washes and what doesn't? What is this book going to tell you? Who is Anuj Dhar? Ah, I'm just a conscientious journalist. Around four years back, the online branch of *Hindustan Times,* one of India's top dailies, launched a probe into the Subhas Bose mystery. I was part of the team that rummaged through the evidence and rejected the crash theory. When the professional job ended, I started my personal quest.

My findings are same as those of *Hindustan Times.* There is a compelling body of evidence against the crash theory. Netaji Subhas Chandra Bose did not die on 18 August 1945. The ashes, parts of a skull to be precise, currently enshrined in Renkoji temple are not his. The Government of India, I have the mortification to allege, is the most unreliable party *vis-à-vis* the Bose mystery. They have stubbornly withheld information from the people of India. I will prove my point just now. The Prime Ministers of India have been visiting Renkoji temple with an ostentatious purpose of paying obeisance to "Netaji's ashes" kept there since 1945. The truth is, the alleged "ashes and other remains" of Bose were "received by the Minister of External Affairs from our Embassy in Tokyo" in 1954. I have a PMO paper from a hitherto "missing" file saying this. It is as simple as it gets. Prime Minister Nehru himself was the External Affairs Minister then. Those "ashes and other remains" should now be lying in some vault in the South Block.

If Netaji did not die in 1945 what happened to him? There are good reasons to believe that he made it to the USSR after his "death." Hold on, you would read about it all. As for the Bhagwanji legend, there's something in it for sure. The reasons for that are varied and startling: The whys and wherefores of several oddities which make up the Netaji mystery can only be explained by the information Bhagwanji has left behind. The commissions headed by late Justice GD Khosla and Justice MK Mukhejee came into being due to the efforts of Bhagwanji's followers. Their arguments first forced the Government to overturn their affirmed but misleading stand and then made the judiciary make up for the executive's wrongs. Left to them, the Government would have never formed any commission. Let's get it straight, our Government has been hostile towards Netaji and the INA. It began one day in 1947 when they refused to put up his portrait in Parliament House. They have zero credibility.

It is public knowledge that the Commission's work has been stonewalled by the Government. Justice Monoj Kumar Mukherjee has himself made statements to that effect on numerous occasions. Rather than being proactive in finding the truth, the Government is going about it in a manner to frustrate the efforts to bring it out. The Commission has been trying to explore the angles left out by two previous governmental probes. They want all relevant records; the Government won't oblige them. They want to go to Taiwan to make on the spot inquiry to find out whether or not a plane had actually crashed there on 18 August 1945. The Government has dillydallied and cited unreasonable pretexts. They want to go to Russia to examine a few Russians of standing, but the Government has done nothing. The Commission wants to get the Renkoji temple remains tested by DNA experts, but that is unlikely to happen.

The only breakthrough that has come about concerns the Bhagwanji twist, which Justice Mukherjee has been pursuing despite hollow protests by some Bose family members and media. Gut feelings, prejudices should have no place in any investigation. One has to go purely by the evidence. The Bhagwanji link to Bose mystery is a reality. The Commission has collected much oral and documentary evidence that connects Bhagwanji to Bose. But was he Netaji? To find that out, Justice Mukherjee had the English and Bangla handwritings of Bhagwanji examined by three experts. Two experts, employed with the Central and West Bengal Governments, said the writer was not Bose. But a private expert, the best in India and vouchsafed by *Hindustan Times,* differed. His report was far more credible than what the Government experts had churned out. During the examination, the Commission pointed out loopholes in the two experts' reports. The Central Government expert was served a show cause notice for his initial unwillingness to allow himself to be cross-examined before the Commission. He never answered that. Worse, his senior, who had supervised the testing, never appeared before the Commission. The State Government expert's report gave an impression that the principles of the scientific examination of questioned documents were given a go by in its preparation.

Some premature reading was done by a section of media, with the exception of The *Times of India,* in the report that a DNA test conducted on the teeth of Bhagwanji "disapproved" claims that he was Bose. One TV channel said that this "put a full stop on at least one of the so-called fabricated versions about his (Bose's) death." The channel perhaps did not know that its sister publication had in 1985 fanned the theory that Bhagwanji was Bose and had concluded, on the basis of evidence deduced from Bhagwanji angle, that Bose had not died in 1945. For argument's sake, if the Bhagwanji story was "fabricated," this media group must share the blame. Anyhow, there are cases of good and bad reporting. All I am doing is making a point. We should not jump to conclusion.

The inside story about the DNA report on Bhagwanji is as follows: Seven teeth presumed to be of Bhagwanji and blood samples drawn from some Bose kin underwent DNA profiling at two different Government-controlled labs. The first report was inconclusive for the test on "two teeth" could not "yield DNA suitable for complete analysis." " ... out of the nine loci used for fingerprinting analyses only three loci amplified the alleles." Why rest of the teeth were not used? Anyway, all that was yielded matched with the DNA of Netaji's family. The other report was conclusive. It saw no link whatsoever between the DNA profiles of Netaji kin and Bhagwanji. When Justice Mukherjee had told media about this report, he stated that the DNA findings "did not conclusively prove wrong" the Bhagwanji theory as the teeth allegedly found from his home "could not be confirmed to be his own." That is, some teeth were discovered in Bhagwanji's home. They were presumed to be his and that this presumption could have been right or wrong. Incidentally, the day the Commission discussed the DNA reports, they collected more evidence on Bhagwanji angle.

What happened thereafter would raise eyebrows. The DNA expert was questioned by the Commission over a media report hinting that there might have been a breach in the secrecy of the test. Some of the deponents expressed reservations about the correctness of the report. It was pointed out that the DNA testing was prone to inadvertent and deliberate fudging. Such cases were reported even in the United States. Moreover, as against the foreign labs which kept record of their error rate, their Indian counterparts were in the habit of not disclosing their mistake margins.

The deponents also called in question the enthusiasm of the same expert to carry out a DNA test on the Renkoji remains without paying much heed to scientific norms. Their point was somewhat boosted by the advice rendered by Terry Milton, world's leading DNA expert, to Justice Mukherjee. Milton, an American, opined that before ordering a DNA test, the Commission should ask for an anthropological test on the Renkoji remains to ascertain if those were of an east Indian man who had died aged 48 five decades ago. The idea of anthropological test never occurred to the Indian expert, even as a rumour did rounds that remains of some Bose kin were "planted" in Renkoji temple. When time came for him to appear before the Commission so that he could be cross examined over his "Bhagwanji report," the expert ducked. Not once, but twice, without providing any alibi, which enraged Justice Mukherjee. Insiders said that the Commission had also detected signs of tempering. The expert finally appeared, but only after the Commission had issued a warrant against him.

There is an urgent need to establish the identity of Bhagwanji. The Commission made attempts to get his fingerprints tested with those of Netaji, but the Government expert they had approached assumed strange silence. To ensure impartiality and ward off future criticism, all such scientific tests must also be carried out in independent labs in the United States or Great Britain. The Government of India must, apart from promptly making public all records related to Subhas Bose, reveal who Bhagwanji was and what were his antecedents. There were blippers on the scanner and inquiries were made. Time has come to settle the whole matter for once and all. Netaji's admirers across the world must be redeemed of the tortuous debate about his fate.

I guess this should be just about all you would like to know before pursuing the evidence spread out in the following chapters. They provide an insight into major incidents and issues relating to the Subhas Bose mystery.

Anuj Dhar

1

Game of Death

Subhas is not dead. He cannot die that way.

Mohandas Karamchand Gandhi in December 1945.

The question of Netaji Subhas Chandra Bose's death is, I think, settled beyond doubt.

Jawaharlal Nehru in Parliament in March 1952.

The Prime Minister (Nehru) is in the habit of prejudging issues.

Atal Bihari Vajpayee in Parliament in November 1963.

The flicker of smile on his face was never an index of his mind. For the past five years he had been living dangerously in his quest to rid India of the foreign rule. Adversity hovered over as he made way through Afghanistan, the Soviet Russia, Italy and Germany to South East Asia. He dodged it most of the time but when it stared him in face, he looked through it.

11 August 1945 ushered in for Subhas Chandra Bose, the Head of the Provisional Government of Free India (PGI), the endgame of his chequered life. Visitors began pouring in the sleepy guest house in Seremban, some 100 miles from Singapore. Tadamoto Negishi, a special envoy of Japanese Ambassador Tsubogami in Thailand, brought the VIP occupant a grave but expected news. Trying not the show his dismay, Negishi bowed to His Excellency Kana Kanta (Chandra Bose) and handed over

him a letter embellished with diplomatese. "Did they drop another atomic bomb?"[1] A frightening thought crossed Bose's mind. They hadn't. Nuking Hiroshima and Nagasaki was enough to yield the required shock and awe. "The Japanese Government had finally accepted the Potsdam Declaration on the condition that the sovereign power of the Emperor is to be kept intact."[2] Bose went through the letter without batting an eyelid and gave an assuring look to the panicky messenger. "The Emperor will issue an order for Japan to surrender. You cannot disobey his order .... Japan will be back on its feet some day. So, pull yourself together."[3]

Ominous darkness outside contrasted with Bose's serene oval face lit up by rays from a lamp. He sat in a sparsely furnished room in the wee hours. Facing him were SA Ayer, his publicity and propaganda minister, and two other visitors — the bewildered Dr MK Lakshmayya and Ganpathy. They too had the same news: Japanese surrender was a forgone conclusion. "So, that is that!"[4] Bose broke the chill. "Now, what next?"[5] He thought aloud, making no gesture. The bad news soon spread to Bose's other companions in the guest house. SC Alagappan, Abid Hasan, GR Nagar, Habibur Rahman marvelled at the smiling sang-froid of their leader. His grandiose plan to liberate India had finally withered. Things had gone out of control everywhere. The Japanese Imperial Army-Indian National Army (INA) alliance had been routed by General William Slim's Fourteenth Army with a little help from American B-29 bombers. The plan to launch a guerrilla battle had turned out to be stillborn. The sole ally, Japan, had capitulated and on 9 August the Soviet Russia, only prospective ally left, had opened front against Japan. The struggle was over and the enemy closing in.

Bose appeared to brood for a few seconds before he got up in a flash. He was now in the thinking mode: What was he going to do about those he had led in the war? Could he order them to go on fighting? Would that not mean leading them to mass slaughter? The option of surrender was sensible. The Indians at home would finally come to know of the INA's heroic war.

But how would the INA surrender? Alongside the Japanese or separately? It was a question of national pride. Bose had so far not let his hosts forget that he represented India. "Tell His Excellency that I have been in politics all my life and that I don't need any advice from any side!"[6] He had once sternly told a shocked Adam Von Trott so that he could interpret that to Adolf Hitler sitting bang in front. The Fuhrer had quipped that time was not ripe for Indian freedom struggle. Bose came to Japan with same demeanour, which made some Japanese think that he was too big for his boots. He made them understand that the generous Japanese help was in furtherance of their own national interest. It was self-respect that had made Bose quickly repay a part of what Germany had spent on him and his men. It was self-respect that had made him ensure that the INA remained an independent entity even though it was a dependency of the Japanese Army. It was self-respect that was now going to guide his action in this hour of defeat.

The phone rang at noon. Major General Mohammad Zaman Kiani was on line from Singapore. "Situation is deteriorating rapidly. Netaji and all of you must return," the message was stern. The Seremban sojourn was cut short. En route, Bose's mind kept going to 500 girls of the Rani Jhansi Brigade who had to be evacuated from Singapore before the arrival of British troops. In the evening he reached at his sea-side bungalow where pacing to and fro was Kiani. He was ready with a lowdown of what the Soviet attack on Japan meant. Bose tried to be attentive, but deep in his heart he cried for Japan — India's benefactor.

On the morning of 14 August Japan formally intimated Bose of the surrender to be announced the next day. A messenger from Hachiya Teruo, Minister-designate to PGI, came over with a detailed note. A meeting followed. Bose read out the note to Rahman, Ayer, Alaggapan, Nagar, Kiani and AN Sircar and invited their comments. There wasn't much to think and talk. Bose had his followers in mind and his followers him. Sircar proposed and others seconded that Bose should immediately leave Singapore. "The Allies are going to be very vindictive." "No,"

Bose mildly shook his head in disagreement. "The worst they can do is to put me against the wall and shoot me. I am prepared for it. The sacrifices made by Azad Hind Fauj and the civilians will not go in vain."[7] All fell in line. A surrender by the Fauj (INA) and its Supreme Commander in Singapore was agreed upon. Before the meeting broke, they cleared a golden handshake for the INA and Indian Independence League (IIL) men and women in the shape of three months' salary and ration. The countdown had began. Bose buzzed around keeping his ADC and INA's Deputy Chief of Staff, Lt Colonel Habibur Rahman, and IIL General Secretary, Dr MK Lakshmayya, on their toes. Captain Mrs Thevar, Commandant of Rani Jhansi Brigade in Singapore, was entrusted to carry out safe deportation of the girls.

By 15 August morning Bose, now depriving his body of sleep, had approved the final layout for a column to honour those who had died for India. He ordered his Anglo-Indian Aide Colonel CJ Stracey to raise the memorial for INA's dead in Singapore come what may. In the evening came the local Japanese commander's reaction to the INA surrender plan. He stated he was nobody to concur or disagree with it. All he could say was that Bose should go to Bangkok, where PGI headquarters then were, and confer with Minister Hachiya and Lt General Saburo Isoda, chief of Hikari Kikan — the Japanese military organization liaising with the PGI. The suggestion was understandable. Bose ordered his men to get ready for the Bangkok tour the next day. Since they were to return in two to three days, all of them travelled light. Rahman "carried a travelling bag and a suit case containing a consolidated statement on INA strength in Malaya (west Malaysia)."[8]

At 9.30am on 16 August they took off for Bangkok. The flight was jinxed. A pipe gushed petrol, drenching Bose and others. Eerie silence greeted them at the aerodrome. Allied strafing had wiped out the city's communication system and it was some time before they could move into the city. Travelling in a car, Bose, Rahman and Ayer picked up Major General JK Bhonsle, INA Chief of Staff, and headed to meet Hachiya,

Isoda and his deputy Colonel Kagawa in a bungalow. "They held a conference at which Hachiya spoke in English. They discussed the INA and Japanese surrender. Hachiya and Isoda informed Bose that no orders had been received from the Japanese Government regarding the INA surrender, and, therefore, they were not in a position to advise them on the proposal of a separate surrender by the INA."[9] Hachiya mooted that Bose should go to Saigon and contact the HQ of Field Marshal Count Terauchi Hisaichi. Terauchi, a relative of the Emperor of Japan, was the commander of the Japanese forces in entire South East Asia and had overlooked the INA operations. Bose approved of the idea. Terauchi was his friend and Hachiya and Isoda were sincere enough to offer that they would accompany him to Saigon.

On 17 August morning Bose boarded a plane to Saigon with Rahman, Colonel Pritam Singh, Ayer and Negishi. They were followed by another plane carrying Isoda, Hachiya, Colonel Gulzara Singh, Debnath Das and Hasan. The scene was not much different from Bangkok when the planes landed in Saigon around noon. Rumours were rife that Allied troops were about to begin hunting down pro-Japanese Indians. At the airport, Hachiya and Isoda confabulated with local commanders and reported to Bose that his flying to Terauchi's HQ in Dalat, a few hundred kilometers away, was risky. The surrender had resulted in much disorder so this trip was best avoidable. Isoda volunteered to do the needful and take up the matter with Terauchi and report back. These were no ordinary times. Bose had to simply agree once again. Isoda flew to Dalat, and Bose's car meandered through the deserted streets of Saigon to reach the house of IIL representative Narain Das.

Around thirty past twelve Bose's first deep slumber in days was interrupted. Isoda and Hachiya turned up in Das's house with a message from Colonel Muraji Yano, chief of the India Section in Terauchi's HQ. Bose took them to a room and sent for Rahman. The Japanese were still undecided on Bose's course of action. "Terauchi had received no orders from Tokyo in connection with the surrender of the INA and, therefore, he was not in a position to give any advice on the matter."[10] The wireless link was gone so the only option was to fly to Tokyo itself. This was feasible as the Japanese still effectively controlled the region. In a huff, Bose and Rahman emerged and darted to another room where Gulzara, Pritam, Hasan, Ayer, Debnath were summoned. Bose bolted the door from inside, and stood still with a reconciled look on his face. "Look here, there is a plane ready to take off in the next few minutes, and we have got to decide something important right now. The Japanese say there is only one seat to spare, and what we have got to decide now, in a few seconds, is whether I should go even if I have to go alone."[11]

It was a tough bargain. No one wanted that a head of state recognized by seven countries should embark on an air journey all alone to Tokyo after Japan had announced the surrender. "Why can't the Japanese spare at least one more seat?"[12] But where was the choice? "Sir, please for heaven's sake insist on the Japanese giving you one more seat and if still you cannot get it, then you had better take one seat and go."[13] That looked slightly better. Bose went back to the Japanese and returned in no time. "We are getting one more seat,"[14] he said, running his eyes on all six. He had already made up his mind. "Aap chalengey!"[15] "You will accompany me!" he ordered his loyal ADC. "Yes sir," Rahman replied. Bose told Ayer and Gulzara to come to the airport with their luggage in case more seats were made available. All then rushed to the airport. A plane was already on the taxi strip with its engines running. On board was top Japanese Army commander Lt General Tsunamasa Shidei, staff officer of Terauchi's HQ and would be Deputy Chief of Staff of Quantung Army. Shidei came out of the plane and greeted his Indian guest. Bose turned towards his men to say goodbye. There was some delay as his luggage, packed by Hasan himself, hadn't arrived as yet. In a few minutes a car was driven right to the rear of the plane. Some luggage was transferred into the plane. "Well, Jai Hind, I will meet you later."[16] Smile returned on Bose's face. His men saluted him. They would not know when they would see him again. He wore a khaki bush shirt, trousers and had his INA cap and badges on. He quickly entered the plane and Rahman followed him. The take-off was not smooth. The pilots had to run the entire runway before getting airborne. Bose's men stood transfixed, watching the plane disappear in the sky.

The Mitsubishi Ki-21 of the Japanese Third Air Force soared to a height of 14,000 ft with its dozen or so occupants. It was an obsolete bomber doubling as a transporter and had no seats or parachutes. All passengers squatted on the floor on cushions. In the cockpit were Pilot Warrant Officer Aoyagi and Associate Pilot Major Takizawa. Lt Colonel Tadeo Sakai, Lt Colonel Shiro Nonogaki, Major Taro Kono, Major Ihaho Takahashi were in the rear. Bose was invited to sit on the co-pilot's seat on the starboard side, but he found it cramped. Shidei took it up and Bose made himself comfortable behind the pilot. Rahman sat behind Bose, who was opposite to Shidei, and next to him a petrol tank protruded from the ceiling.

Around 7pm the plane landed in Tourane[17] on south Vietnamese coast. Bose and other officers checked in at the largest hotel in the town. While they rested, Takizawa and Kono jettisoned some unwanted machineguns, ammunition and surplus luggage from the overloaded bomber. It was a sunny day when the plane took off on the morning of 18 August. But hardly had Heito come in sight when the radio message came that the Russians were advancing rapidly. The Japanese got worried and decided to skip to the scheduled landing in this Formosan city. At 2pm the bomber landed at Matsuyama aerodrome in Taihoku, Formosa. The scenic city did not appear what it used to be, though the spectacular mountains Sz-shou, Mu-zhu and Bi-jia loomed all around, and Keelung river fed the lush environs beneath. The air was fresh, but the aerodrome was a picture of devastation after an Allied air assault only a month earlier. Control towers, hangers, offices — nothing was left intact. The skeleton ground staff looked depressed. Tall chimneys jutted into the sky far away and up close was the sole welcome sight of a grand tent. It had been "pitched at the aerodrome for the Japanese Prince Kanin, who was expected to pass through ... to convey the Emperor's orders for Japanese Armed Forces to surrender."[18] Rahman emerged shivering, wanting to change into warmer clothes. He held out a pullover but Bose declined. The visitors were invited for a light lunch laid out in the tent.

When they returned at 2.30pm, the plane had been refuelled and checked. "Major Kono reported that the starboard engine had been behaving oddly, and Major Takizawa carried out an engine test twice, to ensure that nothing was wrong."[19] All took their seats. The plane began to traverse the 890 meters long runway. "In the case of heavy bombers, normally the tail gets lifted half-way down the runway but in this case, the tail was not lifted off the ground until it had run approximately three-fourths down the runaway."[20] It wobbled as it took off and did not remain airborne for long. There was a terrific explosion and the plane swerved violently. The passengers inside heard an ear-splitting noise. Rahman thought some enemy anti-aircraft gun had got them. Captain Nakamura's heart came to his mouth. He was the Maintenance Officer at Matsuyama aerodrome. From the runaway, he saw parts of the ascending plane shot out. The propeller and port engine blew off and spiralled down. Plane nose-dived with a wailing sound. "Turn off the switches,"[21] Kono screamed. He tried to get up, but "could not get up because of the centrifugal force of the falling plane."[22] The pilots made desperate attempts but the time and space wouldn't allow any manoeuvers. Rahman covered his face with both hands. All baggage began to tumble down on him and from the windows the ground began to rush in.

The plane hit the ground on its belly with a thud at a velocity of 400 kmph. It screeched through for some 30 meters and was brought to a halt by pile of rubbles. The front of the plane ruptured and caught fire. "Nonogaki was in the gunner's seat, and was thrown to the ground, almost unhurt; he managed to escape behind a stone wall. Sakai, Takahashi and Arai were knocked unconscious by the impact, but came to very soon and sprinted out the plane."[23] Major Kono was lucky to have his wits about him. He was "almost in the middle of the plane, and when the crash came, a fuel tank landed between him and Bose."[24] He saw the gory sight of Pilot Takizawa's face pierced by the joystick and Aoyagi lying with his head downwards. General Shidei had been flung onto the starboard in front of him and was hit from behind by the fuel tank, fracturing his skull and bringing about instant death. Kono broke through the windscreen and jumped out. Bose and Rahman were trapped in the middle of the plane. From this time to all times, Rahman could recall the ensuing events in freeze-frames.

"I wonder now whether I did any thinking at that time. But I must have thought that the end was only a matter of seconds. And in less than a few seconds the plane crashed on its nose and then everything went black for a while. When I recovered consciousness after a few seconds I realised that all the luggage had crashed on top of me and a fire had started in front of me. So exit by the rear was blocked by the packages .... Netaji was injured in the head but he had struggled to his feet and was about to move in my direction to get away from the fire and to get out of the plane through the rear. But this was out of question. There was not an inch of passage through which we could get out. So I said to him 'Aage se nikaliye, Netaji'."[25]

Bose dashed to the front. The entrance door had been blocked. The only way out was through a three to four feet thick firewall. It was touch and go. Bose leapt through the flames.

"He sized up to the situation. Then he started to make way through the nose of the plane which was already smashed and burning ... with both hands he fought his way through the fire .... When the plane crashed, Netaji got a splash of petrol all over his cotton Khaki and it caught fire when he struggled through the nose of the plane."[26] "I followed him through the same flames. The moment I got out, I saw him about 10 yards ahead of me ...."[27]

The Japanese officers watched with horror. The man they had expected would free India was meeting a most horrendous end. Bose emerged from smoke wrapped in fire. He floundered, dashed and tried to take off his clothes. Colonel Nonogaki saw Rahman rushing to Bose and attempting to tear off his clothes with his bare hands. The tight clasp of the bush shirt wouldn't release. By the time Rahman managed to tear it off, it was too late. Bose collapsed, he was severely burnt and had a great gash on the left side of his head. "His face had been scorched by heat and his hair also caught fire and singed. The cut in his head was a long one, about 4" long. He was bleeding profusely. It was a straight cut. I tried to stop his bleeding with a handkerchief."[28] Exhausted and in pain, Rahman fell in a heap. The air reeked of gasoline and burnt metal. A Japanese sat moaning about 20 yards away. Rahman looked at himself. His hands had blistered. His right thigh had been badly cut. Bose groaned. Rahman had no time for himself. Bose was courage personified even in this terrifying situation. *"Aap ko ziada to nahin lagi"*[29] I hope you have not been badly hurt, he enquired from Rahman in Hindustani. Rahman said he was fine. "Has my skin gone?"[30] Rahman could see that Bose's skin had peeled off. He tried to pep up, "You will be all right." "I am done for, I think,"[31] Bose's voice cracked. "Oh! God will spare you. I am sure you will be all right!"[32] Rahman said. "'No,' I don't think so,"[33] Bose murmured.

"I said I am sure you will be alright and actually believed in that. I ... laid him down. We were in that position for about, I think, 15 to 20 minutes when a Japanese ambulance and a lorry with some Japanese nurses arrived there. I think the aircrash took place not more than 1 or 2 miles outside the airfield. It was a plain open land. I noticed a heap of stones near the place where the plane had crashed. The plane continued to burn. I did not see any village or habitation nearby. We were removed in a lorry. We lay on the floor of the lorry and rushed to the nearest hospital."[34]

This was Nanmon (South Gate) military hospital. It was a branch of the main hospital, which, for fear of air strikes, had been shifted away to the safety of the hills. The aerodrome staff had already sounded Nanmon hospital. At around 3pm the victims were rushed in. It was for all to see that the "big-built foreigner," was the most severely injured of the survivors. His whole body had turned ashen gray due to hideous burns. He was wearing only boots. He was in his senses, and could see, but had difficulty opening his swollen eyes. A colonel identified

"Chandra Bose" to medical officer in charge Captain Taneyoshi Yoshimi. "You are not to spare yourself. Give him the best treatment." The young doctor did precisely that.

"When he was laid on the bed, I personally cleaned his injuries with oils .... He was suffering from extensive burns over the whole of his body, though the most serious were those on his head. There was very little left on his head in the way of hair or other identification marks."[35] Bose was running high fever; his temperature was 39 centigrade. The pulse rate was 120 per minute. The heart too had suffered burns. "He will survive," Dr Yoshimi tried to assure Rahman. But he knew that all he could do was to try ease his patient's pain. Sulfonamide was injected to prevent infection. For his heart, Bose was administered four injections of vita-camphor and two injections of digitamine. "Since his body had lost fluids quickly upon being burnt, he was also given Ringer solution intravenously."[36] Yoshimi's colleague Dr Tsuruta Toyoshi applied white zinc ointment and bandaged Bose all over. Dr Yoshimi's problems kept on compounding. The third degree burns had made Bose's blood thick. Pressure on his heart kept on increasing. Yoshimi let out 200 cc of his blood and gave him a transfusion of 400 cc. Bose kept sinking and, oblivious to his injuries, Rahman remained by his side.

"I find it impossible to describe ... those six hours of mortal agony .... In all those six hours not even once did Netaji complain about the writhing pain that he must have been suffering. Except for brief spells Netaji was practically conscious throughout. In one of those delirious moments Netaji whispered the name of Hasan. I was sitting near him and I said '*Hassan yahan nahi hain, saab, main hoon, Habib*. (Hassan is not here sir, I am here, Habib)."[37] What Dr Yoshimi saw was not much different: "During the first hours he was semi-conscious, and practically normal, speaking quite a good deal. The first words I remember him speaking were in Japanese, when he made a request for water, which had to be fed to him through a hospital cup with a spout. As most of his speaking was in English, a request for an interpreter was made, and one was sent from the civil government office named Nakamura."[38]

Juichi Nakamura was stunned by Bose's composure even as the other survivors writhed and cried out in pain. Around 7-30pm Dr Tsuruta informed Dr Yoshimi that Bose's pulse was getting weaker. Yoshimi asked Nakamura to ask Bose "if he wanted to leave his last will and testament."[39] Nakamura dared not use the words but asked Bose what he could do for him. Bose said: "Some of my men are following me, and they should be taken care of."[40] Then he waved to Rahman. "Habib, my end is coming very soon. I have fought all my life for my country's freedom. I am dying for my country's freedom. Go and tell my countrymen to continue the fight for India's freedom. India will be free before long."[41] Bose began to slip into coma. Yoshimi futilely administered more stimulants. Slowly Bose's life ebbed away. "I feel blood is rushing to my head,"[42] he complained for the last time. "I want to sleep a little."[43] Around 9pm he began to snort and then quietly his head dropped on one side. Dr Yoshimi, Dr Tsuruta, Major Nagatomo, Colonel Rahman, interpreter Nakamura and some nurses witnessed the Indian leader's passing away. The Japanese saluted Bose. Rahman knelt by Bose's bed, and prayed for five or six minutes. Then he opened the window and, looking at the sky, prayed again. Everyone sobbed and left, leaving Rahman with the body. He did not sleep the entire night.

Early on the 19 August morning, a screen was put around Bose's body. As per Japanese customs, flowers and candles were placed by its side. Around 10am, Nakamura and an army officer came. Rahman requested that arrangements be made to preserve the body and transport it to Singapore. Dr Yoshimi injected a preservant into the body. Then it was wrapped and put in a coffin with cotton padding underneath. The coffin was nailed and laid on two stools in the same room. On the coffin Bose's name was written. Soon Japanese officers began to line up to pay their last respects. A photographer was called in. Rahman opened the lid of the coffin. The body was covered in a hospital gown. Rigor mortis had long set in. The chest was burnt black. The abdomen was bloated. The hands were burnt too and one finger was crushed. Swollen, the face was coated with white ointment. The upper lip had a rupture. Rahman could not look anymore. "No, not the face," he beseeched the photographer not to take the picture. "I do not want people to see Netaji like this!"

On 20 August morning a Japanese staff officer brought a message from the local commander. There was no chance of transporting Bose's body anywhere. The huge coffin was not going to fit in any of the available planes. Disappointed Rahman was reminded that he could see that in the warm weather of Formosa the body was fast decomposing. Rahman had to give his nod for the cremation in Taihoku. After some time, the coffin was put in a Japanese military lorry. Escorted by two lorries full of Japanese soldiers, Nagatomo, Nakamura, Rahman and the Japanese garrison commander, Bose's last journey began through the streets of Taihoku. There weren't many onlookers and no Indians at all. At the crematorium, which was about four miles away from the hospital, the coffin was removed from the lorry, the escort saluted it. The crematorium had two rows of about a dozen incinerators with metallic doors with bolts outside. The body was taken out of the coffin, laid on a sliding tray and pushed inside. The door of the incinerator was shut by a somber-looking priest holding incense sticks. He held out one to Rahman who somehow grabbed it in his bandaged hand. For about half an hour Rahman watched fire consuming his leader's body. He returned the next day with Nagatomo. The hood was opened and the sliding slate pulled out.

Nagatomo found that "the whole skeleton had still retained its shape, but it was completely burnt."[44] "According to the Buddhist custom, I first picked a bone from the throat with two chop-sticks and placed it in the box. Then I picked a bone from every portion of his body and placed it in the box. The Indian Adjutant (Rahman) did the same after me .... In this way, the whole of the box was filled up."[45] Rahman collected the ashes with his hands and saw a shining piece of gold, leftover of the filling in one of Bose's teeth. The ashes put into the box, the priest told Rahman that he was to carry them as per the Japanese customs. The box was wrapped up in a white cloth and hung from his neck. From the crematorium, the box was taken to

Nishi Honganji temple, where a special ceremony was held. Bose had set out for a journey to Tokyo, and now his ashes were to reach there. He kept the promise he had given to Rani Jhansi Regiment's Datin Janaki Athinappan in 1944. "Don't worry, the British will never take me, dead or alive."[46]

At home in India, Subhas Bose's death jolted everybody. His dare-devilry during the most volatile period of human history had caught everyone's imagination. His was the last story that the colonial British had wanted the Indians to know at that juncture. They used every trick up their sleeves to counter his rapidly-rising influence. George Orwell was employed by the *BBC* to counter Bose's pep talks from Berlin. Propaganda and censorship machinery worked overtime to undermine Bose and his actions. It worked in one respect that the Indian masses remained in dark about Bose's actual activities from 1941 to 1945. But there was no way to contain the exalted perception, at times imaginary, of the man. "At night, we mistook every star for one of Subhas Babu's planes,"[47] a charged up Congressman, expecting Netaji to do wonders, said. Indians had never thought on those lines. Bose had become symbol of the resistance Indians had not known since 1857. And just when they were expecting the man wronged by his Congress compatriots and Britishers to return home, he was declared dead. Shock, disbelief, negation trod on the heels of the death news. On 25 August 1945, which was a Saturday, *Hindustan Times* splashed the "REPORTED DEATH OF SUBHAS BOSE" relayed by Japan's Domei News Agency.

"The Japanese News Agency on Thursday announced the death of Mr Subhas Chandra Bose in a Japanese hospital from injuries received in an air crash, says a London report. The Japanese News Agency said: Mr Bose, head of the 'Provisional Government of Azad Hind' left Singapore on August 16 by air for Tokyo for talks with the Japanese Government. He was seriously injured when his plane crashed at Taihoku airfield at 14.00 hours on August 18. He was given treatment in a hospital in Japan, where he died at midnight."

And less than half way through the copy, the first smattering of doubts had sneaked in:

"The death of Mr Subhas Chandra Bose reported by the Japanese has — if true — relieved the British authorities of a difficult problem, but has undoubtedly caused new pain in the heart of millions of Indians, writes Preston Groer, Associated Press of America staff correspondent .... At the same time many (Indians) questioned whether the Japanese had co-operated in giving him an opportunity to 'go-underground' and escape punishment for opposing Allied forces."

"London Indians sceptical," reported the *Hindu*. "The death of Subhas Chandra Bose was a front-page news in the early editions of all the three London evening newspapers today. With its top of column report of the accident the *Evening Standard* published a photograph of Mr Bose and *Evening Star* recalled the chief incidents in Mr Bose's stormy career. The news was received with surprise and certain amount of scepticisim in the Indian quarters in London. Mr VK Krishna Menon, Secretary of the India League, said, 'We cannot comment on his death. Any expression of opinion is best sought in India.'"

Hindustan Times had another story. Of and for doubting Thomases.

"'BOSE DEAD' STORY NOT BELIEVED IN LONDON"

"Today's Japanese reports of the death of Subhas Chandra Bose are taken with a grain of salt in circles close to Far Eastern official quarters. It is pointed out that reports of a somewhat similar character were put out by the Japanese two years ago, after which Subhas Chandra Bose embarked upon one of the most active periods of his career. Opinion expressed is that the Japanese reports savour too much of imitation, that the timing is too good to be entirely fortuitous and that Subhas is probably seeking 'an easy way out with the intentions of not returning to India' .... The news was received with surprise and a certain amount of scepticism in Indian quarters in London. Mr Pulin B Seal, chairman of the Committee of Indian Congressmen, who was at one time secretary to Mr Bose, said: 'I await definite proof that Mr Bose is dead ....' Mr VVS Sastry, founder and former secretary of the Federation of Indian Associations in Great Britain, made a similar statement, adding 'The truth will be known after the Allied occupation of Japan.' ... The *Evening Star's* diarist writes: 'I expect the India Office will be most anxious to get official confirmation of the news ....'"

Elder brother and political associate Sarat Chandra Bose was devastated nonetheless. On 25 August, in a dingy cell of Coonoor jail he lamented: "Today's *Indian Express* and *Hindu* brought the heart-rending news of Subhas's death as the result of an aeroplane crash. Divine Mother, how many sacrifices have we to offer at your altar!"[48] Few days on, still in jail, he could not help but note that suddenly there were many takers for his brother's legacy. He was not comforted by the good words of Subhas's former colleagues who had "insulted him by their malevolence".[49] "Mahatma Gandhi and Jawaharlal Nehru ... found it easier to deal with him in death than in life."[50] Gandhi was still a captive of the past when he first reacted. "Subhas Bose has died well, he was undoubtedly a patriot though misguided."[51] Nehru said he was shocked. "I always had great regard for him in spite of our mutual differences .... I earnestly pray that the departed soul may rest in peace."[52] Then from nowhere doubts appeared. Gandhi and Madan Mohan Malviya went to the extent of telling Bose family in Calcutta to "not to perform *Sraddh* ceremony but to hold mild prayer." The family took their word. The mood of the city reflected in the proceedings of Calcutta Municipal Council. On 28 August 1945 the Mayor moved a resolution condoling Bose's death and asked all to stand up in silence. But the European members refused.

"Mr Methold, did you not stand up?" Mayor Debendranath Mukherjee inquired.

"We did not, because, after all, we do not believe that this gentleman is dead," JH Methold rejoined.

"Did you stand up, Mr Wise?"

"There is no point in this."

"I ask those who do not obey the Mayor's order to stand up, to go out at once without any argument or explanation," the Mayor was exasperated.

"Is this an example of European discipline and courtesy?" an Indian member asked.

All European members chose to leave and Wise stayed put. He had something to say: "You ask us to condole the death of someone who is not dead and that is why I say that this is not in order. If you order me to stand up, I shall certainly obey your order, but in the face of the fact that I do not believe in view of what has subsequently transpired that this gentleman is dead, I do not see why we should offer our condolences."

The Indians, at higher most level, were entertaining wishful thoughts. The All India Congress Committee held on 21 September 1945 its first general session after the Quit India Movement of 1942. When it came to making obituary references in the memory of the departed leaders, Congress president Abul Kalam Azad declined to name Subhas Bose. He was asked why. "The circumstances in which the news of the death of Bose has reached us and the sources responsible for announcement don't make certain that Bose is in fact dead. Therefore his name should not appear in the list of those who died since the last session of AICC."[53]

The South East Asia was surcharged. In October an INA man publicly aired his conviction. "We are his (Bose's) time-bomb, and will burst when the right time comes. Our leader will return to lead us." On 25 November, 3000 Indians gathered at a meeting in Rangoon. "(The) meeting was convened by one C Pani but he was soon ousted from the chair for having failed to open proceedings with suitable INA songs, those were then sung and the spirit of Bose was appointed chairman ... one speaker saluted empty chair before speaking."[54] In November a graphic account of Bose's death was released by a United Press of America scribe who claimed to have interviewed one of the Japanese survivors. The Chinese Central News Agency relayed from Taihoku on 23 November the "authentic story about Subhas Chandra Bose's death as told by Miss Chen pee Sha, a Formosan nurse in the Japanese military Hospital .... Miss Chen disclosed that the body was immediately cremated after death and his ashes could be found in the cemetery in the suburb of Taipeh (Taihoku)." But the overriding belief in the otherwise soon had the better of such stories.

"Shri Narayan, the war correspondent of the *Hindu* who is on a far-Eastern tour at present, reports, that reliable evidence to substantiate SC Bose's death in a plane crash is not available,"[55] said *Dainik Samachar* on 20 December 1945. A report emerging from Hong Kong said "that the plane in which he was travelling and which is alleged to have crashed was in fact seen in Hong Kong the next day."[56] HV Kamath, ex-ICS and Bose follower, told a crowd in Chinsurah in December that Bose was alive.

Gandhi went into overdrive as the months passed. "If someone shows me ashes even then I will not believe that Subhas is not alive," he told jailed associates of Bose on 30 December 1945. "I believe Subhas is still alive and bidding his time somewhere,"[57] Congress workers in Contai, Bengal were told on 2 January 1946. In an article published in *Harijan* on February 3, Gandhi spoke about Bose in present tense. "The hypnotism of INA has cast spell on us. Netaji's name is one to conjure with. His patriotism is second to none. His bravery shines through all his actions." In March 1946 he met INA heroes Shah Nawaz Khan and Prem Sehgal. "I still believe in my heart of hearts that Netaji Subhas Chandra Bose is still alive." On 30 March 1946, *Harijan* announced that "there was 'strong evidence to counteract the feeling' that Subhas Bose was dead." For once, Jawaharlal Nehru too felt the same. "I have received a number of reports, which have put me in great doubt and I disbelieve the authenticity of the news (of Bose's death)," he briefed media on 11 September 1945. All this had a rippling effect in India and abroad. In a boisterous meeting in Singapore on 23 January 1946, presided over by KPK Menon, a speaker shouted amid the cries of "Chalo Delhi" that Bose was "in hiding" and would "come to India as the free President of a free country." "The British are making frantic efforts ... but they will not find Netaji." Menon spoke as well: "Bose is alive; our great leader Mahatma Gandhi confirms this belief of ours."[58] Sarat Bose's views metamorphosed after he had undertaken a tour of Europe following his release. He briefed the United Press in Bombay on 22 July 1946: "I am led to believe that Netaji Subhas Chandra Bose is alive. The story of the plane crash connected with his death is a myth." He owed a part of his newly discovered information to Dr Lily Abegg of the Swiss journal *Weltwoch.* Abegg was in Japan at the time of crash and she found out that the Allies had thrown discredit on the Taihoku crash.

Meanwhile, on 7 September 1945, Colonel Rahman and Colonel Nonagaki arrived in Tokyo at the Imperial General Headquarters with the ashes. SA Ayer had reached there much earlier. The Japanese contacted S Ramamurti, president of Tokyo IIL. Ramamurti and Ayer took possession of the urn containing the ashes in the presence of Japanese military personnel. It was taken to Ramamurti's house and placed on a pedestal. Tokyo Boys, the INA cadets Bose often referred as his sons, were given the charge of keeping a vigil.[59] Ayer and Ramamurti met Rahman and heard first hand account of all that had happened after the flight from Saigon. By this time the American occupation of mainland Japan had begun. Rahman was expecting to be taken a prisoner so he handed over to Ramamurti a statement he had written on 24 August 1945 in Taihoku about the mishap. Then came the last rites. Ramamurti and others thought to have it in a modest way, so as to avoid unwanted attention by the occupation forces. The venue decided upon was Renkoji temple in Tokyo's Suginami ward. The ashes were placed in PGI minister AM Sahay's house for a day at the request of his wife. Sahay was missing. "*Netaji chale gaye.*"[60] Netaji has gone. Sahay's teenaged son saw a stream of visitors wailing and prostrating before the urn. In a room upstairs was housed Rahman with his hands bandaged and eyes stoic. He could not attend the funeral ceremony on 18 September. The Americans took him away for interrogation. The onus of performing Bose's last rites fell on Ramamurti and Ayer. In a modest procession, Tokyo cadet Virick carried the urn from Sahay's house followed by Indians and Japanese, including some army officers. In the post-surrender period, this was more than what the Japanese could do for their dead friend. In Renkoji temple, two miles way, the urn was put on an altar. A picture of Bose and wreaths were placed.

The temple priest Kyoei Mochizuki performed the ceremony befitting the stature of the man revered by millions.

This would have been the end, but the funeral itself sparked off a controversy among Indians in Japan. "Ashes don't prove who the dead man is; they might be anybody's."[61] A student told media that Bose was either "bumped off his plane by the Japanese on his air trip to Tokyo from Singapore when Singapore surrendered or that he disappeared on his own account to disclose himself after things settled down to normalcy."[62] "Doubts now began to grow in the minds of the Indians as to the truth of the whole story. Those doubts increased even more when one Indian, who discovered where Bose's 'ashes' were kept, asked when the 'funeral' would be held. He was told ... that all Indians would be informed in due course .... But as it happened, no one was informed and everyone was surprised to read in the paper a couple of days later that funeral rites for Mr Bose had been held in Tokyo two days before this Indian had inquired ... all this hush-hush and the evasiveness about the whole affair has certainly not done any thing to remove the doubts in the minds of the Indians in Japan that there is something fishy about it."[63]

On 18 November 1945 Rahman and Ayer left Tokyo in a US military plane and arrived in Delhi on 23. Rahman returned with one memento. Dr Yoshimi had removed Bose's watch after his death. The square watch was partially burnt and had stopped functioning at the time of impact at Matsuyama aerodrome. A sinister moment had been frozen in time. Rahman was to undergo the trauma of recalling over and again the ghastly manner in which Bose was burnt alive in Taihoku. From Gandhi to man on street, everyone queried him. All his frankness notwithstanding, Rahman could not convince some of Bose's die-hard followers.

At time the authorities too fell for rumours. On 2 September 1945, the CID sleuths laid a trap around Gandhi's Nature Care Clinic in Poona wanting to get "Subhas." They got his look-alike younger brother Sailesh instead. In mid-1946 Tibetan traders coming to Assam through Lohit Valley brought news that Bose was being looked for on the borders. A scribe's account of the tale was censored. The story still got leaked. The *National Herald* on 18 June 1946 ran "Hunt for Subhas along Indo-Burma border."

"A batch of experts belonging to the Scotland Yard intelligence service aided by a large number of Indian CID observers is keeping a day-and-night watch along the Indo-Burmese frontier to capture Netaji Subhas Chandra Bose .... The traders say that everyone crossing the frontier into India is subjected to heavy close interrogation by the search parties with a view to capturing Subhas Bose and frustrating his possible attempt to cross into India. It is said that the frantic hunt for Netaji is under the direct supervision of the officer belonging to the Home Department of the Government of India."

"There is no truth in the report," the Intelligence Bureau was to later rubbish the story while admitting that "the Assam Government did stop a wire from the API correspondent in Shillong on this subject."[64]

Forward Bloc denied in September 1946 that Bose was in India. Sardul Singh Caveesher, its president, however reaffirmed the belief that Subhas would return. October was time for Nehru to burst out. "I don't think there is the slightest justification for the belief that Shri Subhas Chandra Bose is alive,"[65] he angrily aired his dismay.

"For some months after the news of his death came, I was rather doubtful of its veracity. Later, when Col Habibur Rahman gave me a detailed eye-witness account of the accident which resulted in the death, I became convinced of it. No piece of news has come to me since then, or has appeared in the Press, that has shaken that conviction,"[66] he added.

31 October 1946. In the Council of States Ahmed Jaffer asked the Home Member (Minister) Vallabhbhai Patel if the Government of India had any evidence whether Bose was dead or alive.

"No," was Patel's cryptic reply.

Sardar Mangal Singh intervened and asked if the Interim Government had made any enquiry whether Subhas Bose was dead or alive.

"No," Patel said yet again. "Government are not in a position to make any authoritative statement on the subject," he added unhelpfully.

Mangal Singh would not let the Sardar go that easily: "A few days ago the Hon'ble Leader of the House (Jawaharlal Nehru) made a statement that Netaji Subhas Chandra Bose is dead. Is that the view of the Government of India or his personal view?"

"The Government of India have no view, either way," Patel yielded.

6 November 1946. Yuveraj Dutta Singh of the Forward Bloc asked in the Council of States: "Are the Government in possession of reliable information relating to the whereabouts of Srijut Netaji Subhas Chandra Bose, about whom conflicting reports are current?" He was given a reply the next day.

"Government are not in position to make an authoritative statement on the question."

Notes:

1 *Netaji Subhas Chandra Bose* by Tatsuo Hayashida. Page 161.

2 Ibid. Page 161.

3 Ibid. Page 161.

4 *Unto Him Witness* by SA Ayer. Page 52.

5 Ibid. Page 52.

6 *The Sign of the Tiger* by Rudolf Hartag. Page 28.

7 Habibur Rahman's statement to Shah Nawaz Committee dated 9 April 1956.

8 Combined Services Detailed Interrogation Centre (CSDIC) report on Habibur Rahman.

9 Ibid.

10 Ibid.

11 *Unto Him Witness* by SA Ayer. Page 68.

12 Ibid. Page 69.

13 Ibid. Page 69.

14 Ibid. Page 70.

15 Habibur Rahman's statement to Shah Nawaz Committee dated 9 April 1956.

16 *Unto Him Witness* by SA Ayer. Page 71.

17 Better known as Da Nang, an American base during the Vietnam war.

18 *Netaji Subhas Chandra Bose* by Tatsuo Hayashida. Page 108.

19 *The End of the War in Asia* by Louis Allen. Page 141.

20 *Netaji Subhas Chandra Bose* by Tatsuo Hayashida. Page 109.

21 Taro Kono's statement in Hayashida's book. Page 148.

22 Ibid. Page 148.

23 *The End of the War in Asia* by Louis Allen. Page 142.

24 Ibid. Page 142.

25 SA Ayer's 1951 report to the Prime Minister.

26 Ibid.

27 Habibur Rahman's statement to Shah Nawaz Committee dated 9 April 1956.

28 Ibid.

29 Ibid.

30 *The End of the War in Asia* by Louis Allen. Page 142.

31 Ibid.

32 Habibur Rahman's statement to Shah Nawaz Committee dated 9 April 1956.

33 Ibid.

34 Ibid.

35 Tenayoshi Yoshimi's statement to War Crimes Liaison Officer Hong Kong. WO 208/3812, The National Archives (PRO), London. A copy of the same report is in file 249/INA.

36 *Brothers Against Raj* by Leonard Gordon. Page 542.

37 Habibur Rahman's statement to Shah Nawaz Committee dated 9 April 1956.

38 Tenayoshi Yoshimi's statement to War Crimes Liaison Officer Hong Kong. WO 208/3812, The National Archives (PRO), London.

39 Nakamura's statement in Hayashida's book. Page 152.

40 Ibid. Page 152.

41 SA Ayer's 1951 report to the Prime Minister.

42 Nakamura's statement in Hayashida's book. Page 152.

43 Ibid.

44 Shah Nawaz Committee Report. Page 41.

45 Ibid.

46 *A Centenary History of the Indian National Congress.* Volume V. Page 602.

47 *Brothers Against Raj* by Leonard Gordon. Page 536.

48 *Brothers Against Raj* by Leonard Gordon. Page 544.

49 Ibid. Page 544.

50 Ibid. Page 551.

51 *The Collected Works of Mahatma Gandhi.* Vol LXXX. Page 161. Letter to Amrit Kaur on 24 August 1945.

52 JL Nehru's statement on Bose's death as quoted by Congressman Jagdish Kodesia before Khosla Commission in March 1971.

53 *Hindustan Standard* on 4 April 1956.

54 The National Archives (PRO), London. WO 208/804A. From SACSEA to BMA (A) SEAC. 10 December 1945.

55 No 11/INC/45. Office of the Dy Inspector General of Police, CIS, Bombay to Intelligence Bureau, Home Department. National Archives (Delhi).

56 *Hindustan Times story* **Netaji is not dead** on 24 March 1946.

57 *Hindustan Times* page 1 story **Gandhiji believes Subhas is alive.** 3 January 1946.

58 S Section, CSDIC (I) letter number ST/19/1008 dated 25 January 1946.

59 Input by 'Tokyo Boy' Captain D Dasan.

60 Input by Ashok Sahay, son of AM Sahay.

61 *Hindustan Times* story **Is Subhas Chandra Bose still alive?** 11 November 1945.

62 Ibid.

63 Ibid.

64 DIB. U/O No C-5-V dated 16 October 1946 signed by LP Biggie, Assistant Director. National Archives, Delhi.

65 *Hindustan Times* report **Nehru says Bose not alive.** 12 Ocobter 1946.

66 Ibid.

2

Vanishing Act

I am writing to you on the eve of a long journey by air and who knows an accident may not overtake me.

Subhas Bose's message to Indian Independence League's John Thivy on 17 August 1945.

You will understand our pressing anxiety to get to the truth of whether Bose is actually and permanently dead. Government wants to know where they stand over the matter, in view of the claims by Gandhi and others in India that he is still alive.

Intelligence Bureau report dated 19 February 1946.

... if it (the plane crash) is a deception plan it is one which has been extremely carefully and ingeniously organized ....

Observations in a British intelligence report dated 1 March 1946.

Throughout his life Subhas Bose remained an enigma for the British security sleuths. And in 'death', he gave them his best shot. Long before he became *Netaji*, Bose was reckoned by the British as one capable of causing trouble in a big way. They pushed him hard right from the time he plunged into the freedom struggle. When he was all of 30, Bose was put in a veritable cage in hideous Mandalay jail, usually reserved for hard-core nationalists, and branded as one of "the most dangerous men in India."[1]

The colonialists watched him grow and master intrigue, the very game of which they were the past masters. They shoved him into jail as often they could. There were times when he escaped death by a hairbreadth. He was exiled to Europe in 1930s for seven long years with the MI6 shadowing him. For a long time they did not allow him — a top Congress leader — to set foot in Great Britain, where he had studied. They banned his book *The Indian Struggle,* which had been praised by the British press. They treated him with harshness that no other Indian leader of his stature would ever know. Yet, all efforts to break Bose down backfired. He went on to become a *chevalier d'industrie,* an artful dodger who outsmarted the authorities many times. Prisoner Bose in Calcutta Jail managed to have a confidential file on him smuggled to his cell to find out the extent of the dope police had on him. He orchestrated in 1941 the greatest escape in modern Indian history. Right under the nose of his captors he vanished and it was not until he had crossed the Indian frontiers that the security services got the wind of his disappearance from Calcutta. Figuring out his whereabouts seemed impossible; it took months. People took him for dead, some said he had become an ascetic; and then one day in October 1941, his resonant voice came through unhindered via Berlin's Azad Hind Radio.

Bose's near and dear ones knew him as an arch secret service man. He could count several degrees of torture employed by the colonial authorities to make people talk.[2] He understood well the techniques of the interrogators and gave tips to his followers on how to stymie them. In Germany, he came up with an extensive plan to uproot the British Raj with the help of a corps of spies. "I am proposing the following plan. It will involve work in Europe, in Afghanistan, in the tribal area (independent zone) situated between Afghanistan and India, and last but not least, in India itself .... Our agents are already at work in this independent zone, which is situated between Afghanistan and India. Their activity would have to be coordinated and a plan drawn up for large-scale raids on British military bases .... Our agents and party members in the various Indian provinces will have to be instructed to hamper the activities of the British authorities in India as much as possible. They should work along the following lines .... Secret action among the Indian units of the Army, toward inducing the

Indian soldiers to engage in a military rebellion ... acts of sabotage against strategic railway lines, bridges, factories, etc."[3]

The grand plan Bose outlined before Reich Foreign Minister Joachim von Ribbentrop could not be translated into action. But when he organized his first free India army in Germany, Bose selected some motivated Indian expatriates for future plans. NG Swami led a group of five who were imparted the know-how of modern espionage by the Germans. "Bose was in constant touch with some underground political organisations in India who kept him informed on all the political developments in the country. 'Maj' Swami, a wireless engineer trained in Germany and Bose's private secretary, was considered to have been controlling this channel of communication."[4] Swami remained Bose's trusted companion and followed him in a submarine to South East Asia. Somewhere down the line, the INA secret service was formed with bases in Penang and Rangoon. Bose kept even his ministers in dark about INA secret service's cadre and their activities. He personally supervised his secret agents and some of them carried out for him the tasks that were the stuff of legends.

Surely, the British had the wherewithal to gauge the threat perception Bose offered. During the war they and their allies kept constant track of his moves.[5] They knew his psychological profile and could well anticipate what he would do when driven to the wall. The Japanese announcement on 15 August 1945 to surrender brought the situation to that pass. It was time to capture the big fish. Suddenly the Japanese announced that Bose had died in an air crash. Who would believe that? Viceroy Field Marshal Viscount Wavell's first reaction on 23 August to the Japanese announcement was that Bose had possibly slipped through the Allied dragnet: "I wonder if the Japanese announcement of Subhas Chandra Bose's death in an air-crash is true. I suspect it very much, it is just what should be given out if he meant to go underground. My first reaction when I heard it was to tell PSV (Private Secretary to the Viceroy) to ask SEAC (South-East Asia Command) to make most careful enquiries into the story as soon as they could."[6]

Supreme Allied Commander South East Asia (SACSEA) Admiral Louis Mountbatten had crushed the military challenge of Bose, and now it was up to get him, dead or alive. Lt Colonel JG Figgess, then on deputation with the Counter Intelligence Corps (CIC), General Headquarters, United States Armed Forces (USAF), was put on the job. But then, there were many more interested parties around.[7] They preferred to catch Bose alive rather than see him die and leave behind a formidable legacy. The Indian leader's activities across Asia and Europe had made many secret service agencies in the Allied bloc take keen interest in him. Though they hardly behaved like a monolithic, these agencies joined hands as they set out on the trails of Bose after the Japanese announced his death.

Leading the pack was Raj's watchdog No 1. The Intelligence Bureau (IB) at that time was responsible for surveillance in India and surrounding regions. Off went at least two teams to South East Asia within days of the crash news with the aim, as one member was to reveal, of arresting Bose if he was alive. Another member, Assistant Director M Johnston, died in a plane crash while on the job. The team which completed work comprised IB Deputy Director PES Finney and his assistants, WFW Davies, AK Roy and Kalipada Dey. They were also joined by top cop and IB man "Rai Bahadur" Bakshi Badrinath. A long-time favourite of Wavell, Badrinath was accredited in the intelligence circles as the man who had resolved the mystery of Bose's disappearance in 1941.[8]

Geography favoured Mountbatten's men. They scrambled first at the places where Bose was last seen. The first signs the SEAC sleuths saw on the ground seemed to back the Viceroy's instincts. On 14 September 1945, the Military Intelligence (MI) prepared a note assessing the intelligence gathered by the SEAC: "The Japanese report of Bose's death is also a matter of considerable importance not only in the political arena but also to those concerned with security: the continued existence of 'Netaji,' possibly underground, would undoubtedly maintain the fervour of many Jifs (Japanese Inspired Forces) military and civilian .... The report of Bose's death was received in most quarters in India with sympathy and regret ... but in Bengal scepticism widely persists .... It is generally believed that the news has been faked with Japanese connivance and that Bose has gone underground to re-appear at the correct psychological moment."[9]

The Intelligence Assault Unit (IAU) of the 7th Independent Division Allied Land Forces, Siam (ALFS) was the second to come in the picture. They started ransacking the INA and Japanese army offices in South East Asia looking for records on Bose's last moments and death. The records would have enabled them with background information against which they could interrogate Bose's Indian and Japanese confidants. But to their disappointment, in Bangkok and Singapore nothing had survived. All had been burnt down on Bose's orders on 17 August. Why would he do that? The suspicions began to spark. Bose's allies too had followed suit as if there was a method in the destruction. "The Germans at the German Embassy at Bangkok reported proudly to the arriving British that they had burnt their *Sonderakten* or special archive, including all their material on Bose."[10] The Japanese too had finished off every paper in Saigon on Bose's last moments.

All that the IAU could trace was a file in Bangkok in September. It contained classified telegrams exchanged by Field Marshal Terauchi's Southern Army Command in Saigon and Hikari Kikan in Bangkok, where Bose had come on 17 August. The subject was "T," the Japanese code for Chandra Bose.

"Today at 1700 hrs (17 Aug), 'T' with Lt-Gen Shidei and others left here for Tokyo via Formosa and Diren. Inform Indian community of this,"[11] the first one said. It was from Chief of Staff, Southern Army, to the Commanding Officer of Hikari Kikan Lieutenant General Saburo Isoda. The second was dated 20 August, and marked "Top Secret." "'T,' while on his way to the capital, as a result of an accident to his aircraft at Taihoku at 1400 hrs on the 18th, was seriously injured and died at midnight on the same date. His body has been flown to Tokyo by the Formosan Army. I have thanked the Formosan Army for their kindness. Further, I have asked that proof of his death in the plane accident — remains, photographs etc — be collected. As for the Centre (Tokyo), I am getting Staff Officer (Colonel) Tada, who leaves Saigon on the 20th to take up an appointment, to provide them with a detailed report. I wish secrecy be maintained in handling the matter."[12] And the third gram had come in just after the death news had been announced. Hikari Kikan had been asked on 24 August 1945 to tell Indians of the death of Bose. "Please ensure that Indian communities are informed of the Domei dispatch regarding T's death."[13]

On 24 September the translated texts of these grams were dispatched by Captain S Hyder. He had included his note of suspicion. How come this particular file survived the systematic destruction of documents? "These telegrams were found in the ordinary files in their proper place and numbered and docketed in the unusual manner. There was nothing suspicious about them and they did not appear to be interpolations."[14] The point was further worked upon under a major general's supervision in Saigon by the General Staff Intelligence (GSI). Hyder was right. On 18 October 1945 the HQ, ALFSEA (Allied Forces South East Asia) was told that "it seems interesting that the signal instructs the recipient (Hikari Kikan) to inform the Indian community of Bose's departure whereas the signal itself was SECRET. It may be that it was part of the plan to prepare the ground for eventuality releasing the news of Bose's death. It is not possible to check these signals at Terauchi's HQ as the records have been destroyed. The general impression (?) from these signals and other bits of information is that all records had been destroyed both at Saigon and Bangkok, except that in Bangkok a file containing these messages was recovered. It may be that this had been deliberately left there for the British and constituted part of the deception plan .... It is rather hard to say conclusively although all sources, both Japanese and Indians, are emphatic that Bose is dead .... A source has stated that after his retreat from Rangoon, Bose believed that he ought to start on a new road to Delhi."[15]

The IAU, in the meanwhile, concluded that the inquiries in Bangkok were not adding much to the brief announcement made by the Domei news agency. "Proofs, if any, might be in

Saigon,"[16] said a 25 September 1945 dispatch. By early October the IB sleuths arrived in Saigon to extract details. Davies found out that the "records of aircraft arrivals and departures have been destroyed"[17] and only the captured Japanese officers and local Indians could offer some information. "Captain Yoshida of the Japanese Air Force staff was interviewed on 5/10/45 in connection with the movements of SC Bose through Saigon during August. Interrogation of local Indians have only elicited the information that Bose arrived by air from Singapore on the 17th at 10.00 hrs and left the same day at 14.00 hrs. According to them, he met a number of Japanese officers at the house of Narain Das but that he did not disclose his intentions to anyone."[18]

Yoshida told Davies that "the aircraft used was a K21 Heavy bomber (Sally) and the final destination was Tokyo."[19] He also gave the list of the Japanese passengers who "had been waiting for transport to Tokyo, where they were proceeding on transfer."[20] With that Davies too hit the wall. The last point in his 7 October 1945 report was the "the ultimate confirmation will be available only in Formosa or beyond. It is not known whether the injured persons especially Habib-ur-Rehman have yet been traced."[21]

Colonel Rahman, the man in eye of the storm, had actually by then been rounded up by the Americans. The Counter Intelligence Corps grilled him on 29 September 1945 and on 8 October, Colonel Figges forwarded the report to the Commander-in-Chief India and the Director of Military Intelligence (DMI). "Rehman revealed that on 16th August 1945 he accompanied Bose on a proposed trip to Tokyo, Japan, to negotiate with the Japanese Government as to the disposition of the Indian National Army, but the plane in which they were riding crashed and Bose was killed .... Rehman stated that he was not rendered unconscious and noticed immediately after the crash that the interior of the plane broke into flames at the nose and tail. Due to the terrific crash the canopy overhead was broken and it was through this opening that those not too seriously injured or instantly killed escaped from the burning plane. He revealed that he had no knowledge of how Bose escaped or was removed from the plane. He stated that upon alighting from the plane he noticed his own coat afire. He removed it immediately and then saw Bose lying by the plane with his clothing afire, whereupon Rehman went to the aid of Bose and removed his burning clothing .... It was later determined that Bose received serious injuries about the head and neck in addition to his severe burns. According to Rehman, Bose recovered sufficiently to carry on a conversation and complained of the pain in his head and asked him to request that the medical authorities check his blood pressure .... "[22]

Figges himself did not feel very confident of the outcome of the interrogation. " ... unfortunately the evidence cannot be regarded as conclusive" he wrote, " ... since we have reason to believe that the Japanese Government also drew on Habibur Rehman for the information submitted to us."[23]

More reports coming in from Saigon and Bangkok began to muddy the waters. SACSEA Commission No 1 reported on 18 October 1945 from Saigon that "it is rather hard to say conclusively although all sources, both Japanese and Indians, are emphatic that Bose is dead. Besides, Bose took with him 4 iron boxes of gold — probably 50lb in weight — and while taking a farewell at Bangkok he indicated that he was not likely to return to that part of the world. All that suggests that he wanted to go underground and the Japanese had undertaken to give the necessary protection to do so."[24] Allied Land Forces South East Asia Weekly Intelligence Review No 57 for week ending 2 November 1945 specifically stated that "the above story (of Bose's death) cannot be taken as final until the photographs stated to have been taken at the spot, and the actual remains of Bose have been examined .... One source states Bose died in Japan, while others state he died in Formosa ...." The Intelligence Bureau rounded up Bose's personal assistant Major Bhaskaran Menon who told that "before leaving for aerodrome (in Bangkok) Mr Bose called the members of his personal staff and made some small presents to them. He was deeply moved and was in tears all the time ... four iron boxes containing golden ornaments were brought from Rangoon and these were taken along by Mr Bose when he left."[25]

The inputs in these reports did not gel with what the Japanese and Indians had so far been telling. Bose was reportedly going to Tokyo when he was killed. He was to work out the surrender and then to return to Singapore. So why would he carry 200 pounds of gold with him and take adieu of his staff in the manner described by Menon?

It was not until PES Finney's arrival that the mystery of the aim of Bose's last flight was uncovered. As Superintendent of Police in Bengal, Philip Finney had for long kept a tab on Bose. He did not take much time to fill in gaps even though more credible evidence emerged later. The IB/IAU report dated 5 October 1945 by him stated: "The general opinion among Indians here (in Bangkok) is that Bose is not dead but has probably managed to evade Japanese control and has made his way to some place occupied by the Russians .... At the time Bose arrived in Saigon, General Isoda was also there, and this fact may be significant if there was any plan on the part of the Hikari Kikan to allow Bose to escape, and to publish a false story regarding his death. This would have been the ideal place for Isoda to put into operation any such plan."[26]

Finney also came up with the strategic decision as to what was to be told to the people of India then. Bose's "death" had occurred two months earlier but a confirmation had eluded it so far. This was not only coming in way of the British government's unequivocal declaration that their enemy had actually died, but also fanning belief among Indians that their leader had "disappeared" like the case was in 1941. Finney suggested a way out. "Considerable time is being spent on these enquiries, and it is therefore requested that any conclusive information, one way or the other, should be circulated as soon as possible."[27] He also tried to spread it by word of mouth. IB official S Majumdar heard him speak on these lines in Bangkok. At the higher level, Finney's suggestion appeared to have found favour. A dead Bose would have helped lower Indians' morale that had gone sky high since the heroic fight of INA had become known. The British subtly allowed the circulation of information that Bose had after all died. And all the while for months on the inputs to the contrary kept on coming.

Finney remained in Bangkok for a while and barely month after he was able to demolish the myth the Japanese had build up regarding Bose's last flight. He backed it up with the testimony of Kinji Watanabe, an interpreter with the Hikari Kikan, who had attended a secret meeting between Bose, General Isoda and others. Within hours of Watanabe's interrogation, Finney, on 12 November 1945, promptly dispatched his report to Director of Intelligence Bureau, General Staff Intelligence Branch (Saigon) and Combined Intelligence Bureau, Malaya and other agencies.

"Watanabe was a civilian interpreter attached to the military branch of the Hikari Kikan. He was transferred from Hikari Kikan to the Embassy on or about 14 August. On or about 17 August he (Watanabe) was called to interpret a conversation between Lt Gen Isoda and Col Kagawa on the one hand and Subhas Chandra Bose, 'Major General' Bhonsle & 'Lt Col' Habibur Rehman. This took place at Gen Isoda's house.

"When Watanabe reached there, the conversation was almost over, and Isoda was speaking without any interpreter. They were discussing how to get Mr Bose to his destination. It was generally understood that he was to get to the Russians, probably to Manchuria.

"With regard to Bose's going to Russia, it was an understood thing in the Embassy and in the Hikari Kikan that he was going to hand himself up to the Russians in Manchuria. W(atanabe) does not know further details nor does he know whether he came to any terms with the Russians. Bose left with Isoda for Saigon on 17.8.45. The next day W(atanabe) heard the talk in the Embassy circles that one of the motors, or the propeller had fallen off the plane in which Bose and Colonel Habibur Rehman were leaving Taihoku airfield in Formosa. Bose died of his injuries along with a Japanese Lieut General. Habibur Rehman was injured. It was generally accepted amongst the Embassy staff that Bose had died, though W(atanabe) saw no papers on the subject."[28]

By late 1945 the scene had shifted to the Red Fort in Delhi. A composite investigation was conducted from here by the Indian arm of the Combined Services Detailed Intelligence Centre

(CSDIC), a worldwide Allied counter-intelligence organisation. CSDIC's Saigon Control Mission told Commanding Officer, Delhi, on 22 November that there was "still no proof of Bose's death though it is assumed."[29] In the backdrop of mounting suspicions, Colonel Rahman, now a prisoner, was subjected to gruelling interrogation for the entire month of December 1945. An Indian police officer was given charge. He also got to study several intelligence inputs. He and CSDIC India head Colonel Stevenson later sent a report to War Office in London stating that Rahman and Japanese had misled the Allies about Bose, who had not died on 18 August 1945.

A little later, in January 1946, a CSDIC report expressed valid surprise over the presence of all of Bose's top men during his last known movements.

"The choice of persons to accompany BOSE is however, we think, strange if HABIB'S story be accepted that BOSE was merely going to arrange a separate surrender. BOSE first calls CHATTERJI and (NG) SWAMI to his side: these two are held up and do not reach him. He then takes GULZARA and PRITAM - both KAMKAZI boys, - HASAN, who knows more about his activities (1941-1944) than any man alive, AYER, his main confidant and secretary on all TOP SECRET matters at any rate recently, DEBNATH, the man closest to him after AYER and with more experience of political underground than any. Our question is 'to what end this wealth of talent if BOSE was only going on a routine INA job which BHONSLE or (Mohammad Zaman) KIANI could have done just as well?'"[30]

On 19 February 1946, the Intelligence Bureau did a re-run on all the evidence on record and found that there were just about too many holes in the news given by the Japanese. IB Deputy Director W Mckwright commented in his report: "We have at last completed an examination of the information available here relating to the alleged death of Bose, and the result is not entirely satisfactory for it reveals many discrepancies which, until clarified, make any definite conclusion on this incident a little doubtful."[31]

"Regarding the crew and passengers of the plane in which Bose travelled, the list of passengers as indicated by Capt Habibur Rahman, seating arrangement ... does not agree with the list, given by Capt. YOSHIDA of the JAF staff forwarded by SACSEA Commission No 1 in a report dated 7 October 1945 .... Yoshida's account also does not agree with a figure of 9 quoted in the Japanese Government's first report on the incident.

"Confined in Appendix C is Southern Army signal No. 393 sent by ISODA from Saigon to the acting OC of the Hikari Kikan in Bangkok. Instructing him to inform the Indian community of Bose's departure for Tokyo. Can you say from your records that it was usual for the Indian community to be informed of Bose's movements in this manner and in the middle of his journey? Incidentally, why was ISODA's signal No of 24 August, asking certain authorities in Malaya and FIC to inform the Indian Communities of Bose's death, not sent to Burma and other parts of South East Asia? He certainly kept some of the Indian communities neatly in the picture regarding this last (?) journey of Bose's.

"The disposition of Bose's remains is obscure. The Japanese Government report referred to above states:

'Aug 20 Placed in Coffin

Aug 21 Cremation

Aug 23 Funeral at the Nishi Honganju Temple Taihoku

Sept 1 HR arrived in Tokyo'

Habib-ur-Rahman's dates are:

'Aug 20 Placed in sandalwood coffin

Aug 22 Cremation

Aug 23 Ashes placed in a wooden box and funeral

Sept 6 Arrived in Tokyo'

Relevant to this and also contained in Appendix 'C' is Southern Army Staff II Signal No 66 dated 20 August, 1945 of which we have another version. The version quoted in Appendix 'C' states:

his body has been flown to Tokyo by the Formosan army.'

The alternative version states:

' ... statements flown to Tokyo'

Our comment on the version No 1 is — how come Southern Army have beer so misinformed as to believe on 20 August that Bose's body had been flown to Tokyo assuming of course, that the Japanese Government's report is correct? If, however, the alternative version is the correct one, what 'statements' were these, which presumably were taken by Staff officer TADA .... You have probably seen the written and recorded statements of K Watanabe formerly of the Bangkok Branch of the Hikari Kikan, forwarded by Finney on 12 November, 1945. I consider that ISODA should be severely re-interrogated on the basis of these statements."

"The SACSEA Commission No 1 report dated 6 November 1945 states: 'It is beyond doubt that he (Bose) had plans to go underground together with a number of selected friends of his movement.' The earlier report from the Commission dated 18th October, 1945 suggested that the Japanese had undertaken to give Bose the necessary protection (to go underground). This may find confirmation through the interrogation of Chatterji and party who absconded to Hanoi .... Lt Gen SHIDEI ... is said by staff officers of the Japanese Army HQ Saigon, to have been travelling via Japan to Manchuria where he had been posted after the surrender. In view of reports Japanese Staff Officers of HQ Southern Army, the Embassy staff in Bangkok, and prominent Jifs that Bose himself was going to the Russians was this coincidence or intention?"

"I enclose a copy of Habibur Rahman's CSDIC report. We find this unsatisfactory. The multitude of discrepancies in account of the actual crash, as given first to CIC in Tokyo and later to CSDIC is being taken up with CSDIC here ...."[32]

The CSDIC too held similar views. Lt Colonel Anderson told General Staff Branch (MI Directorate) in February 1946 that "an examination of all information available here relating to

Bose's death reveals discrepancies in the various accounts."[33] Another dispatch dated 28 February 1946 laid to rest the doubts about Rahman's Tokyo theory. "It has been previously been accepted that for various reasons connected with their recent separations from BOSE, none of the members of this party interrogated by S Section knew what BOSE's aim was. H1459 (AM Sahay), however, says that when (Abid Hasan, Gulzara Singh and Pritam Singh) reached HANOI they told him that BOSE was bound for MANCHURIA. None of them will, even now, admit this knowledge. At all events the story told by HABIB UR REHMAN (B1269) in CSDIC 2 Sec Report 1156 that BOSE was merely going to arrange a separate surrender for the INA and that he would have returned to SINGAPORE, may be categorically rejected, and it may be accepted that B1269 (Rahman) himself probably knows the truth."[34]

The Intelligence Division of SACSEA on 1 March 1946 gave vent to their gut feeling about the crash story: "In conclusion it can be said definitely that Bose left Saigon and probably that there was plane crash at the take-off in Taihoku. It is possible that Bose escaped from the crash unhurt and either hid in Formosa on his own initiative or was hidden by local authorities who took ad hoc decision."[35]

At the instance of Bakshi Badrinath, who was diverted from Bose probe to Royal Indian Navy (RIN) mutiny investigations, Major General Bhonsle was re-interrogated in March 1946. In his earlier interrogation the INA Chief of Staff had misdirected the CSDIC, saying that Bose had "left for Tokyo" on 17 August. In the light of interpreter Watanabe's confessions, now it was impossible for him to hide the truth. "Maj JK Bhonsle (B1189) has been re-interrogated at HQ Jumna area regarding the meeting in Bangkok. B1189 as anticipated, was not anxious to provide further information .... B1189 confirms that the meeting with at Bangkok on about 17 August 45 between Lt Gen ISODA and Col KAGAWA on the one hand SC Bose, 'Maj Gen' Bhonsle and 'Lt Col.' Habib-ur-Rehman on the other, was to discuss how to get Bose to his destination. B1189 also confirms that it was Bose's intention to try to find his way into Russia .... B1189 gave the impression that he — and some others — had some idea of Bose's plans in Russia, but refused to commit himself. He evaded all questions relevant to this subject, merely saying that 'if Bose's exact plans were known by his trusted henchmen, none of the later would ever reveal them now.'"[36] The Intelligence Bureau was further told in April 1946 that "it seems clear that Bose and his staff were trying to make a get away to Russia" and that "Habibur Rehman, Pritam Singh, Gulzara Singh and (Abid) Hasan ... have lied, or withheld their knowledge."[37]

The CSDIC continued to investigate into Bose's death until June 1946 and possibly weren't finished even then. Their last (known) report showed that Habibur Rahman was lying and still being evasive and as such the results were "far from satisfactory."[38]

The US intelligence too made some inquiries about the death of Bose. The Office of Strategic Services (OSS), the forerunner of the CIA, had been keeping a watch on Bose since 1941, apart from running small offices in Delhi's Firozshah Road and Tollygonge in Calcutta. The OSS[39] recorded on 24 January 1946 that "'a good proportion of Indians and British believe that he (Bose) is alive and hiding in some place,' and characterised the story of his death in an air-crash 'as untrue and made up by the Japanese'."[40] At the close of the war, the Americans were much better positioned than the British — even in this respect. During the war, they intercepted and decoded most secret Japanese messages. "Ten days after his death, US intelligence noted a dispatch from a Japanese mission in Saigon ... on the 17th, at his own request, Bose set off by air for the – [place name uncertain, probably 'Manchukuo']."[41] Manchukuo was Japanese for Manchuria. So the Japanese did lie for Bose. He wasn't heading to Tokyo. Another intercept read that the "the Japanese embassy in Bangkok suggested that Tokyo avoid 'suspicions among the enemy' by not releasing any information regarding Bose's fatal accident."[42]

General Douglas MacArthur's forces marched into Formosa in early September 1945. The OSS already had an agent in Taihoku. Mainland Japan was soon after occupied by the

Americans, and they had laid hands on all personnel and documents of Japan. Colonel Habibur Rahman was arrested and interrogated by them before being handed over to the British. In May 1946 American Consulate General in Bombay, Howard Donovan, was drawn into the vexed issue of Bose's death by Lt Colonel Hannessy, the area chief of British Military Intelligence (MI).[43] Hannessy requested Donovan to find out if he could "ascertain (from his government) whether American Intelligence substantiated the fact that Bose actually died following the plane crash at Taihoku on August 18, 1945." Hannessy told Donovan that "the hold which Bose had over the Indian imagination was tremendous and that if he should return to this country trouble would result which ... would be extremely difficult to quell ..."

"I personally am not sufficiently familiar with events in Formosa in 1945 to know whether British or American agents did in fact make any inquiries regarding Bose's death," Donovan noted. On May 23 he wrote that "if the (State) Department could furnish any information on this subject (Bose's death), it would be most helpful ... positive proof of some kind that Bose is dead would be most interesting."[44] The State Department forwarded the letter to the Pentagon. In June 1946 the State Department reverted to the Consulate: "War, Military Intelligence Services, advises under date of June 20, 1946 that Subhas Chandra Bose was killed in a airplane crash at Taihoko (sic), Formosa, despite the public statements of the Japanese to that effect."[45]

Admiral Louis Mountbatten was not so much straightforward 30 years hence. In 1978, the then Indian High Commissioner in UK, NG Goray, implored the first Governor-General of India to tell the truth about Subhas Bose's death. "As you took over from Lord Wavell it will not be wrong to presume that you must have come to know every detail about the incident. Will it be possible for you to shed some authentic light on the Subhas episode, so that we at this late hour at least shall know what happened to that intrepid, great and beloved leader of ours?" Goray wrote, and packed the punch:

"You would say: 'Why rake up the past?' My answer would be: Because there is a deep suspicion in India that Sri Bose took asylum in the USSR and all this was known to you, to Nehru, and the Soviet Government. But all of you preferred to observe silence, an intriguing silence, I would say, because the British did not want to pick up a quarrel with their erstwhile ally and Nehru did not want to have a rival."

Lord Mountbatten replied on 10 March 1978 that "there was no official record of Subhas Chandra Bose's death in his archives."[46] That is, he could not vouch for Bose's reported death even after so many years.

Any record of Subhas Bose's death couldn't have been in the treasure trove of the man who undoubtedly knew better than anyone else about India of that period. Even the British Government did not seem to have credible record of Bose's death. For if there had been any, they would have long ago officially announced their *bête noire's* death. The record was not there because the evidence was sketchy: Bose's body was never found. The pictures taken by the Japanese did not show his face and those showing the plane wreck were doubtful. The only worthwhile evidences were the testimonies of Rahman and the Japanese. What price their words were when they had hoodwinked the Allies from the start? The British intelligence network groped for answers about Bose's whereabouts. A note was prepared on 8 April 1946 for a meeting to be chaired by one Wagstaffe and Intelligence Bureau's PES Finney. On agenda was discussion on intelligence gathered from India and abroad. Doubts had been cast at the outcome of Allied inquires made in Taihoku, Russian sources had emphatically disclosed that Bose was in Russia and, most curiously, attention had been drawn to what India's top leaders were up to.

"Gandhi stated publicly at the beginning of January that he believed that Bose was alive and in hiding. He has not offered any satisfactory reason for the belief he says he possesses, ascribing it to an inner voice. Congress circles have elaborated in some cases. Some reports declare that Congressmen believe that Gandhi's inner voice is secret information which he has received.

"We have nothing in the way of intelligence which helps directly to disclose the grounds Gandhi has for saying what he did or the reasons why he did so. There is, however, a secret report which says that Nehru received a letter from Bose saying he was in Russia and that he wanted to escape to India. He would come via Chitral, where one of Sarat Bose's son should meet him."[47]

The outcome of Finney-Wagstaffe meeting remained unknown. But on 2 May 1946, nine long months after the death story had been circulated, the Indian Political Intelligence (IPI) sent the India Office a most interesting dispatch: "The D.I.B. (Director of Intelligence Bureau) during his recent visit to London mentioned the receipt from various places in India of information to the effect that Subhas Bose was alive in Russia."[48]

Notes:

1 *The Indian Struggle* by Subhas Chandra Bose. Page 147.

2 Input by Bose's niece Shiela Sengupta.

3 Memorandum by Subhas Bose. No 300 195/139137-43. From US Department of State. Documents on German Foreign Policy. Series D. Volume XII. A number of documents concerning Bose from this series were published under Project South Asia, a joint project of the Office of the International Programs at South Dakota State University and the Institute of International Studies at Missouri Southern State University, USA.

4 File No 249/INA. Page 5.

5 The National Archives of Australia, Melbourne, were generous enough to present the writer a declassified dossier comprising items of communication intelligence on Subhas Bose. Dated 18 September 1945, it had been prepared by a Royal Australian Navy Commander.

6 *Wavell: The Viceroy's Journal* edited by Penderel Moon. Page 164. On 21 September 1945, Wavell noted: "According to the Japs at Saigon, SC Bose definitely is dead, but I shall be sceptical till further confirmation." Ibid. Page 174.

7 In *Intelligence and the War Against Japan*, Richard J Aldrich, an authority on wartime espionage, refers to Lt Col Arthur Trevor-Wilson, who headed an MI6 counter intelligence section. Trevor-Wilson had many of Bose's ministers arrested in Vietnam after the war and 'was looking for Chandra Bose.' Page 349.

8 Input by Air Vice Marshal (Retd) Kuldeep Bakshi, son of Bakshi Badrinath.

9 No 10005/3/GSI (b). The British Library. Oriental and India Office Collections. London.

10 *Intelligence and the War Against Japan* by Richard J Aldrich. Page 458.

11 South East Asia Translation and Interrogation Centre (SEATIC) Document No128. Signals No 4,5 and 6.

12 Ibid.

13 Ibid.

14 Ibid.

15 No 63/2/10/GSI (b). HQ SACSEA Commission No 1, Saigon.

16 Interrogation report on Major Takayashi Kiyoji of the Hikari Kikan. SEATIC/IAU.

17 Subhas Chandra Bose Saigon Enquiry report by WFW Davies.

18 Ibid.

19 Ibid.

20 Ibid.

21 Ibid.

22 Report by Counter Intelligence Corps, GHQ, on Bose's death.

23 General Headquarters, United States Armed Forces, Pacific. Report CZ/49 dated 8 October 1945.

24 No. 63/2/10/GSI (b), HQ, SACSEA Commission No 1, Saigon.

25 Statement of Bhaskar Menon Basi received with AD(X)'s memorandum No DIB/P 19. 23 October 1945.

26 PES Finney's report. He was with 7 Division in Bangkok.

27 Ibid.

28 PES Finney's report dated 12 November 1945.

29 UB/DO/4. Saigon Control Mission. SEAC to OC, CSDIC.

30 ST/12, S Section CSDIC (I), SEAC, 15 January 1946.

31 No C-5, Intelligence Bureau. National Archives, Delhi.

32 Ibid.

33 MI Directorate report.

34 ST/12/104. S Section, CSDIC (I)

35 From Top Secret Letter No SLO/CC/1 dated 1 March 1946.

36 No 1300/SE, CSDIC, Red Fort, Delhi.

37 INA File No 273. Document C-4, Part-IV. National Archives, Delhi.

38 From File No INA/249.

39 Officially, the OSS was wrapped up in October 1945. But that doesn't mean the US did not have any intelligence network from this time to 1947 when the CIA was formed.

40 From the paper *Darkness at Dawn* by Bose biographer Subodh Markandeya, whom the writer interviewed.

41 *Subhas Chandra Bose: A Biography* by Marshall J Getz. Page 110. Getz sourced this information from United States War Department, Office of the Assistant Chief of Staff, G-2, MAGIC Diplomatic Summary No 1250, SRS 1772, August 27, 1945. The writer also interviewed Getz for *HindustanTimes.com*.

42 Ibid.

43 Friends of India Society International, California, obtained a dossier of heavily censored declassified US documents on Bose and forwarded it to Indian newspapers in 1994. Apart from RSS mouthpiece *Organiser*, perhaps none made use of them at that time. In January 2005, Mukherjee Commission obtained the copies of some of these documents in their uncensored form from NARA. The writer received this particular set soon after the publication of the book. The current edition, as a result, gives revised information about the identity of Donovan.

44 Confidential Airgram number 274, from American Consulate General Bombay to Secretary of State, 23 May 1946.

45 Airgram A-78 dated 28 June 1946. Copy received by Mukherjee Commission in January 2005 (See note 43).

46 From booklet *Country Must Know What Happened to Netaji* by Samar Guha. Page 9.

47 File No 273/INA. Document C-4, Part IV. National Archives, Delhi.

48 IPI series. Document No L/PJ/12/217. The British Library, London. Oriental and India Office Collections.

3

Stalking Dead Man

I am quite clear in my own mind that all the enquiries we could make have been made and the result is a conviction that Shri Subhas Chandra Bose died as has been stated. There is an abundance of evidence on this, which I consider convincing. In the circumstances, I see absolutely no justification for appointing a commission to make further enquires.

Prime Minister Jawaharlal Nehru in a note to Deputy External Affairs Minister BV Keskar on 13 February 1953.

You ask me to send you proof of the death of Netaji Subhas Chandra Bose. I cannot send you any precise and direct proof.

Prime Minister Jawaharlal Nehru in a letter to Subhas's brother Suresh Bose in 1962.

"If he is already in Moscow or on his way, you must reach him as early as possible. There will be plenty to do. So, we stand down in your favour, and we want you to go."[1] Abid Hasan surmised for SA Ayer, concealing his fears. Pritam Singh and Gulzara Singh acquiesced. Gulzara had had second hand information about Bose's "destination unknown," but Pritam knew that it was the USSR for sure. On 13 August night, at the dinner table, Bose had discussed with him the implications of the Japanese surrender. "What should we do now?"[2] "We should open another front,"[3] the fighter in Pritam Singh replied. "Surrendering would not serve any useful purpose."[4] Bose was determined to go on fighting. He whispered to Pritam that "contact had already been established with Russia and we shall try to move towards that direction."[5]

This was Saigon. Two days had passed since Bose had left and his men were waiting to be united with him. The Japanese were being unusually secretive and had yet not told the Indians of the tragedy. "A plane is leaving for Japan tomorrow. Colonel T is going by that plane. One seat can be spared in that plane for one of your party,"[6] they said. The remaining, the Japanese added, could be flown to Hanoi in Vietnam. Here, PGI's General Secretary Anand Mohan Sahay had been involved in some special work. "What else can he (Bose) do now, except to start doing some propaganda,"[7] Hasan reasoned Ayer out of his great reluctance. He was PGI's Publicity and Propaganda Minister, a former *Reuter's* correspondent, the most suited to follow Bose to the USSR. On 20 August morning all five — SA Ayer, Debnath Das, Abid Hasan, Pritam Singh, Gulzara Singh — assembled at Saigon airport. The plane to Hanoi went first. The party arrived at Sahay's place and soon dropped in Major General AC Chatterjee and John Thivy. They had "got instruction from Hikari Kikan at Singapore that Netaji desired them to proceed towards Netaji's direction, and accordingly they came."[8] Then came the death news on radio, but none believed in it for obvious reason. Pritam Singh and Debnath Das went to Japanese staff officers and asked them what that was all about. "The plane crash is only a cover,"[9] Colonel Enamoto of Marshal Terauchi's HQ said.

A week after the reported death of Subhas Bose, the chief of the Japanese military intelligence department met Debnath Das in Hanoi. "*Netaji no hikoki ochiru kotown shinio shimasan* ...," he said in Japanese well understood by Das. "Don't believe the plane crash as a real crash. You adjust your movements and plans in accordance with the alternate plan of Netaji."[10]

Back in Saigon, the Japanese began to brace themselves to tell Ayer of "the crash" as soon as his colleagues had left. First wandered in a Domei scribe and then showed up Rear-Admiral Chuda. In the roar of the bomber he was about to board, Ayer heard the naval commander say "Atherji is dead!" He thought he heard "Chatterjee." "CHANDRA BOSE KAKKAA (Excellency

Chandra Bose),"[11] Chuda yelled out. Before the news could sink in, Ayer was bundled in the plane. At Canton airport, Colonel Tada took Ayer into a hangar. He spoke in Japanese and Aoki translated. He gave a blow-by-blow account of the air crash in Taihoku. Ayer wouldn't believe. He shrugged it off. "Not a single Indian ... will believe this story unless you produce conclusive proofs ... take me at once to Taihoku. I must see Netaji's body with my own eyes .... Don't tell me afterwards that Netaji's body has been disposed off ...."[12] The bomber soon landed in Formosa but Taihoku was given a miss. Ayer never saw Bose's body, which anyway had been disposed off. But in time, the much annoyed Ayer was persuaded by the Japanese to write the death news Domei was to splash world over.

About five years later, India witnessed a surge of inquisition over Bose's death. The man who brought it to the Parliament was a fervid nationalist, the second Indian after Bose to have quit the Indian Civil Service (ICS) to join the freedom struggle. HV Kamath made dogged attempts to gauge the stated conviction of the Government in the death story. He asked on 31 March 1951 about "the various communications and reports Government have received so far about Netaji Subhas Chandra Bose's death or about his being alive." The long answer by Deputy Minister for External Affairs Dr BV Keskar on 19 April 1951 was short on substance. "Questions regarding the death of Shri Subhas Chandra Bose have been put and answered on the floor of this House on many occasions since 1946. After due enquiry and the collection of whatever evidence it was possible to gather, the Prime Minister made a statement on 12 October 1946 to the effect that there was little doubt that Shri Subhas Chandra Bose died on the 18th August 1945 .... The latest communication that Government received was from Major General Bhonsle of the INA Committee on the 30th March, 1951 in which he stated that the ashes of Shri Subhas Chandra Bose were deposited in a Japanese temple in Tokyo on September 18, 1945 .... Government are unable to furnish the dates and sources of various communications they have received regarding this matter."

On 6 March 1953 Nehru himself dispelled the doubts. Lok Sabha member AN Vidyalankar asked him "whether Government have in their possession conclusive evidence that Netaji Subhas Chandra Bose is dead and the ashes said to be his really belong to Netaji?" The Prime Minister replied the "Government have enquired repeatedly into this matter and a resume of the evidence in Government's possession was placed on the table of the House on 5th March 1952. All possible steps were taken by the Government and they are satisfied that the report of Shri Subhas Chandra Bose's death is correct. The facts ascertained have been made public."

It trickled out that SA Ayer had visited Japan in 1951 to authenticate the story he had written in 1945. On records, it was the Chief Secretary of Bombay who had asked him to make enquiries about the death story and the gold Bose was carrying with him. De facto, it was the Prime Minister, a believer in Bose's death, who had wanted to know if it was actually true. Ayer submitted a detailed report of his enquiries to the Prime Minister on 26 September 1951. Nehru read out aloud in the Lok Sabha on 6 March 1953 a line from the last passage of this report. "In conclusion, I (Ayer) would repeat that I have not the faintest doubt in my mind that the ashes that are enshrined in the Renkoji temple are Netaji's."[13] There were counter questions, which Nehru answered with his hallmark panache. "This is the fullest account that we have had. Whether it is the last word or some further information may come later I cannot say, but it does seem now that it is a fairly convincing account."

Earlier, on 1 March 1952, the Prime Minister sent to Dr BC Roy, Chief Minister of West Bengal, a copy of Ayer's report. "'I have no reason to doubt as to correctness of the report and I think I must accept the final conclusion also.' The Prime Minister asked Dr Roy to ascertain the wishes of Subhas Chandra Bose's family regarding the disposal of his ashes .... According to Dr Roy's reply of March 11, the Bose family were disinclined to move into the matter and did not want it to be pursued for the time-being."[14]

Niharendu Dutt-Majumdar, former Bengal minister and noted barrister, in January 1954 stoked the talks of setting up a commission to look into Bose's death. He sent Nehru a draft resolution for his perusal and clearance. He intended to place the final version before Congress Working Committee (CWC) and then, at Nehru's behest, before the session of Congress party at Kalyani. The draft said that "a special fact-finding commission on Netaji Subhas Chandra Bose should be set up as soon as possible by the Government of India, consisting of persons commanding public confidence in this behalf and be invested with plenipotentiary powers and rank of Ambassador, with a view to collect facts and evidence on the spot with the help of Government and the people of all friendly powers concerned, including Japan, USA, UK, USSR, China and others to whom also a request in this behalf should be made by the Government of India for their help and co-operation in the Commission's work."[15]

There was something about Majumdar's suggestion that irked the Prime Minister. His 21 January reply to Majumdar was laced with rudeness. "I have just seen your letter of the 16th January. So far as the Working Committee is concerned it has finalised the Resolutions of the Congress .... I really do not understand what more the Government of India can possibly do about finding facts in regards to Netaji Subhas Chandra Bose. We have done everything possible within our ken and got all the facts that were available. I have no doubt in my mind about them. From time to time, members of Forward Bloc say that Netaji is alive. Anything more irresponsible, I find it difficult to imagine. Evidently the Forward Bloc has got no politics at all left except to repeat the statement. All the countries you have mentioned in your draft resolution, excepting Japan, would refuse all facilities for such a formal enquiry. As for Japan, we have had the fullest enquiry there."[16]

In a meeting of Berhampore Municipality Commissioners on 7 July 1954, someone broached the question of Bose's death. Going a bit far, the municipality adopted a resolution, urging the Government of India to conduct a "thorough enquiry in order to ascertain the truth and to dispel misgivings and misunderstanding." A copy of the resolution reached Teen Murti Bhawan. The PM's office promptly routed a reply couched in Nehruspeak. "All the enquiries that the Government of India could make have been made and result is conviction that Shri Bose died in the fatal air crash. No further enquiries in the matter are considered necessary,"[17] ML Bazaz, Private Secretary to the Prime Minister, wrote.

This was then the story from the Government's side: The facts ascertained have been made public ... No further enquiries in the matter are considered necessary ... What more the Government of India can possibly do? ... Government are satisfied that the report of Subhas Chandra Bose's death is correct ... If only it could be brought out those days, the inside story would have put the Government in a spot. Never mind the public posturing, the correspondence at the highest level had little to inspire such conviction in the crash theory. Discreet inquiries, made with the help of former Bose-men-turned-Nehru's aides, had tipped off that Bose might have slipped into the USSR.

The first case involved Anand Mohan Sahay. If they had wished to find out, it would not have taken long for the Nehru Government to know what the old papers said about him. Sahay was possibly the first of Bose's top men to crack under the Britishers' pressure. Sahay "is the only one who has talked at all freely on this subject,"[18] complimentarily noted an intelligence dispatch dated 28 February 1946 while dwelling on "The last plans and intentions of Bose." As Commissioner for India in Port of Spain in 1952, Sahay was more supine and forthcoming. On 17 January 1952, he wrote a "Top Secret" letter to Foreign Secretary Subimal Dutt. The letter was earmarked for the NGO section of the ministry. "Not to Go to Office" it meant, and it served to safe keeping highly sensitive records in this side of the South Block. The reason why Sahay's correspondence was classified as such was evident in its startling disclosures. Sahay's proximity to Subhas Bose was unquestioned. He was his diplomatic pointsman — the one who did crucial talks and undertook sensitive missions. What he had written to

Dutt ideally should have made the Government fidgety. He called the death story "a show" and revealed that, courtesy the Japanese, he had come to know of Bose's "death" before it took place.

"Please refer to your letter No. 758/51-S, dated the 1st November 1951, and reminder of Miss Leelamani Naidu, No 25/4/NGO, dated the 21st December 1951, about the late Netaji Subhas Chandra Bose. I am sorry for the delay in sending the promised statement. I herewith enclose it. I hope this will be of some use. There is one thing extraordinary in the whole show which needs some explanation from the Japanese. So far as my information goes, Netaji was removed to a hospital after the accident and he died there. How is it that the crash took place on the 18th and the announcement regarding his death was made on same day, or was it that the plane crashed on the previous day? Perhaps Safrani who is working under you as an Under Secretary may be able to say when Netaji left Saigon for Tokyo."[19]

But in the enclosed "promised statement," Sahay packed enough gunpowder to blast the official version that from Saigon Bose had flown towards Tokyo. He knew the truth better than many. He had himself received a communication from Subhas Bose on 16 August for a rendezvous in Manchuria — the gateway to the USSR.

"While I was visiting Shanghai in January 1945, Netaji passed that way on his way back from Tokyo. He stayed there for a couple of days. He informed me that the Japanese would no more be able to lend much support to our (INA's) fight in future. Japan was being attacked by American air force regularly, inflicting heavy losses on the Japanese, making it impossible for them to send their air support to our army in Burma or Manipur.

"Netaji said that he could see the end of the war in course of months and he wanted me to try to persuade the Japanese to allow us to establish direct contact with the Soviet Embassy in Tokyo. I was in Tokyo in the beginning of February 1945. I met General Tojo and the Chief of the General Staff and discussed the matter at length. I told them that if we could deal with the Soviet directly we might be able to help in improving the Russo-Japanese relations that was necessary to strengthen Japan's position.

"The plan was to proceed to Manchuria and be there when the end of war comes, so that we may be within Soviet sphere after the surrender of the Japanese .... War came to an end on 15th August. A special messenger from Netaji came to see me on 16th from Bangkok with a letter from him asking me to get ready to secure transport from the Japanese and to leave for Manchuria, and to meet him there. He suggested that although Soviet had declared war against the Japanese, it would be desirable to be arrested by the Soviet authorities in Manchuria because we could later negotiate with them and might persuade them to accept us as their friends and not enemies. This was the last time I heard from Netaji.

"On 18th August 1945, at about 5pm Major General Chatterjee, Col Gulzara Singh, Col Pritam Singh, Mr Thivy and Mr Abid Hassan arrived from Saigon and gave me the message that Netaji had left for the north (towards Manchuria). Being aware of the plan, I was already negotiating with the Japanese to take me to Tokyo. I thought of proceeding to Manchuria from Tokyo on my own ...."[20]

Sahay's dope on Bose's secret flight towards Manchuria was wee bit compared to Ayer's precise inputs. When he spoke in the Parliament in 1952 about Ayer's report, the Prime Minister did not tell the nation the full story. Ayer had actually sent at least two different reports. The one selectively quoted in the Parliament was perhaps meant for public consumption. Ayer had filed it on 24 September 1951 from his Churchgate, Bombay residence. He reproduced verbatim the suspicious story of Habibur Rahman. On the whole, he simply conjectured along the Governmental line.

"I paid a brief visit to Japan towards the end of May 1951. I was in Tokyo from May 24 to June 10. During my stay there I tried to meet as many Japanese nationals as I could with a view to checking up thoroughly the truth of the story of Netaji's aircrash .... I called at the house of General Tojo on June 3, and the next day Mrs Tojo and family were my guests at a dinner at the Tokyo Hotel. I did not ask the Japanese journalists or Mrs Tojo family any direct questions about Netaji's death but I must say I am convinced beyond the shadow of a doubt that the report of the crash is hundred per cent correct .... It was obvious that the Japanese journalists and General Tojo's family assumed that I had no doubt whatsoever about Netaji's fatal air crash."

Ayer's other report was "Top Secret", written in pencil, and sent across pronto to the Prime Minister when he was still in a Japanese hotel on 5 June 1951. In 1972 or so, when the Government forwarded some classified files on Subhas Bose to Khosla Commission, this report, or a part of it, was deemed so sensitive that its number was not disclosed. Even the PMO file it originated from was not identified. The introduction only said "Item No 36 of Listed documents/SA Ayer's report" and the contents were based on Ayer's confidential talks with Colonel Tada, Staff Officer of Field Marshal Terauchi in 1945. The same Tada who had told him about Bose's death in Canton. The same Tada whose sudden surfacing along with Hikari Kikan chief Lt General Isoda before Bose's disappearance had raised suspicions of the Allied intelligence sleuths. Some had averred that the duo turned up to execute a "deception plan." Six years on, Tada hinted to Ayer that they were right. Contrary to what was earlier given out, Tada was actually able to contact Marshal Terauchi over Bose's request. He also laid bare the actual reason Bose and the Japanese had met in Narain Das's house in Saigon on 17 August 1945.

"Col T filled certain important gap in my information regarding certain events that happened immediately before and after Netaji's fateful flight from Saigon. Soon Netaji & party (including myself [Ayer's comment]) landed at the Saigon airport from 2 planes from Bangkok at about 10am on 17.8.45. Col Tada flew to Dalat, contacted Field Marshal Terauchi, Commander-in-Chief, Southern Command (starting from Burma to China and Manchuria) and conveyed Netaji's request for facilities to fly to

Russian occupied territory in Manchuria to enable him ultimately to reach Moscow .... Field Marshal took the responsibility on his own shoulders and without referring the question to the Imperial (Military) Head Quarters in Tokyo and told Col Tada to tell Netaji that all facilities would be given to him to reach Russian held territory. Count Terauchi had great respect and affection for Netaji and wished to let Netaji have his wish and do whatever he liked on his own responsibility, whatever the consequences might be.

"A plane was leaving for Diren and to Tokyo, General Shidei who had been ordered to proceed forthwith to Diren to take charge as Vice Chief of Staff was going by that plane. Netaji could take the only seat they could spare and General Shidei would look after Netaji up to Diren. Thereafter Netaji would fall back on his own resources to contact the Russians .... Japanese would announce to the world that Netaji on his way to Japan had disappeared from Diren. That would absolve them of all responsibility for the safety of Netaji's person in the eyes of the Allies. Col Tada, on return from Dalat at about 2 or 3 pm conveyed this message to Netaji in a secret conference at Narain Das's bungalow, offered him first one seat, then one more (surrendering his [Tada's] own) .... Count Terauchi had told Col T that if Tokyo asked him about Terauchi's decision to help Netaji to reach Russian held territory, Col Tada was to tell Tokyo that Terauchi had done so on his own responsibility."

This was for the first and last time Colonel Tada opened his mouth before an Indian. He died young — around the time Ayer gave Nehru his second report. British intelligence reports showed how badly they wanted him. "I think our only worthwhile move is to get hold of Tada," said a 1 March 1946 dispatch. They did get him eventually. What was the outcome? There was no way to know! It emerged in 1956 that "records of interrogations" of Minister Hachiya, Lt General Isoda, Colonel Yano and Colonel Tada — all those who had worked out Bose's last known flight — were unavailable at the Intelligence Bureau's Delhi HQ.

Notes:

1 *Unto Him Witness* by SA Ayer. Page 75.
2 Pritam Singh's deposition before Mukherjee Commission.
3 Ibid.
4 Ibid.
5 Pritam Singh's deposition before Khosla Commission.
6 *Unto Him Witness* by SA Ayer, Page 74.
7 Ibid. Page 75.
8 Debnath Das's deposition before Khosla Commission.
9 Pritam Singh on a Star TV show hosted by Vir Sanghvi. Both he and Debnath Das told the same to Khosla Commission.
10 Debnath Das revealed this in a letter dated 27 March 1953.
11 *Unto Him Witness* by SA Ayer. Page 79.
12 Ibid. Pages 84-85.
13 File No F 25/4/NGO/-Volume III. SA Ayer's report to Prime Minister.
14 File No 2(64)/56-PM, Volume I. Page 19/B.
15 File No 2(64)/56-PM, Volume I. Letter dated 16 January 1954.
16 File No 2(64)/56-PM, Volume I. The Prime Minister's reply.
17 File No 2(64)/56-PM, Volume I.
18 ST/12/104. S SECTION, CSDIC (I).
19 File No F 25/4/NGO/-Volume III. DO No 13-Com/52. The Foreign Secretary, obviously, must have queried Abid Hasan Safrani. No related paper has come to the writer's knowledge, though.
20 Ibid.

4

Command Performance

All presumptions, therefore, are that he (Subhas Bose) died and the real inquiry would largely be about the circumstances ....

Jawaharlal Nehru in a Prime Minister's Secretariat note dated 2 April 1956.

So, although there cannot be absolute certainty, nevertheless, it can be said that, in all probability, the ashes kept in Renkoji temple, Tokyo, are the ashes of Netaji Subhas Chandra Bose.

Shah Nawaz Committee Report

My colleagues, both connected with the Government, have tried their utmost to secure and to manipulate the evidence, so that it could easily conform with the Prime Minister's statements.

Suresh Bose on Shah Nawaz and SN Maitra in *Dissentient Report.*

And they thought Subhas Bose was their stooge! A sitting of International Military Tribunal for the Far East (IMTFE) in Tokyo provided the foreign judges a spectacular rebuttal to what had been drummed about during the world war. The "war criminals" stood up, former premier Hideki Tojo included, and bowed when the name of their ally Chandra Bose was taken. Crestfallen and facing death rows, the Japanese top brass graciously displayed their reverence for the Indian.

This struck a chord with an American judge. He broached up the topic with the Indian judge sitting next. Justice Radha

Binode Pal, the only Asian to sit in judgment at one of the most significant trials in human history, briefed the American about Bose and the evident respect the Japanese accorded him. Taihoku crash was naturally discussed and the American made a disclosure. In intelligence agencies' estimation Taihoku plane crash was a subterfuge. Pal was taken aback. The Americans were in a position to know. Passing on the information was a judge who had seen official papers. Pal did not let one-off information override his judgment. He dug out more and returned home well-briefed by the American, the British and the Japanese sources. On 23 January 1947 Justice Pal revealed in a public meeting in Calcutta that as per the Americans no plane had crashed at Matsuyama aerodrome on 18 August 1945. The only plane that had gone down there during that period was an American one. There was no denial from any side to his statement. In 1953 Pal wrote a letter to AM Nair, a former Bose aide, scotching a rumour that he had visited Renkoji temple to see "Bose's ashes":

"It is really surprising that my name should be used in that manner. I did not go to any temple either with or without the ambassador to see the alleged ashes. As a matter of fact, I could not accept as true the story of Netaji's death at Formosa. In any case I feel that the whole thing demands a thorough investigation. Statements by individuals made here and there will not convince me as to the truth of the story given out. I have reasons to doubt its correctness ...."[1]

Little did Pal know that he would one day become one of the reasons for the Government of India to launch the first official probe into Bose's death. In 1950s recurring demands were made for an inquiry, but the Government had its heels dug in. Prime Minister Nehru himself ran over many such attempts. On 5 March 1952, in reply to a question put in the Parliament by HV Kamath, he said: "I have no doubt in my mind — I did not have it then and I have no doubt today of the fact of Netaji Subhas Chandra Bose's death .... There can be no enquiry about that."[2]

In a privately circulated letter dated 27 March 1953, Debnath Das broke his silence. "It is beyond our comprehension to think why the Government of India have chosen not to set up an Investigation Commission ...." He explained that the reasons for Bose's associates keeping quiet since Independence was that "some allowance" had to be made for "Japan's extremely delicate position," "war criminals' trials," "other international complications" and "the disguised hostility of the Power that be in India towards Netaji." "There was a historical necessity too in case everything was done according to the plan, for Netaji's remaining underground for obvious reasons only to appear at the historical moment for shaping India's destiny." Das rued "complete disintegration of the INA," "beggarly conditions" of its veterans and "somersault of some of our colleagues," which was a barb aimed at SA Ayer, JK Bhonsle, AM Sahay and others who had taken up governmental assignments. "Why did the Government choose to send just one man (Sri SA Ayar) to Japan for the said investigation — a man who had been in Japan just for a month or so and did not know the language and country well and had to yield to a conducted tour? ... why should he choose to keep his findings secret from us who are all pilgrims to that 'journey's end'?"

On 29 September 1955 Nehru rose again in the Parliament to reply to the question persistently put over and again by Kamath. "In a matter of this kind, the only enquiry that is to say, satisfactory enquiry that can be made is by the Japanese Government. The matter is in Japan the whole thing is there. We cannot impose ourselves or an Enquiry Committee on the Japanese Government. Of course, if they choose to enquire we will gladly cooperate and give such help as we can. But we cannot simply enquire into their territory .... And as I said, the initiative must come from the Japanese Government ...."[3]

Many were naturally disheartened by the Prime Minister's stand that he would rather have a foreign country take a lead than himself try and find out the truth about the fate of a national hero. Pushed at the tether's end, Bose's followers began pressing for an unofficial inquiry. And that was when Justice

Pal's name again started doing rounds. It was argued that Pal had earned immense goodwill in Japan due to his pro-Japanese verdict at the Tokyo trials. Therefore, if he went there as head of an inquiry team, the Japanese would be more helpful to him than anybody else. The showdown took place on 6 September 1955 in Calcutta. At a meet of Netaji Memorial Committee, presided over by former INA Major General Shah Nawaz Khan, the participants voiced that enough was enough. Shah Nawaz, then a Congress MP, himself inadvertently triggered the backlash. He informed them that the Prime Minister was not ready for an official probe. A resolution envisioned a public-funded, non-official committee which would have toured all over India and abroad for clues. In pursuance, Shah Nawaz met Suresh Bose, one of Bose's brothers, in October and appraised him of the development. He volunteered that he would take up the issue with the Prime Minister and seek his help in extending governmental facilities to the committee. He promised Suresh to be back soon with the plan of holding a big meeting of Bose's supporters.

That was the last time Shah Nawaz Khan was heard to voice his opinion on the side of those who doubted the crash theory. Gone was the man who had on 23 January 1951 had told a public gathering that Bose would return to India.[4] No one knew what happened in Delhi, but suddenly the Government sat up to Shah Nawaz's eminence. Soon it transpired that there would be an official committee and Shah Nawaz would head it. A captain in the British Indian Army who wasn't actually very close to Bose, Shah Nawaz possessed little acumen to conduct an international enquiry. But to some the Parliamentary Secretary to the Railway Minister was a better bet than fiercely independent Justice Pal.

The Prime Minister on the 3 December 1955 announced in Parliament the formation of Netaji Inquiry Committee (NIC). Shah Nawaz was to be assisted by Shankar Moitra (Maitra), a nominee of West Bengal Government, and Suresh Bose, a former magistrate, represented his family. There was more than what met the eye. Non-political, gentlemanly Suresh Bose, someone said, was included to keep out some other Bose kins known to be holding fiery belief that Subhas Bose was alive after 1945. And his being in the Committee certainly did not mean he would be able to pull the strings. That was the prerogative of the chairman, who was to take orders from the Ministry of External Affairs (MEA). Prime Minister Nehru himself was the External Affairs Minister and as such it was he who was to call the shots. So what came about was a puppet on Government's strings. The Committee had no trappings of a commission: It wasn't independent, it was to work in camera, away from media scrutiny. From the day one, the dotted lines were made known in the NIC's terms of reference:

"To enquire into and to report to the Government of India on the circumstances concerning the departure of Netaji Subhas Chandra Bose from Bangkok about the 16th August 1945, his alleged death as a result of an aircraft accident, and subsequent developments connected therewith."

That is, the Government had already concluded that there had been a plane crash in Taipei on 18 August 1945. Bose's death was anyway a *fait accompli* to them. Never mind that they were planning to inquire into its veracity, the Government upheld the death story in secret correspondence barely a few months before the Committee began to work. It all started with the sudden decision of the Renkoji temple priest to hold memorial service to mark Bose's death anniversary. Indian Ambassador in Japan, BR Sen, lobbed the ball into the South Block. His telegram "No 71" dated 26 July 1955 began with the prefix all governmental correspondence of the day on Bose used as a rule.

"Late SUBHAS CHANDRA BOSE. Chief Priest of Renkoji Buddhist Temple who has all along had the custody of ashes proposes holding for first time formally a memorial service on the 18th August. Temple authorities ask Embassy approval for this and request presence of Ambassador and others at the occasion. Please advise action desired."[5]

In its initial response, the MEA asked the Ambassador two days later to elaborate his views and refer to a communiqué,

DO No FS (I) NGO (1) dated 23 June 1954, sent earlier by former Ambassador Dr MA Rauf to "Kaul" over the matter.

The explanation from Tokyo came pronto: "No 73. From Ambassador. Your telegram No 28434 dated 28 July. Late Subhas Chandra BOSE. My views generally same as RAUF's. Main question is whether Government are in a position to publicly accept fact of death. If they are then there could be no objection to Embassy participating in memorial services here. It will be realized that participation in memorial service here will also involve Government in other actions which must logically follow. Whole issue seems to be obviously tied up with repercussions at home and I feel can best be decided at policy level in India. Japanese feelings or those of community here not much of importance."[6]

What were Rauf's real views? Jagdish Kodesia, Delhi Congress chief in 1958-59, met Rauf, a fellow Allahabadi, in August 1954 in Tokyo. Kodesia wanted to see Bose's ashes but Rauf dissuaded him from "wasting" his time, saying that "they are not the ashes of Netaji." On his return, Kodesia told both the Prime Minister and Home Minister Lal Bahadur Shastri about his experience. "Shastriji was slightly inclined to listen to me patiently. But Panditji simply laughed at what I said."[7]

Anyway, Sen's views were conveyed to the Prime Minister, who stepped in to issue the following instructions to the MEA: "I suggest you send the following reply to the attached telegram from Tokyo: 'Your telegram 73, July 29th. We think that our Embassy should participate in Memorial Services for Subhas Chandra Bose. Prime Minister stated in Parliament two years ago that in the circumstances we had to accept fact of death. Therefore, there is no difficulty in our taking up this position publicly.'"[8]

Netaji Inquiry Committee got cracking. It began its work early in April 1956 and was through with it in flat four months' time. In all 67 witnesses were examined, bulk of whom were Indians and Japanese. The outcome looked as credible as Shah Nawaz Khan's good name. The NIC Report was a compact narration, comprising six chapters spread across 78 pages with pictures of the plane wreck and the urn in Renkoji temple. The first chapter — "Last Plans of Netaji Subhas Chandra Bose" — cursorily portrayed Bose's last plans as a series of knee-jerk reactions. Caught in between the original Japanese version and evidence that punctured it at many places, the Committee could just about manage to say that "there were a number of reasons for Netaji to go to Tokyo, although his ultimate aim was Russia via Manchuria." It went on to speculate that "there was no time then to contact Russian authorities or to make out detailed plans ahead. Russia was at war with Japan, and the Russian armies were advancing into Manchuria. Even if Netaji reached Manchuria what would happen to him and the few trusted lieutenants, whom he wanted to take with him, was uncertain." This twisted insight was based on the evidence given by, among others, an impressive array of Bose's closest aides like Abid Hasan, Pritam Singh, Gulzara Singh, SA Ayer, etc, all of whom had last seen Bose in Saigon on the evening of 17 August 1945.

The vagueness of the first chapter gave way to the graphic details of the next three. "The Air Crash at Taihoku (Formosa)," Chapter 2, drew from the testimonies of six of the seven survivors. Partition had snatched away Rahman along with several other INA greats. The Pakistan Central Administrative Service official Habibur Rahman crossed over to India first and last time. Among the Japanese survivors all but one were traced. Lt Colonel Nonogaki had become a manager in a company, Major Taro Kono had taken to printing business and Captain Arai had been teaching at universities. While Rahman gave evidence at Delhi, the Japanese were examined in Tokyo, where the Committee received a rapturous welcome by the people and press of Japan. One after another, the survivors recounted the horrific details with Major Kono showing off the lasting havoc the fire had wrecked on his body. Dr Yoshimi shut down his clinic for days and travelled over 1,400 Km to give his testimony that formed the bulk of Chapter III — "The Death of Netaji Subhas Chandra Bose." For the fourth part — "Cremation of Netaji's body" — a number of witnesses, including Rahman, were at hand. Part V — "Netaji's ashes" — detailed how Bose's ashes had reached Renkoji temple.

Much as they had wanted, the committee members could not visit Taipei (Taihoku), "which was the actual scene of occurrence of the plane crash, Netaji's death, and his cremation. There were difficulties in doing so, as there were no diplomatic relations between the Government of India, who informed the Committee that they did not consider a visit to Formosa (Republic of China) feasible. So the attempt had to be given up."[9] The Committee report recommended in the last chapter that Bose's ashes be brought to India and a fitting monument be erected in his memory. On 11 September 1956, a reassured Prime Minister presented the NIC report in the Parliament. Papers world over carried the news prominently the next day. "Anti-British Indian Dead, Inquiry Finds," the *New York Times* reported. "Death of Netaji established: Overwhelming evidence obtained," was the *Hindu* lead.

"The conclusion that Netaji Subhas Chandra Bose died as a result of an air-crash at the Taihoku airfield, in Formosa, on August 18, 1945, and the ashes now at the Renkoji temple in Tokyo are his ashes, has been reached by the Netaji Bose Enquiry Committee, Prime Minister Nehru told the Lok Sabha today.

"Making a statement on the report, which was placed on the table of the Lok Sabha today, the Prime Minister said, 'Government feels that this conclusion of the Committee about Netaji's death should be accepted as the evidence adduced in the report is practically overwhelming .... The Report of the Committee is signed by the Chairman and Mr SN Maitra, one of the other two members. The third member, Mr Suresh Chandra Bose, brother of Netaji, has not signed the report nor has he submitted a minute of dissent' .... The Prime Minister added that Mr Suresh Chandra Bose had gone to Calcutta when the report was completed. He had not signed it. A fortnight's time was given to Mr Bose to give his note of dissent or his own report. But he did not submit anything. Ultimately Government felt that they should not delay the report any longer. 'I cannot say to what extent Mr Suresh Chandra Bose agreed with the report or he does not. All I can deduce from his behaviour is that he does not like the report as a whole. What part he likes or dislikes I cannot say.'

"... against the mass of evidence that Netaji had died as a result of the plane crash, the Committee has taken into consideration the view of those who believe this can be divided into two categories: the first, mainly consisting of certain members of the Bose family, believe that, although Netaji is alive, nobody is in touch with him and for reasons of his own, he is in hiding and will re-appear in India at a chosen time. The Committee does not accept this line of reasoning."

The air in Rajya Sabha was somewhat hostile, so the Prime Minister resorted to put downs. "... Mr Nehru said Government felt that the evidence put forth in the report was adequate and no reasonable person who read it could come to any other conclusion. If a person had an unreasonable mind, it was difficult to reason with him ...."

The Prime Minister was able to silence the MPs, but in Calcutta, a bitter Bose family and followers rallied around Suresh Bose to put up his case. There was an another side to the story. Suresh Bose and the Government had run into a collision course at the very outset of the Committee's work. On 1 April 1955, which was the day one of the Committee's work, an upset Muthuramalingam Thevar, Bose's friend and Forward Bloc leader, descended on the scene. He had taken umbrage at the wording of letter sent by Shah Nawaz to him, refering to "circumstances of Netaji's death." To him the phraseology indicated a foregone conclusion on the Government's part. Thevar gave Shah Nawaz a piece of his mind and for the people's benefit, he held a press conference in Delhi on 3 April.

Thevar claimed that "he would furnish conclusive proof that Netaji Subhas Chandra Bose was alive if the Inquiry Committee appointed by the Government of India to go into this question was reconstituted." He said "he might tell the Prime Minister also about Netaji if he was sympathetic." "This Committee is an eyewash .... Dr Radha Binode Pal should be invited to function as the Chairman .... The Government must make it known categorically to the public whether Netaji's name is still in the list of war criminals and if not, when it was removed and how?"[10]

There weren't many takers for Thevar's claims, though no one came forward to contradict him. Neither the Government nor the press felt the need to raise any questions or examine him. Suresh Bose, however, picked the threads. In a letter dated 2 April 1956, he sought clarifications of the Prime Minister on some points:

"The External Affairs Department in their letter dated 3.2.56 to me have mentioned '... circumstances of the disappearance of ....' whereas the same department in the later dated 16.3.56 to me have stated 'circumstances of the death of ...."

"With due respect to Shri Shah Nawaz Khan, I am of opinion that as this enquiry is more or less of a judicial nature and not pertaining to military matters, his position in the Committee as Chairman is not appropriate because he does not appear to be in a possession of additional information, which would be helpful to the Committee regarding the places to be visited by us or regarding the subject matter of this enquiry.

"It is considered important by me on behalf of the Committee to know whether the name of Netaji Subhas Chandra Bose was and still is in the list of war criminals drawn up by America and her allies. If his name still exists and if they request the Government of India to hand him over to them, if he be found on Indian soil, for being tried as a War Criminal, whether this Government will have the option of handing or not handing him over to them for the aforesaid purpose.

"As I consider this Enquiry to be a very important one and as it will be of great concern to millions of persons throughout the world, it requires mature deliberations and sound judgment. As such, it is my humble opinion that Dr Radha Binode Pal be requested and persuaded to join the Committee and lead it."[11]

The next morning Suresh Bose bumped into Nehru and took the opportunity to set forth all the points. By evening Nehru's response had been duly recorded: "Our effort should be to get as many facts as possible about Netaji Subhas Chandra Bose's last days — the disappearance or death or whatever it was. Apart from direct evidence which we have thus far received and which may further be obtained, it seems to me almost inconceivable that Netaji should be alive. Over ten years have passed since the aircraft accident. Even if he had escaped then I cannot conceive how he could possibly remain silent during all these years when it was very easy for him to communicate in various ways with India ....

"I pointed out to Shri Suresh Bose that Dr Radha Binode Pal's appointment to this Committee was not suitable because of the part he played in the War Criminals' trial. He is, of course, a very eminent criminal jurist and is well known in Japan and elsewhere. But, in the circumstances, his functioning in this Committee might not be liked by some foreign countries like the USA ....

"I told Shri Suresh Bose that the question of War Criminal does not arise and we are not going to ask the USA or any other country as to whether Netaji is in the list of their War Criminals. Possibly, their answer would be that they believed he was dead. Anyhow, we do not propose to do anything in the matter ...."[12]

Suresh's version was different. The Prime Minister was blasé throughout the meeting. He remained absolutely mum on the war criminal issue when he should have rebuked Suresh for propping up such an absurdity. Subhas was his friend after all. Suresh never got any reply from Nehru. Twelve days later he himself resumed correspondence, this time to complain about Shah Nawaz's selective leaks to the press.

"As the public and the press have not been allowed to be present during the deliberations of the Committee, I was taken aback, when I first saw a report of the deliberations of the Committee in the newspapers. On asking Sri Shah Nawaz Khan about this publication, he said that some persons enquired of him in the lobby of the Parliament and he had told them something about the matter. There have been some other irregularities, and I think your instructions are very necessary for our guidance."[13]

This time the democrat Prime Minister obliged him by answering on the same day. He had a nugget of advice to offer: Keep media out. "It is desirable that members of the Committee should not give any interviews or make any statements to the press. They should avoid even informal talks on this subject with others who might give the information to the Press."[14] As for the growing mistrust between Suresh and Shah Nawaz, Prime Minister did anything but firefighting. Shah Nawaz got a copy of the letter sent to Suresh with a stinker that "Suresh Babu also says that something appeared in the Press, apparently because you had had a talk with someone in the Lobby. I think this should also be avoided".[15] Nehru's jibe worsened the relations between the two. On the eve of crucial visit to Japan, Shah Nawaz told Suresh that as ordered by the Prime Minister he would examine only a few witnesses in Japan and write the report. On their landing in Tokyo, Suresh attracted media's attention as he was Bose's brother. Shah Nawaz did not like that a bit. "Talk to me, I am the leader here!" he yelled, and outlined to the Japanese press his agenda: "My mission is mainly to interview people who might offer direct evidence or Subhas Bose's death."[16] Which was what he did. Only those witnesses whose statements conformed with the official line, and who were ushered in by a Japanese foreign office officer, were given patient hearing by Shah Nawaz. Whereas those differing were discouraged or shunned.

"Whenever any witness made a statement that did not fit in with his opinion, he (Shah Nawaz) would make a suggestion to him as to whether he remembered it definitely, as the incident took place about 11 years ago or would put other questions or suggestions to him to confuse him and to make him modify his answer or change his definite statement to a vague one. Another unimaginable conduct of his was that when a statement made by a witness did not suit his purpose, he would modify it, while dictating it to the stenographer."[17]

"Capt M Nakamura ... said he was at that time the Ground Engineer and the Airforce Officer in Charge of the Maintenance Unit at Taihoku aerodrome. He stated that a serious accident took place there on 17-8 or 18-8, in which Mr Subhas Chandra

Bose, Gen Shidei and others were involved. He then stated that he was 90% sure that it could not be on 18th as on that day, about 30 American planes came and left on that day and he attended to all of them. As this date, viz, 17th did not fit in with what the Chairman wanted, he started manipulations .... and eventually succeeded in getting from the witness that the American planes did not come on the 18th and succeeded only partially, when the witness said the crash took place either on the 17th, 18th or 19th of August, 1945."[18]

Some witnesses were allowed to read from prepared text, while others were shown the door for fear they might say something unwarranted. This sort of selective screening of witnesses had in fact been going on in India as well. N Dutt Majumdar and LN Roy Chowdhary arrived at the Committee venue to find the Chairman missing. Roy Chowdhary had served with the intelligence branch of the Fourteenth Army, which had taken on the INA, and claimed to have seen reports that suggested that Bose had escaped to the Soviet Russia.

In Japan, Shah Nawaz turned way some 20 independent witnesses. Bondai Mori, a businessman, was so much irritated that he vent his ire before media persons. Why Shah Nawaz could not afford to let people of his ilk have their say became clear when three such witnesses sneaked into the venue. SN Sen, who had been living in Japan for two decades, deposed that Bose was not on the plane that had crashed in Taihoku. Shah Nawaz brushed him aside and called on M Miyoshi, a medical orderly in the Taihoku hospital at the time of Bose's reported death. Contrary to his expectations, Miyosgi could just say that he and three others were ordered to lift a coffin containing an unknown body and loaded it on a truck. He added that he never heard that Subhas Bose had been under treatment in the hospital or that his body had been kept there for over two days.

K Satoh[19], a bomber mechanic posted at Taihoku Aerodrome in 1945, offered an altogether new insight. He said that there indeed had been a crash, but it took place at 7 in the morning and not 2.00pm as Habibur Rahman had said. There were only two passengers in the plane. Satoh said that one of them jumped out while the other one was pulled out. The one who had jumped out appeared Subhas Bose to Satoh. He added that both passengers were unscathed, and he saw them talking to each other after the crash.

On return from Japan, some drama took place in Bose's city. Jawaharlal Nehru had handed over to Sarat Bose a partially burnt watch, which he said was brought to India by Colonel Rahman. Habib's story was that it was given to him by Dr Yoshimi who had it removed from the person of Bose. At the Red Fort, fearing the worst, Rahman stealthily passed this watch to Shah Nawaz Khan. In time, Shah Nawaz handed over the watch to INA defence counsel Bhullabhai Desai, who in turn gave to Jawaharlal Nehru. But Dr Yoshimi flatly denied that he had ever passed any watch to Rahman leave alone his removing one from Bose's body. And, Bose never wore a square watch! Close acquaintances told the Committee that he unmistakably wore a distinct round golden watch till his disappearance. Shah Nawaz knew that for himself. But the square watch episode was a part of the death story he had to uphold. When Bose's nephew Dwijendra Nath Bose tried to set the record straight, Shah Nawaz would not know what to do. Making a mockery of judicial norms, he disallowed Dwijen to make any statement saying that some other witness had already made statements on the watch. Shaken by this brazen misconduct, SN Maitra was compelled to dumb down the procedure for the benefit of the Chairman of the Committee. "If a red shirt was hung up against a wall, a person could state that it was so, another could say it was green and not red, a third could say it was white and not red and so on, and so this witness should not be prevented from speaking about that wrist watch."[20]

Hence the fact of the matter emerged. Bose's prized possession throughout his adult life had been a round Omega gold watch. He was so much attached to this present by his parents that he would refuse to part with it even in jails. Yes, he did have a number of other watches. Many square watches were gifted to him by Joseph Lural, the President of Philippines.

He had all those distributed among all the INA officers, including Habibur Rahman and Shah Nawaz. Both of them were wearing these watches when they were brought to Red Fort as prisoners. Dwijen drew the attention of the Committee to the burnt watch. The mark left by fastener on leather strap was not where it would have been in case it was worn by his uncle. So whoever wore it had a bulkier wrist than Bose. Bose family suspected that Rahman had passed off his own watch as that of Bose's. Rahman had been asked about his own watch. "I had it with me there at the Red Fort, but someone stole it," he said. The Committee's report had little choice but to say that "the case regarding the watch remains inconclusive." Dwijen differed. "They did not do anything about it."[21]

In June 1956 when he was finalising the report, Shah Nawaz's thoughts went to papers in the possession of the US and the UK Governments and the Intelligence Bureau. "The Committee is now in the final stages of writing out the report," he wrote in similarly worded letters to Home Minister BN Datar and Foreign Secretary S Dutt on 19 June and requested them to forward the relevant files. The IB dossier encapsulating inconclusive reports on Bose's death was dispatched on 22 June. Shah Nawaz had no time to study them; the report had to be made ready. On 23 June he asked Suresh Bose what his findings were. "It's too early for me to form an opinion," Suresh said with surprise, adding it would "amount to putting the cart before the horse."[22] Restive Shah Nawaz persisted that he needed to know Suresh's mind before the report could be jotted down. Suresh insisted that it would be possible for him to reach to some conclusion only after he had evaluated the evidence. On June 30 the three committee members met. Shah Nawaz set the tone by asserting that they were dealing with three issues: Bose's death, his cremation and his ashes and "the last two would go a long way in proving the first one."[23] Suresh objected to his line of thinking. The ashes were not identifiable; they could be of someone else's, he countered.

Another surprise was in the offing. The Shah Nawaz Committee's report was not to be written by Shah Nawaz.

The MEA had more faith in seasoned bureaucrat Maitra, the ghost writer. The members met on 10 July to discuss Maitra's first draft. By July 14 serious differences had cropped up. Suresh listed a number of serious discrepancies and contradictions on all major points concerning the Taihoku crash and Bose's death, which Shah Nawaz and Maitra tried to paper over. On 15 July Suresh put his foot down. He said what with the flimsy evidence and the contradictions made by the witnesses, he was veering towards believing that there had been no plane crash at all in Taihoku on 18 August 1945. Shah Nawaz told him that in that case he would have to write a separate dissenting report. Suresh agreed and demanded that copies of draft report, relevant papers, including exhibits and photographs etc be given to him so that he could proceed.

The last meeting Suresh Bose had with Shah Nawaz was on 16 July. Shah Nawaz frowned at him and told him to vacate the Committee's office. The Government too began to view Suresh Bose as a spoilsport. He had been urgently needing a government accommodation in Delhi, which was denied to him. He was humiliated and eventually forced to leave Delhi. All the while, not once did Shah Nawaz bother to ask 68-year-old elder brother of his Netaji if he would be his guest at his sprawling MP bungalow. From Calcutta, Suresh wired Shah Nawaz, asking for the papers so he could write his report. He wouldn't get any. On 29 July he received a stinker. Shah Nawaz asked him to submit his dissentient report by 31 July which was an impossibility. Suresh began to see the Government's hand behind Shah Nawaz's tactics. Few days later a news item appeared in a Calcutta paper. "Netaji died in a Formosa hospital during last war - enquiry findings." It was leak and had something disparaging about Suresh Bose. He immediately sent a letter to Shah Nawaz and marked it CC to the Prime Minister. The PM's reply on 13 August brought him little succour. Nehru wrote that the leak "was some kind of an intelligent guess by some reporter or some clerk in our office here. Obviously, the Chairman of the Enquiry Committee had nothing to do with it."[24]

Suresh Bose reacted angrily. He called the government officers "callous, non-obliging and indifferent" for the way they had treated him and accused Shah Nawaz of "making diabolic false statements." "When the Chairman curtly turned down my request for relevant papers, I suspected that without inspiration from higher ups, he would not have had the audacity to decline the legitimate request of his colleague. My opinion has now been confirmed .... " The Prime Minister did not respond to this scathing attack that amounted to saying that his Government wanted to muffle Suresh's opinion. A controversy was the last thing the Government needed at that point. After some days Bengal Chief Minister Dr BC Roy, Gandhi's confidant physician and long-time Bose opponent, entered the fray. Those were rainy days for Dwijendra Bose. The CM began to call him. He evaded. Roy finally had him on other side of the receiver.

"Hello! Dwijendra, I am in search of you. Why are you afraid of seeing me. Come to my office my dear." The discussion resumed in the Chief Minister's office. "What are you doing in this business, earning a thousand here or a thousand there. How will you keep your family prestige with this paltry income. I will give you business." Dwijendra wasn't averse to the idea. "You are a friend of the family. Rather you were - in the 30s and in the 20s. If you are in love with the family again, I am here, you may give me business. I will take it." The CM made his move. "You get the report of Shah Nawaz signed by Suresh and I will give you whatever business you want," he proposed. "No, not at that cost. I will never ask my uncle. And for argument's sake, why would he listen to me? He is an independent man," Dwijendra responded. Roy was nobody's fool. He persuaded Suresh Bose to come to the Writers' Building and rephrased his proposal. "Subhas is dead. How come you are stating to the contrary?" was his introductory remark. "Who told you that Subhas is dead?" Suresh shot back. Roy counted the evidence of some witnesses and Suresh discounted it by recalling findings of intelligence agencies. Roy asked Suresh Bose if he would like to be a Governor. This led to an exchange of heated words.[25]

Suresh Bose somehow finished his report by October with the help of notes and copies of some secret papers. He had to publish it on his own in November 1956 for neither the Government not any publisher was willing. *Dissentient Report* ended with an appeal to Indians that they should ask the Government "to place at their disposal, the whole of the evidence that was made available to the Committee" and "form their own opinion after careful perusal and consideration of the same." "... if the general opinion be that the aircraft accident did not take place and that Netaji Subhas Chandra Bose did not die ... demand an impeachment of all those, who have taken part in this nefarious game."[26]

The *Dissentient Report* of Suresh Bose was never widely read, though another edition came out in 1961. A part of the blame lay in its Victorian English. Suresh Bose was soon lost in oblivion. For Shah Nawaz and SN Maitra, it was alleged, the committee stint proved quite useful. Shah Nawaz was promptly made Deputy Minister for Railways and Maitra, for a start, became India's Deputy High Commissioner in Pakistan. In his personal encounters, Shah Nawaz came under fire from those who did not agree with his findings. Lawmaker HV Kamath pressed him on why he would not go to Taiwan, where Bose's plane had reportedly crashed. "Suppose a murder takes place and the police investigate the case without going to the place where the murder took place, what will be the credibility of their investigation?" Shah Nawaz wriggled out saying that he "got all the evidence he wanted sitting in Bangkok and Tokyo and other places."[27] There was not much for him to say when he confronted a niece of Subhas Bose's. "*Kya bhaijaan, deputy ministership ke liye aapne Netaji ko maar diya*!" (Brother, you killed Netaji for deputy ministership!)

The story certainly did not finish with the submission of the report in 1956. Defensive Shah Nawaz appeared as witness No 1 before Khosla Commission and later came Suresh Bose. The angry old man described Shah Nawaz "a dark specimen of an unparalleled treachery to Netaji." "He has been a traitor to Netaji by supporting Prime Minister Nehru in his report that

Netaji had died which was clearly against the oral and documentary evidence adduced and for which he was awarded." Suresh Bose let loose a volley of allegations: "Shah Nawaz Khan falsely coined his rank as Major General instead of his correct rank as Colonel in the Azad Hind Fauj ... he fought well in the initial stage of the war but subsequently played Netaji false .... He was rightly suspected of passing over some INA secrets to his brother and others in the British Indian Army opposing them for which he was given an important assignment away from Netaji's headquarters. Some loyal officers were placed with him for reporting about his conduct and he was not allowed to meet Netaji during his last four and half months' stay in South East Asia .... the order of court-martial was passed against him but it was not carried out as the war suddenly came to end."

The *Times of India* on 6 November 1970 quoted Suresh Bose telling the Commission that "Jawaharlal Nehru did not agree that it was very necessary for 'us' (members of the Committee) in our inquiry' to inspect the site at Taihoku, where the alleged plane crash involving Netaji was reported to have occurred .... Shah Nawaz had later told him that there was no diplomatic difficulties for visiting Taihoku, the Prime Minister, Mr Nehru, did not like it .... Nehru did not agree to include Dr Binode Pal in the Committee either as chairman or a member because he (Nehru) said that Dr Pal was of the opinion that Netaji was not dead ...."

Suresh's views were backed by some other witnesses. Sham Lal Jain, who had in 1946 worked with the INA Defence Committee, testified on 31 December 1970 that he had "typed the personal files relating to Mr Shah Nawaz Khan." "Khan was never a Major General." A diary of Lt Colonel Ehsan Qadir, a Minister in PGI, "revealed that this Shah Nawaz Khan created communalism in the INA by inciting the Muslim members of the INA ...." Jain quoted Qadir (later a Pakistani) writing that "I saw ... with my own eyes ... what sort of work this Shah Nawaz Khan was doing to ruin the INA .... I brought this fact to the knowledge of Netaji ... who took a serious view and immediately ordered for the court-martial ...." INA's Colonel Thakur Singh stated that "the very first day when I put the company of SN Khan on duty, those handpicked by SN Khan defected. Netaji came to know about this."

Aware of what all his detractors thought of him, Shah Nawaz emotively refuted all charges. His story was that Suresh Bose "appended a dissenting report relating to Netaji's death, apparently 'under family pressure' to keep the issue alive for political reasons." He said that Nehru learnt from Mountbatten that Bose had died. He denied ever making a public statement that Bose was alive. He affirmed that the Prime Minister had nothing to do with the Committee's skipping a visit to Taiwan. "The Japanese were prepared to make arrangements for the Committee to go to Formosa, (but) the consensus of the Committee was that no useful purpose would be served in going there."[28]

Khan lied through his teeth so far as Formosa affair was concerned. A sneak peep into official papers showed that they did not proximate with Shah Nawaz's statement absolving the Nehru Government of throwing a spanner in the works. In May 1956, Shah Nawaz strongly mooted to the Embassy of India in Tokyo about inspecting the scene of the crash in Taiwan. Ambassador BR Sen immediately sounded the MEA. In his reply, the ministry conjured up unfounded assumptions to the prejudice of the inquiry relevant for India.

"Your telegram No 44 May 19. Matter has been placed before Prime Minister. We had to make it clear to Committee in Delhi that it would not be practicable or advisable for them to visit Formosa. The only possible advantage of going there might have been to see entries in hospital registers .... At the Committee's request we had approached UK High Commissioner here to get this information for us but have not had a reply yet. The Japanese Ambassador in Formosa would be in a better position to handle this matter than the British who have only a Consul .... We have considered the matter again and are not in favour of the Committee visiting Formosa. Japanese good offices may enable the Committee to land there but it is unlikely that the Formosan Government will give any facilities. In fact they may put obstacles and suggest degrading conditions. Apart from this, politically this will be very embarrassing for us and might lead to complicating situation."[29]

But it turned out the next day that far from what they had been portrayed by the MEA, the Taiwanese were nice enough to be willing to help the Indians despite the lack of formal ties. Officer "Kaul" sent a telegram to Ambassador Sen. Without assigning any reasons, he again began casting aspersion on Taiwan's bona fide offer: "Reference our telegrams No 28407 May 22. UK High Commission have just informed us that their Consul in Taipeh has telegraphed that Formosan authorities are willing to allow 5 Chinese whose names were given by the Committee to be examined by British Consul in the presence of Formosan officials. They are however not prepared to let them to go to Hong Kong to appear before our Committee .... Formosan authorities' refusal to allow witnesses to go to Hong Kong is significant. It is possible that they may tutor their witnesses and make them give wrong statements which may only complicate the work of the committee. Our opinion therefore that the Committee should not visit Formosa confirmed."

The Taiwanese had no reason or need whatsoever to tutor any witnesses. Some fear had been creeping up in the South Block. On 25 May 1956, AK Dar, First Secretary in the Indian Embassy in Tokyo, conveyed to Shah Nawaz that he was not to visit Taiwan. "The Ministry of External Affairs feel strongly that any attempt to visit Formosa may well turn out to be embarrassing all round and lead to frustrating complications without any advantage for the Commission (sic) .... This letter has been written in the absence of the Ambassador and, if the Commission so desires, confirmation of the above reply from the Ministry of External Affairs can be secured when the Ambassador returns to Tokyo." Ambassador Sen returned and Dar hammered into Shah Nawaz on 28 May that the visit was out of question. "I am desired to say that the Ambassador has on return to Tokyo confirmed the contents of my two letters .... The Ministry of External Affairs feel after reconsideration of the matter that they would not be in favour of the Commission visiting Formosa ... it is not likely that the Formosan Government would extend any facilities .... Under the circumstances, I am to request for advice of further action desired in the matter of securing authenticated copies of the entries in the hospital registers at Formosa."

A Franklin, the British Consul in Tamsui, Taiwan, did go ahead with the task entrusted by the British High Commission in Delhi. What he found out was neither revealed in Shah Nawaz's report nor ever made public by the Government. The Government of India's specific queries to the High Commission had been inspired by the findings of journalist Harin Shah who had conducted some on-the-spot inquiries in Taiwan in 1946 and had concluded that Bose had died there in a crash. Shah immediately disclosed his findings to the Indian Ambassador in Nanking, China. "Ambassador Shri KPS Menon was friendly and most considerate. From that very evening ... we agreed that we should take care to see that the papers bearing on Formosa investigation that I was wanting to send to India should not be lost or miscarried on the way. I think, he permitted me to send the Formosa material to India through the courtesy of the Diplomatic Bag. I believe those papers reached India under a British escort."[30]

Shah returned to India in 1947 and caught up with Home Minister Vallabbhai Patel in his early morning walk in Delhi's Lodi Garden to tell him of his findings. Patel asked Shah to try convince Sarat Bose. He did that in early 1949 in Prague, but failed. Shah did not publicize his findings for a decade or so until Shah Nawaz Committee was formed. Suddenly, he came out with tear-jerker of a book — *Gallant End of Netaji* — and made a killing. It carried statements and photographs of many Taiwanese witnesses to the crash and Bose's death. Shah Nawaz made full use of Harin Shah's evidence to prove the Taipei crash even as Suresh Bose differed. "I fail to understand the utility of this ridiculous piece of evidence to prove Netaji's death."[31]

After Shah Nawaz Committee had been formed, the Government asked the British High Commission in Delhi to trace the witnesses cited by Shah, get their testimony and obtain copies of the hospital entries and cremation certificate for Subhas Bose. "Indian official concerned was obviously embarrassed at making this request. Nevertheless I think there is some advantage in trying to establish the facts in this case and to put a stop to legends about Bose's survival,"[32] the High Commissioner wrote to the Consul on 3 May 1956. The specific queries were forwarded to Chairman of Taiwan Provincial Government, CK Yen, who ordered the Department of Health to look into the matter. Official Kang Fu Chaing, who supervised all crematoria on the island, conducted inquiries. His findings, reported to the British High Commissioner on 4 July 1956, in no way proved Bose's death. There were no old records left in the hospital and the cremation certificate said to be for Bose actually turned out to be for some Japanese soldier. The eyewitnesses Harin Shah had quoted had either disappeared or they knew nothing. The rest had nothing to prove it was Bose who had died in Taipei on 18/19 August 1945. One witness to "Bose's cremation" clarified that he saw a body "packed in powdered lime, swathed in white cloth"[33] whose "only the eyes, the nose and the lips were visible (all black in colour)."[34] "We were not acquainted with Bose in his lifetime, it therefore follows that we could not identify him after his death. We can only speak according to what we remember of what took place at the time",[35] Chen Chih-Chih said.

The last statement Shah Nawaz Khan publicly made on the Bose death controversy was in 1978. He called for closing it. There was a minuscule view that he had been "forced" to profess what he really did not believe in. Before Khosla Commission an acquaintance reminisced about Shah Nawaz's confessions. "It is foolish to think that Netaji is dead," PS Lavania claimed Shah Nawaz had told him in early 1950s. He went on to say that in Tokyo Shah Nawaz was confided in by some Japanese witnesses that he should not worry for "Bose was safe." Lavania said Shah Nawaz had brought this to the notice of the Prime Minister. Thirty years on someone said Lavania might have been right. INA veteran, and a friend of Shah Nawaz's, Colonel AB Singh said it happened some time before Shah Nawaz's death in 1980. They were at the dining table and, as usually, Singh egged him on until Shah Nawaz became teary-eyed. "AB, I made the blunder of my life as Chairman of Netaji Inquiry Committee."[36]

Notes:

1 *Dissentient Report* by Suresh Bose. Appendix BB.

2 Ibid. Pages 2, 3.

3 Ibid. Pages 19, 20.

4 Intelligence Bureau's 'Daily INA Report No. 56' dated 5 February 1946 says: "In the Punjab, the rumour that Bose is alive is also current. Shah Nawaz and Ehsan Qadir are both stated to have said recently that they greatly doubt the reports of Bose's death." (National Archives, Delhi). Shah Nawaz had met Habibur Rahman in Red Fort and heard about the crash.

5 File No 2(64)/56-PM, Volume I.

6 Ibid. Secret Telegram. CCB No 7827.

7 Jagdish Kodesia's evidence before Khosla Commission on 1 March 1971. It appears from Kodesia's testimony that Rauf was shifted to some other country and that he died soon after.

8 Ibid.

9 *Netaji Inquiry Committee Report.* Page 3.

10 *Hindustan Standard.* 4 April 1956.

11 File No 2(64)/56-PM, Volume I.

12 Ibid. Prime Minister's note dated 2 April 1956.

13 Suresh Bose's letter to Prime Minister. File No 2(64)/56-PM, Volume I.

14 Ibid. No 792-PMH/56.

15 Ibid. No 793-PMH/56.

16 Suresh Bose's account in *Dissentient Report.*

17 *Dissentient Report* by Suresh Bose. Page 16.

18 *Dissentient Report* by Suresh Bose. Page 83.

19 Amiya Nath Bose, son of Sarat Bose, told Khosla Commission that when he tried to search for Satoh, the Ministry of External Affairs told him that no such person ever appeared before the committee. But he managed to find Satoh in Tokyo and had his statement recorded in a tape, which he duly produced before the Commission.

20 *Dissentient Report* by Suresh Bose. Page 17.

21 Dwijendra Nath Bose's testimony before Khosla Commission. Habib had told CSDIC that on August 18 "Bose was not wearing a wristlet watch ..."

22 *Dissentient Report* by Suresh Bose. Page 37.

23 Ibid.

24 No 414-PMO/56. Reproduced in *Dissentient Report*.

25 This account is based on the testimonies of Suresh Bose and Dwijendra Nath Bose before Khosla Commission. Suresh Bose also told Justice Khosla that "had I signed this report my reward would have been the Governorship of Bengal which the Prime Minister Nehru for fear of inviting insult from me did not offer it to me himself but had it done through the Chairman (Shah Nawaz) who told me in Tokyo 'Mr Bose you could become the Governor of Bengal if you choose to'." Record of Proceedings of Khosla Commission. Volume II, page 729.

26 *Dissentient Report* by Suresh Bose. Page 181.

27 HV Kamath's testimony before Khosla Commission.

28 Shah Nawaz's testimony before Khosla Commission.

29 CCB No 3318. Telegram No 28407. File No 2(64)/56-PM, Volume I.

30 *The Gallant End of Netaji* by Harin Shah. Page 117.

31 *Dissentient Report* by Suresh Bose. Page 168.

32 Confidential *Inward Telegram to Commonwealth Relations Office*. Ref C 1852/1. The National Archives (PRO), London.

33 Taiwan Provincial Government's report to AAE Franklin, Her Majesty's Consul at Tamsui. The National Archives (PRO), London. Ref c 1852/6. File No. FO 371/121012.

34 Ibid.

35 Ibid.

36 Input by AB Singh. Colonel Singh deposed the same before Mukherjee Commission.

5

Sham Commission

If such a step is not taken without delay, posterity will never forget the Government and the people of India for their neglect and indifference to ascertain actual facts about one of the mightiest architects of India's liberation.

A 1967 memorandum to Government of India, urging a judicial probe into Subhas Bose's death.

I am convinced beyond any shadow of doubt that Netaji is alive. So, this inquiry is of no value to me.

Dwijendra Nath Bose to Khosla Commission during his deposition in 1972.

It (Khosla Commission's finding) was something like QED. This was to have been proved; this has been proved.

MP Sasankasekhar Sanyal in Parliament in 1977.

The mystery surrounding the death of Subhas Bose peaked following the Government's acceptance of Shah Nawaz Committee report. Those were the years when very very strange things were heard. A top Naga leader openly voiced belief in Bose's continuing existence. Bose was "spotted" in Tibet and Uttar Pradesh. A booklet said he had assumed the identity of a top Chinese general. The 1962 India-China war turned a catalyst, one would not know why. Some one said Bose was alive and Home Minister Lal Bahadur Shastri knew about it. People jumped from their seats in cinema halls; caught on camera was "Netaji" in Teen Murti House in Delhi. MPs accosted

Prime Minister Shastri in Parliament over a spitting image of Bose by Nehru's bier in May 1964. Shastri told a fellow Congressman soon after Nehru's cremation that mammoth crowds would gather if it were announced that Bose was coming. Then there was one "Subhas Chandra Bose" who made a speech on Moscow radio after the 1965 Tashkent Agreement, etc.

The offshoot that led to most brouhaha came from obscure Shoulmari pocket in Cooch Behar district of West Bengal. A holy man's ashram near the international border became talk of the nation in early 1960s. Armed men roamed about there, allowing no one inside unless a detailed form was filled in. Ascetic Swami Shardanand or Shoulmari Baba lived a fanciful life. The first outsider to penetrate his amazing abode was one Radhey Shyam Jaiswal, a school teacher, who straightaway reported to the Prime Minister. In his letter to Nehru, Jaiswal accused Shoulmari Baba of spreading rumours that he was Subhas Bose. Jaiswal zeroed in on the intrigue that the administratively-run ashram harboured foreign agents. Baba was painted as an unusual holy man – he spoke in English and puffed imported cigarettes. No one knew for sure what action Nehru took on Jaiswal's letter. Heard through grapevine was a story about some investigation by the Government.

Within months of Jaiswal shooting the letter to Nehru, an old follower of Subhas Bose's came out of hibernation to claim that Shardanand was indeed Subhas Bose. In his press conference on 13 February 1962, Satya Gupta repeatedly harped on Shardanand's "real" identity while offering no clue about his whereabouts since 1945. "There is no mistake in identifying my master and there is no doubt that Shoulmari Sadhuji is Netaji. Existence of the sun and moon may be questioned but my meetings with Netaji is beyond all doubts."[1] Satya Gupta's statement was synchronized with the activities of Haripad Bose, joint secretary of the ashram. Everyone wanted to reach out to the Prime Minister. Haripad sent Nehru a telegram saying that his "lost friend" was at Shoulmari. The ashram denied the claims and expelled Haripad. In February 1962 itself, N Dutt Majumdar, a former Bengal minister, met Shardanand and told press that he was "an extraordinary person but not Bose." Unmindful of counter claims, Haripad and Satya Gupta went all over India and caused much furore with their stories.

The Prime Minister finally intervened but would not say much. "We have inquired into this matter," he wrote to the editor of *India Reformer* on 18 April 1963, "and we are quite sure that the story about his (Shardanand's) being Netaji is completely without basis."[2] Atal Bihari Vajpayee drew his attention in Parliament on 22 August 1963 over the "propaganda carried on by some self-appointed persons and organizations" and asked "whether any enquiry has been made?" "We are aware of such propaganda which was carried on. It has faded now more or less," Nehru replied. "But such enquiries we have made and the Government of West Bengal have made have conclusively established that Swami Shardanand is not Netaji Subhas Chandra Bose, and he himself denies it absolutely."[3]

Over a period of time, Satya Gupta was forgotten and no trace was left of Haripad. Their place was taken by Uttam Chand Malhotra who immediately clicked due to his antecedents. He could rightly claim to have played a vital part in helping Bose escape to Germany.[4] What had happened in 1941 was not a Sisir Bose show all the way. There were multiple players and arrangements. Subhas began to sound his confidants of his plan much before the D-day. Niranjan Singh Talib took message to Acchar Singh Cheema, and Cheema spoke to Akali leader Master Tara Singh. Bose eventually sneaked into Afghanistan in the guise of a Pathan. For days, he hid from the enemy agents in Malhotra's Kabul residence. In July 1962, Malhotra met Shardanand, and, together with Hira Lal Dixit, he set out on a decade-long propagation that he was Bose indeed.

The subsiding of the Shoulmari tales in second half of 1960s was followed by the rise of the restless Samar Guha. Freedom fighter, chemistry professor and Bose votary, Guha burst on the national scene on 3 April 1967 — his first day as an MP in Parliament. He made an emotive case for a "joint enquiry by the Government of Japan, the Government of Formosa and Government of India." This was the shape of the things to come. Going solo, Guha resorted to tactics like sit-ins at Parliament to make himself heard. When Indira Gandhi's Government showed no inclination to consider his demand Guha roped in like-minded persons, including Atal Bihari Vajpayee and Madhu Limaye, in and out of the Parliament and formed a "national committee" to pressurize the Government. Success came their way as a record-breaking number of MPs cutting across parties threw weight behind the cause. A memorandum signed by 350 MPs representing every nook and corner of India was sent to President Zakir Hussain. The old Nehru loyalist, nevertheless, wasn't impressed. " ... an inquiry into the matter like this after a lapse of 22 years can hardly help in bringing to light any further material set at rest, whatever doubts people may have ...,"[5] Principal Secretary to the President wrote on 24 May 1968. The MPs bounced back. A delegation marched into the Rashtrapati Bhawan and pleaded again before the President. The vibes were bad still, so a letter signed by 45 leading MPs landed in the Prime Minister's Office. Indira Gandhi treated the issue like it was the dirty end of the stick. A response came on 30 July 1969, but from the perennial External Affairs Minister Dinesh Singh. "As you are aware that this matter has been raised in Parliament on several occasions and the Government have adequately explained their stand, last year, when members of Parliament had given a memorandum, the Government considered it in some depth. However, Government reiterated that a further inquiry into the death of Netaji was not warranted."[6]

This was a blow. After some frustrating days, the national committee got the chance to do some arm-twisting. The intra-party contradictions had destabilised Indira's Government. Things came to a head with the split in the Congress in 1969 over the defeat of Congress nominee in the presidential elections. Though Indira sided with the winning candidate, two setbacks came her way. The split made her minority government dependable on a combination of MPs, bulk of whom were signatory to Guha's memorandum. More importantly, the new President, VV Giri, was empathetic to travails of Bose's admirers. MPs turned on the heat. Emotional pleas resounded in power corridors. Guha and others led a number of abortive representations to the Prime Minister. Then it was up to the President, who heeded and forwarded Indira the memorandum with his favourable comments.

Home Minister YB Chavan dithered in a December 1969 meeting attended by leading MPs, Bose kin and followers. After months' wait Amiya Nath Bose, MP and Bose's nephew, vented his anger in Parliament on 3 March 1970. "So far as the inquiry, if one can call that farce to be an inquiry, that was held by Shri Shah Nawaz Khan ... is concerned, it is best to consign it to the dustbin of history. It is unfortunate that the fate and the life of a person who dedicated his entire life to the service of this country was being inquired into by persons who were thoroughly worthless and incompetent for the job .... I ... call upon the Government of India to appoint without delay a judicial inquiry commission ...." On March 6 hurt ministers fumed in a Cabinet meeting: "Government should not have given the impression that it was against a fresh inquiry when millions of people were interested to know what had happened to Netaji. The Government's rejection of the demand both in and outside had created a wrong impression among some people that there was something to hide."[7]

The Government gave in. On 11 July 1970, orders were issued for the formation of a One-man Commission and a month later GD Khosla, a retired Chief Justice of the Punjab High Court, took over as its Chairman. Suave Gopal Das Khosla, a celebrity in his own right, had graduated from Cambridge and excelled in the judicial branch of the ICS until his retirement in 1961. A footnote for him had already been earmarked in history. He was the sentencing judge in the Gandhi murder case. A prolific writer, he had to his credit many outstanding works. He wrote in 1949 *Stern Reckoning*, a benchmark work on the tragedy of the partition. In 1963 was published *Murder of the Mahatma & Other Cases from a Judge's Notebook*. Khosla's circles of friends was fabulous: Khushwant Singh, Nirad C Chaudhari, and above all Jawaharlal Nehru. "Justice Khosla was closely associated with the Nehru family. He had shared his literary interests with Jawaharlal Nehru at Manali where they spent a good deal of time together trekking through the forests and hills."[8]

And there was the fly in the ointment. Khosla nursed a grouse against Subhas Bose ever since his London days. "In his golden years, savouring the rewards of a loyal mandarin of British India and also of Nehru's India, Khosla recalled Subhas's Cambridge successes with unconcealed envy .... Khosla disliked Subhas at Cambridge where the latter towered above the peer group, both physically and scholastically."[9] At Fitswilliam House Khosla had had an unforgettable encounter. He saw Bose surrounded by Indian students. He went over and heard Bose saying that he had decided to discard the heaven-born service. "When he learnt that Khosla was preparing for the ICS examination, Bose gave him a withering look of contempt and condemned his act as unpatriotic .... Bose's earlier treatment was bound to rankle in Khosla's heart."[10]

GD Khosla began in style. On 14 October he called a press conference and made a string of promises. He said that all relevant matters would be looked into and that he would approach the Governments of the UK, the USA, the Soviet Union, Japan and Taiwan for "evidence about disappearance of Netaji in 1945."[11] The opening session of Khosla Commission was held in Delhi's Vigyan Bhawan on 16 October 1970. First witness was grim-looking Shah Nawaz Khan. He began with some extravagant histrionics, saying he should be "hanged in public" if it was proved that he had "played a fraud on the nation." "Yes! You are a traitor to Netaji Bose,"[12] Amiya Bose screamed at the top of his voice. The next venue was even hotter. Commission's second sitting in Calcutta on 18 November 1970 was marred by ugly events. Khosla adjourned the session early in the day, which made the people infuriated. He tried to leave but couldn't. They dragged him out of the lift and forced him to take the chair. "The personal appeal by the Secretary of the Commission Mr DK Das to the impatient crowd to help keep the sanctity of the Court yielded no result. The agitated people stood up on the chairs, scaled the galleries, rushed towards the Judge's Bench and continued shouting slogans."[13]

The issues Khosla faced were multitudinous. However, he chose to give the Shoulmari episode more than a fair deal. Protagonist Uttam Chand Malhotra appeared before him under media glare in December 1970. Kholsa indulged in his never-ending tales that went into 220 typed pages. Perhaps the idea was to accentuate the absurdities that were going around in Bose's name. In his report, Khosla freely played up many instances of inane depositions.[14] He concluded that Subhas Bose sightings and suchlike episodes were bunkum and propagators were either hallucinating or seeking cheap publicity. That was the long and short of it, but not the full story. There were fishy parts GD Khosla hushed up while writing his report. Dwijendra Nath Bose, for one, alleged before him that Swami Shardanand was a prop set up by the Government. "This is being done to bewilder the people with the names of these sadhus. There are three sadhus today running in the name of Netaji .... The people who propagate that these sadhus are Netajis are all financed by the Government."[15]

"Yes, I had gone there. There was much propaganda about this sadhu ... it (Shoulmari ashram) was full of CID people. This SC Mukherjee, this Bhola Mullick were there. This SC Mukherjee was next to Handoo. This man (SC Mukherjee) was made the administrator of the ashram. He posed before me that he was an ICS .... I enquired and came to know that this gentlemen was an assistant of Handoo who was the Chief Security Officer of Nehru and belonged to the Intelligence Department .... There was another one Bhaumick. He also belonged to intelligence. There were other fellows, but I have forgotten their names. All of them were CID people."

The "CID people" were Intelligence Bureau's top guns. Bhola Mullick was BN Mullick, India's numero uno secret service man and GK Handoo was once a deputy director in the IB. Dwijendra was not alone in thinking that way. *Ananda Bazar Patrika's* political correspondent Barun Sengupta, one of the finest reporters in the country, pointed up his version. The *Patrika* had done some investigations and had published a report of Sengupta's on 6 November 1970. The substance of the report was that more than 20 years after his "death", Subhas Bose was a subject under surveillance. Enquiries were carried out at the northern and eastern borders of India. Sengupta told the commission on 6 July 1972 that Nehru was behind these enquires.

"As reporters we very often used to talk to (CM, West Bengal) Mr PC Sen. Once he went to Japan and after coming back from Japan he said certain things about Netaji's disappearance. Then I asked him one day 'Mr Sen, the late Prime Minister was also interested to know about all these things?' He admitted, 'Yes.' I said, 'These enquiries were being made through Dr BC Roy (former CM), through you and Mr (Assam Chief Minister BC) Chaliha?' He said, 'Yes.' But he did not like to go into details of these things. This is about the Chief Minister. Then about the ex-followers of Netaji .... Surendra Mohan Ghosh ... he was being deputed for this work."[16]

Sengupta was asked to elaborate what Sen had let slip on his return from Japan. "He said that some people told him that there was no plane crash." On Shoulmari tales, the *Patrika* report was quoted to Khosla: " ... we have heard about many saints and monks masquerading as Netaji. The central Intelligence Bureau knows fully well about all of them." This prompted some more questions and intrepid Sengupta was all game: "When the Shoulmari sadhu affair came up very prominently in West Bengal, I was asked by the editor to investigate into all these things .... I had no belief in this from the very beginning, but as a reporter I had to go and investigate. I went to the local intelligence people, the State Intelligence Bureau as it is called, the intelligence branch of the West Bengal Police. I asked one of the chief men who was supposed to be dealing with this section, 'What is this about Shoulmari?'"

"Off the record, I can tell you one thing. We wanted to investigate into the affairs. The Central Intelligence has submitted a certain report. They have submitted some report which we do not believe," the official said much to Sengupta's surprise. "And when we do not believe a certain thing about the Central Intelligence, we have to make a through enquiry about it by going into details and all that. So, knowing fully well that it is a very serious matter .... I sought permission from Dr BC Roy, the then Chief Minister of West Bengal to go into the matter deeply. But the Chief Minister told me not to bother about these things."

Sengupta revealed that the IB was on lookout for a dead freedom fighter.

"Whenever there is a rumour or a story, the Central Intelligence people and the state Intelligence people go and investigate into it. They also come to us for further enlightenment and to know whether we have any information ...."

"He (BN Mullick) was also entrusted with the Netaji Inquiry affair because I was told by so many Intelligence Officers working in the eastern regions of the country that it is Mr Mullick who looks after all these things. Personally also he used to visit all these northern and northeastern borders of our country. (In connection with the Bose mystery) .... I never talked to Mr Mullick and I knew that Mr Mullick will not tell me anything .... Mr Chaliha, Mr PC Sen and Dr BC Roy knew certain things. There are certain things which do not go beyond the Chief Minister's level."

Barun Sengupta wasn't imagining things. BC Roy and BC Chaliha had died but PC Sen, Chief Minister of West Bengal from 1962 to 1967, was summoned by the Commission. He wriggled himself out saying little. He said during his 1965 Japan visit he was told at a tea party that Bose did not perish in 1945. It did not strike Khosla that a Chief Minister could have been so naive as to lend ears to such gossips when the Government of India had declared Bose's death. "Friends came to me and said that this sadhu was not Netaji," Sen said on Shoulmari Baba. He was more forthright while giving his overall impression. "This matter of Netaji's death or Netaji's remaining alive, is a controversial matter." Sen's ambiguity was surpassed by SR Mirchandani, a Deputy Director in Research and Analysis Wing (R&AW) at the time of his deposition on 24 July 1972.

Mirchandani had been called because Barun Sengupta had named him. It did not take Amar Prasad Chakravarty, the counsel for Forward Bloc, to make out that Mirchandani had no intention to help the inquiry. So he first tried to get around him by asking him to define the work the IB did. The idea was to tie him up with the claim that the IB had been looking into the Bose controversy. Once the officer had accepted that the Government could have been asked to reveal what the agency had found out. This was easier said than done.

"Q: Mr Mirchandani, I want to understand a little about this Intelligence Bureau under Ministry of Home Affairs as you have said. What is the main job of this department which is called Intelligence Bureau?

A: About political activities of various parties.

Q: And about the individuals of political importance also?

A: They would also come. They have been included in the political parties.

Q: Does this department collect this intelligence of its own accord or when it is directed to do so by the Ministry?

A: It is a regular function. There is no day-to-day direction; it is a regular function of the Intelligence Bureau to collect about what is happening in the country.

Q: May I take it that supposing something is reported in the newspapers — some story — which has a political bearing, it would be the function of your department to investigate about that?

A: If the Government asks for it.

Q: Otherwise not?

A: Otherwise not.

Q: That is why I asked you in the beginning that is it the function of this department to collect intelligence of its own accord, or as and when directed by the Home Ministry.

A: It is the routine function of the department to collect intelligence and the directions are given by the Ministry of Home Affairs.

Q: It is not clear to me. Supposing if a political news or something appears in the press which has political importance and which can excite the public mind, will you wait for the directions of the Home Ministry or is it your function to collect on your own?

A: That depends upon the importance of the news item.

Q: I say, news about any political leader of consequence. Of course, no one is going to expect you to collect intelligence about the PM.

A: It would depend upon what the contents of the news items are. May be that the news items would be a cock and bull story.

Q: But how can you say it is cock and bull story unless you investigate it? If a cock and bull story appears in the press, would you or would you not investigate?

A: Yes, I would."

That is, the IB would, *suo moto,* collect information about stirring news items, even if they were of cock and bull variety. The next line of reasoning, as put up by commission's counsel TR Bhasin, was that surely the IB must have seen reports about Bose mystery and must have snooped around. But the officer ducked the queries.

"Q: Suppose something appeared in the press about Netaji Subhas Chandra Bose after 1945. Would it be the function of the Central or Subsidiary Intelligence Bureau to investigate into that aspect?

A: It was only of a local significance which appeared in the Shillong paper.

Q: Whether it is of local significance or national significance will you not investigate that?

A: If it appeared in Calcutta, then I will not do that.

Q: If it concerned the Central or Subsidiary Intelligence, will you not investigate?

A: That is something which only the Director (Intelligence Bureau) is qualified to answer.

Q: That is a very evasive answer. Are you not in the CIB? (Central Intelligence Bureau).

A: I was.

Q: Then are you not expected to know whether the Central Intelligence officer has the duty to collect the intelligence or not?

A: I would say, that that was not part of the CBI (Central Bureau of Investigation). "

Amar Prasad Chakravarty had a go, again.

"Q: But the Subsidiary Intelligence Bureau is to look after the political development within the country. Is it so?

A: That is right.

Q: It is your evidence, I take it, that you had no occasion to enquire into the whereabouts of Netaji.

A: Throughout my service, I have never been asked to enquire about Netaji.

Q: But Mr Mirchandani, I say that you know many things but you are not disclosing them before the Commission. You know many things regarding Netaji.

A: I have never handled any paper, files, report, source report, newspaper report, about Netaji.

Q: My question is that you know many things about Netaji.

A: I know many things but I never handled this subject.

Q: But you know something.

A: I know nothing officially.

Q: May I take it you had knowledge of all the political affairs except this?

A: Netaji was not relevant in Assam (where Mirchandani was posted in 60s). The question does not arise. Even in my services I had not dealt with that subject because

> I had not handled it .... He has been dead for the last 20 years nor does the question arise about my enquiring about him.
>
> Q: If he is dead, why is this Commission sitting?"[17]

Strictly, Mirchandani was not wrong. Chakravarty's choice of words was wrong. The IB was not an investigating agency. Their job was to simply collect intelligence. Making enquiries was the responsibility of other agencies, like the CBI. When cross-examined about his talks with Barun Sengupta, Mirchandani, looking shifty, said, "I cannot divulge the official secrets."

The next month, BN Mullick, Director of Intelligence Bureau in 50s and 60s, and his successor in 1972, A Jayaram, appeared before GD Khosla in Delhi. Mullick's reputation had preceded him. He was the man who had rebuilt and nurtured the IB in independent India. Forever in the good books of Prime Minister, he had single-handedly controlled internal and external intelligence of India much longer than anyone else. Khosla set the tone of cross-examination by raising heckles of an otherwise servile TR Bhasin.

"Ask Mr Mullick if he has information about it. He can reply from his memory. If he says that he will like to refer to those files, then he can refer to those files; or if he says he knows nothing then you can refer him to these (IB) files."[18]

"That he cannot say — he knows nothing," Bhasin told Khosla. "There is no justification to become the Director of Intelligence Bureau if he says he has nothing to say; or he knows nothing about it. He can say, of course, he prefers to say nothing."

Khosla wasn't amused. "I am not quite sure what sort of information is sought to be obtained from him .... I think it was Mr (Amar Prasad) Chakravarty who suggested that we should examine the head of the intelligence of that time."

Mullick's deposition began. He spoke evasively, like he knew nothing, in contrast with sincere witnesses like Barun Sengupta.

As would be the wont of a seasoned intelligence man, he seldom gave a straight answer to a question. Selective amnesia remained a problem throughout and the words/phrases he often employed were "no," "I do not know," "I do not remember," "probably," "vaguely" etc. Here was the man who perhaps knew more about India of 1950s and early 1960s than anyone else, but when it came to Bose mystery, he behaved as if he had been living in a cave.

Mullick was put questions similar to those faced by Mirchandani. Bhasin asked him to describe the basic function of the IB. "To look after the security of India," Mullick said, admitting that in pursuance "any matter that agitated the public mind or created a sensation" would come on the agency's scanner. Bhasin wondered if Bose mystery too agitated the people. "It did," Mullick admitted.

"Did the Intelligence Bureau deal with this aspect?" was the counter question.

"No. During the entire period that I was Director of Intelligence Bureau, we were never asked to make enquiry about this aspect."

"Do you remember that there were number of questions on the floor of the Parliament?"

"Yes. I remember that."

"May I take that none of them were referred to the Intelligence Bureau?"

"None of them were referred to the Intelligence Bureau during the time I was the Director of the Intelligence Bureau."

Quite naturally, Mullick was queried on the Allied intelligence reports on Bose's death.

"As Director of IB do you know at that time that there were files with the Intelligence Bureau relating to Netaji's disappearance or alleged plane crash?"

"There were some papers relating to enquires made by the then IB about Netaji's alleged death."

"Had you any occasion to look them up?"

"I had occasion to look them up to make myself acquainted as to what were the facts."

"Would that be correct that from that material nothing conclusive was established?"

Khosla got restless at this and butted in. "It is not important if he drew the conclusion whether Netaji had disappeared or not." Mullick went on to invent a story that "Sarat Bose believed that Netaji had died in the plane crash" and claimed that he did not know any of the war-time investigating officers. Truth was that he knew well Bakshi Badrinath, then leading a retired life in Delhi. Khosla too was aware of the Badrinath's role in the Allied probe, but he made no efforts to trace him. Badrinath and PES Finney, the IB Deputy Director in 1945, remained friends until the Britisher's death in early 1970s. The deposition progressed with Mullick turning increasingly hostile. His reaction was sought on the stories of Bose being alive.

"I do not know. I think the place I know and a hint was made that Sadhu of Shoulmari as Netaji but then that was disputed."

"May I take that you had something to do in proving into mystery of Baba of Shoulmari?"

"We made no enquires about the Baba of Shoulmari. I am talking about my time."

"Supposing if there was responsible statement made on the floor of the Parliament that Director of Intelligence Bureau has submitted report, that would be incorrect."

"In my time, it would be incorrect."

"You were never asked by the Government, by the late Prime Minister Pandit Nehru about Baba of Shoulmari?"

"As far as I remember, I was never asked by the late Pandit Nehru about the Baba of Shoulmari."

"On your own, did you not consider it as matter of any importance."

"On my own, I did not consider it as a matter of importance."[19]

So here was Mullick, reiterating with his stiff body language that when the whole of India was engulfed in Bose mystery, the IB was doing nothing. Fine. Next day, 9 August 1972, was the turn of the incumbent DIB. Jayaram turned out to be a greenhorn in dodging tactics. He too wouldn't give a straight answer on Bose mystery and initially gave the line that Shoulmari episode wasn't looked into.

"Has your department been dealing with the subject of Netaji Subhas Chandra Bose?"

"As DIB I can only say that the Intelligence branch has wide possibility and whatever the government wishes to know, we will do it but it is difficult for me to say what we do or what we do not."

"Have you ever been asked specifically to make any inquiry relating directly or indirectly with Netaji since you took over as DIB?"

"Since I took over, I have not been asked."

"You were not asked but did you of your own accord ... and for good reasons direct or conduct any such inquiries?"

"No. Since I took over my office."

"Can you say that the Intelligence Department has not at all been dealing with any news concerning Netaji?"

"I cannot say that but we have presented whatever material we have."

"Not producing old files but doing a positive act. What ... (we) want to know is have you ever, your department, done enquiry?"

"Not that I know of."

"Can you say that your Intelligence Department has never conducted any inquiry into Baba of Shoulmari Ashram?"

"I can only talk from my memory. This subject did come up some years ago and when we use the word enquiry, not in the form of police inquiry."

"I am talking as a layman!"

"Inquiries will be done by the police organisation. In this particular case by West Bengal Government and they would send their reports or pass their reports both to the Government and to us."

"There were certain enquiries?"

"Certainly."

After bit of hum and haw Jayaram admitted that Shoulmari case was looked into during Mullick's time. In other words, Mullick had lied. Jayaram's disclosure provoked the moot question from a counsel. "When the Government of India has accepted Shah Nawaz Committee's report that Netaji is dead then how is it that the Intelligence Department goes after every news when it appears that Netaji is not dead and he is alive?"[20]

Surendra Mohan Ghosh, former MP, came as well. He admitted that he had been personally asked by Nehru to find out if Swami Shardanand was Subhas Bose. He went to Shoulmari ashram on 11 September 1962 along with lawmaker NR Ghosh, who had made all arrangements. He met the man who people said was Bose. He was nothing like Subhas – dark looking with a protruding neck, and having a scar above his eye brow and a squint in his eye. A copy of Ghosh's report dated 4 October 1962 to Nehru was produced before the Commission. "This man is not Subhas Bose," he wrote for the benefit of Prime Minister who seemed unsure of his public postures. The testimony of Ghosh and others did not ring any bell to Khosla. Without mentioning a single word about Sengupta, Mirchandani, Jayaram and perjure Mullick, he wrote in his report: "The matter was referred to the Intelligence Bureau and enquired into. Several reports on the working of the ashram were submitted."

What about the findings of Anglo-American agencies? Nothing suspicious about them too! This Khosla strongly felt after seeing secret files and hearing the men who were part of the investigations. For BC Chakraborty, a retired Deputy Inspector General of Police, this was the second go at telling what he knew. The first time had been a bad experience; Shah Nawaz had cold-shouldered him. This time he was determined to tell about the man he had come to admire while on deputation with Combined Services Detailed Interrogation Centre. In Delhi's Red Fort, Chakraborty had interrogated front-ranking INA men. Habibur Rahman's turn came. Chakraborty surveyed the reports filed from SE Asia; took Rahman to secluded Bahadurgarh camp near Delhi and put the screws on him throughout December 1945. On 30 December he submitted his 75-page report. His senior Colonel Stevenson saw it, put down his signatures and sent it across. Chakraborty recalled the CSDIC findings before the Commission:

"The only available evidence (of Bose's death) was the statement of Lt Col Habibur Rehman. When he was subjected to questions, he failed to give pertinent answers to all the questions ... he was not delivering the truth .... After analysing all the reports that were in hand at the time in the CSDIC, it was obvious that Colonel Habibur Rehman told lies or the Japanese Government concealed facts. Their reply was nothing other than a product of conspiracy regarding the movement of Netaji Subhas Chandra Bose on the 18th August, 1945 .... There were other informations leading to different conclusion that there was either no plane accident or even if there had been an accident Netaji escaped death."[21]

Khosla adjudged that Chakraborty — winner of President's Medal — was a reckless liar. He did so because the Government said they did not know of any 75-page report filed by Chakraborty. " ... a 25-page closely typed report, was subsequently made available to the Commission, and I have no doubt at all that this is the material collected by Shri Chakraborty and the material on which he professes to base his doubts and his disbeliefs of the crash story .... (Chakraborty's) argument is seen to be nothing but a string of false assumptions and non-sequiturs. The file containing the record of the interrogation carried out by Chakraborty, and his report was produced before the Commission by an officer of the Government and I have carefully pursued the long interrogation as well as the report. This report is dated 31-12-1945, the date mentioned by Shri

Chakraborty in the course of his statement before the Commission."[22]

The pot was calling the kettle black. No Government officer ever turned up before the commission with a CSDIC report signed by Chakraborty and Stevenson. The 25-page report Khosla so boldly discussed was a figment of his imagination. What actually came was an undated, unsigned, incomplete 13-page report just outlining the turn of events before and after Bose's death. Gobinda Mukhoty, a noted lawyer who represented the national committee, charged the Government of not producing the real 75-page report "because it did not affirm the truth of the crash story."

The judge put his own spin on British vintage reports and the testimony of another officer. Inspector Kalipada Dey, part of PES Finney, HK Roy, WFW Davies team, deposed before Commission. "The witness (Dey) went on to say that the substance of the police report was that Netaji had died due to air crash at Taihoku on the 18th August. This is borne out by the copy of the report supplied to the Commission .... The sworn testimony of Dey, corroborated by the copy of his report supplied to us, leaves no doubt whatsoever that there was no question (for the British) of disbelieving the report of the crash or of any concealment of evidence .... The enquiry merely confirmed the news which had been originally broadcast."[23]

There was no confirmation! Dey too never stated that his team reached a conclusion that Bose had died. His exact words during the cross-examination were that their investigation yielded "no direct evidence" of Bose's death and the death story was based on "heresy." HK Roy's testimony before Shah Nawaz Committee, available to Khosla, had clearly stated that "although the Central Intelligence were aware of the alleged plane crash and death of Netaji, they did not believe it and considered that it might have been a hoax. We were sent to arrest Netaji and to find out the truth or otherwise of the statement about the death of Netaji which had been broadcast."

Khosla's sins of omission continued as time rolled by. He was shown official papers containing doubts about Bose's death. As an inquirer he was supposed to read in between the lines and seek clarifications from the Government. There was this Top Secret file – 273/INA — comprising a number of reports. One was clear that Bose was in Soviet Russia after August 1945, and that this was known to Gandhi and Nehru. Khosla brushed the file aside. "There is nothing ... in this file which can be said to have any relevance to the inquiry," he wrote in the forwarder. On 31 May 1972, he gave another illustration of his blinkered approach. Debnath Das listed out documents he wanted the Government to furnish. "Lord Wavell's Government's intelligence report, West Bengal Government's intelligence report and some reports from Japanese military HQ ...." At this TR Bhasin introduced an unreasonable rider. "He (Das) must give a brief substance of these documents." That is, Das was to provide a sneak preview of the classified records lying in custody of different countries. Khosla gave his assent to Bhasin's line of thinking. "He must tell us what are the contents of these documents and how they are relevant. Then you (Bhasin) can judge as to whether they should be called for. They should tell us why they consider it relevant; what is in those documents which throw light on the subject."[24]

Amar Prasad Chakrovarty became a victim to Khosla-Bhasin's queer logic.[25] He found out that one Defence Ministry file was a copy and felt that the original might contain some extra papers. He raised the matter only to get the duo started.

"GD Khosla: What is there in the original file? You must mention that there is something particular in the file otherwise being a responsible counsel you would not go on calling the files.

Bhasin: Obviously there are so many parts of it. You enlighten us which part do you want?

GD Khosla: He must say that this important instruction or this important evidence is contained in the file. For instance a person who is claiming to be a witness should say that the file contain the signature of Netaji or something of that type, something definite.

Bhasin: Any person saying anything about should say it in an affidavit."[26]

In his report, Khosla made a vehement defence of the Indira Gandhi's Government accused of not providing all necessary files to the Commission. "As and when I received information regarding files and documents which could throw light on the subject matter of my inquiry, I sent the appropriate requisition to the Government. The requisition was invariably complied with and all files and documents asked for were made available, except one file which was said to have been destroyed in the ordinary course of routine according to which old and unwanted files are destroyed to lighten the burden of the record rooms."[27]

Too bad for him, by mistake the Home Ministry had actually admitted before Khosla that about 30 classified papers and files on Subhas Bose were either missing or destroyed. The files and papers were once in personal possession of Nehru, who had been assisted by his Confidential Secretary Mohammad Yunus in maintaining them. One look at the indices, and one knew that by no stretch of imagination could they be of "unwanted" type that might have been thrown away or destroyed "to lighten the burden of the record rooms." Prime Minister Secretariat File No 23(156)/51 was *Indian National Army (INA) in the Far East.* 23 (11) 56-57 was the serial number given to the one about *The INA Treasure*. And, file 12(226)/56-PM — *Investigation into the Circumstances Leading to the Death of Subhas Chandra Bose* — was most sensitive of all, for Prime Minister's eyes only.

Khosla, who had earlier boasted that he was "not only an inquirer but also an investigator," did not question any Government representative why and under what circumstances and rules these most important files were destroyed. It did not bother him that so many classified papers had gone missing from the PM's office at the time Bose mystery was being hotly debated. He did not inquire if any attempts were made to trace these official papers. He declined suggestion to summon Yunus so that he could throw some light on, say, UO Note No D/S-8666, dated 24 August 1953 from PM's Secretariat to him. Here was a clear-cut case of criminal negligence on the part of PM's office, but Khosla would not smell a rat. Instead, he had the gumption to write in his report that "I have, at several places, in the course of this report stated that the Government unhesitatingly placed all material in its possession at the Commission's disposal."[28]

Atrocious was the manner in which Khosla dealt with certain individuals. He spitefully rapped Justice Radha Binode Pal, Suresh Bose and former MP Satyanarayan Sinha for the views they held. Putting down the great jurist was quite easy since he had passed away in 1967. Khosla rubbished his publicly known view by casting aspersions on his ability to judge: " a subsequent request to Nehru to name Dr Radha Binode Pal a member of the (Shah Nawaz) Committee was rejected. Dr Pal had made statements which indicated that he could not bring an impartial, unbiased and unprejudiced mind to bear on the subject."[29]

Suresh Bose was seen as the villain in the piece and for him was reserved a demeaning treatment. The virtual duel Suresh Bose and Shah Nawaz engaged in before the Commission brought lot of bad press to the Nehruvian legacy. The elder Bose came down heavily on late Prime Minister, particularly on his refusal to allow the Committee to visit Taiwan. Khosla turned a blind eye to the official papers proving Suresh's point and Shah Nawaz giving misleading statements. At various places in his report, Khosla portrayed Suresh Bose, like BC Chakraborty, a liar: "It will be seen that Suresh Chandra Bose is drawing inferences which are not warranted by the facts[30] ... (he was) at pains to enlarge upon his grievances real or imaginary[31] ... (his) testimony in the present proceedings was a long diatribe against Nehru and Shri Shah Nawaz Khan[32] ... (his) testimony ... let me say at once, is wholly inadmissible in evidence and has no probative value whatsoever[33] ... the examination of Suresh Chandra Bose's evidence is a pointless exercise."[34]

Khosla left no stone unturned in putting down Suresh Bose's evidence, which was in stark contrast to his kid-glove way with the Japanese witnesses. Whenever a crash survivor made a howler, he ascribed it to lapse of memory. He allowed them to read out from prepared text even though they should have known all about the incident. But from Suresh Bose he wanted a verbatim reproduction of everything. Once he cribbed that Suresh was making use of notes on the vexed intelligence inputs he had studied as a member of Netaji Inquiry Committee 15 years earlier. Khosla would not care that while the forgetful Japanese were in their 50s and 60s, Suresh Bose was an octogenarian, the oldest surviving member of the Bose family, and dying. More then once, right in front of his eyes, the old man's health broke down and he had to be taken away for medical care. Suresh Bose died within months of his deposition before Khosla Commission.

Dr Satyanarayan Sinha, former Ministry of External Affairs officer turned MP, was one of the reasons the Commission had been formed. Spurred by inputs from Russian-German sources that Bose was in a Siberian camp, Sinha made a visit to Taiwan in 1964, and more specifically to the site of the 1945 crash. Strangely, none of the people he met there could recall any such crash. One such person had been working as a firefighter in 1945. "Do you remember any airplane crash during the period of your service?" Sinha asked him. "Yes there was one in October, 1944," pat came the answer. "Was there any other accident in August, 1945?" Sinha put to him. "Never heard of any accident in 1945. If there was one, I could have known about it, because, we from the fire brigade are the people who rush to the site of the accident first."[35] On his return, Sinha told *Amrita Bazar Patrika* that as per his inquiries the alleged plane crash never took place. In 1966 he came out with a book — *Netaji Mystery* — to detail his case.

Thanks to the gift of gab he possessed and shock value of his information, Sinha's deposition before Khosla Commission was much talked about. He called Shah Nawaz's report "a procured document." He said "the photographs of an aircraft published by the Shah Nawaz Committee was similar to one photograph which was published in *Taihoku Nichi Nichi Shimbun* (newspaper) sometimes in October 1944 .... Dr Sinha was confident that Netaji was alive and that he was in Russia ... he believed ... Prime Minister Mrs Indira Gandhi ... could get information about Netaji ...."[36]

The Commission made no attempts to find out the veracity or otherwise of Sinha's Siberia story. Instead, Justice Khosla asked irrelevant questions and heaped insults on Sinha. "By nature a boastful exhibitionist, he has adopted a flamboyant style in his speech and in his writing ... he never felt abashed nor was he ever embarrassed on being confronted which left the impression of a persistent braggart, a consummate though transparent liar and a wholly unreliable witness."[37]

But there were people who took Sinha seriously. The officials from Soviet Russian embassy in New Delhi accosted him and acted in a manner that ideally should have caused much commotion in the official and media circles. "Do you want Kozlov to be shot in Russia?"[38] they asked him, reminding him of his Russian contact. When Sinha reported the matter to the Commission, he was rebuffed. Khosla reacted as if the USSR officials were within their rights to threaten an Indian national, an former Member of Parliament, right in the heart of the Capital. Sinha pleaded that the "the Prime Minister, Mrs Indira Gandhi, who was expected to stop over in Moscow on her way to the UN, to request the Soviet Prime Minister, Mr Kosygin, to give protection to Mr Kozlov. The Commission, however, said it was not responsible if anybody was put in prison if his name figured before the Commission."[39]

The Taipei angle, brought to fore by Sinha, acquired bigger proportions as the Commission neared the end of its work. GD Khosla received first hand information to the effect that the alleged plane crash in which Bose reportedly died never ever took place. Coupled with it was the Government's mistrustful reluctance in allowing the Commission to pay a visit to Taiwan.

HV Kamath, the old Bose guard, had been at it, battering at the edifice of perceived falsehood of Bose's death. He chanced to meet Varanasi-educated P Shein, Vice Foreign Minister of Republic of China, in Delhi in 1966 and found him to be kindly disposed. Kamath requested him to look into the reported mishap. In December same year, Kamath received an invite from Taipei. When he reached Taipei, Kamath was briefed by Dr Lin, a ROC Foreign Ministry Official who had himself been entrusted with the inquiry. On 31 May 1972 at Delhi's Vigyan Bhawan, Kamath told Khosla Commission that Lin's conclusion was that there was "no confirmation."

"The evidences do not confirm that Netaji or any Indian for that matter had been killed in an aircrash on the 18th .... The people whom he (Dr Lin) questioned could not tell or remember whether there was an air crash on that particular date."[40]

Worth noting was Kamath's recall of his discussion with then ROC Foreign Minister Chein Hua. "We have done what we can. We have appointed Dr Lin and he must have met you and told you what had been done in this matter and he said if your government wants to peruse the matter further we will be only happy to collaborate with the Government of India in this matter." Kamath implored Khosla to make uses of the good offices of ROC Government to get to truth about the crash, but was interrupted by TR Bhasin. "Mr Kamath are you aware that we have no diplomatic relations with Taiwan?" Kamath retorted that that would hardly come in the way as nations maintained relations with each other despite their not having formal ties. "President (Zulfikar Ali) Bhutto will be coming here and President (Richard) Nixon went to China recently though America has no diplomatic relations with China ... our agricultural (Green) revolution is supposed to have been boosted by Taichim paddy from Taiwan." Kamath said he hoped the "Government would not be so perverse as to stand in Commission's way to go to Taipei in the national interest."[41]

Kamath's information was boosted by sworn testimony of a distinguished Member of Parliament. In 1966 itself, a delegation of Indian lawmakers visited Taiwan on the invitation of ROC Government with the aim "to better the friendly relations between the two countries." As luck would have it, the officer liaising with them was Dr Lin. During his testimony on 30 May 1972, Mulka Govinda Reddy,[42] an MP since 1958, was examined over what had transpired in their talks with Dr Lin.

"Since Dr Lin was with us all the time, during our stay in Formosa, we (MPs of delegation) asked him some questions particularly regarding the incident that appeared to have occurred wherein Netaji Subhas Chandra Bose died in that air crash ... he was good enough to tell us (that) he was asked by his foreign ministry, Vice Foreign Minister specially, to investigate into this question and he told us after examining all relevant records, he came to the conclusion that there was no positive evidence to show that Netaji died in that air crash. And he also told me and other members of the delegation that on 18th of August, no air crash appears to have occurred ...."[43]

"Not on 18th August?"

"Not on 18th August and in no air crash Netaji appears to have died."

"But he told you that he had collected some material?"

"Yes, he told us he had collected very valuable material in this connection. He also told us there was one Mayor of Taipeh at that time, who is still alive. He appears to have told him that no such aircrash occurred on that day and that at no time Netaji Subhas Chandra Bose appears to have been involved in any air crash in Taipeh."

"Had you any occasion to met the Vice Foreign Minister of Formosa?"

"Yes, we were his guests for a dinner party and he also confirmed what Dr Lin said and he assured us that the Government of Formosa will be ever ready to cooperate with the Government of India if a commission or an officer is appointed to go into this question."[44]

Another member of the delegation, former MP Prakash Vir Shastri, reiterated before the Commission that "the whole delegation (of Indian MPs) met (Taiwanese Premier) Chiang Kai-shek and during the course of interview, we asked him about the reported aircrash. He said ... if Government of India made an enquiry, his (Formosan) Government would give all necessary help." Shastri stated that on return he and nine other MPs raised a question in the Lok Sabha in July 1967. "The question we asked was whether the Shah Nawaz Committee had gone to Taiwan and if not how the Committee had reached any conclusion without seeing the place of occurrence .... The question we asked was, if the Government of Taiwan was prepared to assist in any enquiry regarding the alleged aircrash of Netaji's plane. We also asked if the Government were contemplating in sending a delegation to Taiwan for the purpose? The reply given was that the Government of India had not received any such intimation from Taiwan Government and that in view of the report given to the Government of India, the sending of the such a delegation was not necessary."[45]

Why in the world should Taiwanese Government have extended any intimation to the Indian Government? A magnanimous offer was still made by the Generalissimo himself to Indian lawmakers and yet the Government refused to consider this offer of help which was solely in India's interest. Taking a stand that what was sauce for Shah Nawaz was also sauce for GD Khosla, the Government on 10 May 1972 told Khosla that they would not allow the Commission to visit Taiwan. The old pretext of the absence of diplomatic relations was held out once again. To Satyanarayan Sinha this was bereft of logic:

"What an inquiry is imaginable which is not done at the actual scene of occurrence? The Nationalist Government of China at Formosa is a leading member of the United Nations, and if approached by India, could have never turned down any request for facilities to make inquiries which are concerned only with the noble human aspects. India has no diplomatic relations with the Soviet zone East Germany, but when myself was accredited with diplomatic rank to the Indian Military Mission, Berlin, I ... visited East Berlin and East Germany a number of times with other members of our Mission there, to carry out the instructions of our External Affairs Ministry. If the Communist East Germany could be visited without any diplomatic relations with that country, why not the (democratic) Nationalist Republic of China on the Formosa Islands?"[46]

Stark facts lay behind the charade of "absence of diplomatic ties" between India and Taiwan. Generalissimo Chiang Kai-shek was a friend of Indians, who responded in same kind. Even

Subhas, who was otherwise in opposite bloc, had implored the Japanese to buy peace with the nationalistic Chinese. The Generalissimo visited India in 1942, and was a good friend of Nehru's. "Jawaharlal was one of the first persons to congratulate the Generalissimo upon the surrender of Japan."[47] Both had communicated with each other in late August 1945 as well. It was Nationalist China that India had recognized from 1945 to 1949. The Independence Day greetings from the Generalissimo were deemed so important that they were read out on 15 August 1947 in the Constituent Assembly by its President Rajendra Prasad immediately after the message of the British PM and the Archbishop of Canterbury. The first delegation of nine Indian MPs led by Dahyabhai Patel visited Taiwan in June 1964 at the invitation of the Ministry of Foreign Affairs of Republic of China. This visit had been cleared by Prime Minister Jawaharlal Nehru himself.

Since all this was well-known, the MPs began to exert pressure on the Government. Led by Atal Bihari Vajpayee, twenty-six of them jointly wrote to the Prime Minister on 26 May 1972 that the Commission "should be given facilities to visit Taiwan" for "a good deal of information may come to light if the Khosla Commission is enabled to visit Formosa." "The MPs ... pointed out that many Indian Government officials visit Formosa every year even though India has no diplomatic relations with the island."[48] The Government had to relent, and, at the fag end of the Commission's work, on 11 July 1973, GD Khosla landed at the very site where Bose mystery had begun. The old Matsuyama aerodrome was now part of an enlarged international Taipei Songshan Airport. Waiting for Khosla here were local officials and sombre-looking representatives of national committee — Samar Guha and Sunil Krishna Gupta. Aviation Minister "Maharaja" Karan Singh had refused to grant some concession to Guha over air-fare even though such largesse were usually given for all sorts of international conferences. Worse, Guha-Gupta did not know that Khosla had come with a stratagem conceived by External Affairs Ministry hell-bent on sabotaging the inquiry in Taiwan. "Mr Guha, you have done a great job," Khosla tried to cosy up to Guha at the airport. Back in India, a newspaper had reported that Guha had managed to trace the nurse who had treated a dying Bose. Guha hadn't found anyone; his detractors had launched a counter information offensive.

The second time Guha met Khosla in Taiwan, the latter was holed up with some local reporters in his hotel room. Guha objected to the secret briefing and a flustered Khosla dispersed the reporters. But the damage was done. Next morning a report ran in local papers: "According to Mr Khosla, Chairman of the Inquiry Commission, all the Japanese witness confirmed Bose's death report." This was not as innocuous as it seemed. Taiwan had good ties with Japan and could not have openly contradicted a friendly nation over a matter that after all did not mean anything to them. But then, as a democratic polity, the Taiwanese would not have declined to state facts had someone duly approached them. Guha-Gupta soon found out that someone was not going to be Justice Khosla. Perturbed by the judge's strange behaviour in Taipei, they pressed the Secretary of the Commission to know what Khosla was up to. Khosla, it emerged, had received a directive from MEA, barring the Commission from contacting not only the ROC Government but also any other non-official agency. Infuriated Guha went over and yelled at Khosla. "Why did you come here then? Why did you not tell us this in Delhi?"[49]

"Why have you come to Taipei after 27 years?" people asked Samar Guha as he scoured Taipei even as GD Khosla luxuriated in the hotel. The ROC Government soon came to know of the presence of a foreign judge who intended to run an inquiry without notifying them. This amounted to undermining their sovereignty and the obvious action they intended to take was to give him the boot. Khosla evidently preferred that to conducting the inquiry, which was likely to throw up facts contrary to the Government's line. Satyanarayan Sinha had warned: "The Government of India and their intelligence, renowned for their cleverness, are definitely afraid of the real truth about Netaji coming out, and for this reason did not allow even their own trusted NIC members (Shah Nawaz

Committee) to visit Formosa. The barrier of diplomatic relations is only a pretence to keep Netaji and his brilliant historic role covered in darkness."[50] Guha-Gupta pleaded with the Taiwanese officials and politicians for leniency. Thanks to lobbying by political luminary Dr Ku Cheng Kang, they succeeded in convincing the ROC Government that for the sake of Indians the Commission be allowed to function.

Least bothered about it all, Khosla went on to do nothing. "Please write a letter to the Government of Taiwan," Guha implored him repeatedly. "There are many things in the archives there — the report of inquiry conducted by the Mayor of Taipeh; also the correspondence between Panditji and Chiang Kai-shek; they have instituted some inquiries." Khosla wasn't ready for this or a visit to the scene of the alleged August 1945 crash. Guha-Gupta worked out all formalities to visit to the restricted unused old airstrip where the Sally bomber had reportedly crashed, but still had to pester Khosla no end before he stepped out of the hotel. At the airfield Khosla acted up: He would not get off his car and then began gazing aimlessly into the yonder. Guha-Gupta did Khosla's job. They took out copies of three pictures of the plane wreck taken by the Japanese on 19 August and matched them from different angles with the actual scenery. They weren't matching. Apparently the Japanese had fobbed off to the Allies pictures of debris of more than one plane lying in different spots in the same area. His adrenal running fast, Guha turned to GD Khosla. "Look at the pictures! Look at the hills in the background! They don't match! These pictures were planted! They do not show a single crashed plane! Do they?" "What am I to do with these pictures?" Khosla became blazing mad. "I have nothing to do with them." He turned away and barged into his car.

If only Khosla could turn his back on realities all the time. Journalist Harin Shah's 1946 investigation in Taipei was finally nailed. *Gallant End of Netaji* had carried statements and photographs of many Taiwanese witnesses to the crash and Bose's death. One picture was of nurse Chu Chow Tse, who looked after injured "Bose" until the end. Guha-Gupta gave

Tse's picture and other details to newspapers. In response, they got to meet some nurses who were present in the hospital where Bose had allegedly expired on 18 August 1945. But none had ever heard about either Bose's death or the existence of any sister Tse. Harin Shah had also published the photo of a man he identified as the caretaker of the crematorium where Bose's body had been cremated. GD Khosla, Samar Guha and Sunil Gupta visited the crematorium and met the caretaker whose father was in charge in August 1945. "Not my father," he said when the published photo was shown to him. Guha-Gupta also contacted some other people mentioned in Harin Shah's book. Most of them denied the statements attributed to them. Hiren Shah was alive at that time and had earlier sat through the Commission's proceedings. Khosla did not feel it necessary to summon him and ask him at whose instance he had spread half-baked stories and lies over such a crucial incident of Indian history.

In Taiwan, the Commission anyhow examined seven non-official witnesses and the report declared them to be saying things that proved the crash. This was a distortion. None of the witnesses said that they saw a plane crashing. Opposite to what was attributed to him in the report, YR Tseng, the last witness before Khosla Commission, averred that no plane had crashed in Taipei on 18 August 1945. He recalled, just as Satyanarayan Sinha had informed, that some time in September/October 1944 a Japanese plane crashed near the site of the alleged 18 August 1945 crash. Khosla haggled with Tseng over the year and month. This got on the Taiwanese's nerves and he walked out saying he would bring in the next day a dozen of his former schoolmates, all of whom had helped clear the wreckage. GD Khosla suddenly decided it was time to pack up. Guha begged him that one day's wait was worthwhile, but there was more important assignment on hand. Khosla spent his last day in Taipei shopping around for a gift for Indira Gandhi, the Prime Minister and the daughter of a friend.

On return, an exasperated Guha asked Indira Gandhi about the MEA directive. "I don't know anything. Why they have done so, I don't know," she feigned ignorance. When nothing came out of the lip service, Guha blasted off in the Parliament, accusing the Government of wrecking the inquiry.

"If the Ministry of External Affairs had not issued any instructions to the Netaji Enquiry Commission ... perhaps the Netaji mystery would have been finally resolved .... When I met Taiwan leaders, they never raised any diplomatic or political issue. They did not even ask the Commission to write to their Government. But they pointed out that for holding the court proceedings in a foreign country, permission from the Government would be necessary. There was a little bit of legal technicality here. The Commission was required to write to the foreign department of that country to seek their permission to hold a court proceedings there. I say they were eager to give all the necessary help to us ... 69 Indian ships of both the public and private sectors were at Taipeh. Directly, our government had also their export-import trade with the Government there, of transport equipment, ores, concentrates, mica, silicon etc .... I know something more but I do not want to disclose that in the interest of the nation. Are these not contacts with the Taiwan Government? If a judicial body contacted them indirectly that would amount to contact. But when our officials regularly visit the place, is that not contact? .... What kind of logic is this?"[51]

The Lok Sabha Speaker GS Dhillon did not take kindly to Guha's words. "These are matters which are under inquiry ... why does the Honourable Member now make a speech on these things?" "Sit down. You are discussing the conduct of the Commission which is not permissible under the rules."

Guha continued: "I repeat that the object of the visit has been frustrated by this instruction. We owe it to the nation, we owe it to posterity, we owe it to ourselves, we owe it to anything that is in the conscience of the nation to find out what happened to our great leader."

Swaran Singh, the External Affairs Minister rose to launch a personal attack on Guha. He complained about Guha's "agitated manner." "You do not feel agitated?" angry Guha joined the issue with him. "This posture, as if he really is the only person in this country who has reverence for Netaji Subhas Bose is, if I may say so, completely misplaced," the minister retorted. Guha demanded that the secretive directive be placed on the table of the House. But Singh wanted to get away with a brief statement. "To save the time of the House I made a briefer statement .... there is really nothing I should answer, but probably he (Guha) wanted to unburden himself, which he has done .... this attempt to monopolise the conscience of the nation is, if I may say so, much too pretentious."

Guha flew off the handle: "For all those 27 years what did you do? Did you care to hold an inquiry? Did you care to visit the alleged place of occurrence of the plane crash?" He reiterated his question. "Is the Government going to place the text of the suggestion (to Khosla) on the table of the House?"[52]

"No, (Mr Speaker) Sir I have no intention," Singh flatly turned down the request. Backing Guha's demand, Atal Bihari Vajpayee and Madhu Limaye "argued that the minister had no right to deprive the members of information if no public interest or national security was involved."[53] The Minister said it was "not customary" for him to produce the directive in original; Limaye countered if unless it wasn't against national interest, the minister really should not have made a mountain out of molehill. Shyamnandan Mishra noticed the streak of insult in Speaker's conduct. "You are taking it lightly. Please do not laugh it away. It is a serious matter which has to be considered." "Where is the point of order?" Speaker rejoined. "My submission is," Mishra said, "that this State (India) has been carrying on some kind of activities with Taiwan. So why is this State not also allowing the Commission to have some contacts with the Taiwan Government for the purpose of an inquiry of this kind?" Dhillon did not know what to say, so he silenced Mishra. "Sit down. Do not lose your temper all the time."[54]

All said and done, the Government did not produce the copy of the instruction and with that, the last hurdle before the Government was removed. The defence counsels put up resistance in Delhi but their voices were muffled. Gobinda Mukhoty's arguments meant zilch for Khosla. "Why Your

Lordship was not allowed to correspond freely with the Formosan Government? Why Your Lordship was not allowed to ask for the report, which they claimed, to have with them as far as this inquiry is concerned?" Khosla's shoddy job in Taiwan cast its shadow in his report. More than half of his argument revolved around the degrading Samar Guha — the man who made the Taiwan visit possible. No mention was made of what HV Kamath, Mulka Govind Reddy and Prakash Vir Shastri had stated. Instead, brazenly, Khosla wrote that "the Commission did not learn that the government of Taiwan at any time held any inquiry into Bose's disappearance."[55] Afterwards, he made disparaging remarks about the Mayor of Taipei. "The official who was in charge of the crematorium in 1945 was dead, so was the Mayor of Taipei who arrived there some time after August 18, 1945, and who is said to have made some sort of enquiry into the matter. Not that the Mayor's report, if available, would have been admissible in evidence, for it would be nothing more than the opinion of an individual."[56]

It took little commonsense to see that the Mayor of Taipei city was not an individual but its head. His views were not his, but of the Taipei government. To get to the truth about the alleged crash that killed Bose, the writer contacted Dr LM Singhvi, Member of Parliament and former High Commissioner of India to the United Kingdom. Dr Singhvi was taken aback when asked to comment on the visit he had made to Taipei as a young MP along with Mulka Govinda Reddy, Prakash Vir Shastri, Ram Sevak Yadav and Uma Shankar Trivedi. A *Hindustan Times* reporter succeeded where Justice GD Khosla had failed. In a short but meaningful talk, Singhvi admitted that he had been to Taiwan and that the issue of Netaji figured prominently during the visit in 1966.

The writer then made a request to Taipei Mayor Dr Ying Jo Ma in 2003 via e-mail. The reply on 12 March 2003 denied outright that any plane had crashed in Taipei on 18 August 1945. "According to the historical documents in Taipei city archives, there is no such record of a plane crash in Taipei on that day." In an instant it all fell into place. Encouraged, I pleaded to ROC President Chen Shui-bian to verify the fact for the sake of millions of Indians across the world. The President was as kind and noble as Mayor Ma. I felt ashamed for the language my country's officials had used against the Taiwanese in 1956. What they had tried to cover all these years was now laid bare. President Bian's office forwarded the matter to the organization in charge of relevant records, Ministry of Transportation and Communications (MOTC), for a formal reply. On 5 August 2003, MOTC Minister Lin Ling-San himself spelt out details. A thorough analysis of the records left by the Japanese showed that there had been only one major air crash during that period. An American C-47 transporter carrying about 26 released POWs had crashed near Mount Trident in Taitung area around 200 nautical miles away from Taipei. That was in September 1945. What about 18 August 1945? There was "no evidence" to show that any plane carrying Netaji had ever crashed in or around Taipei between 14 August and 25 October of 1945. Justice Radha Binode Pal's information was right.

Netaji Inquiry Commission Report, upholding Bose's death following the "Taipei crash," was submitted to Home Minister Uma Shankar Dikshit on 30 June 1974. It was produced in Parliament in September and approved in a jiffy. Furious Guha shredded his copy. His anger stemmed from both the conclusion and the manner in which it was drawn. Using derogatory phrases, Khosla had tried to degrade Japan and Subhas Bose. In something about two dozen places in his report, he depicted Bose as a "puppet" of the Japanese. He tried to belittle Netaji's contribution to India and painted him as an impractical hothead. Khosla's worldview reeked of the anti-Bose tirade of the 1940s and his phrases were vicious. Bose had "styled himself the Head of the State;" his cabinet members "blindly submitted to his orders without question;" the Japanese "looked upon (him) as a puppet, a tool which could be discarded and ignored, when deemed no longer useful;" his proposal that the INA men should lead the charge into India was "the proposal of a zealous but impractical patriot;" INA "campaign was a failure" and that "Bose entering India with Japanese assistance could only mean one thing, viz India would become a colony or a suzerainty of Japan."[57]

Khosla's report card was messier than anyone who headed a commission of inquiry in independent India. Even as he headed Netaji Inquiry Commission, he accepted the Government's proposal to head a commission to review working of the National Academies and yet another regarding Film and Television Institute. Such a "misconduct" today would have invited the Opposition and media's wrath. India of those days was different. As he worked on Bose inquiry, Khosla also did what in our times would have brought hell on earth. Khosla wrote an eulogistic book on Indira Gandhi, which must have been put to good use in the ensuing Emergency. Months before he finished his inquiry, Khosla's staff was fired, and he began writing his report. The excerpts were leaked to some Calcutta papers.

But the biggest blot was Khosla's writing a book on the basis of his report and releasing it alongside the report to fill in his coffer. *Last Days of Netaji* was an attempt of GD Khosla to be the Indian Trever Reeve, but it proved to be his nemesis. Bose's followers took offence to its contents with Dwijendra Nath Bose filing a case against him under the Indian Penal Code. For more than a year Khosla evaded arrest and eventually on 1 April 1978, he, a retired Chief Justice, apologised in a Metropolitan Magistrate's court. "I ... tender my unqualified apology to ... Dwijendra Nath Bose and other members of the family of Netaji and to our countrymen, who have felt hurt and aggrieved owing to the impugned passages in the said book concerning one of the greatest sons of India and his nephews. I would also express for myself that I sincerely share in common with my countrymen the deepest regard for Netaji who is regarded as the LIBERATOR of our MOTHERLAND and was christened by no less a person than Mahatma Gandhi, the Father of the Nation as "THE PATRIOT OF PARTIOTS - THE PRINCE OF PATRIOTS" as one of the greatest sons of India. I am prepared to make due and adequate amends to have the case compounded according to law and also undertake to have the apology herein contained published fully and adequately through advertisement inserted in leading newspapers in Calcutta, Delhi, Bombay and Madras and other state capitals of India as also in newspapers of countries where the said impugned publication has been circulated, to freeze stocks of the impugned book left with me, my publishers and their agents and not to sell or reprint the same and also to supply copies of the apology to the leading booksellers where the book has been displayed for sale, requesting them to hung up the same in public view."

In mid-1970s, India was sucked into the Emergency vortex and with that ended the little protests against the "failure" of Netaji Inquiry Commission. All prominent opposition leaders like Samar Guha were pushed behind bars. Then Janata Party came to power and Guha made a sensational comeback with his book, the strangely titled *Netaji: Dead or Alive?* In 1977, he moved a motion in the Lok Sabha seeking a new inquiry into Bose's death. The marathon debate culminated with the rejection of Khosla's report by Prime Minister Morarji Desai. Twenty-two years after it accepted the report of Bose's death, the Government of India thus reverted to its older ambiguous stance.

Notes:

1 *Bhumigat Subhas* by Ranjeet Panchalay. Page 55.

2 File No 2(64) 56-66 PM Volume II. Letter 1039-PMH/63.

3 Rajya Sabha debate on 23 August 1963.

4 Malhotra recounted his days with Bose in a series of articles in *Hindustan Times* in 1946. *When Subhas was Ziauddin* was later published as a booklet.

5 *Netaji: Dead or Alive?* by Samar Guha. Page 37.

6 Ibid. Page 38.

7 *Hindustan Times* report **Govt may order fresh probe on Netaji.** 7 March 1960.

8 The *Tribune* article **Did Netaji actually die in 1945?** by historian VN Datta. 19 August 2001.

9 *Hindustant Times.com* editorial **Khosla disliked Netaji** by Sitanshu Das.

10 The *Tribune* article **Did Netaji actually die in 1945?** by historian VN Datta. 19 August 2001.

11 The *Tribune* story **Netaji Commission to probe into all relevant matters.** 15 October 1970.

12 The *Times of India* report **Opening Day's session ends on dramatic note.** 17 October 1970.

13 *Amrita Bazar Patrika* report **Kholsa heckled by unruly crowd.** 19 November 1970.

14 Example: "Whenever (Rajaram) Dixit (witness No 26) came out of his house in Bombay and wherever he went he 'was surrounded by hundreds of foreign girls,' who were all spies of different nationalities. This strange assembly of girls, known to be spies, however, did not arouse the curiosity of any one, and not even the police took any notice of their unconcealed, almost brazen, subversive activities. Once an attempt was made to shoot Dixit by Nanavaty, an officer of the Indian Navy, who became notorious for killing his wife's paramour. According to Dixit, Nanavaty's and his wife were 'first class spies of Britain.' One day Dixit was taking the air and walking along the road by the sea-side, when 'All of a sudden, a healthy and stout man, guarded by another man, came to me. And the moment he came near me, he said, 'Look here. I am Netaji.' He was dressed in the dress of Kabuliwalla. And I had a serious and thorough look at his face like this, to see whether he was Subhas Babu or somebody else. And I was convinced that he was Subhas Babu. Then I began to dance.' The witness suited his action to the words, by performing a brief terpsichorean act." Netaji Inquiry Commission report. Page 107.

15 Proceedings of the Netaji Inquiry Commission. 8 August 1972.

16 Proceedings of the Netaji Inquiry Commission. 6 July 1972.

17 Proceedings of the Netaji Inquiry Commission. Volume X. Examination of SR Mirchandani. Pages 3076 to 3093.

18 Proceedings of the Netaji Inquiry Commission. 8 August 1972.

19 Ibid.

20 Proceedings of the Netaji Inquiry Commission. 9 August 1972.

21 Proceedings of the Netaji Inquiry Commission. 5 September 1972.

22 Netaji Inquiry Commission report. Page 63.

23 Ibid. Page 61. Khosla's report also says: "Indeed, in the earlier enquiry carried out by the personnel of the British Intelligence the finding was that Habibur Rehman's story was true and that Bose had, in fact, died." Page 49.

24 Proceedings of the Netaji Inquiry Commission. 1 June 1972.

25 *Amrita Bazar Patrika* reported on 3 November 1970 that " ... in his submissions before the Commission, Mr Amar Chakravarty on behalf of his party, Forward Bloc, contended ... it was imperative that the Central Government actively participated in this enquiry and placed all secret papers, files and documents at the disposal of the Commission and also permitted its top officers, including those who were once in Defence Services, to appear before the Commission ....

Mr Jusrice Khosla: Mr Chakravarty, you are anticipating events. Why are you supposing that the Government is not submitting papers and files?

Mr Chakravarty repeated that those secret papers and files in the possession of the Central as well as the foreign governments together could only reveal the truth. 'Is it not a planned conspiracy to cripple your hands by not submitting those documents?' he asked.

Judge: Mr Chakravarty, please do not repeat those points and arguments which I have already heard."

26 Proceedings of the Netaji Inquiry Commission. 1 June 1972.

27 Netaji Inquiry Commission report. Page 113.

28 Ibid. Suresh Bose during his deposition on 17 November 1970, recalled seeing as part of Shah Nawaz Committee what might have been one of the files listed missing/destroyed. He said: " ... Anglo-American military intelligence officers made a thorough search in all the areas where they thought Netaji could have been living. They did so and as a result of the enquiry which covered 40 pages which was in the custody of the External Affairs Department or probably the Defence Department of the Government of India from where it was given to us for our perusal. The report said, 'We have made a thorough enquiry and we do not think that anything else has been left to be done but the final result is that far from getting evidence about his death it is to the extent that he is alive and he is hiding somewhere.'"

29 Ibid. Page 55. Justice Radha Binode Pal is a reverend figure in Japan. At a gathering of Japanese lawmakers in Tokyo on 11 December 2001, visiting Indian Prime Minister Atal Bihari Vajpayee said: " Half a century ago, Justice Radha Binode Pal brought our two nations closer ...." Similar views were echoed by Hiroshi Hirabayashi, Japan's Ambassador to India, in Kolkata on 23 January 1999: " One ... personality ... we Japanese can never forget is Justice Radha Binode Pal .... (Pal) gave a dissenting judgement on high moral grounds ... Such personalities provided an unbroken link of empathy and friendship between the people of India and Japan."

30 Ibid.

31 Ibid.

32 Ibid. Page 93.

33 Ibid.

34 Ibid. Page 94.

35 *Netaji Mystery* by Dr Satyanarayan Sinha, Page 12.

36 *Amrita Bazar Patrika* report **Shah Nawaz report on Netaji called a fraud**. 3 November 1970.

37 Netaji Inquiry Commission report. Page 73.

38 The *Hindu* report **Soviet questions to Netaji probe witness**. 20 October 1970.

39 Ibid.

40 Proceedings of the Netaji Inquiry Commission. 31 May 1972.

41 Ibid.

42 Octogenarian Govinda Mulka Reddy lives in Bangalore. Recently he was honoured by President APJ Abdul Kalam in the Parliament House.

43 Proceedings of the Netaji Inquiry Commission. 30 May 1972

44 Ibid.

45 Proceedings of the Netaji Inquiry Commission. Vol X. Pages 3068-3070.

46 *Netaji Mystery* by Dr Satyanarayan Sinha. Pages 21-22.

47 Ibid. Page 48.

48 *Hindustan Standard* report **26 MPs want Khosla to visit Taiwan.** 27 May 1972.

49 Samar Guha's account in *Netaji: Dead or Alive?* The writer also spoke to Sunil Krishna Gupta.

50 *Netaji Mystery* by Dr Satyanarayan Sinha. Pages 22-23.

51 Lok Sabha debate. 23 April 1973.

52 Ibid.

53 *Hindustan Times* report **Govt 'sabotaging' Netaji inquiry.** 24 April 1973.

54 Lok Sabha debate. 23 April 1973.

55 Netaji Inquiry Commission report. Page 121.

56 Ibid. Page 114.

57 In a paper on Bose, noted historian TR Sareen wrote: "The myth of Japanese grabbing India was propagated by the British to malign Japan in order to win the support of the Indian political parties for winning the war. Even the British conceded after thorough interrogation of the Japanese high officials that ... the conquest of India was not one of Japan's ambitions." In Tokyo's Yasukini Shrine for Japan's war dead appears the following inscription based on a letter written in 1998 by Captain SS Yadav, the general secretary of INA veterans' association: "We the members of the Indian National Army pay our highest and most revered tributes to our comrades-in-arms members of the Japanese Imperial Army who laid down their lives on the battlefields of Imphal and Kohima for the liberation of India. The Indian nation will ever remain grateful to valiant martyrs of Japan and we pray for eternal peace of their souls."

6

Death That Wasn't

Narration of a true incident, even after a lapse of ten years, could not be so discrepant and contradictory.

Suresh Bose on eyewitnesses' accounts of the Taipei crash.

There is no way of reconciling these different statements and they must remain as they are.

Shah Nawaz Committee report on the statements of the eyewitnesses.

What to speak of your Lordship, even a fool will not believe in these stories.

Gobinda Mukhoty to GD Khosla.

Taken on the face value, the dozen or so witnesses to Subhas Chandra Bose's death said all that could be said. Evidence gathered in reams before the governmental panels on the last-ditch efforts of a braveheart whose luck ran out in Taipei. What was left to be done then? Analysis. One couldn't have cursorily gone only by one side of the story. The matter concerned a man with a clout strong enough to change the destiny of a huge chunk of humanity. The evidence had to be scrutinised, the bottom of the barrel had to be scraped to erase the last vestiges of doubts.

One could well have begun with recreating a scenario where Subhas Bose had actually been killed. The starting point would have been Bose's last movements that must have been documented. He was a head of state moving around with several officials, therefore, the Japanese and INA authorities would have kept papers at Bangkok, Singapore and Saigon. He spent the 17 August night in Tourane, so there must have been some records or eyewitnesses there. The authorities at Taipei too would have maintained some record of the arrival and the mishap.

The eyewitnesses' accounts of the crash would have been incontrovertible. The plane crashed in a city airport in daytime. The survivors watched everything unfolding before their eyes and so one expected them to give out concordant details. At least on major points: Like how Bose was rescued from the burning wreck. The dissemination of news should have been prompt and unimpeded for the plane had crashed in view of aerodrome staff. Fire brigade personnel must have been pressed into action. Local top officials would have rushed to the crash spot, and within minutes or hours the Japanese and Bose's ministers would have received the news. At hospital some papers must have been maintained. Bose must have been put under close observation and his last hours must have been carefully noted. He remained conscious for a couple of hours, so quite naturally local military brass must have paid visits to him.

Bose's death came in the presence of many — those moving details could not have been missed. The disposal of the body must have been done ceremoniously. It would have been photographed and a death certificate issued by a doctor. The cremation would have been attended by local commanders. The last thing the Japanese could have risked in the times was to arise suspicions of Bose's cabinet members and the Allies. The British, therefore, would have been told of their foe's death. Due attempts would have been made to bring the PGI cabinet members to Taipei so that they could attend the funeral or take possession of Bose's remains. Lastly, the Japanese would have conducted a routine inquiry, however perfunctory, into the mishap which killed an ally and a most senior military officer of theirs.

Well, things did not go the way they should have been and that aroused suspicions. The Government inquisitors looked through them all. Shah Nawaz, the man in a hurry, roughshod with his conclusion that Bose's death anyhow took place. GD Khosla had all the time so he put a veneer of precision details on his version of the crash story as if he had himself witnessed "the last days of Netaji": "The Japanese bomber left Saigon at approximately 5pm ... arrived at Touraine at 7.45pm and ... arrived at Taipei in Formosa at 2pm ... the plane took off 2.35pm but within a few seconds one of the engines flew out and the plane crashed near the fringe of the Taihoku airfield ... two days later, Bose's body was cremated and his ashes carried to Tokyo in the beginning of September 1945 ...."[1] But for Suresh Bose and Samar Guha's efforts, the wishy-washy reports would have gone away unchallenged. They chanced to look at the evidence, reached diametrically opposite conclusion and blew the whistle. What made them highly suspicious was the very foundation on which Bose's death was sought to be based. They scratched the surface to find the eyewitness accounts to be grossly inconsistent. The body of evidence was crammed with a slew of discrepancies and contradictions spread out in every point. The eyewitnesses made statements which would not gel with not only those of others but also what they had themselves made on different occasions. They frequently checked, prepared notes and still said things that were poles apart. All this could not have happened had they been recalling actual events they had lived through.[2]

The fumbling began with the very plane — Mitsubishi K-21[3] — in which Bose had travelled from Saigon to Taipei. Why in the world Bose required a different plane at Saigon? What became of the 12-seater Japan had gifted to him? Shah Nawaz Khan the witness told GD Khosla that he hadn't enquired what happened to this twin-engine plane with INA insignia after "Bose's death." Another witness claiming to be one of the pilots of this plane told the Commission that Bose's plane was destroyed in Bangkok airport in June 1945. One war-time intelligence report contested this. General Isoda, who certainly knew the truth, revealed before the Commission that Bose flew in his own plane to Bangkok on 16 August. Then why did Bose let go of it and flew with Shidei and party at his behest? The British saw

Hikari Kikan imprint in the move: "It is also suspicious that Bose had to change planes at Saigon and go on in another plane with one of his staff officers. It would appear more likely that a person of Bose's importance even though he may have been discredited, would still be allowed to travel in his own special aircraft."[4]

Could it be that the Japanese changed planes to isolate Bose from his ministers, who were not to be taken to Manchuria? On 17 October 1945, Director of Military Intelligence (DMI) in China reported about the interception of a secret Japanese message advising Bose "to be separated from his fellow travellers at the time of his journey from Burma in an aircraft."[5] "DMI's supposition is that though Bose's family were in that plane that crashed, Bose was not there and he subsequently escaped ...."[6]

How many people travelled in the ill-fated plane? The complete list of passengers could never become known. GD Khosla counted Bose, Rahman, Sakai, Nonogaki, Kono, Takahashi, Takizawa, Shidei, Aoyagi "and some others, whose names need not be mentioned".[7] Guha mocked Khosla saying that he wrote "as if he knew the identities of the rest of the passengers and could mention their names if he so wanted."[8] Correct. GD Khosla examined four survivors as against six by Shah Nawaz Khan. Still, the former INA officer hadn't been able to dispel the confusion over the exact number and identification of all. Different witnesses put the figure at anything from ten to fourteen. While most passengers were identified, there were "one or two engineers," wrote Shah Nawaz "whose names have not come out."[9] In their communications to the Committee and the Commission, the Japanese Government did not provide any inkling of the fate of Sergeant Okista and Radio Operator Tominaga. That meant that some people remained unaccounted for. General Isoda had to fly to Dalat to disturb Field Marshal Count Terauchi for seats for His Excellency Chandra Bose. That is, all personnel on board were so important that none of them could be dropped to accommodate two or three cabinet members of Provisional Government of Free India. So how was then that no one knew about three to four of these important people? Suresh Bose in 1956 gave an interesting break-up of the survivors and the victims. Those heading towards Russian border — Bose, Shidei, pilots — died, and the rest survived with minor injuries. Samar Guha did not think it was a coincidence. "Such extra-ordinary and fortuitous selection of the list of dead and the list of survivors, even the Providence perhaps would not have dared to plan! But it appeared to Shah Nawaz Khan or Khosla as nothing intriguing or unnatural. They found nothing suspicious in the narration or selective deaths and selective survivals."[10]

Things got complicated when the plane reached Tourane. Colonel Rahman told Shah Nawaz Committee that they spent the night at a hotel in Tourane. Shah Nawaz wrote in his report that "there is reason to believe that the hotel in question was Morin Hotel, which the Committee visited."[11] Suresh Bose, who had accompanied him to Morin Hotel for cross-checking, observed that they "made serious attempts to get evidence everywhere, including the hotel staff about Netaji's stay at Tourane, (but) such attempts on our part ended in miserable failure .... Netaji's name and fame in the Far East was immense. If he had come to the small town of Tourane and stayed in the biggest hotel there, its staff and the people round about there would surely have known about it and we would surely have got several persons of good standing and position, who would have known about Netaji's stay there .... "[12]

The only "witness" Shah Nawaz could fish out was an Indian expat Mir Ghulam Dastgir who said that "sometime in 1945, he was asked by Mr Suziko, the Japanese Administrator of Tourane, to meet Netaji, who, he said, had arrived there."[13] Despite several attempts, Dastgir failed to see Bose but Shah Nawaz saw in him a "witness" to Bose's stay in Tourane on the 17 August night. To Suresh Bose the sum of Dastigir's evidence was zero. "It is quite clear that the deposition of this witness has absolutely no bearing on the fact that has been attempted to be established that Netaji stopped on the night of 17 August 1945 at the biggest hotel there."[14] Khosla too visited Tourane and he was helped by none other than AM Sahay, former PGI Cabinet minister and then India's Ambassador to Vietnam. Between them they too failed to get even any independent evidence to prove Bose's alleged visit 25 years earlier.

The hotel stay claim was contested by Colonel Sakai in his statement to Shah Nawaz. He was confident that having reached Tourane airfield, they all spent the night at "Supply Base Billet." GD Khosla had many options to choose from. One witness said they stayed in the army barracks while another claimed it was the airport itself. Nonogaki offered a two-in-one pick. Before he was cross-examined he held the view that Bose and Shidei were put up in army barracks. Afterwards, he said "no, they stayed in a hotel." Playing safe, Khosla kept away from the issue and did not touch upon the night stay — hotel or elsewhere — in his report. The witnesses who said that Bose stayed in a hotel could not proceed on similar lines. Arai said all of them dined together and at the dinner table Bose, General Shidei and he, a much junior officer, discussed the future of Japan and Germany. For Nonogaki only the dining part was right. In his version, Arai, he and others sat quietly trying to make sense of what Bose and General Shidei discussed with each other in German. Major Takahashi neither recalled having any such dinner nor seeing Bose at the hotel. Major Kono and Major Takizawa missed the dinner Nonogaki and Arai claimed was attended by all. They dined separately and never came face to face with the Indian dignitary at the hotel.

Quite possibly, Bose and Shidei were separated from the rest. Perhaps that's why the eyewitnesses' accounts began to blur from the evening of 17 August 1945.

The time of the plane's arrival at Taipei and halt was something the witnesses were not expected to forget about. This was a prelude to the most horrifying experience of their lives, and, as such the memory of that day should have got etched in their minds. Khosla maintained that the plane "arrived at Taipei in Formosa at 2pm" never betraying that no witness before him actually mentioned this particular hour. This was Rahman's version and he had not given evidence before the Commission. The fact of the matter was more clearly admitted by Shah Nawaz Khan: "The landing time has been stated by different witnesses to be between 11 am and 2 pm."[15] The unexplainable 4-hour gap was carried forward to the exact time the party rested under a tent pitched near the airstrip. "Different witnesses have given time of halt at Taihoku Airfield from half-an-hour to two hours,"[16] the Committee's report said. Nonogaki, one of Khosla's star witnesses, continued to be mercurial. At first he said the plane halted at Taipei for half an hour. Then he changed it to one and half hours, and his final count was that the plane halted at Taipei for two and a half hours.

Contradictions aside, Taihoku authorities did know that Subhas Bose was going to land there on the afternoon of 18 August. Despite this not a single local high officer cared to formally receive the dignitaries. Khosla looked at this with a view steeped in the war-time propaganda that depicted the Japanese as barbarians. His report, an insult to those who had helped India attain freedom, portrayed post-surrender Japan as a place where civility had ceased to exist along with the hostilities. Khosla did not think it was odd that the local commanders did not accord Bose a welcome. Time and again, he spewed venom on Japan:

"It does not need a great deal of perspicacity to understand that the Japanese were interested in the INA not in order to help India free itself from British bondage but to make use of the INA in their campaign against the Allies in Southeast Asia. They had realised that Bose commanded a great deal of respect and following amongst a vast number of Indians in Southeast Asia and that he was in a position to draw upon the wealth of the richer Indians for a patriotic cause. Their respect for Bose began and ended with his usefulness to them. After their surrender Bose could be of no assistance to them .... The war had come to an end and so had Bose's usefulness to the Japanese."[17]

This ungrateful man should have known that unlike the Indians serving in British Indian armed forces, Imperial Japanese Army personnel were not mercenaries. Yes, there was disorder following the surrender, but it was not that the Japanese had gone berserk. The Imperial Army's set-up was largely intact. On 15 August 1945, Japan announced its decision to surrender to the Allies and terminate hostilities with the Anglo-American bloc. However, they remained engaged on the Manchurian front. It was on 23 August that General MacArthur issued an order calling for grounding of Japanese military aircrafts in mainland Japan. The actual surrender took place on 2 September 1945. For South-East Asia the date was 12 September, when Marshal Terauchi surrendered *in absentia* to Admiral Mountbatten.

Taihoku, thankfully, was not Hiroshima and, facts would bear out, the Japanese would have been the last to mistreat Subhas Bose. They shared with him, in their own words, a "spiritual relationship."[18] Their respect for Bose had not diminished in the least as Khosla had alleged. "Nippon Government pays deep respect with its whole heart to Your Excellency's co-operation with Nippon on the moral strength to the utmost in order to attain Indian Independence ... without resorting in the least to the opportunism ...."[19] This was what they had conveyed to him in June 1945 with the obvious hint to fair weather allies who had deserted them. Japan deemed Bose so important a person that they informed him within hours of their requesting Swiss Charge d'Affaires ad interim Max Grassali to convey to US Secretary of State James Byrnes their desire to surrender. Regard for Bose was widespread even when Shah Nawaz Committee visited Tokyo in May 1956. The Committee's report noted that "Netaji's name was still a household word in Japan, and a great deal of interest was taken about him both by the public and the press .... The members of the Committee were much struck by the interest displayed by the Japanese public in their enquiry."[20]

In this context, it was rather strange that not even single person showed up to receive Bose and Shidei at the Matsuyama aerdrome. The latter was Deputy Chief of Staff of the Quantung Army facing the Red Army at Manchuria. That the Japanese army men followed rules was evident from a disclosure by Major Kono that in the plane a particular sitting arrangement had been insisted for the pilots as one of them was a noncommissioned officer. Moreover, GD Khosla's deduction was contrasted by the views of Shah Nawaz Khan, an army officer himself. General Harukei Isayama, Chief of General Staff of the Formosan Army, appeared before Netaji Inquiry Committee in Tokyo. Isayama and his boss General Rikichi Ando, commander of the Formosan Army and Governor General of Formosa, were No 2 and No 1 of the area and were stationed in Taihoku itself on August 18. In his testimony, Isayama failed to offer any satisfactory answer as to why General Shidei and Chandra Bose were not received at the airport. Much to his annoyance, Shah Nawaz heard that some days after the crash, the successor of General Shidei, General Tanaka, and Dr Ba Maw passed through Taihoku and this time an official welcome was accorded to them by Ando and Isayama personally. In Japanese esteem both were nowhere close to Bose and Shidei. If the situations were chaotic on August 18, they were surely worse a week later. General Ando followed protocol even though he was wrecked by the outcome of the war and was to commit harakiri soon after. Then how was that same Ando reportedly "shut himself up in his house ... and did not come out"[21] (and did not even send anyone on his behalf) when Bose and Shidei had arrived?

For all we know, Bose and Shidei never arrived in Taihoku on 18 August 1945.

It was not that one expected the witnesses to be in unison about all the details about the crash. Human sensory perception cannot with cent per cent accuracy register the split second events of a plane crash. The flip side, however, was that the survivors of the Taihoku air crash were war-hardened soldiers with plenty of flying experience. Three of them were air force officers. Major Kono knew how to fly and both he and Nonogaki could fix up aircraft glitches. Most survivors were daredevils. The plane hit the ground at around 400 kmph, got ruptured and dragged on for quite a while before abruptly stopping and catching fire. These people tumbled inside as they were no seat belts and yet many remained unruffled enough to make their way out and even rescue others. Due importance had to be given to such men's words. Being the only Indian survivor, Colonel Rahman was most sought after to describe the crash. In his written statement to Shah Nawaz Committee, Rahman wrote: "After taking off, the plane circled over the air-field at a few hundred feet height and then it turned north or north east. We were no more than 5 or 6 minutes in the air and the plane was still gaining height when suddenly I heard a deafening noise ...."

During cross-examination Suresh Bose asked Rahman to specify what he meant by "a few hundred feet." "I think it was about 1000 feet or above," Rahman replied. Captain Arai guessed it was higher — 1,600 feet before the plane plunged.[22] That was way up than what the rest of the witnesses would say. Major Kono, for one, said hardly had the plane attained an altitude of around 100 feet, when it started descending rapidly. Nonogaki told GD Khosla that the "plane did not nose dive or fell vertically" as Rahman had said. Major Takahashi offered a variety of versions. What he told Shah Nawaz was tantamount to say that the plane had belly-landed. He continued that the impact made him unconscious and when "he regained sense, he found himself thrown out of the plane." To GD Khosla he said that the plane "leaned on towards the left side and broke. I lost consciousness." When cross-examined, he put a new spin and said that the plane "nose-dived but after falling on the ground it stood in natural position enabling him to "crawl out of the plane." He was reminded of his previous statements that he was supposed to have lost consciousness after the impact. "What I told Shah Nawaz Committee was wrong" he blankly replied. Nonogaki and Tara Kono earlier said that the plane fell leaning towards left. During cross-examination before the Commission, they felt the plane leaned on the right. Tara Kono said earlier that the left engine and the propeller broke off, but later he said it broke but did not fly off. He moved with a lightening speed as the plane came down. He was sitting before Bose when the propeller and engine broke away. He sprang into the cockpit, switched off the engine, watched the pilots struggling — all within 3 seconds taken by the plane to fall from 150 feet.

The deeper one went, the more one saw the jumble. Nonogaki told the Committee that the plane hit the ground, swerved and broke into two. Tara Kono thought the "plane was broken into three parts." Their impressions were certainly not formed immediately after the plane had plunged to the ground. They got out, remained in the vicinity for some time and saw what had become of the plane. And obviously they got to discuss the incident with each other many times over in the coming days and years. Khosla did not feel the need to touch upon this part. The man he described as a most "alert witness," Nakamura, Maintenance Officer Matsuyama aerodrome, who came at the crash spot within minutes for rescue, testified that the plane's body was intact.

Unanimity eluded in pin-pointing the place the plane had crashed. To say that it was towards the south-end of the airport near a temple was way off the mark. Shah Nawaz wrote that "some witnesses, like Lt Col Nonogaki, have stated that the plane crashed on the concrete runway; on the other extreme, Col Habibur Rehman has said that the crash took place one or two miles outside the aerodrome."[23] Tara Kono said "the plane hit the right-wing against the dyke within the compound of the airport." Nonogaki's story was that "the plane crashed at the end of the runway in a bomb crater."

All said, experts could have made out from the evidence whether or not the Taihoku plane crash was plausible. Shah Nawaz sought the expertise of AMN Shastri, an aircraft accident inspector of the Directorate General of Civil Aviation. Shastri, incidentally was the last witness before the committee and for reasons known to Shah Nawaz, Suresh Bose was kept out of loop in this regard. Shastri was later found to be talking evasively. "It is not possible," he told Shah Nawaz "to establish the exact cause as to how the propeller came off from the engine from the details available."[24] That is, notwithstanding graphic evidence of the survivors, three of whom were air force officers, the expert could not bring himself around to say that such a crash was possible. Shastri tried to see reason in Major Kono's statement about the craft having some trouble at Saigon, which was not corroborated by others. Suresh Bose saw little fault of Shastri's. He revealed in his report that the government servant had little option to speak his mind. "He (Shah Nawaz) continued calling for new witnesses and examining them not with the intention of arriving at the truth, but to fill up the gaps in the evidence and for explaining and reconciling discrepant and contradictory statements that stood in the way of his coming to the conclusion that the plane had crashed and that Netaji had died."[25]

Shastri's bewilderment over the propeller coming off found an explanation a decade later. Hayashida and Fred Saito, Bose's biographers, consulted a number of Japanese war-time aeronautical experts. The experts' opinion on the Taipei crash amounted to rubbishing the official theory in general and testimonies of Nakamura and Taro Kono in particular. Their view was that this plane crash was one of its kind. "The entire Japanese air-operations before and during Pacific war did not record any other case of propeller falling out during take-off. If the plane dived to the ground, it could have only smashed itself into bits, killing all aboard instantly."[26] Nakamura's "eyewitness" account of the plane crash was dubbed by them as "completely irrelevant and illogical." And as for the "overloading" theory upheld by Major Kono among others, the experts observed: "That 13 men with personal effects did not exceed the load limit was proven by the standard 7-hour flight from Tourane to Taipei."[27]

GD Khosla saw the opinion of a senior IAF officer. Air Vice Marshal DAR Nanda too was at a loss for the reasons for this strange air crash. "From the statements, there is such a lack of essential details that it is humanly impossible for any person to give any sensible assessment for the things even at this stage."[28] The photos, the Air Vice Marshal noted, "did not make any sense. No specific details could be obtained from them."[29] He also made one observation that put in spot Major Kono's evidence that he had walked on the left wing after he managed to break off the hood. Keeping in mind the story of the propeller and engine falling, "the tendency would be for the aircraft to have leaned leftwards and left wing down and the nose would come down.'[30]

The crash *per se* did not kill Bose. Almost unhurt, he ran out but was caught in flames. Five survivors claimed they saw this occurring from close range, but when asked to recall, they gave out incredibly different stories. This was the central part of the crash story, and it took the cake. Rahman gave a most detailed account before Shah Nawaz. Bose jumped through the fire and his petrol-soaked clothes caught fire. Rahman then removed the burning clothes from Bose's upper body. Nonogaki's story was somewhat similar. He saw Bose near the left wing of the plane. Rahman was having difficulty in removing Bose's "woollen sweater," which Rahman said Bose was not wearing. Nonogaki was sure that Bose was stripped of all his clothes and he was "absolutely naked," which was backed and contradicted by other witnesses. Major Kono's version of the event had it that Bose standing very near the burning wreck facing away from it. He stood erect with his legs apart, arms stretched and fists clenched. "He was completely naked and was wearing only his shoes." Kono did not see any fire on his body. And then Rahman pounced and dragged Bose away from the flames. Major Takahashi said after the crash, he found himself lying near the plane with his ankle injured. He crawled up to Nonogaki, who told him that both Bose and Shidei were trapped in the plane. After some time Bose emerged from the left front portion of the plane desperately trying to take off his burning "coat." Takahashi moved towards Bose and caught hold of his legs and told him to roll on the ground to put off fire. Bose did just that and all the while Rahman stood there doing nothing. Take that! The major saw that "only patches of the clothes on the upper part of his (Bose's) body were burnt and as his trousers were slightly burnt." While other witnesses claimed in varying degree that Bose's clothes were stripped, Takahashi said he had them on.

Nakamura provided the ringside view. He was not in the plane when it crashed so the chances of his making an erroneous statement were nil. Immediately after the crash, he rushed to the spot with 30 of his men. He found the plane intact and burning in the front. Luckily, one of the doors could be opened and through it he and his men rescued all survivors. Bose was the last person to have come out and he came out walking. Suddenly a flame leapt and despite Rahman's caution, Bose was caught in it. Nakamura and three of his men laid Bose on the ground and stripped him naked. Shah Nawaz was put off by Nakamura's testimony, and did not know how to make sense of different stories. But there was a job to be done. "This version is completely uncorroborated by anybody else," he made a weak defence, "and may perhaps be put down to confused recollection after such a lapse of time."[31] When it suited him, Shah Nawaz described same Captain Nakamura as "most credible" witness. This was the modus operandi: Take selective passages from the witnesses' testimonies, paper over cracks, provide alibis and make the death story believable. Shah Nawaz's slip showed at times; GD Khosla removed the suspicious parts altogether.

The survivors had to wait about 15 minutes before they were removed to hospital. How? Shah Nawaz had no precise answer. "There is some discrepancy between the witnesses, as to who travelled in which vehicles, and who arrived first (at the hospital)."[32] Who took them? Some nurses and medical orderlies whose identities were never established. How fast? On the spot observation in Taipei by Samar Guha and Sunil Krishna Gupta revealed that the crash site, separated by river Keelung, was located a mile away from the south end of the runway. There was no bridge in sight and hence it appeared most unlikely that the survivors could have been rescued in fifteen minutes as was stated by witnesses.

What happened to the items on Bose's person? Rahman returned India with his "watch" but there was no trace of his burnt dress, his spectacles, his rings, fountain pen, cigarette case, camera, insignia as Supreme Commander, INA & IIL badges, and a firearm he must have been carrying. Immediately after the crash, the Japanese had cordoned off the wreck site and were able to secure delicate objects like paper knife, belt buckle, pendants and some leather stuff but could not find these objects, when these should have been lying away where fire was beat out of Bose's body.

M Kazuo, a medical orderly at Nanmon Military Hospital in August 1945, told Shah Nawaz Committee that he saw a well-built foreigner lying on a stretcher, wearing the full uniform of an air force officer. Kazuo said that this man's trousers were slit open with a pair of scissors to expose the burns on his legs. No other witness said that Bose received burns in his legs or that he wore the uniform of an air force office. Then "the foreigner" was taken to a special ward. The witnesses made conflicting statements about their position in relation to Subhas Bose in the ward. Rahman said that he only shared a room with Bose but others said there were more patients. Nonogaki's claim was that it was he who was all along by the side of Bose. Takahashi punctured his claims, saying he, Nonogaki and Sakai were together in the ward next to where Bose was admitted. Taro Kono compounded the situation by saying that the very evening he and Nonogaki were taken to a different hospital.

Dr Tenayoshi Yoshimi and his junior Dr Tusruta supervised Bose's treatment until the last. Along with the statement of Rahman, Captain Yoshimi's testimony ranked as the most formidable "evidence" of Bose's death. Here was the man who had himself tried to save a badly burnt Subhas Bose and pronounced him dead! However, just as was the case with Rahman, Dr Yoshimi, when subjected to scrutiny, made a series of gaffes. Almost a year after the end of the war, a British officer interrogated Dr Yoshimi in Hong Kong's Stanley jail on the death of Subhas Bose. Shah Nawaz and GD Khosla had the copies of Colonel Turner's report as a ready-reckoner. During the cross-examination, Yoshimi, a man of extremely sharp memory, said different things every time he opened his mouth. He gave in his testimonies an impression that he knew in advance and all along who his patient was. But in 1991 he appeared in a BBC documentary and stated that it was only after he had passed away that he came to know that his patient was Bose. He could never be sure of the exact time when Bose was brought at the hospital. To Turner, he said it was 5pm; to Shah Nawaz 2pm, and 12.30pm to GD Khosla. He also missed as to exactly who bandaged and applied ointment on Bose. Turner and GD Khosla were told it was he himself. Shah Nawaz got the version that it was in fact Dr Tsuruta. The doctor was liberal with words while describing how badly burnt was the man who was brought before him on the 18 August. He told Turner that Bose was suffering from extensive burns all over his body, "so much so that very little was left for his identification." Yet, when a picture of Bose was shown to him in the presence of GD Khosla, he was quick to say, "Yes, he is the person I treated in the hospital." Yoshimi had never seen Bose until a disfigured man was brought to him in August 1945.

In his zest to convince others that Bose had died, Yoshimi told Shah Nawaz that Bose's heart had suffered burns. Such a condition would have been instantly fatal: Layers of thick muscles above and below the rib cage are destroyed when heart sustains burns. After such injuries, no human can survive even for minutes. But Dr Yoshimi, forgetting earlier part of his statement, went on to tell how Bose carried on conversation with some people. He realised his slip up before Khosla Commission and retracted from the statement he had given to Shah Nawaz Khan. The claim of Dr Yoshimi that in the course of treatment he had let out "approximately 200 cc blood" of Bose and gave him "400 cc of fresh blood" was admitted as "a more serious discrepancy" by Shah Nawaz. Dr Tsuruta, who claimed to have remained by Bose's side denied that this was ever done. As a result, Dr Yoshimi retracted from this part of his statement too before Khosla Commission.

Yoshimi was crystal clear while enumerating how many shots of Vita-camphor and Digitamine he had given to Bose. He could recall the exact temperature and blood pressure Bose had. He admitted that Bose's death shattered him. Shah Nawaz wrote in his report: "Dr Yoshimi says that tears were rolling down Col Rehman's eyes. The nurses were crying loudly. Everybody present in the room was crying. In fact, describing this poignant scene (of Bose's passing away) before the

Committee, Dr Yoshimi himself broke down and sobbed audibly."[33] And yet, the maudlin doctor, who also prepared Bose's death certificate, made howlers about the time of Bose's death. He told Turner that Bose had died at 11pm. Shah Nawaz heard that it was around 8pm. Foxed, he noted in his report: "According to the telegram sent by the Chief of Staff, Southern Army, to OC, Hikari Kikan, on the 20th August 1945, which was recovered by British Military Intelligence, the death took place at midnight .... The evidence of the fellow injured persons does not help to establish the correct hour."[34] In an interview to a Japanese newspaper in 1969, Yoshimi said Bose had died at 10pm.[35]

Contradictions continued to mar the statements of different witnesses to Bose's death at hospital. Shah Nawaz noted many minor ones. "Although Lt Col Nonogaki named two staff officers who came on the receipt of the information when Netaji was alive, the staff officers, Col Miyata and Major Nagatomo said that they arrived after Netaji died." Suresh Bose observed a serious one. "These are the six persons, who are alleged to have received injuries along with Netaji, and who were also taken along with him to the same hospital for treatment. It is unique that except Col Rehman, none of the five others had any knowledge of Netaji's death, nor had any personal knowledge of Netaji's death, nor had any of them even seen his dead body, though he is said to have died in the same hospital."[36]

Did anyone from the local army command come to see Bose when he died? Shah Nawaz Committee report stated that only a junior officer of the rank of a major was sent to the hospital. Two distinguished witnesses to this particular episode then made totally contradictory statements. The same report said: "Major Nagatomo says that immediately after receiving information, General Ando, commander of the Formosan Army, went to the hospital to see Netaji. He also says that General Ando attended the subsequent funeral ceremony."[37] There was more in the report: "General Isayama, Chief of the General Staff, who should know what the Army Commander was doing, gives a completely different story. He says that neither he nor

General Ando went either to the hospital to pay respects to Netaji's body, or attended any funeral ceremony."[38] Which version represented the truth? Khosla hammered on the scenario that the Japanese discarded Bose. Suresh Bose was positive that Subhas was never brought to the hospital.

The real date of the cremation of Bose's body was contentious. Rahman gave three different dates ranging from 20 to 23 August within months of the crash. The other witnesses too sounded confused, but Khosla wasn't. He wrote that "Bose succumbed to his injuries the same night (18th August) ... two days later Bose's body was cremated."[39] Shah Nawaz would not do a similar guess work. "There is some discrepancy about the date of cremation."[40] Samar Guha improved upon the language: "According to witnesses, the date of the cremation could be August 19, 20, 21, 22 or 23, 1945."[41]

Following an inquiry by Counter Intelligence Corps, a British officer on deputation sent a report on 8 October 1945 with four photographs supplied by the Japanese Government. Three of the photographs showed the wreck of the plane at Taipei, one showed a bandaged Rahman sitting in the hospital and the last one showed "Bose's body" fully covered with a sheet. There was no explanation why no picture of Bose's body could be taken. When the photos were examined, they proved nothing. The one that purported to show Bose's body in a coffin was particularly off-putting. Suresh Bose could not make anything of this picture. " ... (It) does not show any coffin whatsoever, as stated by the Colonel. It shows a white background which, I regret, I am unable to understand what it could possibly signify ...."[42] Bose was photographed as late as the afternoon of 17 August 1945 in Saigon, but the next day the Japanese cameras malfunctioned. Rahman said he did not allow a picture of Bose's face to be taken because it had been disfigured. That did not pass muster as according to his testimony the face was nevertheless identifiable. Such a picture had to be taken for record if not for publications in newspapers. Suresh Bose argued that "the Japanese Government, for warding off any calumny or treachery, that may have been suggested against them, if not for anything else, would have decidedly taken pains to maintain correct and detailed photographic records of the true incident for the satisfaction of the Indian people, for the Japanese nation and for the world at large."[43]

"I am definitely of opinion that no better photographs than these four could be available to the Japanese Government, as a plane crashing with Netaji in it, as Netaji with injuries and burns near a crashed plane, as Netaji being treated in a hospital for those injuries and burns, as a dead Netaji in a hospital, as the dead body of Netaji being cremated and being put inside a furnace of a crematorium were not available to the Japanese Government for being photographed, because such incidents did not take place at all and therefore, it was not possible for them to obtain these photographs."[44]

Shah Nawaz did not trouble the readers of his report with such complexities. He simply produced the pictures as appendices as evidence of the crash and death. GD Khosla knew that all these pictures hinted that there had been a cover-up and so refused to consider them. "The same photographs were produced before the present Commission, but as they are not relied upon, as in the absence of Habibur Rehman who alone could have testified to what they depict, they cannot be held to have been proved. Moreover they are inadmissible in evidence as they do not constitute direct or primary evidence of air crash or Bose's death."[45] Khosla expected others to forget that the pictures were produced by the Japanese Government. Samar Guha retaliated: "Figges team accepted them and Shah Nawaz Committee also accepted them as part of evidentiary materials and all their reports formed part of the exhibits of the Khosla Commission, which he very often quoted as and when they served his convenience to support his findings. But on further scrutiny, as these photographs were likely to explode the whole story of the air crash and Netaji's death, Mr Khosla on a very fragile legal pretence refused to recognise them as admissible in evidence."[46]

There was not a shred of paper to show that Subhas Bose came to Taipei in August 1945, or that his plane had crashed there or that Bose was treated in Nanmon Hospital. No entry was made in the airport log book or the hospital register. There were no records in police and fire departments. No medical chart was prepared and neither any paper showed description of treatment. The case of the "death certificate" and the "cremation permit" for Bose was the mystery wrapped inside an enigma. Journalist Harin Shah, who went to Taipei in 1946, was able to secure the two documents from Municipal Bureau of Taipei. Harin Shah appeared before Shah Nawaz and produced the documents saying they had to be issued in the name of a soldier as the Japanese wanted to keep the news of Bose's death a secret. But what was the need for secrecy when Bose had "died"?

Shah Nawaz cross-checked facts from the Japanese government who discussed the cremation permit but overlooked the death certificate. The Japanese Secretary of the Asian Bureau told the First Secretary at the Indian Embassy at Tokyo that the " 'doctor's report' and 'police report' ... could not be traced,"[47] but the copy of the cremation permit was available. It was the same that Harin Shah had brought. Japanese government affirmed that the permit "must correspond to Mr Subhas Chandra Bose."[48] It had been issued for an unnamed, Tokyo-based soldier cremated on August 22. The applicant was Chcaz Chi jin, the deceased's "close friend." The date of death and birth were stated to be "same as in Doctor's report" and the name of the "applying Japanese Officer of the police station" was Yoshimi Yani Yoshi — that is Dr Yoshimi. Shah Nawaz readily accepted the documents as evidence of Bose's death, but GD Khosla, a judge, could not. Unlike Shah Nawaz he had a number of counsels around him. He wrote: "The death certificate described the deceased as Ichiro Okura, male, born on April 9, 1901. The cause of death is mentioned as heart failure, the illness manifested itself on August 19, 1945 ... it is clear that neither the name nor the date of the birth of the deceased in these two documents is truly descriptive of Bose. Neither document mentions the cause of death as burn injuries sustained in an air crash."[49]

The evidence of the two doctors who had treated Bose ran contrary to the details given in the certificate. Dr Yoshimi was firm before Shah Nawaz and GD Khosla that "on August 18, I had issued a medical certificate in respect of the deceased person, writing his name in Japanese (Kata Kana) as 'Chandra Bose' and giving the cause of death as 'burns of the third degree'." Once Dr Tsuruta claimed that actually it was he who had certified Bose's death "due to heart failure." In circumvallating the issue of bogus death certificate, GD Kholsa came up with an alibi that only a judge of his stature could think of. Faced with the prospects of accepting documents that could not prove Bose's death, he refused to take them into consideration saying, "The two documents have no evidentiary value at all, neither of them prove or disapprove anything. They relate to totally different persons and not Bose at all."[50] This rattled Gobinda Mukhoty, who reminded him that the documents related to Bose and as such were proofs that the man declared dead by doctors in August 1945 at Nanmon hospital was not Subhas Bose. The objections provoked GD Khosla to resume: "The argument is in the nature of a non-sequitur, for what does not relate to an event, cannot be used to disapprove it. It is tantamount to raise a phantom and then destroying it. I do not, therefore, accept the contention that these documents relate to Bose and they disprove the factum of his death."[51] The bottom line was that these documents did relate to "Bose" and his "death"! The death news was given by the Japanese and they had officially stated that the death permit was for Bose. The moot point was to find out the need for the Japanese to raise "phantoms" after Bose's "accidental death"?

The Taipei crash also killed 49-year-old Lt General Tsunamasa Shidei. It was out of question for the Japanese to treat this case with indifference and secrecy. Shidei was one of the seniormost military commanders of Japan and there was no way he could have been meted out the contemptible treatment, GD Kholsa alleged, Bose was given in his last days and after death. Surprisingly, very little was heard of Shidei after the plane hit the ground. Only three witnesses could provide some sketchy details about the general's fate. Kono said that moment plane hit the ground, a petrol tank fell on the general and he died on the spot. Nakamura said that along with the pilots, the general too perished in the flames. Arai contradicted them, saying Shidei was taken to hospital, where he expired. No one knew when, how, by whom and in which condition the general was extricated from the wreck. Suresh Bose wrote that along with the general, the death of the whole crew was doubtful. "The Service entries, regarding Major Takizawa, Chief Pilot and NCO Aoyagi, Co-Pilot, and the other members of the crew, alleged to have died, have not been produced either. The evidence regarding the death of both these pilots is also very insufficient and shaky and that, regarding their remains, is even worse."[52] IIL's AM Nair, who had good contacts in the Imperial Japanese Army, interestingly, wrote in 1981, that "it was said that some persons were also killed in the alleged crash, but to the best of my personal knowledge, every one of the passengers listed as killed, was living for long periods after the reported incident and supposed death."[53]

At hospital no one remembered to have seen or heard about the general or his body. In fact no one bothered to. Nonogaki ran around the plane after the crash yelling out for the general, but once in hospital, he too became unconcerned. Doctors did not see or heard about the general or his body and the question of issuing any death certificate did not arise. Nakamura claimed that Pilot Takizawa, Co-Pilot Aoyagi and General Shidei died instantly, and "he helped to bury their entrails and put their ashes in three boxes."[54] But the British intelligence had reported that Ayogi died in Namoon hospital more than a month after the crash. Witnesses said he had been pulled out of the plane alive. General Isayama, Chief of Staff of the Formosan Army and a batch mate of Shidei's was clueless about his friend. He was told that on his arrival General Shidei had inquired about him. But that did not make Isayama feel like going to see his friend at the airport. He did not see his body and nor did he have any knowledge of Shidei's funeral. A week after when General Tanaka, the successor of General Shidei landed at Taihoku, everything had turned normal. Isayama and General Ando came to the airport and General Tanaka himself took possession of "Shidei's ashes." The ashes were dispatched to Kyoto city, where Shidei's family lived.

As was the case with Subhas Bose, the Japanese Government could not produce any substantial record of Shidei's death. Shah Nawaz Committee received what the Japanese called "Military record of the Death of late Lt General Shidei." But it turned out to be an anonymous 1947 application for posthumous promotion of the general made to or forwarded by Chief, Korean and Manchurian Affairs Section, First Demobilisation Bureau. The Japanese government must have had better record on general but they seemed unwilling to part with those. Along with this application, the Japanese Foreign Ministry had attached a brief note on the career of the General. Shah Nawaz took these two papers as proving the general's death. So did GD Khosla, but not before making a concession to Gobinda Mukhoty. Khosla had to agree that these documents appeared to be "fraud." Samar Guha was suspicious that "Manchurian Section" should describe general's "death by war." The Soviets took around 60,000 Quantung army personnel prisoners in Manchuria in August 1945. "If General really died at Taihoku, the application should have been made to or forwarded by either the Chief of the Southern Army Command Affairs Section, or by the Chief of the Formosan Command Section ... this (document) clearly shows that Lt General Shidei's death was caused definitely within the area under command of 'Korean and Manchurian Section of the Japanese army' ... (it) unmistakably points out that Lt-Gen Shidei reached the active war area and died in Manchuria after assuming his command there, which means he did not die at Taihoku."[55]

The manner in which the Japanese broke the death news to Bose's confidants and the world was anything but usual.

They destroyed all but one record of Bose's last movement. The Southern Army Command informed Saigon and Tokyo of Bose's death, but for two days after the crash, Pritam Singh, Gulzara Singh, Abid Hasan, SA Iyer and Debnath Das were kept waiting in Saigon. It might have been OK to hide facts from ordinary INA officers, but these men were Bose's top brass. Rather than being told of Bose's death, they were moved around with the feeling that they were going to join Bose. Pritam Singh, Abid Hasan and Debnath Das were flown to Hanoi on the 20th and it was only after that they reached there that they were told of the mishap. JK Bhonsle, INA Chief of Staff, was told of the crash on 21 August, when the body had been disposed off. Pritam Singh could never make sense of the delay. "If the plane had crashed on the 18th, then why did the Japanese authorities provide us with a plane on the 20th August, 1945 for the purpose of following Netaji?"[56] Stranger was Japanese officers' telling Debnath Das and Pritam Singh that the crash was a cover. Subhas Bose's personal physician Dr RN Kasliwal told Khosla Commission that the Indian officers held a memorial service for Bose after the news of his death was circulated. But to their surprise, not a single Japanese officer turned up and neither did they send wreathes.

In Tokyo, the Imperial Headquarters assumed strange silence on Bose's fate. No official note was prepared to announce the death of Subhas Bose and General Shidei. When SA Ayer arrived in Tokyo on the 21st August, he was told to write the death news. Ayer never made it to Taipei. He never saw the body and nor did he wait for Rahman to come. What the world got to know via Domei news agency five days after the Taipei crash was Ayer's copy verbatim – complete heresy. In Taipei, the authorities were all the more secretive. Nothing was heard of the crash for days before local intelligence department circulated a misleading press brief on 25 August. The Japanese did not seem interested in conducting even a cursory inquiry to find out the reason for a crash that killed two important people. Shah Nawaz Khan had it confirmed from General Isayama, who spoke in two voices. "Since the aeroplane in question did not belong to Formosan Army, the headquarters of the Formosan Army had no responsibility to hold inquiry into the matter."[57] Isayama then changed tack. "It was the duty of the commander (his boss General Ando) within whose area an air crash took place to enquire and report to the higher authorities. In this case, a report was submitted to the Imperial headquarters by my staff officer, Lt Col Shibuya through me."[58]

In a double blow, both the Colonel and Japanese Government denied that any such report was ever sent. "Shibuya," Shah Nawaz wrote, "denied the knowledge of any such inquiry, and said that the responsibility of holding it lay with the Air Division concerned."[59] The final word came from the Japanese Foreign Office on 4 June 1956: "As a result of investigation ... it has been revealed that no official inquiry commission to determine the causes of the accident was held so far."[60]

Under detention in Rohtak jail during the Emergency, Samar Guha, with future Prime Minister Atal Bihari Vajpayee and Deputy Prime Ministers Devi Lal and Lal Krishna Advani giving him company, spent most of his time in analyzing the notes prepared by Gobinda Mukhoty. He got out to make his case in his book and then in the Parliament. "What will the nation do now?" he asked while concluding the debate on 28 August 1978. In response, Prime Minister Moraraji Desai made a statement that took care of the "findings" of the "inquiries" conducted by messrs Shah Nawaz Khan and Gopal Das Khosla.

"The Shah Nawaz Committee and the Khosla Commission held the report of Netaji Subhas Chandra Bose's death following a plane crash as true. Since then, reasonable doubts have been cast on the correctness in the two reports and various important contradictions in the testimony of the witnesses have been noticed. Some further contemporary official documentary records have also become available. In the light of those doubts and contradictions and those records, government finds it difficult to accept that the earlier conclusions are decisive."[61]

Notes:

1 Netaji Inquiry Commission report 1974. Pages 123, 124.

2 In *Netaji: Dead or Alive?* Samar Guha listed out scores of anomalies in the death story to prove that the eyewitnesses had been tutored. Suresh Bose explained why the Japanese had "lied" over the years: "These witnesses ... are citizens of Japan, and whose unbound patriotism is probably unique in the world. They have made statements to different authorities at different times, supporting the aforesaid plan of their Government. As such, I consider it an impossibility for them to go beyond their previously recorded statements and thereby disgrace themselves as well as their Government, who, after all, had done a magnanimous act by giving succour to their friend and ally 'Mr Chandra Bose'." *Dissentient Report.* Page 10.

3 Allied code name "Sally." Some witnesses said that the crashed plane was brand new whereas others thought it was old.

4 No SLO/CC/1, dated 1 March 1946. "Apparently Bose's plane was not allowed to go beyond Saigon for reasons which are not quite clear," commented PES Finney in one of his reports.

5 Mukherjee Commission's status report dated 12 December 2001. Page 7.

6 *Hindustan Times* report **Guha motions to probe Netaji mystery.** August 3, 1977. Guha referred to Telegram I 2822 of 17.10.45 from British troops in China to SACSEA contained in Mountbatten Diaries. This document was produced before Khosla Commission but has now gone missing.

7 Netaji Inquiry Commission report 1974. Page 123.

8 *Netaji: Dead or Alive?* by Samar Guha. Page 72.

9 Netaji: Inquiry Committee report 1956. Page 15.

10 *Netaji: Dead or Alive?* by Samar Guha. Page 99.

11 Netaji Inquiry Committee report 1956. Page 16.

12 *Dissentient Report* by Suresh Bose. Page 88.

13 Ibid. Page 87.

14 Ibid. Pages 87, 88.

15 Netaji Inquiry Committee report 1956. Page 17.

16 Ibid.

17 Netaji Inquiry Commission report 1974. Page 31.

18 The website of the Ministry of External Affairs states: "India as the country of origin of Buddhism and Netaji and INA's association with Japan during the war also invoke friendly feelings among section of the Japanese society." http://meaindia.nic.in/foreignrelation/japan.htm.

19 Netaji Inquiry Committee report 1956. Page 56.

20 Ibid. Page 2. It goes without saying that the older generation of the Japanese hold Netaji in highest esteem.

21 Ibid. Page 43.

22 Mitsubishi Ki-21's climb rate was 19,685 feet in 13.2 minutes.

23 Netaji Inquiry Committee report 1956. Page 19.

24 Netaji Inquiry Committee report 1956. Page 25.

25 *Dissentient Report* by Suresh Bose. Page 109.

26 *Netaji Dead or Alive?* by Samar Guha. Page 101.

27 Ibid.

28 Proceedings of Khosla Commission. Volume XV. Page 4415.

29 Ibid. Page 4416.

30 Ibid. Page 4417.

31 Netaji Inquiry Committee report 1956. Page 23.

32 Ibid. Page 27.

33 Ibid. Page 37.

34 Ibid. Page 30.

35 Hayshida wrote that Bose died at 8pm, whereas the account given by the Japanese Foreign Office put that to 11.40pm.

36 *Dissentient Report* by Suresh Bose. Page 127.

37 Netaji Inquiry Committee report 1956. Page 43.

38 Ibid.

39 Netaji Inquiry Commission report 1974. Page 40.

40 Netaji Inquiry Committee report 1956. Page 40.

41 *Netaji: Dead or Alive?* By Samar Guha. Page 113.

42 *Dissentient Report* by Suresh Bose. Page 114.

43 Ibid. Page 115.

44 Ibid. Page 116.

45 Netaji Inquiry Commission report 1974. Page 61.

46 *Netaji: Dead or Alive?* by Samar Guha. Page 117.

47 MEA file No 24 (13)- FEA/56. Letter dated 24 July 1956 from Hisaji Hattori, Chief of 4th Section, Asian Affairs Bureau, Gaimusho to AK Dar, First Secretary. Embassy of India, Tokyo.

48 Ibid.

49 Netaji Inquiry Commission report 1974. Pages 41, 42.

50 Ibid. Page 42.

51 Ibid. Page 43.

52 *Dissentient Report* by Suresh Bose. Page 172.

53 *An Indian freedom fighter in Japan: Memoirs of AM Nair.* Pages 274, 275.

54 Netaji Inquiry Committee report 1956. Page 23.

55 *Netaji: Dead or Alive?* by Samar Guha. Pages 242, 243.

56 Examination of Pritam Singh before Mukherjee Commission.

57 Netaji Inquiry Committee report 1956. Page 24.

58 Ibid.

59 Ibid.

60 Ibid. Page 64.

61 Lok Sabha Debates, Sixth Series, Volume XVIII Part II. 28 August 1978.

7

His Leader's Voice

Cool, calm and solid as a rock, a devoted follower of his Netaji and a most selfless worker for Indian independence.

Shah Nawaz Khan on Habibur Rahman in 1946.

Throughout the protracted questioning (over Bose's death), resentment was visible from B1269's face and he made no bones about it.

A 9 June 1946 intelligence report on Rahman's interrogation.

It's a word of honour I have given to Netaji; don't question me further.

Rahman to Bose's Confidential Secretary Major E Bhaskaran in 1946.

We wanted to accompany Netaji wherever he went .... Japanese told General (AC) Chatterjee that it would not be possible to conceal a group of men but Netaji alone could well be concealed and kept away from the enemy. We asked why Habibur Rahman was going with Netaji and the Japanese told us that he too would be left behind in the last stage.

INA's Colonel Thakur Singh during his cross examination before Khosla Commission on 3 March 1971.

Not many people were around when Zain-al Abdin Hasan Safrani made that statement before Khosla Commission in the summer of 1972. Fewer still got its import. Abid Hasan, as he was well-known, was one of those Bose loyalists who had found some favour with India's first Prime Minister. For the first and last time since Nehru had picked him for a posting in the Indian Embassy in Cairo in 1948, Hasan was reminiscing about Bose's last days in a public forum.

Hasan hadn't just witnessed history, he had had a precious share in it. Before he joined Bose in that perilous undersea voyage from Germany to Japan, he had helped coin the two words that the Indians would be exulting in for all times to come. People close to him knew him as "'Jai Hind' Safrani" and to some INA compatriots he was a haunted man. The fear of Bose languishing in a Siberian dungeon after 1945 never left this Hyderabadi till his death in 1984.

Deep down, Hasan was his former self while being quizzed before GD Khosla over his friend Lt Colonel Habibur Rahman Khan. He made an astonishing remark. When he had met Rahman in 1946, he never asked him anything about the Taipei crash. Why? "(Because) for finding out whether that accident took place or not, that one person could not be Habibur Rehman,"[1] he muttered. There wasn't slightest solecism in the MEA mandarin's words. They carried a deeper meaning that Khosla had no inclination to fathom. Years later, Colonel Pritam Singh, another INA top gun, who had, like Hasan, remained with Bose up till 17 August evening, was to better Hasan's words before Justice Monoj Kumar Mukherjee. After being taken prisoner by the British, Singh met Rahman in Delhi Cantonment's Kabul Lines but never ever asked him about the crash. "Habibur Rahman did not tell us anything about the alleged place crash. Nor did we dare to ask him about that. It might be that he was under such an oath of secrecy to Netaji ... he would not divulge anything even on pain of death ... (such) was our loyalty to Netaji. Even if the heaven fell, we would not do anything against his wishes."[2]

The mystery of Subhas Bose's death revolved solely around Habibur Rahman – the sole credible witness. In Taipei, he was the only man who knew Bose and could, therefore, vouch for the death story. The Japanese survivors had never seen Bose before he boarded their plane in Saigon (Ho Chi Minh City). Conviction though Rahman's testimony did generate for many, it left some others dissatisfied. They thought that Rahman had lied. To keep his leader out of harm's way, he had just done what he was told.

Son of an aristocrat, Raja Mansur Ahmed Khan, Rahman followed a family tradition by joining the British Indian Army in 1936. He was a captain when the British suffered their most humiliating defeat at the hands of the Japanese in Burma in 1942. Like others, he was taken a POW and was exhorted by Major Mohan Singh and Major Iwaichi Fujiwara to join the newly-formed INA. While most shirked at the start, Captain Shah Nawaz Khan one of them, Rahman jumped at the very idea. He became the Commandant of Officers' Training School, which was to re-orientate the officers of the INA. Bose took little time to deposit his faith in Rahman and quickly promoted him. Rahman became a Lt Colonel and *Aide de Camp* to the INA's Supreme Commander. In February 1945, Rahman took over charge from the INA Chief of Staff Major General JK Bhonsle of the INA forces in Malaya and Singapore, some 23, 000 of them, and continued in this position till 15 August 1945.

These distinctions made Rahman perhaps the most important INA officer — a shadow of his leader from early 1944. And hereafter, not one person with either pro or anti INA leanings ever questioned Rahman's unflinching loyalty to Bose. Shah Nawaz Khan admitted before Khosla Commission that "Rahman was so devoted to Netaji that he would not have hesitated one minute even to sacrifice his life (for Bose) ... any order or instructions given to him (by Bose), he would faithfully carry out, even at the cost of his life." Colonel Mahboob Ahmed, Bose's military secretary, explained to Khosla why it was so: "(The) loyalty of most of us to Netaji is something which cannot be believed unless you were in that organization (INA) itself. We fought for India, but India was something very vague .... Netaji was the symbol for which we fought."[3]

The news of Bose's death made Rahman British India's most wanted, though it were the Americans who rounded him up in Tokyo. The bonhomie between the Allies did not extend to their secret services who were wary of each other. Even after the questioning of Rahman by the Counter Intelligence Corps

(CIC) in Tokyo on 24 September, the Intelligence Bureau remained in dark about his whereabouts. On 12 November, PES Finney wrote from Bangkok that for proper investigations "tracing and examination of Col Habibur Rehman" was vital. This led to Admiral Louis Mountbatten's HQ in Candy, Sri Lanka, requesting US General Douglas MacArthur's HQ to hand over Rahman. Thereafter, the Americans brought Rahman, Lt General Saburo Isoda and SA Ayer to Delhi on 22 November 1945. By this time the British had figured out that there was something fishy about the death story. Rahman was handed over to the CSDIC so that they could coerce Rahman into telling the truth. The CSDIC interrogations were carried out by several officers, and, in contrast to what GD Khosla tried to portray, they did not end with BC Chakraborty's turn in December 1945.

Sessions with Rahman at the Red Fort and elsewhere did not satisfy all. He clearly mislead his interrogators on the most crucial aspect of Bose's activities in his last known days. He told the CSDIC that on "13 August Bose retuned to Singapore via Seremban" and on 14 August "a messenger from Hachiya handed Bose a note that the Japanese Government had decided to surrender and asked Bose whether he had anything to communicate to them." The reality was that on 11 August at Seremban itself the Japanese Government had communicated to Bose that they were going to announce the surrender. The Japanese messenger, Neigishi, had himself travelled with Bose, Rahman and others to Singapore. Rahman continued that "in the afternoon (14 August) Bose called a meeting" of his men and "read the message of Hachiya and then invited suggestions as to their further line of action. At the meeting it was decided that the INA would also surrender and that every one was to stay where he was, including Bose who decided to surrender at Singapore." The reality here was that in the meeting PGI ministers had earnestly requested Bose to keep the freedom struggle alive by escaping to Russia.

Rahman said that on the 15 August midnight he was summoned by Bose and ordered to get ready for a journey to Bangkok on the following morning. "The plan then was for Bose and B1269 to return to Singapore within 2/3 days," a

CSDIC report recorded. On the 16th in Bangkok "they met Bhonsle who took them in his car to a bungalow where Lt Gen Isoda and Hachiya were living ... they held a conference at which ... they discussed the INA and Japanese surrender." The truth was that in this meeting the agenda was to give a final shape to the modalities of sending Bose to the Russians. "After this discussion," Rahman's version continued, "Bose went to a bungalow in the suburbs of Bangkok" and was visited by Major General JK Bhonsle, Ishar Singh, Col Gulzara Singh, Major Abid Hasan, DM Khan, Colonel SA Malik, Debnath Das, Parmanand and Lt Rizvi. "B1269 disclosed to some of them that Bose was likely to return to Singapore within a couple of days." This was never the case. Everyone knew that Bose was not coming back.

The British drew the obvious inference: Rahman was drawing a red herring. The Commandant of the "S Section CSDIC (India)" told his superior on 28 February 1946 that Rahman's deposition "may be categorically rejected." As a result, Rahman was re-interrogated by Major Hyat Khan. On 25 March 1946 Hyat reported that "Habib-ur-Rehman has been questioned again on his knowledge of Bose's plans. He has adhered to his earlier attitude of ingenious denial ... B1269 adds that at the meeting one of the senior Japanese present asked what Bose himself intended doing ... Bose told the Japanese that he had decided to remain in Singapore and surrender with the ... INA.

"B1269 states that he is not aware of any other talk ... regarding his (Bose's) ... move into Russia. It is considered that even if B1269 was in the know of Bose's plans, he would not disclose them. His manner is not very convincing. He talks in secretive way even if no one is about."[4] On the instructions of Intelligence Bureau, another round resumed in June. It was recorded that Rahman had retained "an attitude of ingenious denials under the cloak of forgetfulness" and was taking "undue advantage" of "his stuttering habit": "Capt Habib-ur-Rehman, CSDIC No B1269 has been re-interrogated on the lines indicated in the questionnaire enclosed with DIB UO No SA/661 dt 2.4. 46. The results obtained are far from satisfactory and do not take us such further from the original position. Habib-ur-Rehman has shown little co-operation during the course of this re-interrogation .... "[5]

Had it not been for the strong public pressure, Rahman would have been hanged along with the other INA "war criminals." He continued to be in detention even as others were let off. After the release he was bombarded with queries by all those who chanced to meet him. This continued till the partition madness dwarfed all other issues. Some of Rahman's relatives were killed by the very people he had fought for, forcing him to migrate to his native place in Pakistan. He was instantly forgotten like all of Bose's warriors. When he returned to India ten years later to depose before Shah Nawaz Committee, Rahman was a Pakistani civil servant. For both governments of India and Japan, his testimony was still the most reliable evidence of the Taipei crash. On 6 February 1956, Indian Ambassador in Tokyo BR Sen forwarded to Foreign Secretary Subimal Dutt a Note Verbale prepared by Gaimusho, the Japanese Foreign Office, on Bose's death. The Ambassador was worried over reports emanating from Calcutta.

"It will be seen that the Note clearly mentions the presence of Colonel Rahman 'at the moment of his death.' Annexure IV gives the sketch of the room where Subhas Bose died and where Colonel Rahman was seated at the time of his death. I am, however, told that Rahman, in a statement made in Calcutta recently, denied having seen Subhas Bose's dead body .... If Rahman now really denies having been present at the time of the death of Subhas Bose, then the correctness of the Japanese report on the whole matter will be open to grave doubt and criticism. In this connection, you might also consider whether the Committee should examine Rahman before they leave India."[6]

Point was well taken and Shah Nawaz Commitee made it a point to examine Rahman in Delhi before they left for Tokyo. Shah Nawaz himself went over to Pakistan High Commission to receive Rahman and take him to the Committee venue. Much to the Government's relief, Rahman stuck to his old stand. Curiously, he submitted a signed statement, but there were no complains as it made the right noise only. There were no lawyers representing different parties. The scribes have been kept away. Suresh Bose, using the analysis done by his Indian Air force officer son-in-law, did put some questions, but the colonel was too smart for him. Before Suresh Bose could begin to dispute the matter, Rahman was back in Pakistan never to return to India again. The last time he publicly voiced his views about the issue was in 1965. T Hayashida, the man who had carried "Bose's ashes" from Taipei to Tokyo along with Rahman, caught up with his old acquaintance in Rawalpindi. Rahman's devotion to his former leader was intact "Netaji Subhas Chandra Bose," he told Hayashida, "was the greatest revolutionary that the Indian sub-continent produced in the present century ... the flame of freedom lit by him is still burning and will continue to inspire the freedom fighters all over the world for all times to come."[7]

The formation of Khosla Commission ignited the hopes of those who had doubted Rahman's statements. The forum of a judicial panel would have enabled them to have the colonel grilled by a battery of lawyers. They anticipated that with the kind of discrepant statements he had been making, the Commission would find it impossible to accept his version as reliable. Their hopes diminished when Rahman either himself refused to cooperate or was restrained by the circumstances arising out of turbulent India-Pakistan ties of early 1970s. "A letter of request issued through our High Commission brought back the reply that Habibur Rahman was not willing to come to India to make a statement, nor would he make himself available for such purpose in Pakistan. He said he had nothing to add to the statement which he had made before the previous Committee,"[8] GD Khosla wrote. Pakistani Government also would not have been much pleased to host GD Khosla, the head of the Fact Finding Organization that had recorded in graphic details the horrifying stories of refugees coming from Pakistan to India in 1947.

For Khosla, Rahman's non-appearance was a blessing in disguise. He rooted out the very foundation of the doubts by setting aside the reports filed and cleared by top intelligence sleuths of British India. Selectively interpreting the Indian Evidence

Act, he stated in his report: "I do not propose to take into account any of the previous statements made by Habibur Rahman for any purpose whatsoever. These statements cannot be used to support the story of the crash nor to disprove it by invoking the argument that discrepancies prove Habibur Rahman to be a false witness."[9] "The previous statements made by Habibur Rahman are wholly inadmissible in evidence .... Even the statements made before Shah Nawaz Committee are inadmissible in this case, if for no other reasons than that Habibur Rahman was not subjected to any cross-examination and parties and counsels were not represented before the Shah Nawaz Committee."[10] Having boldly said all this, Khosla went on to make use of details provided by Rahman in his report. The timings of Bose's stopovers from Bangkok to Taipei, and the crash, were all lifted by Khosla from the figures provided by Rahman.

Critics said the reason Khosla "discarded" Rahman's evidence was that there was a contrasting body of evidence. From the day he was arrested by the Americans to the time he spoke to Hayashida, Rahman stuck to his guns that the aim of Bose's last flight was to go to Tokyo. But everyone else who met Bose in his "last days" said that he was heading to the Soviet Russia. The Japanese too changed tack in due course of time when they saw that this point could not longer be concealed. General Isoda himself told GD Khosla that "it was finally decided in that meeting (at Bangkok) that Netaji will go to Russia via Manchuria and the Japanese government will give him monetary and other help," adding "he knew it definitely that Netaji was going to Russia ... he was going to Russia via Saigon ...." Minister Hachiya too reluctantly accepted that "perhaps his (Bose's) intention was to go to Manchuria (on Russian border)" and that "he informed Netaji that the Government of Japan was willing to make arrangements for shifting him to some safe areas." To cap it all, the official Japanese version, which was made known in 1956, countered the report given out in 1945. This time, they said that Bose "met with the fatal accident while flying to Manchuria over the strong objections of the IGHQ (Imperial General Head Quarters) in Tokyo."[11]

Samar Guha discussed threadbare "What Habibur Rahman revealed." "If Netaji had really died, the whole story ended there, Netaji was then gone forever. Then Habibur Rahman should have nothing to conceal either from the British Government or his compatriots ... even a casual perusal of the reports of interrogations and the nature of perceptible contradictions found in his various statements unmistakably showed that he tried to conceal all vital facts about Netaji, indicating thereby that he was determined not to divulge truth about his leader."[12] The various statements Rahman made within months of the crash clashed with each other. The crux of his statement before Shah Nawaz Committee was that he heard a loud noise when the plane was in air. He thought the plane was struck by enemy mortar fire. The plane crashed and he found himself and Bose trapped between a blockade and a firewall. On his advice, Bose headed to the front and jumped through the fire to get out of the plane. Rahman followed him and managed to cross the fire without his clothes catching the fire. Bose wasn't lucky and Rahman saw him turn into a human torch. He rushed to Bose and with his bare hands tore down his clothes and suffered burns on his hands in the process. Badly burnt, Bose fell to the ground soon and before help could reach them he gave Rahman his last message for Indians. Bose died in hospital hours later in the presence of Rahman and a few Japanese.

In his five notable statements — in Taipei on 24 August 1945; before SA Ayer in AM Sahay's house in Tokyo in second week of September; to Counter Intelligence Corps in Tokyo on 24 September 1945; to Shah Nawaz Khan on his return and to the CSIDC sleuths in late 1945 — Rahman fumbled on many points. He told Shah Nawaz Khan that it was "probably a vulture that had hit one of the propellers" and soon after the crash he "leaped out of the plane and pulled Netaji out of the burning mass." To CIC interrogators he said that "he had no knowledge of how Bose escaped or was removed from the plane" and that "upon alighting from the plane he noticed his own coat on fire." But at CSDIC he stated that "his clothes were not burnt at all and he wore them at the time of the interrogation." In his written statement of 24 August, he noted that "as soon as I got out, I saw that Netaji's clothes were on fire, from head to toe." CIC got the version that "Bose (was) lying by the plane with his clothes on fire." At CSDIC, however, his feeling was that he saw "Bose in a standing position about 12 yards away with smoke coming from his garments (on the upper part of his body)." SA Ayer was told that Bose "stood with his clothes burning and himself making desperate efforts to unbuckle the belts of his bush coat and around his waist."

The Taipei account had it tnat "within 15 minutes (of the crash) we were rushed to the nearest Nippon Army hospital." Before CSDIC more details emerged about the rescue party, comprising nurses and medical orderlies. This was way off from what Ayer had been told. "The next thing I knew (after Bose and he collapsed) was that I was lying on a hospital bed next to Netaji." Rahman's biggest goof up was on the part where he revealed Bose's "last message" to his countrymen. His statement to Shah Nawaz Committee put it as taking place near Matsuyama aerodrome soon after the crash at around 2.30pm whereas in the 24 August statement, and the one given before Ayer, this happened in Nanmon Hospital at around 9pm.

Furthermore, Rahman's statements were at variance with those of the Japanese. He said that Bose received a deep cut on the back of his head, which Dr Yoshimi denied. Rahman said Bose was taken to an operation theatre and in fact told BC Chakraborty that he died there. Again no corroboration came from the doctors' side. The most controvertible part here was that Rahman could not be sure of the day he performed Bose's last rites. How could he possibly miss on that? He told the committee that the cremation took place on August 20. But his Taipei statement had put it to 22nd. CIC was told that this had taken place on 21 August. To one CSDIC interrogator Rahman said it was 23 August. BC Chakraborty, however, recalled Rahman telling him that "on the 18th August it (the body) was put in the furnace. Furnace was switched on the 18th night ...."

There was more to Rahman's telling the story of Bose's death. Every time he narrated it, he did so with a demeanour calibrated to impress the listener. When he conversed with Ayer, a former correspondent, he introduced the element of drama. "Then a sudden deafening noise, what on earth is this? I thought an enemy fighter had spotted us taking off from Taihoku and had come swooping down on us and had taken a potshot at us. What is pilot going to do? Can he make a forced landing or is the plane going to crash? .... The port engine is out of action. One starboard engine is still working. The plane is already wobbling, the pilot is making a supreme effort to balance the whole weight of the plane on the star board engine. We are losing height pretty fast. I turned round and looked at Netaji. He was absolutely unperturbed. He could not have looked more composed if the plane was about to make a perfect landing after a long flight. But I am sure he must have seen the acutest distress in my face .... I dashed up to him (Bose) and tried to help him remove the belts. My hands were burnt in the process. As I was fumbling with his belts, I looked up and my heart nearly stopped when I saw his face, battered by iron and burnt by fire ...."[13]

Bose's physician, Dr Vasava Menon, testified before Khosla Commission that Rahman "had told him that before the Japanese applied a dose of morphia on Netaji as first aid, he had seen Netaji crawling with burns at the site of the plane crash." When he came to senses, Rahman was "told by the Japanese officer ... that Netaji had been dead and cremated."

Colonel Mahboob Ahmed must have been a mushy man to have got those weepy performances in Red Fort. "What used to happen normally when we sat, the topic came round about the (death) story that we wanted to know from him. When he started the story, he would come to a stage of weeping like a child. After some time we gave up asking about this from him."[14] It was a defiant colonel that the CSDIC interrogators faced. In June 1946 when "his interrogator put him a direct question whether he was prepared to allow himself to be taken to Taihoku and point out all relevant places, he thought for moment and then replied in the negative with a retort saying: 'I have volunteered all the information that was in my possession, and it would not at all have been difficult for the authorities to verify the truth of my statement if investigations were taken up on the spot. Except worrying me for nothing, the Government appear to have taken no step to arrive at a definitive conclusion regarding SC Bose's death. It appears that whenever some irresponsible person makes some sort of statement in the press with the intentions of keeping up the spirits of ex-INA personnel the Government gets unnerved and someone rushes on to me with a new volley of questions."[15]

And when CSDIC's BC Chakraborty broke that resolve by citing many of his contradictions, Rahman began to sidestep. "After recording the statement of Habibur Rehman I (Chakraborty) myself cross-examined him on various points, I myself recorded the answers he gave on cross examination. I asked him, why he was not anxious to see the face of the dead leader when the doctors announced Netaji died on the operation table. His answer was that he was not allowed to stand there for long. Secondly, when he was told that the body would be carried to the furnace, I asked him, 'was it not your duty as the second in command of the INA to accompany to the furnace?' To this, he looked at my face and could not give me any answer. He jumped at his feet and shouted, 'I can say with Koran in my hand that I was not allowed to accompany the dead from the operation table to the furnace.' Thirdly, when in the morning i.e. on the 19th August, 1945, a colonel of the Japanese army and a doctor of the Japanese base hospital handed over to him a brass pot saying that this pot contained the ashes of Netaji he could not forward a pertinent answer. He admitted that his only duty was to hand it over to ... (INA Chief of Staff JK) Bhonsle. Fourthly, when I asked him 'under whose advice you had been to Tokyo ..., he did not give me any reply. When I questioned him that he was hiding in Tokyo instead of trying to communicate the information of the death of one of the leading statesmen of our country, he remained mum; he did not give any answer."[16]

The other side of the story — that Rahman had been lying — had quite a following. Many heard Rahman hinting in private that he was obeying orders. Some, like Hem Raj Batai, a businessman who deposed before GD Khosla, felt that Gandhi too took "the cue." "I know the guru (leader) was not telling the truth," Batai heard Gandhi saying after meeting Rahman, apparently recalling his some earlier experience with Bose. "And the *chela* (follower) was also not telling the truth." "Rahman just gave me a soldier's statement," another version had Gandhi saying after the meeting in Delhi in April 1946. The Bose family members got to meet Rahman many times over and most formed the same opinion. Sarat Bose, the closest sibling of Subhas's, went on record to say till his death that his brother had not died in Taipei.

"When the story of (the aircrash) came out, I was in prison. I shall confess that as long as I was in detention, I felt upset. I had not had any materials then to enable me to judge whether the aircrash story was true or not. But even then when I was in detention, I felt it was somewhat strange that the aircrash story should have been revealed to the public five days after the crash was supposed to have happened. After I came out of the prison in 1945, I had the opportunity of talking to Colonel Habibur Rahman of the INA .... The impression left in my mind that he had orders from his chief to come out with that story ... if Col Rahman had orders from his Chief to keep his whereabouts a closely guarded secret, he would not to tell that ...."[17]

An encounter took place in a Bose family meeting. Shiela Sengupta, Suresh Bose's daughter recalled that this was early 1946 when INA men and women would throng the residences of Subhas's kin. "Shah Nawaz would often drop in at our place and stay back for the night; it was one such family gathering that evening when Shah Nawaz and Colonel Rahman came. Habib stayed over at our place that day." Dr Satyen Dutt, Bose's *mama* (maternal uncle), raised the issue and Rahman began recalling the story for the umpteenth time. "See!" he stretched out his hands, having recalled how he had had them burnt trying to douse the fire on Bose's clothes. Dr Dutt had a careful look: The burn marks were there, on the dorsal and upper arms. "Habib!" he queried, "How is it that you don't have any burn marks on the inner side of your arms?" Everyone realised that going by his claims, Rahman should have had burn marks in his palms and inner arms. "You know, Colonel Habib was wearing the same uniform that day, and it has not been damaged at all," interjected Colonel Raturi. "Sit down!" Rahman got up on his feet. Raturi, who had merely repeated Rahman's claim with an implied inference, left the room but Bose's uncle was charged. "What is Raturi talking about? Is this the same uniform you were wearing when the crash took place? Call Raturi back and clear the matter right away!" Rahman wasn't ready for this. "This is all I have to say. I don't know anything more," he mumbled and left.[18]

Dr Dutt was not alone in raising the question of misplaced burns marks and undamaged uniform. BC Chakraborty had his own. He had had Rahman's burns examined by two surgeons. Dr RN Kasliwal, Bose's personal physician, offered an opinion. "Many things can happen and those burns could come up due to acid," he told Khosla Commission. "Burns can be self-inflicted by carbolic or sulphuric acid." Dr SN Dutt appeared before the Commission and stated that Rahman's burns could have been caused by acid. Aurobindo, Bose's nephew, said he often "complimented" Rahman for creating realistic burn marks with acid. "Habib either used to keep mum or smile at this suggestion," he told GD Khosla. His cousin Dwijendra Nath Bose too recalled Rahman telling him that "I tried to put out the fire with the palms of my hand," but on examination he found the burn marks on the back side. A businessman dealing in garments, Dwijendra knew something about warps and woofs. He saw the cut marks on Rahman's body but failed to locate the corresponding marks on the dress he said he was wearing that day. "On the upper portion he (Rahman) had tunic, shirt-cum-bush shirt and a long trouser .... The sewings were intact ... not a mark of any burning or any repairing. When he lifted the trousers to show me the cut mark on his right knee, I marked his trousers and there was no mark of any stitching there."

"So, I asked Habib Saheb," Dwijendra told Khosla Commission, "'Tell me confidentially that the plane crash had not taken place .... I am not going to let it out before the public, because, I think as we were tutored, when Netaji left India, not to give out the story of his going. So you might have been tutored by him also. Unless your palms are burnt, unless you had a cut mark in your trousers also, I am not going to believe the story that you say'. Then he told me. 'You are a nephew of Netaji. You were a collaborator of his plans of going out of India, you were in politics with him. I never expected such silly questions from you!'"

"What did you conclude?" a counsel asked Dwijendra.

"I concluded that he gave me an idea in a round about fashion that you should not have asked me this question: you should have surmised yourself, that there was no plane crash, that he did not die ... that was my conclusion."

"Because he was under an oath, he could not say it himself? It was for you to have guessed it?"

"Yes!" Thereafter, I remember one thing — I do not know whether I have told it before the Shah Nawaz Committee. I asked him: Habib Sahib, tell me, frankly tell me, what is the position? He said: 'I can't tell you anything. You are not the person who can order me .... I can take orders from Netaji; I cannot take your orders.'"[19]

All this boiled down to a little known expediency of the freedom struggle. The quasi-religious oath the revolutionaries from Bengal and elsewhere would undertake to maintain confidentiality of specific information against all odds. Bose was known to administer similar oaths to his followers. His nephews Dwijendra and Aurobindo underwent the ritual when he was planning the 1941 escape. To get to the truth, the British tortured Dwijendra in Lahore Fort, but got nothing. More than thirty years on, in August 1972, Dwijendra appeared before Khosla Commission with nothing changed. He told the Commission that the oath bound him to a strict rule and he could not divulge anything till the time Bose himself asked him to do so. Repeated questions and provocations from TR Bhasin failed to budge him from his position.

"Were you related to Netaji?"

"I am the son of his eldest brother, the late Satish Chandra Bose."

"From what period to what period you were in jail?"

"From April 1941 to September 1945."

"May I take I that you were taken into confidence along with other two cousins, that is Aurobindo Bose, Sisir Bose and sister Ila in the matter of his disappearance from India?"

"Yes."

"In 1941?"

"Yes."

"Could you tell us briefly about Netaji's early life? One aspect is about his secretive nature."

"I cannot give you the entire story of his departure because I am under an oath to Netaji. Unless I am asked by Netaji, I cannot do that."

"I am not on that at all. In order to supplement the view that you have taken about Netaji's secretive nature, right from his childhood because in your previous statement you have mentioned two instances before the Shah Nawaz Committee about leaving his house in Cuttack."

"He did not consult anybody. He went to Jaipur, served the cholera patient and came back. When he was studying in the Presidency College, he left home in quest of a guru. At home also he did not consult his own mother who was living in the next room. My father was alive, who was eldest to him. He used to meet Netaji daily. He was not informed also."

"When he had completely made up his mind, you were taken into confidence!?"

"That I do not know. But I was taken into confidence when he needed."

"And that was the penultimate stage?"

"That I cannot say because I am not in a position to say. I am under oath."[20]

Aurobindo was more strict in observing the oath. This made his younger brother and veteran journalist Pradip Bose see uncanny similarity in the behaviour of Rahman and his brother:

"I see a strange similarity in the pattern of the story of his escape from India in 1941 and his 'planned escape' to the Soviet Union in 1945. At least seven members of the Bose family knew about some aspects of his escape from India. But Subhas came to the conclusion that if all of them pretended they did not know anything about his escape then at least some of them would be arrested interrogated and even tortured to get at the truth. To avoid such a possibility he constructed a story of his withdrawal from worldly affairs in order to meditate in an undisturbed environment. He withdrew behind a curtain and only one person, his nephew Aurobindo, was allowed to enter into the 'prohibited area' late in the evening to know about his requirements. While Aurobindo knew that Subhas had left Calcutta on 17th January, 1941, he told the police that he had seen Netaji on 25th January, as Subhas had asked him to do. On the 26th January an announcement was made that he was no longer in his room. Aurobindo was a 'viable witness' swearing that he saw Subhas Bose on the 25th night, while actually he had already crossed the Indo-Afghan border.

"Aurobindo never wrote about this in spite of repeated requests from friends and relatives till he died in 1988 i.e. 47 years after the event, because he said that he was bound by an oath of secrecy of Netaji. This seemed a little odd because some governments release their top secret documents after 30 or 40 years but he was not convinced by that argument. At least 5 or 6 persons in the provisional Government of Azad Hind knew that Netaji was planning to escape to the Soviet Union after the end of the war but only one person Habibur Rahman was chosen to fly with him. He was the sole Indian witness to the event of his death. Or, was it yet another non-event, as vouched for by Aurobindo on an earlier occasion?"[21]

Upholding the sanctity of the oath was certainly not limited to Bose family and Rahman. Colonel Gurbaksh Singh Dhillon recalled in his 1988 memoirs one of many forgotten stories. In Delhi's Salimgarh fort INA secret service's Major Maghar Singh and Major Ajmer Singh were "daily tortured but they refused to disclose any information about the INA and the Japanese dispositions. When they felt that they might not be to keep the secret under daily torture, they planned to snatch a guard's rifle one night and committed suicide."[22] Colonel Thakur Singh, second in command of Shah Nawaz, narrated another example before Khosla Commission. "Abid Hasan had come from Germany with Netaji (in a submarine) and had been in my regiment for training. I asked Abid Hasan how Netaji had come from Germany. I piled him with drinks. And when I thought he was full, I put him this question. He threw his glass and the bottle and .... said even if the British had cut him into pieces, he would not have revealed the fact. And who was I to want to know about this matter?" Singh also recalled the days of incarceration with Rahman. "Habib and I were kept in the Red Fort a month longer than the others because the British wanted to know from Habib where Netaji had gone and I was kept because I had organised a special regiment .... One day Habib said that Mahatma Gandhi may go on making all kinds of statements but he (Habib) would never tell the truth about Netaji's whereabouts."[23]

Colonel Mahboob Ahmed, then Chief of Protocol in the Ministry of External Affairs, was examined on the same aspect before Khosla Commission to the same outcome.

"If a secret was entrusted to Colonel Habibur Rahman, in your (Ahmed's) estimation, his character is such that he would keep it a secret all his life, unless countermanded by Netaji himself?"

"That is my assessment of Habibur Rahman."

"Supposing Netaji had selected you to go with him in the last journey to a place of safety, and if he had asked you to carry some news regarding Netaji, would you at any stage disclose it if Netaji had asked you not to disclose it?"

"No. My loyalty to him was so great that I would have done anything for him."[24]

Anything and for all the times to come. The stories of fierce loyalty and absolute secrecy trickled down to the present. On 4 April 2001, Mukherjee Commission took the evidence of Captain Bipul Kumar Sarkar of INA secret service. Sarkar recalled one meeting with his friend Habibur Rahman. He said that he heard the whole story but found no burn or scratch mark on his shirt and on his palm. "Thank you Colonel Saheb. I got the message," he interposed. Rahman paused for a thought and said, "Sarkar, you too are intelligent," and extracted a promise that Sarkar would not "disclose this to anybody for thirty years". "I honoured the promise," Sarkar testified before Justice MK Mukherjee during his brief appearance.

The *Indian Express* on 22 April 2002 carried a story about then Home Minister LK Advani playing host to a reunion of the INA veterans in Delhi. Among those present, octogenarian Captain John Jacob of Singapore was conspicuous in his full INA uniform with a Netaji pin and INA insignia right on their places. Jacob had told the *Patriot* in 1971 that the "only man who could solve the mystery of Netaji's disappearance was ... Rahman." "Colonel Habib-Ur-Rahman might have been ordered by Netaji not to disclose his whereabouts at any cost." In 2002, Jacob had the following to say when the *Express* reporter sought to know from him the functions of INA secret service he had worked in. "I am still in uniform. I have taken an oath not to reveal what went on in these corps, and I won't."

Colonel Rahman passed away in Pakistan in 1991. Shah Nawaz once said that sometimes in 1970s, Rahman had sent across a message about bringing "the ashes of Bose" to India. Major Bhaskaran Menon, never a believer in the crash theory, said that some time before his death, Rahman had made an abortive bid to contact him. Would he have told him something? "No!" Shiela Sengupta strongly felt. "Habib *bhai* would not have done that come what may. Just like my brother Aurobindo."

In Calcutta, two notable men have reasons to assert that Rahman at times did give away "the truth." The first is the Editor of *Bartaman* — one of largest selling Bangla newspapers. Barun Sengupta, dashing in his 70s, told Mukhejee Commission on 23 November 2000 that he had himself seen "a report with an intelligence officer in Delhi." It quoted Rahman telling a "British Intelligence Officer that he was not with Netaji in the aircraft which crashed." As one who devoted his whole life to Netaji, septuagenarian Sunil Krishna Gupta's *raison d'être* is far more compelling. He heard from the horse's mouth. On 6 April 1956 at the Pakistan High Commission in New Delhi, Gupta, accompanied by Amar Majumdar, met Rahman moments before he left to depose before Shah Nawaz Committee. They drew his attention to a recent newsitem in Lahore's *Civil and Military Gazette*, which had quoted him saying that Bose had not died in the plane crash.

"Majumdar and I put many questions to Colonel Rahman. We asked him why he did not contradict the news. In reply to our question Colonel Rahman said that the newspaper had misquoted him. We asked 'Why have you not sent a protest when the news was published? Have you sent any kind of contradiction till now?' Colonel Rahman replied that he 'punctiliously avoided the reporters because they always misquoted him.'"

"We asked again, 'why don't you give a fitting rejoinder?'"

"Oh, they will again misquote me!" Rahman smiled mischievously and wondered why they were being so "anxious to demolish a story which has no basis?"

"Let them declare that Netaji is dead. It would be a double gain when he will return!" Rahman said after a pause.

Gupta strained his ears. "Why it would be a 'double gain'?" he asked.

"Keep it to yourself, will you? One, we shall get Netaji amongst us. Two, the people who are trying to establish the plane crash story will be exposed."[25]

Notes:

1 Record of the proceedings of Khosla Commission. Volume X. Page 3246.

2 Record of the examination of Pritam Singh before Mukherjee Commission on 22 July 2000.

3 Examination of Mahboob Ahmed before Khosla Commission on 3 March 1971.

4 File No 400/INA. No 1400/23/SE.

5 CSDIC report "Re-interrogation of Capt Habib-ur-Rehman" dated 9 June 1946.

6 F 25/4/NGO-Vol-III. D.O No. F.5 (1) NGO-1.

7 *Netaji Subhas Chandra Bose* by Tatsuo Hayashida. Pages 140, 141. Late Anil Mukherjee, when he was Deputy Speaker of West Bengal Assembly, told the writer that in 1975 General Mohan Singh met Rahman in Pakistan and asked him about Netaji's death. Rahman broke down saying he was "duty bound" to follow orders. "Beyond this I do not want to say anything," Rahman told Singh.

8 Netaji Inquiry Commission report. Page 118.

9 Ibid.

10 Ibid.

11 *Subhas: A Political Biography* by Sitanshu Das. Page 587.

12 *Netaji Dead or Alive?* by Samar Guha. Page 164.

13 File No. F 25/4/NGO-Vol-III. SA Ayer's report to the Prime Minister.

14 Examination of Mahboob Ahmed before Khosla Commission on 3 March 1971.

15 CSDIC report "Re-interrogation of Capt Habib-ur-Rehman" dated 9 June 1946.

16 Record of the proceedings of Khosla Commission. Volume XII. Page 3703.

17 Extracted from a newsitem published in Sarat Bose's newspaper the *Nation* on 7 October 1949.

18 Based on the account by Shiela Sengupta to the writer and *HindustanTimes.com*. See: **Comrade challenges Habib's crash theory,** *Hindustan Times.com.* Subhas Bose probe phase 1.

19 Record of the proceedings of Khosla Commission. Volume XI. Pages 3354-3355.

20 Examination of Dwijendra Nath Bose. Record of the proceedings of Khosla Commission. Volume XI.

21 **Did Japan lie about Bose's death in air crash?** by Pradip Bose. *Hindustan Times.com.* Subhas Bose probe phase 1. Pradip Bose also gave the same account in his book *Subhas Bose and India Today.*

22 *From My Bones: Memoirs of Col Gurbaksh Singh Dhillon.* Page 537.

23 Examination of Thakur Singh before Khosla Commission on 3 March 1971.

24 Examination of Mahboob Ahmed before Khosla Commission on 3 March 1971.

25 Input by Sunil Krishna Gupta and the account in *Netaji: Dead or Alive?* by Samar Guha. Pages 171, 172.

8

Russian Connection

It's a gossip from chandukhana (den of opium addicts).

Jawaharlal Nehru's alleged retort to Satyanarayan Sinha in a Paris party in 1950s when the latter claimed Subhas Bose was in the USSR after August 1945.

If Bose comes with the help of Russia neither Gandhiji nor the Congress will be able to reason with the country.

Mohandas Gandhi's aide Khurshed Naoroji to an Advisor of US President Franklin Roosevelt in a July 1946 letter.

They (American intelligence sleuths) told me that they followed a man whose description matched with that of Netaji up to the Russian border.

Lakshmi Sehgal during her cross-examination before Mukherjee Commission in June 2001.

These dreadful stories first appeared in 1945 and have not ceased till date. The mortification of picturing Netaji chained up in a frosty Siberian dungeon fell on Bose kin and the ordinary people alike. In Calcutta, an engineer kept his mouth shut for four decades after he had been threatened by an Indian embassy staffer. He had met in Soviet Russia a German whose eyes twinkled when he came to know that his colleague was an Indian. He took him to one corner and whispered, "Don't tell this to anybody. I met Netaji in Berlin. I met him again up there in Siberia in 1948." In Germany, Emilie Schenkl confided in to

Surya Kumar Bose, son of Bose's nephew Amiya, that "Raimund Schnabel, a German journalist who had settled down in East Berlin after the World War II, had told her in early 1950 that he had been informed that Netaji was in the Soviet Union after 1945."[1]

That he could go to the USSR to boost the freedom struggle was not a brainwave which occurred to Subhas Bose at the end of world war. The first known signs of it manifested six years earlier when the battlelines were still being drawn. Bose looked up to the Soviet Union. Geography dictated that Indians felt attached to the Russians and the Chinese and not to the Germans or the Japanese. The Bolshevik revolution had inspired the Indian struggle and indeed the Soviets sympathised with the Indians.

Amiya Bose came to Calcutta from Cambridge during summer vacation in June 1938. He brought his uncle a message from his friends in Europe that the world was about to go to war. For Subhas this was a window of opportunity. Great Britain was now going to be absorbed in wars away from India making the Raj vulnerable. On his return, Amiya took "a very important letter to be delivered to the CPGB (Communist Party of Great Britain) leader for onward transmission to Moscow. This was Bose's letter seeking Soviet help".[2] More feelers were sent. When the war broke out, Shankar Lal, general secretary of Forward Bloc, left for a dangerous mission "to Japan to seek advice and help from the USSR through the Soviet Ambassador in Japan." "Lal came back to Calcutta from Tokyo incognito after finalising the agreement with the Soviet Ambassador in Tokyo and through ... Sarat Chandra Bose ... the message of agreement was communicated to Netaji in Calcutta jail."[3]

In January 1941 Bose made his way into Afghanistan mostly with the help of those with the Russian connections. Bose had meager means to get out of Afghanistan and had much less chances of remaining alive had it not been for the Russians. The NKVD was not at all surprised when Hans Pilger, the German Ambassador to Afghanistan, met Russian Ambassador V Kozolov over taking Bose out of harm's way with Italian assistance. The Soviets agreed and the order for issuing a visa to Bose, travelling incognito as Italian Orlando Mazzotta, was personally given by A Vyshinski — the deputy Foreign Minister of the USSR. The Soviets not only secretly hosted an enemy of their ally Great Britain, but also arranged for his onward journey. They did so because they thought good of Bose. The Indian leader had been consistently backing the USSR even when most weren't. He was "the only political leader in India who (had) supported the sending of the Soviet Army to the Finnish border on the ground of the Soviets' border security. Even the National Front (CPI) leaders had no courage to support the Soviet move."[4] Some people were of the opinion that Bose left India in 1941 to seek help from the Russians only. When it was denied, he turned to the Germans. Be that as it may, Bose did not conceal his soft corner for the Russians when he mingled with the Nazis. In his conference with Adolf Hitler's Foreign Minister Joachim von Ribbentrop on 29 April 1941, Bose made it clear that the Indians did not think much of the Nazis until they had entered into an alliance with the Russians:

"Thereupon the Foreign Minister asked (Bose) about India's attitude toward Germany. Bose answered that he wanted to admit in all frankness that feeling against the National Socialists and the Fascists had been rather strong in India .... Not until after the German-Russian Pact was concluded did the mood change. Many Indians had greatly welcomed this Pact by reason of their social and anti-imperialist views and as a result they had arrived at a different attitude toward Germany .... When the Foreign Minister asked about India's attitude toward Russia, Bose answered that on account of the anti-imperialist attitude of the Indians the Soviet Union enjoyed a certain sympathy."[5]

The Nazi attack on Soviet Russia came as a rude shock to Subhas. He aired his dismay openly, unmindful that it could pave his way to a concentration camp. "Once, during the last week of July 1941, when (journalist) Dr (Giselher) Wirsing went to see Netaji in his hotel, he found him sitting in a lotus posture in deep meditation in front of a world map. He occupied his seat silently .... Bose at last broke his silence, shaking his head unwillingly and said, *'Das kahnnicht gut gehen'* (This cannot go well)."[6] Bose told Ernst Woermann, head of the political division of the German Foreign Office, the same month that "the realization of his plans looked gloomy as a result of the outbreak of war in the East ... he spoke in detail concerning the repercussions of the German-Russian war on public opinion in India. The Soviet Union had been popular in India, especially among the intelligentsia, from which the leader group came, because in India they believed that the Soviet Union was an anti-imperialist power and thus the natural ally of India against England. The German-Russian pact of 1939 had been a climax for India. It had made it possible for the basically anti-National Socialist intelligentsia now to regard Germany and Italy as those powers which, in friendship with the Soviet Union, would put an end to the British rule in India .... In the German-Russian war the feelings of the Indian people were very decidedly on the Russian side, because the Indian people were sure that Germany was the aggressor and thus also an imperialist power dangerous to India."[7]

Woermann obviously did not like the runaway Indian's wearing his heart on his sleeves. The endnote on the record of that meeting stated rather ominously that "Bose's statements indicated that, away from Berlin, he is strongly influenced by the Soviet thesis even in the question of the origin of the German-Russian conflict, so that it will be one of the first tasks to set him right, on this point." Bose's open backing of the Russians brought him under the surveillance of Reich Main Security Office (RHSA),. which directed the Gestapo (secret police). RSHA "spied on him and its boss Walter Schellenburg used shadowy informants to conclude that Bose was on the Soviet Union's side."[8]

Shah Nawaz and GD Khosla falsified facts to undermine Bose's plans to go to the USSR when it became clear to him that direct or guerilla offensive wasn't feasible. Shah Nawaz told Khosla Commission that there was no "deception ploy" in Bose's disappearance. His 1956 report stated that Bose might have been thinking about going to Russia, but at the time of his "death" he appeared to be heading to Tokyo. "There was no time then to contact Russian authorities or to make out detailed plans ahead .... the details were uncertain, the purpose was fixed. Netaji himself described his last journey as an adventure into the unknown."[9] GD Khosla altered this to say that Bose intended to go to Russia but his plan was "amorphous and vague." "No cut and dried plan of conveying Bose out of the area under the Allied control could be prepared ...,"[10] he wrote. Suresh Bose, however, held an opposite view:

"When the time came for the Japanese to surrender, their Government expressed great sorrow at the failure of Netaji's mission and which they ascribed to their defeat and they then decided to 'respect his last wishes,' in whatever manner it was possible for them to do under such changed circumstances. Netaji, accordingly, requested them to take him to Russian territory. This request they could not comply with, because, they said, it would embarrass both the Russians as well as themselves, as they were negotiating for surrender and treaty terms with the Anglo-Americans through the Russians. Netaji accepted this, and as a next alternative, requested them to take him to Manchuria, which was still under occupation and he told them that he would make his own arrangements for entering into the Russian territory. This plan was agreed upon ...."[11]

"... and Lt General Shidei ... was specially deputed to accompany Netaji, as he knew the territory well and also the Russian language and who would look after Netaji there and help him to enter Russian territory. After the General succeeded in carrying out the job entrusted to him he would come to Japan and report the matter to his Government, after which it would be announced, and which was done on 23.8.45, that Mr Chandra Bose had died at Taihoku on 18.8.45 as the result of a plane crash there, as was Netaji's plan. The five days', delay in the announcement of Netaji's alleged death is satisfactorily explained by General Shidei's conduct in Manchuria, as stated above.[12]

Suresh Bose did not live to see Khosla repudiating his evidence. The opinionated judge had the gumption to do so for he knew that the classified reports and the inside stories would never go public. But unluckily for him, he was under watch. In

Netaji: Dead or Alive? Guha imputed malafide to Khosla's observations: "After having all the evidence before him about the plan it was difficult for Mr Khosla to ignore it and deny the fact that Netaji indeed intended to go to Russia. However, if he accepted the position that the plan was drawn up and executed by the highest military authorities of Japan, then it would have been difficult for him to resist the inference that the story of Netaji's death was fabricated and the Tokyo Radio's announcement of his death was pre-arranged."[13]

The information the writer has been able to cull bolsters the views of Suresh Bose and Samar Guha. On 6 November 1945, the South East Asia Command received a report filed after interrogation of staff officers of the Japanese Army HQ in Saigon. This classified document, seen by Shah Nawaz and GD Khosla like many other secret reports, revealed that Bose had seen into the future that the Russians' bonhomie with the Allies would not last long. He conveyed his views of rapprochement to the Japanese who, as usually, treated them with respect. Bose's plan to move to Russia was afoot a couple of months before his death was announced:

"In December 1944, SUBHAS CHANDRA BOSE suggested that it would be expedient for the Japanese Govt to come to terms with CHIANG KAI-SHEK and further seek friendship with Russia. BOSE's theory was that China would only too gladly accept a suggestion which would extract her from the convulsions of a long and weary war. In regards to RUSSIA, he explained that he was convinced that the Russian alliance with GREAT BRITAIN and AMERICA was brought by force of circumstances and that with the completion of German defeat, Russia will repudiate her present mask of friendship and will openly revert to her well-known hostile status towards GREAT BRITAIN and USA.

"The Japs (derogatory Allied usage for 'Japanese') were in favour of such a move as they realised that their defeat was inevitable unless a paramount political event of this nature occurred. But they were doubtful, if BOSE was capable of procuring this new tripartite alliance. The Japanese therefore rejected the offer and conventionally reiterated their belief in their eventual victory as they intended to produce a large-scale counterattack which would turn the tide of war in their favour .... There are indications that the Japanese Government evinced a keen interest when BOSE put forth these suggestions and in fact, plausible as these looked to them, it was in this connection that Bose visited TOKYO in December 44.

"Again in July as the situation was fast deteriorating for the Japanese, BOSE sought permission, this time to enter USSR via Manchuria with a few selected members of his movement. No formal reply was made to this but BOSE was advised to proceed to TOKYO in view of his request .... In the absence of any specific answer from TOKYO, BOSE intended to give himself up to Chinese or American Forces, if on his own arrival in Tokyo, the Japanese Government did not permit him to enter Soviet Russia. But the fact remains that from Saigon Bose actually traveled in a plane which was taking Lt General SHIDEI to MANCHURIA .... Another source contends that there was no need for the Japanese to ask the Russians for BOSE's entry because BOSE wanted to go to Manchuria from where he thought he would be able to get in touch the Russian forces and obtain necessary admission independently. It was in view of this that SC BOSE had left SINGAPORE on August 16 ...."[14]

On 15 January 1946 a confidential CSDIC report revealed that "in June 45 (General AC) CHATTERJI went to SAIGON commissioned by the Cabinet to ask the Japanese to consider moving 'certain number of the PGI Cabinet' to Manchuria."[15] An IB report dated 19 February 1946 stated that their information "seems to establish that Bose was definitely interested in the possibility of transferring himself, and perhaps even some of the personnel of his movement, to territory under Russian control, with the collapse of the Japanese in the Far East .... There are indications that he had similar ideas about his 950 Regiment (German INA) and the rest of his movement in Europe .... Our belief is that this motive lay behind his last journey, during which he is reported to have been killed."[16]

The men who would be in a position to know about Bose's plan to shift to Russia were those Japanese and Indians who were privy to his last known acts. Many of these appeared before GD Khosla and in addition the commission was provided with reports on interrogations of some of them. Anand Mohan Sahay was interrogated by CSDIC in Red Fort in late February 1946. "1459 (Sahay) ... says that when he was in JAPAN in 1944-45, he called, as a minister of the PGI, on SHIGEMITSU, the (Japanese) foreign minister, SWADA, his deputy, and on KODAKI, who was in charge of the Indian section of the Japanese Foreign Office. From what they said he had gathered that BOSE had wished on his last visit to Tokyo to contact the Russian ambassador .... ISODA confirmed this to H1459 when they met in SAIGON in July 1945. In May or June 45 BOSE himself told H1459 that he had asked the Japanese Army authorities to arrange a passage for him to RUSSIA via MANCHURIA."[17]

After much dilly-dallying, Major General JK Bhonsle told his interrogators that "SC Bose wanted the Japanese Government to contact Russia with a view to accepting his presence in Russia and harbouring him against the British. But as TOJO, a personal friend of Subhas Bose, was no longer in power, Bose was not meeting with success. Bose therefore decided to proceed to Tokyo himself to try and arrange his passage into Russia. He hoped to do this by meeting the Japanese Foreign Minister,[18] who was also a friend of Bose, and, if necessary by approaching the Japanese Emperor through his cabinet to take the matter up with Russia .... Bose was certain that once the Russians agreed to take him, they would give him all the necessary protection .... B1189 (Bhonsle) states that Bose selected efficient officers/ civs to accompany him because he wanted an efficient staff with him in Russia. Asked why he himself was not selected by Bose, B1189 stated that Bose ordered him to stay behind and look after the interests of the INA."[19]

Minister Hachiya Teruo told Khosla Commission in Tokyo that after Japan's surrender he told Bose that the Japanese Government was willing to transport him to a safe place. INA Major General SC Alagappan said that on Bose's orders he prepared a route chart detailing how to go to Russia. "We came to the conclusion that only Russia could give a habitance to

Netaji," Alagappan told the Commission in Madras. The list of such witnesses was long. At Madras only, Bose's personal physician Dr S Vasava Menon recalled a long conference on 17 of August in Bangkok where Japanese officers, Colonel Raturi, Colonel Habibur Rahman, Major Bhaskaran and CN Pillai discussed Bose's plan to go to Russia. Menon said Bose was going to Manchuria because "the Japanese did not want him to be caught as a war criminal."

Lt Colonel Morio Takakura, a staff officer at the Imperial General HQ in Tokyo, told the Commission that "two months before the surrender of Japan I went to Bangkok where I met General Terauchi, Chandra Bose and Lt Gen Isoda. As a result of our conversation. Mr Chandra Bose agreed to cooperate with the Japanese forces in southern area. There was a decision among the Japanese military circles that it would be better for Chandra Bose to go to some area where he could have the freedom of action than coming to Japan because he might have been arrested had he come to Japan. So, it would be better for him to go to such a place, for instance, Soviet Russia-Manchuria border .... Lt General Shidei was on transfer to Kwantung Army ... that is why Chandra Bose went with him. The headquarters at Tokyo accepted the plan for Netaji's going to Russia via Diren and the headquarters directed Lt Gen Shidei to accompany him."[20]

More details had been recorded in the written statement Hikari Kikan interpreter Kinji Watanabe had given in November 1945 to Intelligence Bureau's PES Finney. Watanabe avowed that "Bose proposed to see the Russian Ambassador to Tokyo through Nippon's (Japan's) intermediation."

"My impression is that Bose, having been already fed with Nippon, wanted to open a new sphere of activity. Bose seems to have stressed that if he could see the Russian Ambassador he might possibly do something to improve the relationship between Japan and Russia, this enabled him to get some help or other from Russia. From the very beginning Bose's standpoint was very clear: He was ever ready to accept any assistance from any nation if only it desired India to be independent. No doubt he wished to get nearer to Soviet Russia after the telling blow was inflicted upon Japan and his troops, which made him almost give up hope to advance into India from Burma.

"Bose's point was: 'In order to destroy our common enemy Britain, both Japan and the Provisional Government should try every possible means and help each other. Therefore, I earnestly request Tokyo to act as 'go-between' and let me approach Soviet Russia. Once I have been given an interview with the Russian Ambassador, I have perfect confidence in my success in persuading Russia to help our independence movement and at the same time I am sure that I can do something to improve the relations between Japan and Russia, and it might serve to decrease the menace Japan is feeling on the Manchurian side. I trust if I succeed it will result in killing two birds with one stone.'

'And if my trial proves unsuccessful, I shall only lose my face, that's all. I am nothing but head of a Revolutionary Government .... I will do this attempt in my private capacity. I do request Tokyo to let me have a trial. I'll chance it.'

Takakura asked Bose on which he put more stress, the armed struggle in the Far East for Independence or the political way of propelling things by approaching Russia. To this question Bose replied like this: 'I am very sorry to be asked such a silly question. Your question well shows that you do not understand me from the very beginning. I am fully prepared to fight till the last drop of my blood. I am misunderstood like this; this is why I strongly insist on going up to Tokyo myself and have direct talks with the responsible persons.'"[21]

Though he wasn't very forthcoming, Hikari Kikan's chief Lt General Saburo Isoda accepted before the Commission that "the purpose of his (Bose's) flight was to go to Soviet Union" and to continue the struggle for independence. This plan, he said, was discussed by Bose, Colonel Tada and himself. In 1951, Tada had told SA Ayer about his appreciation of why the Japanese took a long time to decide: "Netaji had been making this request to Tokyo ever since March or April 1945 and had been pursuing it since the collapse of Germany. The Tokyo command had been strongly opposing this idea for only one reason, namely, Tokyo feared that the chances of their using Russian good offices to convey Japan's peace overtures to the Allies one day later might be jeopardized if Netaji, (ally of Germany who in turn was Russia's mortal enemy) reached the Russians earlier and contacted the higher-ups in Moscow .... However, now that the war was over and Japan had surrendered to the Allies, Field Marshal (Terauchi) took the responsibility on his own shoulders ...."[22]

If Bose had planned an escape to the USSR, the "plane crash" had to be a part of "the plot." It surely was, SC Sengupta and Major Bhaskaran Menon told GD Khosla. Sengupta was Bose's Japanese interpreter and part of the elusive INA secret service. Like everybody Bose's inner circle, Sengupta disclosed that in his presence in the early hours of 17 August, Bose, getting ready to escape to Russia, dictated to Major Bhaskaran a letter in which he referred to a plane crash. Sengupta also claimed that at about 5am the same day Bose gave him a note and asked him to flee from Bangkok. That note, Sengupta told the Commission, said that Bose was heading to Manchuria to cross over into the Soviet Union as "the plan had been approved by Stalin and (his Foreign Minister) Mikhailovich Molotov through Jacob Malik (Soviet Ambassador in Tokyo)."

Everyone in the INA knew who Major Bhaskaran Menon was. He remained Bose's Confidential Secretary until 17 August 1945 and thereafter he assisted Sarat Bose in the same capacity until the latter's death. Bhaskaran thought back to what had happened in the wee hours of 17 August. Bose was dictating letters for his confidants: Ishwar Singh, JK Bhonsle and then John Thivy. He paused for a moment and said: "I am writing all this to you (Thivy) as I am on the eve of taking a long journey by air, and who knows an accident may not overtake me." When the plane actually "crashed," Menon understood that premonition was not the case. He told all this to Khosla on oath. Khosla was not impressed with either Sengupta or Menon. "Bhaskaran's statement has been seen to be wholly unreliable," he wrote in a passing way.[23]

It was criminal that Shah Nawaz and GD Khosla should have glossed over what the British had gathered from different sources. On 9 April 1946, senior directors of the Intelligence Bureau sat down to discuss the intelligence picked up from the Russians. " ... a report said that the Governor of the Afghan province of Khost had been informed by the Russian Ambassador in Kabul that there were many Congress refugees in Moscow and Bose was included in their number. There is little reason for such persons to bring Bose into fabricated stories. At the same time the view that Russian officials are disclosing or alleging that Bose is in Moscow is supplied in a report received from Tehran. This states that Moradoff, the Russian Vice Consul-General, disclosed in March that Bose was in Russia ...."[24]

It was abundantly clear that the British made inquiries about Bose's presence in the USSR. There was nothing in 1946 to stop the victorious British to obtain information from any part of the world. Khosla was not shown the records of such investigations and neither did he evince any interest in procuring them. He did not even question why the documents provided to him came with numerous missing links. What became of the interrogation reports of Field Marshal Terauchi, Minister Shigemitsu, General Isoda and chief of Imperial Japanese Army intelligence? Were any inquiries made in Taipei? What explanation did the Japanese Foreign Office offer in post-surrender period? Was Soviet Russia ever asked by the British or Government of India to clarify if Subhas was indeed with them? These were the fair corollaries that could have been looked into but never were.

It transpired during the proceedings of the Commission that Soviet Union, India's foremost ally, had all along maintained a stony silence on the disappearance of the Indian icon. Up to 1970 there had been only one occasion when they had made an unofficial statement on Bose's presence in Soviet Russia. To Samar Guha the outburst by Politbureau's mouthpiece *Pravda* in 1946 was a smoking gun. Khosla disagreed with him vehemently. "(Guha) ... mentioned an article in the *Pravda* in which it was stated that Bose could not be given asylum in

Russia. Prof Samar Guha did not say that he had read the article himself, nor did he mention the date upon which this article appeared, although from the context it appears that the article was published in 1945. The substance of this article was interpreted by Prof Samar Guha as a cover because he thought Russia was friendly towards Bose and so a contrary assertion in the *Pravda* could only be intended to distract attention and provide an alibi for Bose. The inference drawn by Prof Guha is wholly unjustified. In any event, a copy of the relevant issue of *Pravda* has not been produced, and I cannot hold that such a statement appeared in that paper."[25]

How difficult was it for a judicial commission appointed by the Government of India to check old newspapers files? *Hindustan Times*, for one, on 8 January 1946 had carried the following *Reuters* report quoting *Pravda's* unrestrained fulmination against some reports in Indian newspapers.

"The Soviet journalist, David Zaslavsky in an article in *Pravda* denounced as 'a stupid fairy tale' a report that Subhas Chandra Bose, who headed the 'Free India Government' during the war, is in Soviet Russia, Moscow radio reported. He wrote: 'Indian fairy tales are full of poetic charm. Unfortunately, we cannot say the same about the latest product of the imagination of some Indian newspapers.' He had referred to the report, which he said had appeared in some Indian newspapers on December 31 and declared: 'The language of unscrupulous liars begins to penetrate also the political jungle of India.'

He continued: 'The substance of the fairy tale is as follows: The notorious would-be Quisling of India Subhas Chandra Bose, who at first was in Hitlerite pay in Berlin and then in the pay of the Japanese imperialists in Tokyo, has allegedly fled to Russia .... Such is the stupid fairy tale .... In the interests of peace and friendship among the people, one must nail down newspaper lies .... We are contributing to the spread of useful information for the Indian reading public when we state with perfect precision that the newspapers which published this report are under a newspaper signboard dealing in scrupulous anti-Soviet lies."[26]

The language of *Pravda* was much too surprising. Not shocking. The Soviets needn't have come out with such derisive censure of a man they had not long ago saved. As a close observer of the events, Dwijendra Nath Bose too took this denial for a facade. Khosla heard him on 8 August 1972:

"I told both (my cousins) Sisir and Aurobindo that .... they had published in one very important paper — *Pravda* — that no nation should give asylum to Subhas Chandra Bose. I showed it to Sisir and said: Look here ... do you agree with me or not, if I say that Russia had no business to come out with such communiqué — because Netaji had not fought the Russians; he had not declared war on them."

"Did not Russia declare war against Japan, and was Netaji not an ally of Japan?" Dwijen was reminded.

"Russia had declared war after fall of Japan, after the atom bomb was thrown on Hiroshima and Nagasaki."

"That was on the 12th. The Japanese surrendered on the 15th!"

"Only to grab some territory of Japan," Dwijen answered.

"Do you mean to say that since Netaji or the INA had not fought against Russia and so had not declared hostility against Russia? Therefore, Russians had no business to come out with such a statement?"

Dwijen pressed that the Russians had no reasons to make such "uncalled for statement." "I told Sisir ... that Russia has given shelter to Netaji and he is with them."

If such inferences were not enough, some witnesses made claims that needed to be probed given the seriousness of the charges in them. Former government officials SM Goswami and Dr Satyanarayan Sinha stated on oath that Bose had been held captive in Siberia after 1945. Sinha's evidence carried weight. He had been in foreign service and then had been elected to the first Lok Sabha. Sinha said that on coming to know of Bose's existence in Russia he brought the matter to the notice of authorities only to be pooh-poohed. He had to resign from the diplomatic service "substantially because of growing differences with the Prime Minister Nehru on the issue of Netaji ... (and) matters pertaining to Indo-Soviet diplomatic relations."[27]

Shaken by the outrage provoked by Sinha's statements, the Soviet Union embassy on 3 November 1970 released its first official statement on Bose's disappearance without touching the part whether or not he was with them after August 1945. It was briefly stated "with full responsibility" that the Soviet authorities "had absolutely nothing to do with the fate of Subhas Chandra Bose." On 7 November, Khosla's reaction was sought. Those who expected that the judge would seek further elaboration from the embassy by summoning their representative met with utter disappointment. Khosla sidestepped the issue saying he "did not propose to take notice of the statement of the Soviet Embassy."[28]

Two years after Khosla's report had been accepted by the Government came a bolt from blue. It had been thirty years since India had been granted freedom. Great Britain deemed it fit to fill in the gaps in history by publishing selected documents from the India Office records of the Raj days up to August 1947 in the twelve-part *Transfer of Power* volumes. What came about was this: On 23 August 1945, Sir Robert Francis Mudie, Home Member (Home Minister) sent a Top Secret letter to Sir Evan Meredith Jenkins, Private Secretary to the Viceroy Wavell. Unaffected by the death news, Mudie was solely concerned with how to lay hands on Bose, a natural corollary to Japan's surrender. He sent along the letter a detailed note the Home Department (Ministry) had prepared in consultation with Richard Tottenham, Additional Secretary in Home Department, and Norman Smith, the first police officer to take over as the Director of Intelligence Bureau.

The note began with the premise that "one of the most difficult questions that will confront Home Department in the near future is the treatment of Subhas Chandra Bose." Then it went on to list a number of options ranging from bringing "him back to India and try him either for waging war or under the enemy agents ordinance" to leaving "him where he is and don't ask for his surrender." But could the Home Department hazard a guess about Bose's plans in post-surrender days? They certainly could. The Allies intelligence had penetrated deep into INA, IIL set-up and whatever the Axis secretly deliberated on Bose was known to them.

"Interning Bose in India would lead only to an agitation to let him out and to his release after a short time. He might then escape to Russia, as he did in 1940 .... There is more to be said for detention and internment somewhere out of India. Out of sight would be to some extent out of mind and agitation for his release might be less. Also, escape to Russia would be difficult. In many ways the easiest course would be to leave him where he is and not ask for his release. He might, of course, in certain circumstances, be welcomed by the Russians. This course would raise fewest immediate political difficulties, but the security authorities consider that in certain circumstances his presence in Russia would be so dangerous as to rule it out altogether."[29]

Almost nine months later, the British were anxious about Bose's possible presence in the USSR. In August 1997 several files of Indian Political Intelligence (IPI) were released for public at the British Library's Oriental and Indian Office Collections. The IPI, jointly run by the India Office in London and the Government of India, had been keeping tab on the activities of revolutionaries like Subhas Bose. Since this organisation was transferred to TG Sanjevi Pillai, the first Indian DIB, at the time of independence, most likely the records came into possession of the Government. The IB or any other department or ministry of the Government never mentioned a word about IPI to either Shah Nawaz Khan or GD Khosla. They should have as this organisation had collected some vital intelligence about Bose's "afterlife." On 2 May 1946 the IPI was told on the subject of the "probable death of Subhas Bose" that Norman Smith had information about Bose's presence in Russia. "In some cases circumstantial details have been added."[30] But in the whole declassified lot no other paper detailed the "circumstantial details" that had forced a person no less than the Director of Intelligence Bureau to report the matter in London.

In early 1980s, the first indications surfaced in Russia about the Russians' actual appraisal of Subhas Bose, who had been blacklisted during the glory days of Indo-Soviet friendship. Paying tribute to the role Bose played in Indian freedom struggle, two Russian Indologists contended that the Soviet scholars "have now revised their earlier negative opinion of Netaji and the Indian National Army."[31] Dr Poddubni rejected "the notion that Netaji was in sympathy with fascism." "When Nazi Germany attacked the Soviet Union, Netaji was in Rome and wrote a letter to the Foreign Minister of Germany saying that in a war between Germany and the Soviet Union, the sympathies of Indians would be in favour of Russia .... Nazi leaders wanted Bose to stay in Germany so that they could make use of his presence there for propaganda purpose. He not only refused to stay but, before leaving for Japan, advised Indian soldiers in Germany to refuse to fight against the Soviet Union. Had he not left for Tokyo, he would have landed in a Nazi prisoner camp .... Later the Indian Legion in Germany was asked to march against the Soviet Union on the eastern front, which it refused .... Their refusal to collaborate with Nazi Germany was inspired by Netaji."[32]

The Russians talked more freely in the proceeding years when the USSR began to fall apart. In 1989 an article published in *Soviet Land* discussed the fate of Indian revolutionaries Birendra Nath Chatterjee and Abani Mukherjee who "had disappeared from the Soviet Society without leaving any traces."[33] The unease about Bose was palpable. "Mahatma Gandhi, Bal Gangadhar Tilak, Bhagat Singh, Jawaharlal Nehru, Indira Gandhi and other leaders, heroes and martyrs of the India national liberation movement are well known to the Soviet people. Strange as it may seem, few of them have till date known Subhas Chandra Bose. For a long time Soviet researchers were not allowed even to mention this passionate patriot." In 1992, journal *Echo Plantei* carried an article by A Vinogradov, a former *Tass* correspondent in India. Interestingly, the editorial note on his essay — *The life and death of Netaji Bose* — revealed that the officials in " Moscow and Delhi are keeping silence as regards the true fate of Bose. As far as the unofficial information as are concerned, our correspondent (Vinogradov), who for a long time have profoundly worked with the materials on Netaji's life, had occasions to hear from reliable sources, that in Moscow they are quite highly conversant with the true state of affairs and more than that, they have confirmable documents."[34]

In India, no one knew anything until a plucky lady stirred up the nation's conscience. Dr Purabi Roy, a professor of International Affairs in Calcutta's Jadhavpur University, did what no Indian had done before. She, an expert on Russia and Russian language, made inquiries in Russia and boldly asserted that Bose had made it to the USSR after he was announced dead by the Japanese. It was a very different Moscow Roy visited in May 1994. The Soviet Union was gone and democratic Russian Federation was in place. The new nation had no qualms in disowning its Communist past and had little discomfiture in opening up its archives. Roy's momentous research began with the Asiatic Society of Bengal inking an agreement with the Institute of the Oriental Studies in Moscow to probe the missing links in Indian history. Roy became first scholar to be sent to Russia under the agreement to compile materials in Russian archives pertaining to the Indo-Russian relations from 1917 to 1947. In 1995 Sobhanlal Dutta Gupta and Dr Hari Vasudevan joined the research. Bose mystery was not on Dr Roy's agenda, but she saw that many foreign countries and scholars had been making efforts to salvage relevant records from Russia. Many had even doled out money to obtain priceless documents. The results had been quite sensational. It had been revealed after five decades of Soviet denial that the alleged mass slaughter of some Polish army officers had actually taken place. The world had been shocked by the revelation about the Raul Wallenberg mystery.[35]

When the researchers from not-so-friendly countries could gain access to the Russian archives, why not Indians? Dr Roy felt all the more confident when she found out that Russian Indologists were coming out in open with their research works on Bose. It was during her 1994 visit to Moscow that Roy got to meet Victor Turadzhev, an associate editor in Russian journal

Asia and Africa Today. Turadzhev too had written on Bose, without much understanding and with the presumption that Bose had died in the Taipei crash. Provoked by a 1993 write-up — *The mystery of the death of Subhas Chandra Bose* -- by A Raikov, he had spelt his spin on the life and times of Bose. Though his aim was to negate what he called as "extremely exaggerated" rumours going around among Indians and Russians, Turadzhev ended up helping those whom he intended to criticize. He fished out from the KGB archives an irrefutable evidence that Bose had indeed reached out to the USSR at the close of world war. All of Bose's men had stated that he had tried to contact the Russian ambassador Jacob Malik in Tokyo in 1944-45. The British intelligence too had picked up signs but no confirmation could be seen in available records. It was widely held until 1990s that Malik had received a letter from Bose but had returned it without opening it. Such antics were against the grain of seasoned diplomat who was to became vice foreign minister of the USSR.[36] Turadzhev traced and reproduced verbatim Bose's hitherto non-existent letter.

Yes it had been duly forwarded by A Langfang, the Commissar of State Security (NKGB), to Colonel A Otroshehenko, the Chief of the 5th division of the First Command of NKVD. Bose had written the letter on 20 November 1944 on his official "Arzi Hukumate Azad Hind" (PGI) pad. He began without any frills: "I am seeking help of the Soviet Government through you to fulfil the task of our freedom struggle to free India." The second para was an explanation of his position in the Axis bloc and the fact that he did so for Indian freedom. He stressed that his INA waged war against the Allies but not the USSR:

"I cannot deny the fact that at the moment we are closely associated with the Axis power for a common struggle against the Anglo-American bloc. I am glad to inform you that the Axis power is now having a clear idea about the main problems of India and they have accorded recognition to the Azad Hind State (Free India) for which we are thankful to them. Besides, Japan's relations with the Soviet are strictly neutral, even the Germany can understand fully well and evaluate the fact that we Indians are only fighting against England and America. The German Government has also understood and appreciated the fact that we are not interested to go against the Soviet Russia. Certainly, the activities of my organisations in Europe have generated an exclusive impression that we are only against the Anglo-American bloc and not against the Soviet Russia. This was the understanding of cooperation between the Axis power and our organisation in Europe. In this connection, we have a clear policy and approval from the German Government, as well as the Fascist Italian Government."

Para three encapsulated his views on the future scenario and an expression of gratitude for the help Russians had extended to him in 1941: "I know that now there is an alliance between the Soviet Union, England and America. But I feel that I have clear perception about the prevailing international situation that if the Soviet Union extends its help to our freedom struggle, it will certainly not stand in your way. I am very much thankful to your Government and I do remember the help which was extended by the Soviet Government after I had left India in 1941. I conveyed my thanks to his Excellency Minister for External Affairs Molotov in my letter I wrote from Berlin. I trust his Excellency had certainly received it."

The para four was a much needed dash of emotions: "I have always been encouraged by the fact that Lenin in his time always from the core of his heart extended support to the countries which were struggling against the colonial rule. So far I understand, the Soviet attitude to the problems of the oppressed nations like India has not been changed after his death."

Bose reminded Jacob that his pro-USSR outlook was not new: "As to my party — Forward Bloc, I can say that when the Soviet Foreign policy had been condemned by almost all the political parties of India in 1939-1940, ours was the only party which had openly supported the Soviet Foreign policy in relation to Germany and Finland." He ended with the request that his "earnest desire is to pay a visit to your Excellency and find the way through which your Government can help us for success of our struggle for freedom. The nature of help which the

Soviet Government can extend to us depends on the decision of the Soviet Government in relation to the present situation of war ....″[37] The letter had been written from Imperial Hotel in Tokyo and that Malik did meet Bose was proven by the dispatching of the letter to Moscow.

Turadzhev's article, maybe due to anti-Bose contents and the KGB inputs, caused discomfort in the Indian Embassy in Moscow. The Russian was conveyed that he had better mind his own business. Turadzhev was jolted. When Purabi Roy came looking for him, he couldn't help but tell her that for Indians the stakes were quite high. "Try and find out documents on Netaji since you are here," he told her, and said that her search could commence at military archives in Paddolsk and archives in Omsk. Purabi Roy looked around for more clues. She found them aplenty. During May-June 1995, she met a number of high-profile experts at the Institute of Oriental Studies and not one ruled out the possibility that Bose could have made it to the USSR in August 1945. Dr RB Rybakov, Director, told her to go to Pikhoi, the head of the archival documentation section. When Dr Roy met Pikhoi, he told her that he was helpless. "The request for perusal of the archival document should come from the Government of India."

AA Kutsenkov, Head, Indian Department, turned out to be much more informed person. A former KGB man, Kutsenkov suggested that the KGB archives had many documents and "the Government of India should move to get the files declassified." A Kirichenko, head of the international section, and a specialist of Soviet-Japanese strategy, told Roy that "he is rest assured that some documents related to Netaji are lying in the KGB Cell." He added that he himself had "consulted many documents which were related to Japan, INA and Soviet Union. But to get access to them permission of the Government is essentially required." VI Kluev, senior professor, was earlier in the KGB's India cell. As such he was in a position to know. "He was certain that there were documents relating to Subhas Chandra Bose's arrival in Russia after 1945."[38] In his view it was worthwhile to have a look at Stalin's personal archives.

Having satisfied themselves of the presence of crucial records on Subhas Bose in Russia, the Asiatic Society team turned to the Government of India so that they could gain access. This would have been an easy thing to do given the excellent relations between Russia and India. But much to Asiatic Society researchers' surprise, the Government was hostile to the idea. The Ambassador of India in Moscow, Ronen Sen,[39] denied that Turadzhev had been asked to stop his research on Bose. In Delhi, the Government showed not an iota of interest in felicitating the Asiatic Society's move. The society's general secretary Chandan Roychowdhury wrote a number of letters to External Affairs Minister Pranab Mukherjee, his deputy Salman Khurshid, and then to Prime Minister PV Narasimha Rao — a self-proclaimed follower of Netaji. Many did not even display the rudimentary courtesy of admitting that they had received such letters from such a reputed organisation.

By September 1995 Roychaudhuri and Purabi Roy had run out of patience. They went to media and soon all top dailies were publishing what the scholars had gone through. The *Statesman,* Delhi edition, carried report *Documents on Netaji lying in KGB vaults* on 14 September 1995. The report stated that "the scholars, who spent about 6,000 US dollars for having access to the archives in Moscow, regretted that in most cases, they were not allowed to study the required files and documents. The problems were further accentuated due to 'restrictions' imposed by a section of officials of the Indian Embassy in Moscow."

"The scholars quoted an article ... to say that the Russian agent sought to convey the message to Moscow in September, 1946, that the Soviet Government might have to contact "Forward Bloc as one of the major political parties in India and its leader Subhas Chandra Bose." "These references pointed to Netaji being alive even in 1946." The report further said that "most of the archival materials had been 'sold out' by the Russian Government to the super powers .... The scholars regretted that despite repeated pleas, the authorities in the Russian archives did not allow them to have easy access to

Netaji's war time contacts with the Russian leaders, including Stalin."

Amrita Bazar Patrika, Kolkata, on 14 September 1995 reported that "several documents relating to Netaji Subhas Chandra Bose and his mysterious disappearance are still lying in the inaccessible archives of the disbanded KGB and in the official archives of the Russian President in Kremlin .... Purabi Roy .... said that they also came to know that a Tass correspondent had collected more information about Netaji in 1992 who questioned and found stunning silence was being maintained by both Delhi and Moscow about Netaji's whereabouts."

A report in the *Times of India*, Mumbai, on 15 September 1995 said, "Ms Roy felt that the government of India should impress upon the Russian authorities to permit Indian scholars' access to the KGB and the President's Archives as it might help clear the mystery of Netaji's disappearance. Mr Roychaudhuri said he had already sent letters to Prime Ministers PV Narasimha Rao and the external affairs minister to use their good offices in this matter."

The *Indian Express* was as usually no holds barred in titling its 19 September report. *Govt apathy leaves Netaji's fate buried in Moscow's files* quoted Dr Hari Vasudevan whining that "the Russian government is quite generous about opening up these archives .... But while scholars of most Western countries are making the most of the archives, we are suffering due to the quirky attitude of the MEA." Dr Sobhanlal Dutta Gupta and Dr Purabi Roy "required letters for the MEA to read the two files located at the KGB archives. The letter was a prerequisite to obtain Russian Government's permission. But repeated requests to Salman Khurshid, Minister of State, and even the Prime Minister went unheeded."

For any Government in a democratic polity such a public damnation by top newspapers would have sprung the head of the government to clarify their stand. The Government was charged with scuttling efforts to find out the truth about the fate of a national icon, but Rao and his ministers preferred swallowing the humiliation than opening their mouths. Purabi Roy couldn't keep mum — even when media and her colleagues gave up. She continued to take the Government to task all alone. "If they (Government) are confident that Netaji was actually killed in a plane crash in 1945, why have they always tried to scuttle any fresh investigation? If they are clean, let them provide us access to the two archives and see what's there?"[40] In 1996, she approached Prime Minister of the Russian Federation. Viktor Chernomyrdin mooted the idea of an Indo-Russian Commission to investigate the missing Indian nationals within the territory of the erstwhile USSR. But who was interested in Netaji at home?

Roy submitted applications to Russian archives but no one replied. There was some success in London. Rishi Ranjan Chakravorty, an NRI, enlisted help of Lord Peter Archer whose efforts led to the declassification of a few files on Bose. Certain War Office files were made available at the Public Record Office. On scrutiny, however, Roy noted "mysterious disappearance of notes, paragraphs, pages and references, missing informations and papers."[41] They were very abruptly arranged and most of the documents were incomplete.

While Roy had been wondering why the British and the Russian authorities would do such a thing, efforts were on in India to confuse public opinion and undermine the work done by the Indian and Russian scholars. Some inspired researchers were getting jittery over the developments. In December 1996 one of their tribe came out with "counter-revelations" to the effect that there was nothing more to Bose mystery than what was given in official line. One Joychandra Singh gave media an impression that Russia upheld the death story. This he attributed to a measured response of Colonel Brilev, chief of the Russian Ministry of Defence's Central Archives in Moscow. The spin was deceitful: What that the colonel had actually wrote was that "there is no records available with the archives on Netaji Subhas Chandra Bose's death at Taipei plane crash or his arrest by the USSR Army."[42] That is, as per the information available to him, there was no confirmation of Bose's death in Taipei; and, the Red Army had not arrested him. As regards the second point, Brilev simply denied a presumption without volunteering further information. Bose had himself sought asylum from the Russians and as such they need not have arrested him.

All through his press briefing in Imphal, Joychandra Singh harped on his "12-year-old research" on the issue. Starting with a hypothesis that Bose had died, Singh had written a letter to the Prime Minister Indira Gandhi on 23 May 1984, suggesting her that the "remains of Netaji Subhas Chandra Bose should be brought to India from Renkoji temple."[43] Poor Asiatic Society scholars went all over begging for Rao Government's assistance but no one, including Pranab Mukherjee, who had personal relations with some of Bose's kin, cared to write a line to them. And here in 1984, when a researcher swearing by the official line wrote in, a considerate Government instantly responded. The same Narasimha Rao, who was to see a wolf a decade later, was now graciousness personified. With pleasure Rao wrote to Singh on 21 June 1984 on behalf of the Prime Minister: "I fully agree with you that there should be a national consensus on this question before the Government takes a formal decision so that a controversy in any form is avoided at a later stage. Any efforts on your part towards this end (proving the Taipei crash) would be most welcome."[44] Singh by mistake gave out to the reporters that the "inspiration" for his "research" had come from this letter. Then, steering clear of suspicions arising out of it, he started counting to the impressed pressmen the countries and archives he had visited. He flashed a letter he had received, granting him permission to study old records in some Taipei library, which meant zilch of course.

Unmindful of this farce, Purabi Roy, in the meanwhile, managed to pull off a coup. Among the researchers she had met in 1994, Alexender Kolesnikov had been wanting to get something off his chest. A former USSR general, Kolesnikov had joined the Institute of Oriental Studies before turning to diplomacy. He had been taking keen interest in Bose and in his official capacity had seen some classified papers concerning Bose. In October 1996, when she was in Moscow, Roy heard that an Indian parliamentary delegation was in the city. It comprised Lok Sabha Speaker PA Sangma, BJP leader Sushma Swaraj and

Chitta Basu and Jayanta Roy of All India Forward Bloc. Roy called up Kolesnikov and requested him to tell the AIFB leaders what he had seen. After some persuasion Kolesnikov agreed and a meeting was arranged in the lobby of Moscow's President Hotel.

Chitta Basu requested Kolesnikov to be straight. "Please throw light on the rumours that Netaji was in Russia after August 1945!" Overcome with emotions and wary, Kolesnikov faltered; his English was poor anyway. Chitta Basu suggested that he jot down what he wanted to say. Kolesnikov wrote that Bose was in the USSR in 1946. He told the Indians that they must take up the matter with the Indian Government and seek access to the Russian archives. What Kolesnikov had managed to see was a document in a file that noted the minutes of an August 1946 discussion among Soviet Politburo members Voroshilov, Vyshinski, Mikoyan, and Molotov. They were discussing whether Bose should be allowed to stay in the Soviet Union.[45]

On her return to India, Roy pleaded yet again. "I need only a little support from the Government. I need only a letter from the Government requesting the Russian authorities to allow me to go through classified documents kept in different archives. I am sure I will prove that Netaji was alive after August 18, 1945, and that he was in Soviet Russia."[46] Her imploration fell on deaf ears. Not many eyebrows raised even when Kolesnikov himself made the strongest ever pitch over Bose mystery by a Russian in his article *Destiny and Death of Chandra Bose* in the January 1997 issue of Russian newspaper *Patriot*. Kolesnikov underlined that the memory of Subhas Bose was preserved with gratitude by not only Indians but also their Russian friends. The highlight of write-up based on his research was that at the close of the war an envoy of Bose had reached Omsk in Siberia, suggesting that Russian had recognised the Provisional Government of Free India.

"In January 1941 Subhas Chandra Bose arrived in Kabul with the hope of establishing contact with a representative of the Soviet leadership. Bhagat Ram Talwar, who had links with the representative of Soviet intelligence, Zaman (MA Allahverdov), tried to help him in this but the meeting due to some reason did not take place. However, Bose could manage to obtain a passport in the name of an Italian for travelling to Germany via Moscow. In Moscow Achhar Singh Cheema, an old friend of Bose and one of the leaders of Indian Communists, also tried to organise meetings of the 'transit' guest with the highest leadership of the Soviet Union. Most probably such a meeting took place because Bose later sent a letter to Molotov from Berlin expressing gratitude. It is just possible to guess what was Moscow's reaction to Bose's proposals. Party archives on this still remain inaccessible.

"... since the end of 1944 he (Bose) once again strove to establish contacts with the Soviet leadership. With this aim in view he sent the authorised representative of Bose's interim Government, Kato Kuchi, to Omsk with the rank of an ambassador .... Bose went to Tokyo where he tried to meet the Soviet Ambassador Yakov (Jacob) Malik. Bose's letter was delivered to Soviet Ambassador but history is silent about what happened thereafter.

"(at Taipei) ... the aircraft fell on the ground. Thereafter there was a chain of mysterious evidences every one of which was in contradiction with the previous one thereby confusing the real picture of what happened .... It is quite strange for such an important political figure that there was no documented evidence of his death — photographs, protocols, formal identification, etc. There were no material proofs .... What could this mean? Did Bose disappear himself or was someone instrumental in his disappearance?

"There is one more version: Bose was abducted by Stalin who by then began to 'collect' interned political figures of foreign countries. As a matter of fact on one side Bose was a recognised national leader and on the other the political situation in India was contradictory and unpredictable. Then why should not Bose be kept near him for sometime? Stalin had taken the last emperor of China as his captive. If this version is to be believed, probably there should have been some secret gentleman's agreement between the USSR and Great Britain because Bose was considered an ally of the enemies of the anti-Hitler coalition.

"It is remarkable that none of the special commissions subsequently instituted in India to inquire into Bose's death agreed with any of these versions. This is a mysterious point in Soviet-Indian relations. There was no definite reply from the Soviet side to the repeated statements that Bose remained alive and he was in the USSR."[47]

Kolesnikov's input on Kato Kachu was further taken up. Purabi Roy found out that as per Japanese researchers, Kato Kachu was an alias and this man was possibly an Indian. In March 1999 Pramod Mehra of the National Archives in Delhi presented a seminar paper —"The Declassified Documents from the Ministry of Defence" — in Kolkata. Here he revealed that like Germany, Japan, Italy and Ireland, the USSR had recognised the Provisional Government of Free India.

And so began to appear the contours of Bose's escape to the Soviet Russia: USSR and Subhas Bose are warm to each other from the day one. Circumstances force Bose to get into a bloc which becomes a rival to the Soviets, but the mutual liking remains. The war draws to an end. Bose requests the Japanese to help him go to the Soviet Russia, which is not at war with them, and try work out some arrangements which would be to Japan's and India's benefits. The Japanese Government, or a part of it, approves the plan. Bose writes to the Russian ambassador in Tokyo in late 1944 and in December visits him. Bose's letter is favourably considered in Moscow. A plenipotentiary of the PGI is stationed in Omsk. The Red Army enters then Japanese-control led Manchuria on 9 August. On 11 August, the Japanese tell Bose that their time is up and he, their ally till the last, must move on to continue Indian struggle. Hikari Kikan swings into action with General Isoda himself taking the charge. Bose is constantly kept abreast of the advancement of the Red Army. He reaches Saigon and meets General Shidei of the Quantung Army, which is surrendering to the Red Army in Manchuria. Shidei, an expert on Manchurian topography and the Russian language, and his two superiors, General Yamada Otozo and Lt General Hata Hikosaburo, are to work out the final surrender with the Russians. And he is to follow the orders of Field Marshal Terauchi to see to it that Bose goes to the Russians. The plane takes off on 17 August for Diren in Manchuria. A few hundred kilometers away, Bose's friend, a severely paralytic Terauchi lies on bed having suffered a cerebral haemorrhge. He has taken responsibility for Bose's escape knowing well that death will get him faster than the Allied "justice." On 18 August the plane "crashes" in Taihoku but the news is kept in wraps. General Hikosaburo meets Russian Major General Shelakor to discuss surrender modalities. The Red Army continues to take territories in Manchuria. The Quantung Army, led by General Otozo, finally surrenders to General Alexander Vasilevski of the Red Army in the Manchurian capital on 22 August 1945. The same day, Japan decided to release the news of the "death" of Subhas Bose. On 23 August 1945, General Isoda comforts Bose's aide SC Sengupta: "Don't worry, His Excellency Chandra Bose is in safe custody!"

Was then anything heard of Subhas Bose in Russia? In 2000, Ardhendu Sarkar, a mechanical engineer, broke his decades-long silence. He had been to Soviet Russia in 1962 as an employee of Heavy Engineering Corporation. His senior at Gorlovka Machine Buidling Plant, near Donetesk in Ukraine, was one Zerovin — a German who had met Bose. Zerovin had been brought to the USSR in 1947-48 and sent to Siberia for indoctrination. The gulag where he was kept had some VIPs. One day, in around 1948, Zerovin saw Subhas Chandra Bose. There were two unfriendly guards with him. Zerovin managed a few words in German.

"Sir I have met you in Berlin."

"Quite likely," Bose replied.

"What are you doing here?"

"I don't know what for .... "

"What is your programme, sir? Are you going back to India?"

"I expect it to be very soon."

Zerovin requested Sarker to promise him that he would not divulge this as long as he was in the USSR. Sarkar reneged on his promise within days. He went to the Indian Embassy in Moscow and blurted out before a secretary what he had come to know. The secretary said, "Why have you come to this country? Does your assignment include poking nose in politics?" Sarkar was shaken to bones and the secretary noticed that. "Don't discuss this information with anyone. Just do what you have been sent for." Sarkar returned to his office only to find that the embassy had decided to hound him out of the USSR. Someone from the embassy had lodged a complaint against him in his company. "He is meddling into something which he is not supposed to," was the grouse. Within days Sarkar got the marching orders. He returned home, frightened and worried about his family.[48] What Sarkar came to believe was an Indian nightmare. Netaji was in a Siberian camp and perhaps the Government of India knew about it.

Over the years, the aversion of the Government of India to the issue of Bose's alleged presence in the USSR turned into an obstructionist policy. Thanks to Dr Purabi Roy's crusade, the Government was repeatedly reminded of the gravity of the situation in Parliament by lawmakers, who put questions. But every time it appeared that the authorities did not wish to go beyond a self-drawn line. The governments of Deve Gowda and Atal Bihari Vajpayee, rather shockingly, parroted the response prepared during the time Narasimha Rao was the boss. They denied the Russian connection to the Bose mystery on the basis of just two vague communications made at unspecified official level with the Russian Foreign Ministry in 1992 and 1995. The Russians made qualified response that in certain archives of theirs there was no record of Bose's stay in the USSR after 1945. Were it not the Russians who had told the British that they had no knowledge how Bose had escaped to Germany in 1941? Shorn of gobbledygook, the Government of India's response was that they were disinclined to take up the matter with the Russian government at a proper level; or facilitate any such move by others; or access Russian archives holding intelligence and security related papers.

One man in Delhi did not seem shocked by the Government's behaviour. "They do not want to disturb relations," chuckled Rai Singh, a retired diplomat. "They know Netaji was in Siberia. He was left out in the cold!" Singh had joined the Information Service of India in 1950s, and whenever he got a chance, he dug out information about Bose from politicians and diplomats of different countries. His was an interesting career. One of the first assignment was to listen to the Soviet broadcasts. Then he went on to work in several missions abroad and hold several sensitive posts. In 1960s Singh met Alberto Quarani, the Italian consul in Kabul who had helped Bose escape to Rome in 1941. Quarani had become Information Minister of Italy, but still fondly remembered Bose.

Singh befriended Girija Mukherjee, Bose's aide in Germany. And he had a thought-provoking meeting with Vijaylakshmi Pandit, Nehru's sister, and first Indian envoy to the USSR, about whom some rumours were sought to be scotched by GD Khosla in his report. At home Rai Singh was once closely associated with the groundwork that went into answering certain questions that were raised in the Parliament over India's external affairs. His job required him to be meeting Prime Minister Nehru every third day. Inside the PM office, alone, he saw a discourteous arrogant boss, a far cry from his "avuncular" image.

Singh, in his official capacity, also came to interact with Prime Ministers Lal Bahadur Shastri and Indira Gandhi. But it was his relationship with a professor of Central Asian Studies in the Jawaharlal Nehru University that he came to cherish. Ram Rahul was also a well-known Tibetologist. He had developed personal relations with many renowned personalities, including a judge of the US Supreme Court. Those who knew him knew that he got along well with a big shot in the USSR. Babajan Gouffrav and Rahul had struck a cord in their first meeting in Tashkent. The friendship lasted until Gouffrav died. There was a time when Babajan Gouffrav was one of the most influential men in Moscow. He was one of the two aides that Joseph Stalin regarded as friends. "Only Lavrenty Beria, Stalin's Interior Minister, and Gouffrav could intrude into Stalin's privacy." Gouffrav was the director of then much powerful Institute of

Oriental Studies in Moscow. "Stalin depended on Gouffrav on every issue that concerned south-east and central Asia - especially India, China and Tibet." Gouffrav came to India many times after he had got out of the power and he did meet Rahul. In one of their discussions the subject of Bose was raked up. Rahul could never muster the courage to reveal what Gouffrav had told him until he took seriously ill. In July 2000, he sent for his friend Rai Singh.

"I have something to tell you. I do not want to go to funeral pyre with this. It's about Netaji." Singh's heart sank as the professor confirmed the nightmare. Gouffrav had admitted that "Netaji had crossed over to the Soviet Union in 1945 via Manchuria."[49] "As a 'collaborator' of the Axix Powers, he would have been executed. But Joseph Stalin wanted to use Netaji as a bargaining chip in his future dealings with Britain and India. Thus, he ordered Netaji's detention in a labour camp in Siberia."[50]

"According to Gouffrav, India's Ambassador to the USSR was permitted to have a glimpse of Netaji in the camp on the condition that no word was exchanged with him."[51] Perplexed, the Ambassador was frozen at the very thought of what he would do if Bose wished to speak with him. "It has been taken care of," he was told. "The Ambassador was then taken to one of the labour camps in Siberia and he saw Bose from a distance of 10 metres. On his return, the Ambassador filed a report to the Prime Minister."

"Just who met Bose? ... though Gouffrav did not name the Indian official, Rahul did try find out on his own, and asked if he had later become the President of India. According to Singh, 'Gouffrav refused to deny or confirm it.'"[52] Singh's "hunch" was that it was Dr Sarvapalli Radhakrishnan, the Ambassador-Extraordinary and Minister-Plenipotentiary to the USSR from 1949 to 1953. Radhakrishnan "was not even bracketed with such colourless leaders of little most influence as Tej Bahadur Sapru & MR Jayakar." He watched the freedom struggle "from far beyond India's shores, and if, it roused any feeling of nationalist in him he did not exhibit them openly."[53]

When Radhakrishnan's assignment in Moscow got over, Rai Singh added, Nehru proposed his name as India's first Vice-President in a Cabinet meeting. First, because there was no provision for this post in the Constitution. "Nehru was going out of his way and Azad did not approve of it," Singh related another anecdote he had heard from a Congressman close to Maulana Abul Kalam Azad. "*Kya hum sab mur gaye hain*?" (Are we all dead?) Azad demurred. "Wherefrom this Sir Sarvapalli comes to be our Vice-President?"

Radhakrishnan, who had been knighted by the British King, was conferred with first ever Bharat Ratna. A number of witnesses before Khosla Commission charged that Radhakrishnan and his predecessor Vijaylakshmi Pandit knew something about Bose's presence in the USSR. Satyanarayan Sinha claimed that Ambassador Radhakrishnan had warned him to not to "meddle in these affairs" after he told him about Bose in Siberia. The former President and VL Pandit were made aware of the charges. They filed affidavits to deny it all. "The last time I met Netaji Subhas Chandra Bose was in Darjeeling in the summer of 1940," Radhakrishnan affirmed, and VL Pandit stated that she never met Bose after he left India. This did not satisfy every one. The Commission's counsel himself on 6 July 1972 "reiterated his demand to summon former President S Radhakrishnan, Mrs Vijaylakshmi Pandit and others as witnesses before the Commission, although they had denied having any information about Netaji. The records had shown that these persons did have some information on the subject." "Radhakrishnan to be examined," The *Times of India* reported on 24 December and on and on 24 July 1973 it was stated during the Commission's proceedings that "Mrs Pandit will come on the 26th." No one ever came.

The volatility of Gouffrav's admission was never lost on Rahul. Unfortunately his time came before the situation could become conducive for him to go public. So he unburdened himself before Rai Singh with the last message that Singh should "release this information when India is ready to ask questions about Netaji."[54]

Notes:

1 *HindustanTimes.com* report **Emilie knew Subhas was alive.** Netaji probe phase 1.

2 *Subhas: A Political Biography* by Sitanshu Das. Page 409.

3 *The Patriot* article **Subhas, Soviets and Japan** by Sheel Bhadra Yajee. 23 January 1994.

4 Ibid.

5 Record of Conference Between Bose and the Reich Foreign Minister in Vienna on 1 May 1941. From: US Department of State. *Documents on German Foreign Policy,* 1918-1945. Series D (1937-1945). Vol. XII. A number of documents concerning Bose from this series were published under Project South Asia, a joint project of the Office of the International Programs at South Dakota State University and the Institute of International Studies at Missouri Southern State University, USA.

6 The *Times of India* article **When Netaji was in Germany** by JC Jain. 11 April 1970.

7 Memorandum by the Director of the Political Department. July 17, 1941. See Project South Asia. http://projectsouthasia.sdstate.edu/Docs/history/primarydocs/SCBose/Bose11.htm.

8 *HindustanTimes.com* story **Nazis suspected Netaji's Russian connection** by the writer. 23 November 2002.

9 Netaji Inquiry Committee report 1956. Page 10.

10 Netaji Inquiry Commission report 1974. Page 16.

11 *Dissentient Report* by Suresh Bose. Page 5.

12 Record of the proceedings of Khosla Commission. 17 November 1970. Volume II, page 736.

13 *Netaji: Dead or Alive?* by Samar Guha. Page 182.

14 No 63/2/34/GSI (b). From Commander SACSEA Commission No 1 to HQ, SACSEA.

15 From Comd 'S' Section, CSDIC (I) to Comdt, CSDIC, Red Fort, Delhi. 15 January 1946.

16 DO No. SA/661 from W McKWright of Intelligence Bureau to Major Courtney Young CICB, Intelligence Division, HQ, SACSEA, Singapore. 19 February 1946.

17 ST/12/104 from Comd 'S' Section CSDIC (I) to Comdt CSDIC. Red Fort, Delhi, South East Asia Command, 28 February 1946.

As per a document dated 17 October 1945, made available to the writer by the MacArthur Memorial Library and Archives, Norfolk,

USA, the British had sought the custody of Shigemitsu and his deputies in connection with inquiries over Bose. The Americans responded that while Shigemitsu was ill and "unable to take the trip to Delhi at this time", "the two Vice Ministers (Matsumoto and Swada) will be sent to Delhi." Hachiya was missing. C/S RJM/jrf. From CINCAFPAC ADV to SECSEA. No further details are known to the writer.

18 Mamoru Shigemitsu was Foreign Minister of Japan at the time of disappearance. After the Tokyo trials, he was branded a "Class A" war criminal and imprisoned. Shigemitsu, however, made an amazing comeback and became the Foreign Minister of Japan in 1950s. He was in that capacity when Shah Nawaz Committee visited Japan. In a long meeting with him, Suresh Bose thanked him for all Japan had done for Bose. In a letter published in The *Statesman* of 7 February 1999, BK Bhattacharyya of Guwahati narrated: " ... in August or September, 1956 the Japanese Foreign Minister (Shigemitsu) issued a statement to the effect that Netaji Subhas was alive. Needless to state that we were overwhelmed with joy over the news. It was, however, short-lived as after a few days he contradicted his statement and clarified that what he meant was that Netaji was alive in spirit. Many believed that the Foreign Minister of Japan was under pressure from certain quarters and had to revise his earlier statement."

19 File No 400/INA. No 1300/SE; CSDIC. 21 March 1946.

20 Quoted on page 187 of *Netaji: Dead or Alive* by Samar Guha.

21 File no 273/INA. Extract from written statement by Kinji Watanabe. 15 November 1945. Received with No IAU/1435 from Intelligence Assault Unit, Bangkok. In his deposition before Khosla Commission, Watanabe, however, made no reference to these details.

22 SA Ayer's 5 June 1951 report to the Prime Minister.

23 Bhaskaran Menon was examined by Mukherjee Commission before his death in October 2001.

24 Report C-4, Part IV, dated 8 April 1946. National Archives, Delhi.

25 Netaji Inquiry Commission report 1974. Page 113.

26 *Hindustan Times* report **Soviet outburst against Bose.** 8 January 1946.

27 *Amrita Bazaar Patrika* report **Shah Nawaz report on Netaji called a fraud.** 3 November 1970.

28 *Northern India Patrika* report **Japanese plan for Netaji to seek refuge in Russia.** 7 November 1970.

29 Transfer of Power, Vol VI. Pages 138, 39.

30 IPI series, L/PJ/12/217, folio 108. The British Library, London. Oriental and India Office Collections.

31 The *Times of India* report **Soviet scholars revise opinion on Netaji.** 26 October 1982.

32 Ibid.

33 Dr Purabi Roy's affidavit before Mukherjee Commission. Indologist Yan Rachinski found out that some 45 Indian political activists, including Abani Mukherjee and Sarojini Naidu's brother Birendra Nath Chatterjee, were executed by the Soviets on charges of espionage. *Hindustan Times* story **The truth about Netaji is still out there.** (24 January 2001) quotes Dr Hari Vasudevan as saying that "a number of Netaji's collaborators in Europe were known to have fled to the Soviet Union following the collapse of Nazi Germany. Their fate is unknown. Presumably Moscow also has files on them."

34 Translated into English by Susmita Bhattacharya and published in Scottish Church College's Commemorative volume on Bose.

35 A saviour in the mould of Oskar Schindler, this Swedish diplomat had saved thousands of Jews from the Nazis before he disappeared in Switzerland at the close of the war. Later stories were heard of him being in Siberia, which the Soviets always denied. The Russians eventually admitted that Wallenberg had indeed been kidnapped by the Soviets on suspicions that he was a spy. In 1993 the American Jewish Congress and Swedish and US Governments persuaded the Russian Government to form an international commission to look into facts.

36 Researchers have taken interest in communication between Viceroy Wavell and India Office, and between Jacob Malik and V Kozolov, who was the Russian Ambassador in Afghanistan when Bose arrived in Kabul in 1940. Wavell's letter dealt with some secret matter discussed between Russian Foreign Minister M Molotov and Nehru's emissary Krishna Menon in Paris in September 1946.

37 *Asia and Africa Today*, Edition No 10, 1993, by V Turadzhev. Scottish Church College's Commemorative volume on Bose published its translation by Susmita Bhattacharya.

38 Dr Purabi Roy's affidavit before Mukherjee Commission.

39 Now the Ambassador of India to the United States. According to a *Hindustan Times* report by the paper's foreign affairs editor Pramit Pal Chaudhuri, Sen issued a note verbale to the Russian authorities over the Bose mystery. "Moscow sent a note back, saying nothing doing." "Ronen Sen made it clear that ... (it) was as far as the embassy could go". See **From Russia with silence**. 24 January 2001.

40 *HindustanTimes.com* report **Purabi Roy's appeal on Bose research ignored** by Jaideep Mazumdar. Netaji probe Phase 1.

41 Dr Purabi Roy's affidavit before Mukherjee Commission.

42 The *Statesman* report **Russia has no records on Netaji's "death."** 3 December 1996.

43 Letter No. 1665-EAM/84 from PV Narasimha Rao, Minister of External Affairs, to L Joychandra Singh. Reproduced on pages 156-57 of the book *Sheel Bhadra Yajee* by VL Sundar Rao.

44 Ibid.

45 Chitta Basu has passed away but Jayanta Roy deposed before Mukherjee Commission. The writer met him. Chitta Basu spent years probing the Bose mystery. In 1990s, he sought the help of then Prime Minister Narasimha Rao, HRD Minister Arjun Singh, the Indian Ambassador in Moscow and some officials of the ICHR (Indian Council for Historical Research). The outcome was nil.

46 The *Week* cover story **Netaji Mystery: The Lost hero** by Tapash Ganguly. July 21, 2002

47 From the translation that appeared on 19 July 1997 in the journal *Mainstream* under heading **A Russian Tribute to Netaji Subhas.**

48 Ardhendu Sekhar Sarkar deposed before Mukherjee Commission on 28 September 2000. The writer met him.

49 From Rai Singh's letter published in *Hindustan Times* on 2 Jan 2001.

50 Ibid. Rai Singh appeared before Mukherjee Commission and the writer met him.

51 *Hindustan Times* Big Story **Bose was in Russia** by Sudhi Ranjan Sen. 4 March 2001.

52 Ibid.

53 *With Two Presidents* by Captain CL Dutta. Page 73.

54 *Hindustan Times* Big Story **Bose was in Russia** by Sudhi Ranjan Sen. 4 March 2001. The same story says that a researcher contacted Mikahel Gorbachev over Bose. Gorbachev's foundation had published a book on the activities of a Soviet agent and his dealing with Bose in 1940s. The former USSR premier "evaded a direct answer" to the researcher's query, "and is alleged to have said it was upto both governments to solve the issue once and for all."

9

Nobody's Probe

There has been no positive attempt, it seems, after the statement by the Prime Minister (Desai) in the year 1978 ... for any further or fresh enquiry and no serious effort in this behalf (Bose's disappearance) has been made. It seems lapses have occurred from time to time and public at large is dissatisfied.

Calcutta High Court in its ruling dated 3 April 1998.

What purpose would be served by ordering of yet another enquiry ...?

A newspaper editorial on 29 March 1999.

It is utter nonsense.

Historian Dr Harbans Mukhia's reaction to the formation of Mukherjee Commission.

the matter is very sensitive and important ....

AK Paitandy, Director, Internal Security (Ministry of Home Affairs) in a confidential letter dated 11 April 2000 to Ashok Chaturvedi, Joint Secretary, Research and Analysis Wing (R&AW).

Whatever is relevant on Netaji will be shown to the Commission. But beyond a point, the files cannot be made public. It's too explosive.

Senior journalist Deepak Sharma quoting a Home Ministry official in the *Pioneer* on 23 January 2001.

Samar Guha was beyond his contemporaries. He was an impressive man, a powerful orator and an above average Parliamentarian by all accounts. But what was it that Guha had taken the issue of Subhas Bose death mystery to his heart? Agreed he had had some association with Bose, but there were many around with better record. His peer HV Kamath had been crossing swords with the Government since 1947. Yet, Guha was always different: Surcharged and exceedingly emotional. Before his maiden speech in the Lok Sabha in 1967, he taxed himself so much that he suffered a heart attack. His arguments sounded like he was caught up in a time wrap. Psychologists would have picked up disturbing signs in Guha's not coming to term with the realities. Bose's time was long gone but Guha went on puffing Bose's greatness, always referring to him in the present tense.

"I know that many people feel that I am crazy," he once yelled out to the jeering MPs in the Parliament. "I am a gullible person and I easily believe any kind of rumour about Netaji being alive." Guha knew well what others thought of him. He was forever the same man his friends saw in Rohtak jail during the Emergency. "He was always talking and writing about Netaji," LK Advani reminisced on TV channel *Aaj Tak* while revisiting the jail 25 years later as the Deputy Prime Minister of India.

There had to be a limit to which Guha could go. He waged a long lonely battle and that was bound to bog him down. As he entered in his mid-50s, the frustration of receiving repeated setbacks began to show on him. His pleas to rehabilitate Bose met with little success. The Government did accord some importance to Bose and the INA veterans but the pariah status remained. A commission was formed but its findings poured water over his efforts to prove that Bose had not died in 1945. His reputation downed in public's eye, the ageing revolutionary had hardly begun to prepare for a counterattack when the Emergency was imposed. He made good use of the incarceration to write down his testament, a blow-by-blow rebuttal to GD Khosla's eyewash. But here too he acted strangely. Oddly enough, he titled his book *Netaji: Dead or Alive?* Wasn't the book devoted to proving that there had been no crash in Taiwan? Yes, there was the claim that Bose fled to the USSR, but where from the question of Bose being alive in 1970s came in? In 14 chapters of the book there was no discussion of such sort. So how did Guha justify the title? He touched upon this in the foreword to the book. "What happened to him (Bose) after his escape to Russian territory has not been discussed in this book,"[1] he wrote in a know-all manner. And went on to cite purely speculative scenarios to zero on the one nobody in one's right senses would believe in.

"If Netaji was alive after the alleged air crash, the question naturally arises, is he alive even today? Many probabilities are linked with this pertinent question. Netaji might have met natural death in a Russian prison, or he might have been killed by the Russians as it happened in the case of many other revolutionaries who were kept in the concentration camps of Russia or else he might be still languishing behind the bars of a Russian prison in Siberia, or some other part of Russia. It might also have happened that Netaji succeeded in escaping again from the Russian prison and is living somewhere incognito waiting for an opportune moment, according to his own way of thinking, for reappearance before his countrymen. The author possesses some significant information which indicates that Netaji is still alive. But the author has not said anything about it in this book in support of his belief of Netaji being alive, — for reasons which may become known in the near future."[2]

Subhas Bose living incognito in 1978, waiting for the right time to appear! Now, who was to believe in this twaddle? Commonsense dictated most to not to and indeed they felt that Guha was either out of his mind or up to some cheap publicity stunt. Even some of Guha's supporters felt cheated. After making meaningful arguments for a decade, the erudite professor was talking through his hat. Media had to be rational; so they did not rally behind Guha on this point. "Why is this talk of 'significant information'?" a newspaper editorial wondered. "Why not 'definite and conclusive'? Rather than keep the world guessing, why not those who claim knowledge about Netaji's existence dissolve this recurring phenomena once and for all and prove that they are not bluffing." Guha was not to offer any explanation. But for his this claim, his brilliant book would have received far more acceptance than it did. The editorial continued: " ... what is it that keeps him (Bose) in the hiding? Is it some provision in the international law which threatens some penalty? What is the offence? Or is it something which defies human reasoning for emergence from concealment? Why not persons like Prof Samar Guha act on the 'significant information' they have, and proceed to unravel the mystery once and for all?"[3]

Heedless that his "Netaji alive" claim had damaged the cause, Guha went on with the same gusto. In August same year he was heard reiterating the same claim in the Lok Sabha. Perhaps he thought the situation was ripe: His friends were in the saddle and they had began to show signs that they were on the path to accord Bose's legacy its rightful place. On 23 January 1978 President Neelam Sanjiva Reddy and Prime Minister Morarji Desai unveiled a portrait of Bose in the Central Hall of the Parliament House, fulfilling the demand first made in 1947. Atal Bihari Vajpayee said it was like the nation had "repaid" its debt to Bose though "30 years after independence." It was heartening for his friend Guha to hear the Minister for External Affairs saying the same day at a different venue that "the historians and scholars should find out why the Congress government had done injustice to Netaji by ignoring him all these years."[4]

The importance of what happened in the Lok Sabha on 28 August 1978 never actually dawned on Indians. It was one landmark event that the media failed to break down and explain to the readers. That day Samar Guha forced the Government of India to reverse its stand on Bose's death and discard the accepted findings of two panels it had constituted. For fringe benefits came some statements that were to pave way for the formation of a new commission of inquiry two decades on. The August 1978 debate was the concluding part of a motion moved by Guha in the Lower House of the Parliament on 3 August 1977. The motion had urged the Government to reject the findings of Khosla Commission and set up a new one. On August 28 when Prime Minister Moraraji

Desai braced up to deliver the Government's response, he was weighed down by the sheer force of case Guha had assiduously built up.

Desai had perhaps realised that he was going to get into deeper trouble if some concessions were not made at that stage. "The only other alternative," MP Dilip Chakravarty had stated in August 1977, was "to announce in this session to have a fresh inquiry." Another inquiry meant more debates, more newspaper reports and more demands for declassifying secret files and seeking facts from the USSR and Taiwan. To make the situation complicated, the people who had earlier castigated the Indira Government's actions were now occupying the treasury benches. The same Vajpayee who had shared Samar Guha's disgust about the shenanigans of Ministry of External Affairs over GD Khosla's botched up Taiwan visit was now its boss. Could the Janata Government do what the previous regimes had done? Could Vajpayee follow the footsteps of Swaran Singh to sabotage a judicial commission's work in Taiwan? Could Home Minister Charan Singh, a Bose admirer, tell a commission headed by, say a Supreme Court judge, that Top Secret files on Bose mystery were summarily destroyed and get away with it?

Desai took the middle path, fearing that his Government might not be able to comply with the orders of an upright judge and nor employ artifices of the previous governments. After Home Minister Charan Singh appeared to be giving in, he conceded before the lawmakers that the findings of the earlier probes ran contrary to the evidence on record and new information in secret official papers. Having made clean breast of it, Desai said that "at the same time, Government feels that no useful purpose would be served by having any further inquiry." No, he would not explain the logic of saying so when the earlier findings were fallacious. Instead, the Prime Minister made a personal appeal to Samar Guha. "I hope that in the light of this statement, my honourable friend will withdraw his motion," he said, looking beseechingly into the eyes of the agitated professor. Guha saw in the PM's admission his moment of truth. He rolled back the years of struggle. This was it. "A great day for the whole Indian people," he called 28 August 1978. "Because a mortal sin, a treacherous crime that was committed against the epic hero of Indian freedom has been undone," he told the House as the PM looked on with a baited breath. "If I say Netaji was given burial, out of political conspiracy, it would not be exaggeration. Today, I express my gratitude to the Prime Minister because today ends a crusade that in my humble way I was trying to conduct on behalf of the people of India at least to see that officially and legally Netaji is not declared dead. Now, by undoing the findings of the two reports, at least this much we have achieved that, today, Netaji is neither legally nor officially dead."

Misty eyed and his voiced choaked, Guha then cried his heart out. He put aside the papers. All his articulation was gone. His analytic prowess vanished as he reverted to what he had written in the foreword of his book. And this was in the Parliament, the institution that represented the people of India. "If Netaji did not die in the air crash, then what happened to him?" Guha rhetorically asked. "It is our moral obligation to know what happened to him. The Prime Minister has said that no useful purpose would be served by having a fresh inquiry. I agree. But the reason is different. For me, there is no necessity any more of fresh inquiry. I got the report quite earlier and some important information also from very responsible quarters that Netaji is alive .... Today for me there is no question of indecisiveness in any way. In the name of God, I announce in this House that I know that Netaji is alive."

Shouts and sniggers resounded on all sides, but there was no stopping Guha. Overflow of emotions made his speech incoherent, which was not going to make his case better. "Naturally, my friends will ask the question, why are you not divulging his whereabouts? I am too eager, too impatient to let the country know what I know, but then I have not the freedom yet to disclose what I know .... What I know, if I divulge now then everyone of you will jump up if I say something and if I show you something to prove what I have said. But, I have not the freedom yet. But this much I can say, Netaji is nowhere under duress. He is a free man .... I again pray to God along with all of you so that Netaji keeps well and we get him back in our midst as early as possible."[5]

This went on till the time the Speaker put his foot down. He asked Guha pointedly if he was withdrawing his motion. Fatigue had caught up with Guha, and he resigned himself to the perceptible disbelief in the House in his declaration. As he sat down, he murmured, "There is no necessity of any fresh inquiry because Netaji is alive." The Prime Minister heaved a sigh. Guha withdrew his motion and with that he reduced the potential big bang into a whimper. Guha had let Bose followers down.

There was going to be a third time. A disaster. Five months later, Guha did something that finished off his political career and wiped out whatever credibility he was left with. During the parliamentary debate he had referred to something he had to prove that Bose was still alive. In January 1979 he produced that something — a picture — with much bluster. On 22 January at Calcutta Press Club he brandished a photograph and told media persons, again in the name of God, that "Netaji Subhas Chandra Bose is alive, healthy and free."[6] He said he had no intention of making political gain. "My moral responsibility impels me to let the people know that Netaji is alive."[7] "No more inquiry commissions are needed,"[8] he reiterated.

"While paying our national tributes to Netaji on the occasion of his birthday, let our countrymen offer their prayers to the almighty in temples, mosques, churches and everywhere for his long life and for his early appearance before his beloved countrymen."[9] He held out that photograph. "Let this picture of Netaji taken recently (in India) dispel all certainties and doubts from their minds to know it definitely that their Netaji is living in intense *tapasya* (meditation) for the fulfilment of the unfulfilled mission of his divine motherland."[10]

The photograph was taken in 1978 in a temple the location of which Guha would not disclose. "The opportune moment for (disclosing) this has not yet arrived."[11] He said he had not seen Bose but knew some non-political personalities who had had "the good fortune of seeing him."[12] These people were in touch with him and had supplied the picture to him. He said that he had already shown the same picture to Jayaprakash Narayan and the Lok Sabha Speaker KS Hegde. There were others whom Guha did not name – President Neelam Sanjiva Reddy, Atal Bihari Vajpayee, HV Kamath and Gobinda Mukhoty. Guha claimed that when JP saw the picture in October 1978, he was "overwhelmed with an ecstatic joy and he deemed it to be a proud privilege to have a look at the photo of the great leader who was still alive."[13]

The reporters were not expected to sit quietly after all this. They hurled a volley of questions but Guha did not appear ready to take them. "Please don't cross-examine me. You are at liberty to take it at my word or reject it. I am not authorised to state anything more."[14] "Excuse me, it is not possible at the moment to disclose where he is living."[15] Reporters, nevertheless, plied on Guha and extracted something. "Netaji ... is a Yogi of the highest order .... Netaji will not go the Sri Aurobindo way ... he will appear in public and take to politics again ... the moment Netaji appears in public, there will be a political earthquake in India,"[16] Guha avowed he possessed "a host of information" that "countrymen will know from Netaji himself when he chooses his time to disclose it."[17] He gave away some of it. Bose, he claimed, had been incarcerated in the USSR.

"The story of Netaji's death in an aircrash in Formosa in 1945 was cooked up by his devoted accomplice Habibur Rahman, so as to cover up Netaji's escape from approaching Anglo-American army .... Netaji was in jail for many years in the Soviet Union."[18] Guha hadn't any clue how Bose landed up in a temple in India, but he charged two former prime ministers of playing a villainous role. Desai's statement in the Parliament, Guha said, was "a step towards the present government's undoing of a conspiracy."[19] "The conspiracy of the father and daughter has now been undone by the present Government."[20] Jawaharlal Nehru and Indira Gandhi committed "an unpardonable sin" by misleading "the people about about

Netaji's fate and even undertook to hold a fake inquiry to fraudulently confirm the report of Netaji's death".[21]

The tirade continued till the end of the press conference. "Pandit Jawaharlal Nehru committed the worst treachery ... the people in India would have got the Indian pilgrim back in their midst in 1946. The biggest treachery on the part of the first Prime Minister of India was suppression and concealment of convincing evidence ... suggesting thereby the news of Netaji's death in an air-crash at Taihoku might be a cooked up story circulated to mislead Allied Headquarters and the Government of India."[22] Later in the day, Balraj Madhok came out as the sole man to stand for Guha. Confused though he appeared, the Jan Sangh leader was able to make his point well. "Netaji is alive," he too declared at the same venue and for proof recalled his personal enquiries in Tokyo and Taipei that had led him to believe that Bose couldn't have died in 1945.

The next day, 23 January 1979, all newspapers across India prominently covered Guha's press conference. As expected, the media either downplayed Guha or tore into him. An editorial in the *Tribune* — *Mr Guha's hobby horse* — lamented over the event: "Emotions and reason do not as a rule, go together, and Mr Guha refuses to believe what he does not wish to believe .... Although he is one of several like-thinking Indians, he is the most persistent in his refusal to accept the verdict about Netaji's death. Where sentiments and emotion submerge reason the visible evidence that goes against wishful thinking takes a back seat. The result is a continuing legend sustained by the assumption that what should have happened, but has not, must come about .... The element of mystery is strengthened by the theory of conspiracy, namely that certain senior political leaders after independence, including Jawaharlal Nehru, were against Netaji's return to his homeland and actively connived with a foreign power in circulating the report of his death .... It is pity that political figures like Mr Guha should continue to promote a myth which has no more basis that a loyal and emotional attachment to a great national hero .... The Prime Minister, who is known for plainspeaking should himself show the way by putting the record straight even at this late stage."

In the ensuing Guha-bashing no one noticed that despite a top newspaper calling the Prime Minister Desai to call Guha's bluff, which reflected general mood, the Government clammed up. Here was an MP, making all kinds of absurd claims about Bose being alive and hurling serious charges against two former Prime Ministers, and yet Desai, who knew both Nehru and Guha intimately, did not say anything in contradiction. Same was the case with ailing Jayaprakash Narayan and Atal Bihari Vajpayee, who had been shown the picture.

But Congressmen could not keep quiet. Angered by the charges against Nehru and Indira, some of them decided to take Guha to court. They knew where to hit: Doubts had been cast on the authenticity of the picture Guha had produced. Mediapersons had wondered how could the chemistry professor dare them to do a chemical test on a picture that was an out-and-out fake. A look at it was enough to convince anyone that it was a shoddy trick photography job. The "head" appeared to be poorly touched upon "older Bose." And no matter how many woolen clothes the man in the picture was wearing, as Guha said, the size of the torso was grossly disproportionate. Subrata Mukherjee, general secretary of West Bengal Congress (I) later showed that the "head" was morphed onto a picture of Sarat Bose. Mukherjee dared Guha to prove his claim by producing Subhas Bose as many would like him to.

But then, it was not the claim about Bose that had actually irked the Congressmen. It was an old hat. The pinch was in the vicious charges on Nehru and Indira. On 31 January Additional Chief Metropolitan Magistrate of Calcutta issued summons against Samar Guha for releasing "a false story" about the detention of Bose in the USSR and a fake photograph of his. The defamation case was initiated on a complaint filed by one Lallan Singh. He told the court of a particular assertion of Guha's that had lowered Nehru in the estimation of the Indian people: Bose had written five letters to Nehru from the USSR saying that he wanted to return home, but Nehru, rather than helping Bose, informed the British of Bose's whereabouts. Sharing Singh's revulsion were Congress supporters. They came to his house and said "the accused was a politician" who had "damaged the reputation and character of Panditji for an ulterior motive." Pradip Ghosh told the court that "this imputation against Panditji hurt his feelings ...."[23]

Anyhow, the cases against did not last long, and Guha could never be booked. The people soon forgot about the issue as a bad dream. The media was badly hit. It was almost like the end of the road for them so far as Bose mystery was concerned. The man who was in the forefront of the movement had turned out to be raising false alarms. Little wonder then that in the years to come very little was heard on the issue. Indira returned to power in 1980 and after her assassination her son Rajiv Gandhi became the Prime Minister. The priorities for the media changed. The call of duty was in Punjab, Jammu & Kashmir and Assam. There was no reason to go back to the issue — "dead" for all purposes.

As for Guha, over a period of time, he changed his stand. Not regarding Bose being alive, but regarding a new probe. He could not win any election after 1979. That as Chairman of Lok Sabha's Privilege Committee Guha had been instrumental in sending Indira to gaol for Emergency excesses was hardly the credentials to high life at a time when Indira and her son were ruling the country. Change in the Government gave Guha the chance to revive the issue. He found a sympathiser in President R Venkatraman who took up Guha's requests with new prime ministers. VP Singh was directly approached by Guha and as a result instructions were issued to External Affairs Minister IK Gujral to look into the case. VP Singh Government fell apart, and the new Government saw an old friend of Guha's elevated to the post of Deputy-Prime Minister. Devi Lal received a letter from Guha in February 1991 and he duly sounded Deputy Foreign Minister Digvijay Singh regarding "high level investigation into 'secret documents' on the disappearance" of Bose. Singh's was the only positive official response that Guha received since 1969. He was told that the External Affairs Ministry "has already initiated follow-up action in this regard" and were "awaiting results to our enquiries." The hopes dashed with Chandra

Shekhar's Government going the Charan Singh way and the Congress returning to power with Narasimha Rao as Prime Minister. Guha reminded Rao of his days as freedom fighter and presented his case. He wrote to the last USSR President Mikhail Gorbachev and took up the case with Russian Federation President Boris Yeltsin. His letter to Gorbachev was separately forwarded by two former Presidents — N Sanjiva Reddy and Giani Zail Singh. S Nijalingappa, the grand old former Congress president, too sent a letter to the Russian leader. The letters remained unacknowledged and unreplied. Thus ended Guha's last ditch efforts at the autumn of his life.

Subhas Bose returned in news in 1992 by a miscalculation on the part of Narasimha Rao's government. There was more than what met the eyes in conferring Bharat Ratna to Bose on his 95th birth anniversary. Perhaps the idea was to kill two birds with one stone. One, the Congress party thus would have blotted out the criticism that they had not accorded the due honour to Bose. Two, this may well have started the process of exorcising of the ghost of the death mystery. In tune with the second aim, the Governmental communiqué announcing the award on 22 January 1992 stated that Bose was given the award "posthumously." Acceptance of the award by the Bose family would have amounted to agreeing to Bose's death in 1945. Following this, the Government would have initiated the process of bringing the ashes from Tokyo. This masterstroke, however, boomeranged and led to the opening of a new chapter in modern Indian history.

To Bose's followers and family members the conferment of the award was like picking of the old wounds. The injustice done to Bose, his followers and his legacy could not be whitewashed by one belated gesture. The outrage was vitriolic and universal. Anita Pfaff, Bose's daughter, spoke for all when she said that Subhas Bose "should have been one of the first to receive it!"[24] Why now, she asked, when so many individuals whose standing was nowhere near Bose's stature had long been conferred upon the same title. Rajiv Gandhi, Nehru's grandson, had been declared a Bharat Ratna in 1991, and Dr BC Roy, the man who wanted Suresh Bose to sign Shah Nawaz's report, was conferred upon the title in 1961.

The "posthumous" part became the albatross about the Government's neck. How could they use that word without proving Bose's death? That was the point raised by a young lawyer. Bijan Ghosh thought that what with the inaction of the Executive and the Legislature branch, the redressal was possible only in courts. He approached Calcutta High Court, which noted the national relevance of his writ petition and forwarded it to the Supreme Court. In the meanwhile, a jittery Government had within days of the announcement withdrawn the award. But Ghosh had set his mind on not letting the Government scot-free. He prayed that the Government of India must tell the country how and where Bose had died or else launch a new probe. "Declare full particulars of the whereabouts of Netaji Subhas Chandra Bose from 18th of August 1945 till date on the basis of records and information at their disposal" and "institute a proper investigation" to "furnish full particulars of his stay from 18th August 1945 onwards and his subsequent death and the place and manner of disposal of his mortal remains." Chief Justice MN Venkatachaliah took personal interest in the matter, but the Government was extremely wary of disclosing any records about Bose mystery. They never ever produced even a single record, saying that they were classified, which could have convinced the Supreme Court of India that Subhas Bose had died in 1945.

The order of the apex court which came in 1997 stated that "the sentiments of many people were hurt" by the Government's action. But the court could not do much due to the defeatist stand of the Government, who would not take the bait thrown by Bijan Ghosh. "The matter was closed in the sense that no further steps were taken for the conferment of Bharat Ratna on Netaji Subhas Chandra Bose," was what they had told the court. The judgment stated that "since the award has in fact not been conferred, the question of cancellation or annulment ... does not arise ... the award was, in fact, not conferred and the proposal was dropped. We need not therefore, go into the question whether the word 'posthumously' has been justifiably used in the press communiqué or the wider question whether there is enough material available for reaching the conclusion that Netaji Subhas Chandra Bose died either in the air-crash of 18 August, 1945 or at any time thereafter. This is a wider issue on which undoubtedly in future as in past, there will be divergent views. The real controversy in these proceedings relates to the press communiqué. Since no further steps have been taken in pursuant to the press communiqué and the matter is treated as closed, we declare that the press communiqué should be treated as cancelled."[25]

When the verdict was announced, Inder Kumar Gujral had been elevated to the top job. And Mulayam Singh Yadav was the Defence Minister. Unlike most of his predecessors, Yadav was a Bose admirer. One of the tasks he earnestly undertook was to push for the declassification of over hundreds of INA files. He took his good faith forward and heeding to the pleas of several Indian and Japanese followers of Bose voiced view that he would like to see "Bose's ashes" brought to India. That again stirred the hornet's nest. The All India Forward Bloc (AIFB) turned livid at what they described was a "political conspiracy." Party general secretary Debabrata Biswas gave vent to his anger publicly. On firing line were Prime Minister IK Gujral, SR Bommai and poor Mulayam Singh. "It is ridiculous to assume that Netaji has died when there is no proof to establish that. The Government has to face the mirror and answer some questions. And that too in court. We will take them to the court."[26]

The AIFB leader did not even reflect kindly to the gesture of releasing hundreds of Bose-related files. "Nothing has been declassified. What has been handed over to the National Archives consists only of speeches and sundry unimportant things. What purpose will those serve in unravelling the Netaji mystery? The INA held major discussions with foreign countries to establish diplomatic missions and contacts. Where are those papers? It is as if the history of the INA concerns only Netaji's speeches to PoWs at various gatherings. These papers are a major eyewash.

"The real story is not there in those 900-odd documents. We want all documents on the INA and the alleged plane crash. This Government, and we have no qualms about saying so, is trying to suppress facts and that too at its own peril. A figure like Netaji cannot be played around with. Mr Gujral, Mr Yadav and Mr Bommai will have to do a lot of answering once they are asked to appear in court. They will not easily declassify the secret files. They won't do this for the simple reason that it will mean rewriting India's history. Our history text books tell us that India's freedom was won through ahimsa (non-violence). Now, is that true? If the real story becomes public, then many leaders would be exposed and Indian history would become a 'farce'."[27]

The Government, as usually, was not willing to be sucked into any controversy related to Bose. Their trouble was a blessing in disguise for Bose followers. Just two days after the Defence Minister raked up the ashes issue, on 29 August 1997, quietly the judiciary's door was knocked again. Asim Ganguly pleaded before Calcutta High Court in his writ petition that "without there being a conclusive proof and/or otherwise determined in accordance with law, the Union of India cannot accept that Netaji Subhas Chandra Bose died in Taiwan."[28] This was but an irrefutable fact and the court agreed. Chief Justice Prabha Shankar Mishra and Justice Barin Ghosh consequently ruled on 7 April 1998 that "before accepting the ashes which are allegedly kept at the Renkoji Temple, Japan as that of Netaji Subhas Chandra Bose, the Government shall obtain full particulars and evidence and satisfy itself about the genuineness of the claim that the ashes kept at the Renkoji Temple of Japan are that of Netaji Subhas Chandra Bose and take the people of India in confidence."[29] Even before this could sink in, the same court gave its ruling on a similar but much elaborated and well crafted PIL by advocate Rudra Jyoti Bhattacharjee against the Union of India. The man behind the curtain was advocate Sunil Krishna Gupta, who had rendered much help to Suresh Bose and Samar Guha in writing their books. Chief Justice Mishra and Justice B Bhattacharya in their 30 April 1998 verdict dwelt in detail on the PIL that had been woven around the demands raised by Muthuramalingam Thevar and Suresh Bose in 1956.

The Government had been asked by the petitioner to declassify and disclose all documents relating to Bose, his disappearance and the INA. They were urged to issue a press communiqué categorically saying that Bose's name was not put up in any list of war criminals drawn up after the Second World War. Justices Mishra and Bhattacharya referred to the verdict passed on 7 April and recalled the statement Desai had made on the floor of Lok Sabha in August 1978. They ruled that the statement of the Prime Minister was the official stand of the Government on the issue and the "two deviations/aberrations, however, occurred first when Government of India intended to honour Sri Subhas Chandra Bose by conferring 'Bharat Ratna' award .... and secondly recount by Defence Minister of the country made a statement that Government of India intended to accept the factum of death of Subhas Chandra Bose and bring the ashes which are stacked and kept at Renkoji temple in Japan .... The two aberrations are outside the Lok Sabha. True, one which carried the expression 'posthumoulsy' was a communiqué of the Government of India which in deference to the popular feeling was withdrawn but the other, that is to say the statement of the Defence Minister in respect of the ashes of Netaji was neither a statement in any of the Houses of Parliament nor in communiqué of the Government of India. That was out and out a statement most unwittingly made by the Defence Minister of the country."[30]

The judges then inferred what had been prayed by Bijan Ghosh: "The official stand of the Government of India, thus, is that notwithstanding the reports of the Enquiry Committee and the Commission of Enquiry aforementioned, there are doubts as to the death of Netaji in the manner reports indicated and that there was/is a need to have further probe and enquiry to conclusively establish that Netaji has died, that he died in the plane crash, as alleged, and that his ashes are lying in some temple in Japan."[31]

The judges felt that Government's stand on Bose's death was ambiguous. They ordered the Government to do what it should have done long ago on its own. "Launch a vigorous enquiry in accordance with law by appointing, if necessary, a Commission of Enquiry as a special case for the purpose of giving an end to the controversy."[32] Some political observers averred that the court order had come at an opportune time. In April 1998, Atal Bihari Vajpayee had just begun his second innings as the Prime Minister of India. His unique record was most promising, even from the perspective of Bose mystery. An inimitable link to past, Vajpayee had been in politics since the days of Gandhi, Nehru and Bose. The new Prime Minister took pride in declaring his adoration of Bose and also Nehru. His being the Leader of Opposition for several years, External Affairs Minister in late 1970s and of course a friend of Samar Guha meant that he knew how the previous governments had dealt with Bose, and the death mystery. He did not have to hark back to a bygone era for that; he had undergone an ignominy only the previous year.

On 23 January 1997, at a function at the Red Fort to mark the birth centenary of Bose, he stood up to speak his mind. He did not think the occasion warranted any mincing of words. The Government of Deve Gowda, whose survival depended upon Congress party, had perhaps some inkling of Vajapayee's speech. They couldn't have silenced him in the Red Fort, but the second best option was to cut off his TV appearance. The moment Vajpayee began to talk about the inglorious treatment meted out to Bose by Gandhi and Congressmen, the transmission went off. It did not take many discerning viewers to realise that the speech of the leader of Opposition had been censored. Many grabbed their phones to tell the Doordarshan and newspaper staff of the disgust they felt. The transmission resumed after a gap of almost five minutes when the master orator had finished speaking. The next day, *Hindustan Times* ran a bold editorial *A Goebbels in DD*, chiding the Government and asking it to offer an apology to Vajpayee and explain to the people of India why such a draconian episode had taken place.

A delegation led by Debabrata Biswas met Prime Minister Vajpayee and briefed him about the research done by Dr Purabi Roy. He was told how his predecessors had come in the way of truth. Vajpayee gave them a patient hearing. In time to come, without any publicity, the Prime Minister began taking right steps. His two top Cabinet colleagues started testing waters. Human Resource Development Minister Dr Murli Manohar Joshi made a three-day trip to Kolkata and held informal discussions with some people including Dr Roy. Another meeting was held on 25 May in Delhi. The details never became known but the buzzword went around that the Government meant business. The first clear sign came with the Home Minister LK Advani agreeing to meet a delegation of the AIFB who wanted the Government to quickly set up a new commission of inquiry. Subrata Bose, Sarat Bose's son, emerged from the minister's North Block office to echo the suspicion a chunk of Indians had held for years. "The findings (of a new commission) could prove damning for some senior leaders of the national movements in pre-independence India."[33]

On 18 August 1998, *Hindustan Times* came up with a scooper: The Government, it informed the readers, was "contemplating to either order a fresh probe or publish a 'White Paper' on the dramatic disappearance" of Bose. The signals that the higher echelons in the Ministry of Home Affairs (MHA) emitted thereafter were interpreted by different newspapers in different ways. Calcutta's The *Telegrah* reported on 19 August that the "Home Minister LK Advani has directed the home secretary to approach ... Bose's relatives and his followers in the INA to seek their views on what should be done about the great leader's 'ashes' ...." The report titled *Advani in Netaji ashes return bid* quoted the Home Minister as saying that "the 'ashes' would be brought back to India if the family so desired." Then it downplayed the demands for a new probe saying that the Home Minister "wondered if appointing another commission to probe the matter would serve any purpose. Twenty years ago, former Prime Minister Morarji Desai had rejected a similar demand, saying it would serve no purpose."

Next day, the *Indian Express* presented the accurate picture. The Home Minister had actually kindled the hopes of those seeking a new commission. *Express* captured what appeared to be contradictory signs from the Government's side. "Some reports claimed that Advani hinted the ashes should be brought back to India, while another quoted the Minister as saying that the Government had no intention of bringing the ashes back until the mystery over Netaji's disappearance had been solved." Showing which way the wind was blowing, the report quoted an AIFB leader saying that the "the BJP Government at the Centre had finally found the courage to open the Pandora's box."

Things got slow after the initial burst of events. That was expected given the Government's occupation with many problems including the Kargil war. The mood, as a result, at the time of Bose's 102nd birth anniversary was that of despondency and resignation among his followers. Someone bemoaned that after all "Bose is destined to be, at least officially, a Trotsky of Indian revolution, whom no socio-political change can rehabilitate." The AIFB began to show signs of bitterness for all parties including one they were sharing power in West Bengal. A media report suggested that they "seemed to have developed a little detest about its big political ally, the CPI(M), for its clever indifference on the issue." "Some of the state BJP leaders, who initially spoke with confidence that 'our Government would have the guts to unveil the mystery once and for all and give clearance for the scholars to the thousands of secret documents in Indian and Russian archives,' shy away from queries now." Biswas complained that the political parties were taking advantage of their "lack of strength in the Lok Sabha." "When we talk about Bose, whether it's the BJP or CPI(M) or the Congress, all are united to gag and muzzle the truth," he whined. "Even our friendly United Front Government expressed a strange difficulty in opening the Government documents in archives. The former defence minister Mulayam Singh Yadav, after a lot of pressure, could release about 700 documents and plainly told us that they could not open up the rest, for they were top secret." Dr Purubi Roy shared his feelings. "I had felt that this Government, unlike others, would do something to establish the truth. But now I feel we were made to believe in an illusion."[34]

Bose's followers stepped to press for an inquiry commission after a lull. There was a rally in Delhi on 22 March 1999, where the demand was again raised. The big boost had already come in the form of pro-commission resolutions by West Bengal and J&K Legislative Assemblies following efforts of J&K Chief Minister Farooq Abdullah and Anil Mukherjee, Deputy Speaker of West Bengal Assembly. The Bengal Assembly resolution, passed on 24 December 1998, stated that the people and scholars of India were in dark about Bose's disappearance. It called upon the Union Government to "make necessary arrangements for availability of records in and outside India." Biswas succeeded in taking support of some 30 MPs, including former Defence Minister Sharad Pawar, for the cause. A delegation comprising Bose family members, and activists cum researchers VP Saini, Bose biographers Sitanshu Das and Subodh Markandeya met the Prime Minister on 23 March 1999 and made another representation. The Government had by then given finishing touches to the modalities of forming a new commission.

On March 24, Home Minister LK Advani convened a meeting of nine followers of Bose in the presence of Principal Secretary to the Prime Minister Brajesh Mishra, Attorney General Soli Sorabjee and Home Secretary Kamal Pande. Colonel GS Dhillon, Dr Sisir Kumar Bose, Justice (retd) RS Narula, AIFB's DB Kalamankar attended the meet whereas Captain Lakshmi Sehgal sent her comments in writing. After the meeting it was announced that there was going to be a third commission of inquiry into Bose's death. The next day Legislative Assemblies of Tripura and Manipur too passed motions for the commission, making the demand a national one. Public pressure prevailed on Government of India yet again.

The media's reaction to the Government's decision to form a new commission was nothing to write home about. This time the press failed to rise to the occasion. The journalists who had firsthand knowledge of the issue were no longer around. The new crop of hacks had no reference material at hand. The years of unyielding efforts had also brought about cynicism, which showed in numerous sarcastic write-ups. Editorial writers hit the keyboard without proper homework, relying more on jugglery of words than facts. None had clear idea about what had happened since 1945 and almost everyone confused committee with commission. Taihoku was a strange word to most; someone would not even know where and how Bose had "died," and yet another thought that the BJP Government had out of its free will formed the Commission.

Hindustan Times began in a way which shone like a silver lining. A reasonable editorial on 27 March titled *One more probe* welcomed the probe despite it coming a bit late. The *Statesman* edit on 28 March, on the other hand, lampooned the very idea. *Dead or alive: Politics, Netaji and Bofors* peddled an unwarranted pre conceived notion, which was to adversely affect the new commission's appreciation of media. " .... interesting times lie ahead of the Commission's members," it sneered, expounding that "they will have to travel abroad. To Japan, to Singapore, possibly the entire Far East. To Russia where, according to one school of thought, the leader was put through the Stalinist version of welcome. Why not Germany as well, to reconstruct the submarine ride .... All this constitutes an arduous task. Netaji Commission can perhaps take a few tips from the Parliament Ethics Committee, honourable members of which visited a number of affluent democracies to find out how other countries conduct themselves. There's, of course, the crucial question: who will get to be on the commission, the Forward Bloc, which has spent, its entire career on a single issue, should have the first call. But the CPI-M, which went through a very Marxist volte-face to rediscover Subhas as a patriot — he was initially labeled a fascist — should not be entirely unrepresented. Nor should the BJP, which after all instituted the third inquiry commission on Netaji. If the Congress feels left out, it shouldn't. In case no Congress bigwig is appointed, the principal Opposition party will get an opportunity to question the Right and the Left on one issue: why is scarce public money being spent on a subject that has not been illuminated by any new evidence save the heat generated by a near-irrelevant, regional and small political party."

Same day the *Telegraph*, carried an editorial disparagingly captioned *Much ado about nothing*. Its writer had made up mind that Bose had died in the Taipei plane crash. "The accepted version (sic) is that he died of burn injuries sustained in a plane crash in Taiwan in August 1945 and that his remains are kept in the Renkoji temple in Japan. The matter of Bose's death — or disappearance if one so wants to call it — has been one of the perennial mysteries of modern India and one which invokes strong passion. Matters have not been helped by the Government's secretive attitude. There was an offer a few years back, and by a member of Bose's family, that a DNA test should be done on Bose's remains and then matched with a DNA sample of a member of his immediate family. This would have put to an end to the dispute about the ashes, The Government, then headed by Mr Narasimha Rao, paid little heed to this offer."

While the writer did not see anything suspicious in Government being secretive about an accidental death over 50 years back, he, perhaps out of his political views, chose to attack the Vajpayee Government for obeying the Court's order. "The decision taken by the BJP to set up a commission of inquiry into the mystery of Bose's death is not only belated but also prima facie suspect." And then came the sure sign that the writer was some wisenheimer. Sitting in his cubicle, the writer showed how quickly and easily the mystery could be resolved: "The important question is why a commission is at all necessary. The findings of the Shah Nawaz Khan Commission (sic) and the GD Khosla Commission are gathering dust. A good historian, provided he is given free access to those findings and other evidence, written and oral, and is then allowed to express his opinions without fear or influence, will easily solve the mystery."

The *Tribune* edit exemplified the havoc incomplete information wreaked on facts. On 29 March it screamed *Spare Netaji please:* "What purpose would be served by ordering of yet another enquiry into the disappearance of Netaji Subhas Chandra Bose in South East Asia while mobilising support for the INA?" was the opening sentence. Mind you, there was a new information here: Bose was "mobilizing" support for INA after Japan had been nuked and General Aung Sang had joined the British. The next para made all the more interesting reading. "The nation has more or less accepted the theory that Netaji ... was killed in an air crash and the urn kept in a temple in Japan contains his ashes. It is not that serious attempts have not been made in the past by the government and friends of Netaji to reconstruct the circumstances of the air crash and whether the charred remains were rightly presumed to belong to him."

Then a word for Bose followers and the Union Cabinet: "Without meaning to hurt the sentiments of the countless followers of Netaji it may also be in order to point out that two enquiries have already been conducted for resolving the controversy about his disappearance after the air crash somewhere in the jungle of the South East Asia. The first was conducted by his colleague and confidante, Shahnawaz Khan, in 1956, and the second by Justice BB Khosla (sic) in 1970. Both believed that he was killed in the crash. Yet there are those who insist that a third enquiry is necessary to give the controversy a satisfactory ending! In this context it may be pertinent to point out that a similar question was raised in the Lok Sabha by Samar Guha in 1978. And the reply of Morarji Desai, the then Prime Minister, was that no useful purpose would be served by ordering a fresh enquiry. While taking a decision on the Home Ministry's proposal the Union Cabinet would do well not to ignore Morarji Desai's observation on the issue." Did someone forget that Desai had rejected the findings of the earlier probes?

The *Indian Express'* take — *The Netaji enigma* — was different: "So will the Centre's decision to institute a fresh commission of inquiry once and for all clear the fog surrounding the Indian National Army hero's reported death in a plane crash near Taipei on August 18, 1945? Maybe, given the huge amount of freshly declassified archival material in London, Moscow and Tokyo." The *Hindu* welcomed the probe in its edit *The Netaji legend* on 7 May 1999. "The Union Cabinet's decision to set up a Commission of Inquiry to probe the mysterious disappearance of Netaji Subhas Chandra Bose from Bangkok (sic) over five decades ago may seem odd in the prevailing situation, but it will surely be welcomed by millions of his admirers who believe that the Centre has not done enough to find out the truth."

The reaction of the intellectual fraternity and the Bose family to the Government's decision brought to fore the clashing opinions between those who thought that Bose had died in 1945 and those who felt he had not. On one hand were researchers like Dr Purabi Roy, VP Saini, Sitanshu Das, Bose's niece Chitra Ghosh and nephews Pradip Bose and Subrata Bose. The other side looked much more formidable what with inclusion of renowned historians and those Bose family members and associates who needed no introduction. Leading this group were INA Captain Lakshmi Sehgal and Dr Sisir Bose, Bose's nephew and director of Netaji Research Bureau. Historians went ballistic as soon as it was announced in March 1999 that the matter of Bose's disappearance would be probed afresh. "Why don't we accept that the man is dead and that he died more than 50 years back," Jawaharlal Nehru University's Dr Harbans Mukhia said as he gave vent to his choler over the "waste of time." In Mukhia's progressive worldview "the whole controversy stemmed from the 'old-folk mentality' that great men do not die." He also saw "to some extent" some "political motive behind the Home Ministry's decision" but would not say what it was. "It could be part of a BJP attempt to placate the Left, Right or the Centre — and a fresh inquiry is unlikely to do that either."[35]

Historian Salil Ghosh reckoned the new probe to be a "sheer waste of time and money." "Government is playing a game to please Bengali lobby," was the another shot he had. "At the end of the enquiry, the public should have the right to know about the money and time wasted,"[36] Ghosh, head of Netaji Subhas Celebration Committee of Maharashtra, added. Delhi University historian Dr Sumit Sarkar too upheld the common refrain that "any such inquiry would be a waste of time." Beyond this he did not know what to say so he added that the "subject is so boring and unimportant that I do not even feel like reacting to it."[37]

Purabi Roy took off her gloves on 3 April 1999. In the firing line was Sisir Bose, who was charged with not being serious to know what had happened to his uncle. What had made Roy particularly upset was the rumour that Sisir might be given some place in the new commission. Seething with anger, Roy let out what had up till now been discussed in private circles: "I will file a case in court if Dr Sisir Bose is included in the probe panel," she told the *Pioneer*. "Dr Bose has time and again tried to stall any honest probe and has not allowed any scrutiny of the Netaji Research Bureau activities. I can go on record as saying that he is making money by trying to prove to the world that Netaji died in the air crash at Taihoku. He is also out to prove to the world that the ashes kept in the urn at the Renkoji Temple in Tokyo belong to his uncle. He has a vested interest. .... He is trying to keep the Japanese Government happy at a price tag .... That Government wants to get rid of the urn and the controversy surrounding it."[38] Sisir too went to press, albeit in a sophisticated manner. His reaction in late 1999 followed External Affairs Minister Jaswant Singh's visit to Renkoji temple in Tokyo that had angered many. Not Sisir — he was quite happy. "Enough of controversy over the death of Netaji Subhas Chandra Bose," he said, wondering if the ashes could be brought to Delhi and placed near Rajghat "if possible." "The Japanese have kept it with honour. But why should Netaji's ashes remain there for over 50 years?"[39]

Sisir was vociferous in not seeing anything useful in Purabi Roy's "so-called research" in Russia. "Nothing conclusive was found to dispute Netaji's death in the air crash. All evidence indicates that he died in the air crash. Anything to the contrary is not based on evidence,"[40] was his punch. His son Sugata Bose too joined the fray in near future. He "lashed out at politicians and some social scientists for carrying on an unnecessary and impractical controversy on the so called disappearance of his grand uncle." "As far as I know both as a historian and as a child of the Bose family, there is not even one shred of evidence to prove that Netaji survived the air crash and reached the Soviet Union. All evidence collected so far points to his death in the air crash."[41]

In the midst of arguments and counter-arguments, the Government issued a notification on 14 May 1999, appointing the new Commission. On Chief Justice of India's recommendation, 66-years-old Justice Monoj Kumar Mukherjee, former Chief Justice of Bombay and Lucknow High Courts and then a judge of the Supreme Court, was appointed the Chairman of the one-man probe.

In the later half of 2000, Bose hit the headlines again. On 5 October 2000, the *Indian Express* reported that *Netaji was seen in Siberian 'VIP Camp' in 1948. Hindustan Times* on 29 October carried on page 1 the story captioned *Researchers find evidence Netaji was alive till at least 1946.* The month of January was quite happening. On 23rd, a most caustic statement came from arguably the most famous of INA veteran. It was time to shoot the messenger — Mukherjee Commission — that had brought the bad news. Lakshmi Sehgal told a gathering at Bose's house in Calcutta that the INA leader had died in the Taipei plane crash and there was no need to "set up commission after commission to enquire into his so-called disappearance."[42] The same day, the Prime Minister addressed a gathering in New Delhi and was caught in the debate. He suggested that "the Government was willing to initiate a move in bringing home the ashes of Netaji and keep them in the Red Fort."[43] On 27 January 2001, Debabrat Biswas wrote to him, expressing his displeasure. The reply came on 2 February and in it the Prime Minister made clear where his Government stood on the issue of the 'ashes': "Let me clarify that there is no immediate proposal before the Government to bring the ashes lying at Renkoji temple to India. The reference made to the same was in the context of a volume of correspondence received from different quarters requesting the Government to do the same. Any action in this regard will be initiated by the Government only if there is a broad agreement in this regard. The findings of the Enquiry Commission, of course, will be a fundamental consideration in any such decision."

In a time far cry from the years when ministers chose to talk about Bose's death mystery in hushed tones, Vajpayee's minister publicly aired their apprehensions. Railway Minister Mamta Banerjee announced in Kolkata on January 24 that "the Centre was willing to help the Commission pursue the matter 'objectively' and reach a definitive conclusion about the disappearance of Netaji" and that "the Government will release all documents, whatsoever, asked for by the Commission." Minister of State for Communications Tapan Sikdar got emotional while releasing a stamp marking the 60th anniversary of Bose's great escape. He praised Purabi Roy and touched upon Bose's possible presence in Russia after 1945. But soon Anita Pffaf delivered a jolt. She told The *Times of India* that she believed that her father had died in the crash. In March she came to Delhi and repeated her stand. She told the *Pioneer* that controversy over her father's death was "needless" and an insult to his memory. *Hindustan Times* quoted her as saying that "my father disappeared twice. Once when he fled to Europe. And then he escaped on a submarine to the Far East. So when he disappeared after the air crash, everyone, including my mother, thought he wasn't dead .... Not one of the other theories is convincing. The plane crash is the only reasonably consistent theory."[44]

The *Pioneer* carried a hard-hitting editorial *Truth About Netaji* on 25 January 2001. Based on the documentary evidence given by Dr Roy, it intelligently underscored the need "to unravel the truth about Netaji's fate" as the country "owes it to the leader." The *Statesman* chose to highlight a statement of Sugata Bose in its 25 January edit *Close the chapter: Says Bose's grand nephew.* "What is there left to say about Subhas Bose? We hope that his grand nephew, a historian who teaches at Harvard, had the last word on the subject." On 28 January a PTI dispatch came from London. Of all the Japanese witnesses to Bose's "death," Dr Tenayoshi Yoshimi was the only one to have survived. Yoshimi repeated his yesteryear's claim that Bose had died in Taipei. The news attracted some attention, but many viewed with suspicion the timing and the construction of the copy. It had started with a claim that "the controversy ... has finally ended" despite that a commission of inquiry was functioning. Old timers recalled that in some time before Khosla Commission was formed, the Japanese witnesses had suddenly gone to press to recall their experiences. So the feeling arose in that some "vested interests" were at it again. The editorial writers felt compelled to react to the significant story. The *Hindu* edit on 30 June 2001, *Clearing the Netaji mystery*, read like it was the last word on the mystery:

"The death of ... Bose, taking place as it did in the midst of World War II, was sought to be shrouded in mystery. It may be true that the campaign carried out by a section of those claiming to be Netaji's legatees — that Bose had managed to survive the crash — lacked credibility even at the time when it was initiated .... But then, the political context in which the campaign was taking place — the emergence of Jawaharlal Nehru as the natural leader of independent India and as Prime Minister later on — had given the campaign an unwarranted twist. The narration by Dr Taneyoshi Yoshimi ... must finally put the lid firmly on the decades-long 'controversy' for whatever it is worth .... There were not really many takers for the story that Netaji survived the crash. The story ... was nothing more than a fantasy .... But then, a story of that kind did have its implication (rather, some utility for a section) in the political arena. The legacy of Subhas Chandra Bose was sought to be constructed in a way so that it appeared that there was a permanent conflict between Bose and Jawaharlal Nehru. And it was in this context that tales began to be constructed suggesting that Bose was 'captured' in the Soviet Union; the construction went on to suggest a 'conspiracy' entered into between the leaders of independent India and the regime in the Soviet Union to ensure that Bose did not return to India for ever."

Another interpretation of the development was carried out by the *Tribune*. Apparently, a new editorial writer was at work. "The statement attributed to Dr Taneyoshi Yoshimi," it reasoned, "instead of 'ending' may actually revive the controversy surrounding the circumstances of Netaji's death .... Why the doctor, who lives in northern Japan, broke his silence 56 years after the plane crash in Formosa? It is likely that the report is based on the interview he gave to British intelligence after the crash. However, why the transcript of the interview has been released now through the media in London?"[45]

Around a month later the *Statesman* took a most sensible stand. On 22 August 2001, the editorial *Did the leader die in Taiwan?* raised the moot point. "The question now is not whether he is dead, but whether he died as established by two commissions of inquiry, Khosla and Shahnawaz Khan, in 1945 in a plane crash in Taiwan .... The archives in Moscow must be thoroughly consulted and eye-witnesses found to establish the truth of Bose's sojourn in the Soviet Union."

The net result at the end of it all — this clutter of coverage in the press — was that after a very long hiatus Bose mystery made a comeback.

Notes:

1 Samar Guha's note in *Netaji: Dead or Alive?* Page IX.

2 Ibid. Pages IX, X.

3 The *Nagpur Times* editorial **Mystery deepens.** 14 March 1978.

4 The *Times of India* story **Nation has repaid Netaji's debt: Vajpayee.** 24 January 1978.

5 Quoted from the record of the Lok Sabha debate on 28 August 1978.

6 *Hindustan Times* report **Netaji alive, coming any day: Guha.** 23 January 1979.

7 Ibid.

8 The *Hindu* report **Netaji alive, claims Janata MP.** 23 January 1979.

9 *Hindustan Times* report **Netaji alive, coming any day: Guha**. 23 January 1979.

10 *Amrita Bazar Patrika* report **Netaji is alive, claims Guha.** 23 January 1979.

11 The *Hindu* report **Netaji alive, claims Janta MP.** 23 January 1979.

12 *Indian Express* story **Netaji is alive, says Samar Guha.** 23 January 1979.

13 *Amrita Bazar Patrika* report **Netaji is alive, claims Guha.** 23 January 1979.

14 Ibid.

15 *Hindustan Times* report **Netaji alive, coming any day: Guha.** 23 January 1979.

16 Ibid.

17 *Indian Express* report **Netaji is alive, says Samar Guha.** 23 January 1979.

18 Ibid.

19 Ibid.

20 *Hindustan Times* report **Netaji alive, coming any day: Guha.** 23 January 1979.

21 *Indian Express* report **Netaji is alive, says Samar Guha.** 23 January 1979.

22 *Amrita Bazar Patrika* report **Netaji is alive, claims Guha.** 23 January 1979.

23 *Amrita Bazar Patrika* report **Samar Guha summoned.** 31 January 1979.

24 *Hindustan Times* report **India has done too little for Netaji, feels daughter.** 23 January 1998.

25 AIR 1997 Supreme Court 3019. Spl Leave Petn (c) No 628 of 1994 with Transferred Case (C) No 7 of 1994 D/4.8.1997.

26 The *Pioneer* report **FB to sue Govt on bid to get Netaji's ashes.** AIFB, however, never fulfilled that pledge.

27 Ibid. Historian Dr RC Majumdar rejected the official version that credited Gandhi with winning freedom through Quit India Movement. His version was that the movement fizzled out much before 1947 and was disowned by Gandhi and Congress when it turned violent. Gandhi later apologised to the British for the "madness" of the people who had taken part in the Quit India Movement. The writer has seen papers to this effect, and that the role played by Bose was the chief internal reason for the British to quit India.

28 WP No 1805 of 1997. In the High Court at Calcutta.

29 Ibid.

30 WP NO 281 OF 1998. In the High Court at Çalcutta.

31 Ibid.

32 Ibid.

33 The *Statesman* story **Disappearance of Netaji — Advani asked to reopen probe.** 12 August 1998.

34 *Indian Express* story **Bose mystery still unresolved as leaders shy away from queries**. 24 January 1999.

35 *Indian Express* story **Historians dismiss Netaji dead probe.** 29 March 1999.

36 The *Pioneer* report **'Bengali lobby' & Netaji probe.** 28 March 1999.

37 *Indian Express* story **Historians dismiss Netaji dead probe.** 29 March 1999.

38 The *Pioneer* report **Netaji disappearance probe runs into rough weather**. 3 April 1999. The writer found out that the Government had sanctioned Rs 3,00,00,000 during 1996-1997 towards corpus fund of the Netaji Research Bureau.

39 The *Times of India* report **Netaji is dead, bring his ashes home: Sisir Bose.** 1 December 1999.

40 Ibid.

41 The *Times of India* report **Netaji didn't survive air crash: Grand nephew.** 15 January 2001.

42 The *Hindu* report **Centre to release all documents on Netaji.** 24 January 2001.

43 *Hindustan Times* report **Govt ready to help bring back Netaji's ashes: Atal.** 24 January 2000.

44 *Hindustan Times* report **Stop the search, Netaji is dead.** 9 March 2001. Anita's views on Bose's death and ashes were not shared by majority of Bose family members, most of whom were well-versed with facts. In a letter to Prime Minister VP Singh in May 1990, Bose's nephews Asoke Nath Bose, Amiya Nath Bose and Subrata Bose urged Singh to "not to allow the 'so-called ashes' of the illustrious son of India to be brought to the country from Japan." Amiya Nath Bose told press that "Netaji's entire family was convinced that he had not died in an air crash. The ashes (kept in Renkoji temple) belonged to an unknown Japanese." Amiya charged that "certain interested persons were keen on bringing the 'ashes' and 'foisting on the Indian people'." See *Hindustan Times* report **Netaji's kin plead to PM on ashes.** 13 May 1990.

45 The suspicions were further stoked when Justice Monoj Kumar Mukherjee questioned Dr Yoshimi about the "new" death certificate he had issued in August 1988, and which was given much publicity by some Indian activists/researchers who upheld the Taipei crash.

10

Turning Point

It was indeed a leap in the dark. From this leap he did not return.

Shah Nawaz Committee report on Bose's 'abortive' bid to escape to the USSR in 1945.

Had Netaji been alive he would have definitely come to the country ....

Former Prime Minister Morarji Desai in 1983.

He is alive — in India.

Subhas Bose's close associate Leela Roy to his best friend Dilip Kumar Roy in 1963.

My shot at trying to do something about the mystery of Netaji's disappearance was flukey. On one gloomy day in the *Hindustan Times'* record room, I discovered that time travel was possible. I traversed through the years with the old *HT* editions — 15 August 1947, 30 June 1948, 26 January 1950 — getting the "first hand" feel of those important days in the life of our nation. The August 1945 file looked like it hadn't been touched. I opened it. The 19 August 1945 edition had to have the news of Netaji's death, but there was none. Wondering why, I flipped on and located the death story on 25 August 1945. A full seven days after the Taipei crash. I ran my eyes down the longish 2-column story, and by the time I was finished, I thought I had made a discovery. The mystery about Netaji's death had crept in on the day his death was reported. It was not, as I would think, a 1950s development.

"What's new in it?" my editor asked and I did not know enough to make my point. Luckily for me, it came into his head in January 2001 when some senior colleagues filed stories on Netaji mystery. He made a splendid collage and my story sat at bottom. My effort appreciated, I closed the chapter on a happy note and forgot about my doing anything else about the mystery. Things changed with a new general manager and an editor taking over *HindustanTimes.com*. Sanjay Trehan and Shailesh Shekhar in turn hired Shali Ittaman. This man had some knack for thinking big. He came to *HindustanTimes.com* with Netaji mystery on his mind. He proposed to launch an investigation. The idea was okayed, and my colleague Vijaya Sharma and I were roped in. Shali single-handedly prepared the ground — the best part of which was his roping in an authority of a man on Subhas Bose.

Sitanshu Das had lately released a product of his ten years' inter-continental research that had begun on the advice of Rajmohan Gandhi. *Subhas: A Political Biography* had created waves for its incisive perspective of events that had shaped Bose's struggle. Das was not one of those archetypal wimpish researchers who would not touch this politically sensitive issue even with a bargepole. He had held senior positions in the *Indian Express, Tribune, Patriot* and The *Times of India*. He had made his mark while being on the editorial board of the Fabian Society's journals and his membership of the Royal Institute of International Affairs and International Institute for Strategic Studies in London had broaden his horizon. Oblivious though he was to Internet, he had been a member of the *BBC* programme Advisory Committee and a broadcaster on the British and other foreign TV/radio networked. But this impressive résumé was of no use if Das hadn't had the drive to know the truth. Luckily for us, he also turned out to be quite unassuming and willing to work and tolerate younger colleagues. In his admiration for Bose, Das was still the same teenager who had stood waving the Congress flag as Subhas Bose, the Congress president, arrived in Ramgarh in 1940.

Having received the go-ahead from *Hindustan Times* Editor Vir Sanghvi, we commenced the investigation with a smartly designed announcement. Shali, the copy writer, packed in it the inseparable emotional and political overtones. "Arise countrymen," he hailed and began building up the case "that no Indian can ignore." "Fifty-six years and many inquiries later, India still has no epitaph for the man who almost brought freedom to its doorstep in 1945. All because one question remains unanswered: Did Netaji die in an air crash on August 18, 1945?

"*Hindustan Times* opens a public probe into one of the most enduring mysteries of free India. On August 18, the public will rendezvous online to try and end this mystery, and to thereby, free India from its curse of 56 years — the curse of ingratitude. The work is elaborate and the mission is important. *Hindustan Times* urges all Indians to come forward and help organise the task at hand .... Needless to say, dark secrets may spill during the campaign. It is history's mandate and history will call to account even those leaders it had declared as men of character .... If in so doing, the man on the pedestal falls or an icon breaks, God help us Indians!"[1]

The response was overwhelming. We got to hear from a lot of ordinary and special people. D Dasan who as young Tokyo Cadet of INA had taken "Netaji's ashes" to Renkoji temple contacted us immediately. INA veteran Captain LC Malik told us of his belief that Bose had not perished. Captain Ganeshi Lal of INA intelligence recalled a Japanese officer telling him that "the crash story is false". He also affirmed that if Habibur Rahman "was under an oath by Netaji not to reveal the truth he would not have done so till his dying days!" Of course, there were many who expressed belief in the Taipei crash. BJP stalwart KR Malkani discussed a number of theories including an Anglo-American hand. Madan Lal Verma of Delhi, a wireless operator for the Royal Indian Air Force in 1945, revealed that the British had come to know of Bose's "death" days before it was announced by Domei news agency. For he himself had intercepted a Morse code message from Taipei to Tokyo stating

Bose's death. Verma added that the "Japanese would send 'dummy' messages to confuse Ango-American intelligence agencies." VK Kaul, a former IB Deputy Director, admitted that he had spied on his friend, minister and INA's Major General JK Bhonsle over the death mystery in early 1960s. He "submitted a full account of the matter as recounted by General Bhonsle" to BN Mullick. "It was seen by the highest officers before being returned to me as the originator, for filing. It may be still in the old files," Kaul candidly wrote.

Subodh Markandeya, senior Supreme Court advocate, gave us permission to publish his paper on Bose's death, *Darkness at Dawn*, which had been censored during the Emergency. Researcher VP Saini provided plenty of gunpowder. All India Forward Bloc's Debabrat Biswas and Anil Mukherjee were real help, and Dr Purabi Roy visited our New Delhi office. The Bose family too heeded the call. From Germany, Bose's grandnephew Surya Kumar Bose gave us the "first-ever known reaction" of Emilie Schenkl. Suresh Bose's daughter Shiela Sengupta turned up in the office and had us hooked for hours. Her brother Pradip Bose, a close observer of the issue since the 1960s, cleared numerous points.

For the backgrounder, just three people in all working round the clock gathered and put online all the relevant material that could possibly be collected in about one month's time. The reports of Shah Nawaz Committee and GD Khosla Commission, scanned reports of old *HT* issues from 1945 onwards, pictures of the air crash etc. Sitanshu Das wrote essays on "India in World War II" and Shali pieced together the circumstances leading to the alleged death of Netaji in Taipei. Das also penned scholarly editorials, the likes of which had not appeared before. In *Deal with Bose on the spot* he explained the situation Bose was in at the end of the War. "Bose knew that he was in a veritable snake pit. It is necessary to bear this fact in mind when the story of his death in an air crash on August 18, 1945 is read." Germane to the probe was his elucidation *Time we unravelled Netaji's 'death' story*. "Why is it so important to know what happened to Subhas Bose?" he put forth and squeezed in a few lines the tragedy that had befallen on India. It was not a question of an individual; destiny of India had changed with Netaji's disappearance.

"Yes, it is true that the absence of a relatively young leader at the time when undivided India's future was being decided made a qualitative difference to what happened to India in 1947. Furthermore, what happened then has very largely decided the kind of country we now are .... Generations of Indians have been nurtured on simple-minded narrations of events and developments, with the result that new Indians are a bewildered people ... had our post-independence narrations been more truthful, these new Indians could have known that we were not always 'like this' .... Blatant efforts have been made to misrepresent him (Bose) — to conceal facts in the musty vaults of secret archives in order to spawn myths of modern demonology. History has been portrayed in monochrome."

The *Hindustan Times'* web site announced that "we are forced to conclude that on present evidence it would seem improbable that Bose died on August 18, 1945." Make no mistake, we did not "report" or put words into somebody's mouth. No reputed daily had ever dared to take such a decisive bold stand on this explosive issue. The readers, including Bangladeshis and Pakistanis, reacted favourably all through. The stories shot to the top slots of most read Indian stories on the Internet. In Americas, the Gulf, Europe and elsewhere mostly young Indian professionals spent considerable time to go through them. Many of those who wrote back appeared to be angry with Nehru, and unfortunately Gandhiji, with some even charging them of having a hand in Netaji's disappearance. The flip side, however, was that the *HT* probe failed to initiate a domino effect as we had counted on. The other media simply ignored the Netaji mystery. Such a view of a calamitous national issue reeked of hubris.

When the *HT* probe came out with its findings, Justice Mukherjee Commission of Inquiry (JMCI) had entered the third year of its existence. It had been formed on 14 May 1999 for a period of six months. During this period the Commission was virtually without an office. Then they could not draw any amount up to the end of the November 1999 due to "some procedural snags." The notification announcing the appointment of a Secretary to the Commission could be announced only in late October 1999. As a result, the notice of the Commission, seeking help from all on Bose's disappearance, was published on 3 December 1999. Were these teething problems? Hmm. I had off the record talks with government officials. They were evasive and uneasy about the new probe. Those from the IB and the R&AW refused to say anything more than that the matter was sensitive. The ensuing events were shocking but the media glossed over them. Yes, there were silver linings: Pabitra Ghosh of *Bartaman*, Santanu Banerjee of the *Indian Express* and Anindya Sengupta of the *Statesman* kept people informed. Justice Mukherjee learnt at the very outset that the Government of India was not going to be proactive. He had expected that at least the Ministry of Information and Broadcasting would play a constructive role in relaying the news about the Commission's work. Nothing of such sort happened and having failed to see the officials see reason, Mukherjee shot a long letter to I&B Minister Arun Jaitley on 14 April 2000.

"The DAVP was ... requested by the Commission through the Ministry of Home Affairs to ensure that the Notifications got wide publicity through the national and regional channels of Doordarshan and Akashvani. As it appears, the matter was not telecast or broadcast by the Doordarshan or the Akashvani at the national level. I strongly feel that the authorities of Doordarshan and Akashvani did not give due importance to the matter .... Accordingly I wrote a d/o letter ... to Sri Rajib Shah of Prasar Bharti Corporation of India ... requesting him to take necessary steps .... Unfortunately, no visible action has yet been taken on that d/o letter .... It is really a matter of regret that Sri Shah did not even show the minimum courtesy of giving a reply to my d/o letter although the letter was sent by fax and post ...."

Soon Justice Mukherjee was embroiled in frustrating negotiations. The Government, he discovered, was not interested in hearing out any witnesses. It was as if they already knew what had happened to Bose. The Commission specifically directed on 22 March 2000 to "send a representative of the Government or request the Additional Solicitor General stationed in Calcutta to attend the meeting on their behalf."[2] When until 28 September 2000 there was no sign of anyone, the Commission was forced to state that "since, neither any officer of the Government of India nor any Counsel on their behalf is present nor has any communication been received to explain their stand in this regard, the Commission is left with no other alternative but to presume that the Government of India do not intend to examine any witness."[3] When he saw the Governments of India and West Bengal to be faltering, Justice Mukherjee reprimanded them. Comply with orders or the Commission would "invoke the provisions of the Section 5(4) of the Commission of Inquiry Act, 1952, against the recalcitrant officers of the Government, both Central and State," was one such stern message. "The orders/directions passed ... by the Commission are in exercise of statutory — and not administrative powers,"[4] the Governments were reminded.

The first major roadblock JMCI had hit upon was the violation of the instruction that governmental responses must be accompanied by "affidavits filed by an officer not below the rank of Joint Secretary." The Prime Minister's Office was the first to flout the order. The Commission duly snubbed the PMO: "The Prime Minister's Office has sent an affidavit sworn by an Under Secretary of that office .... The Commission therefore does not take any notice of the contents thereof; and calls upon the said office once more to strictly comply with the orders/directions .... "[5] The malaise was widespread. The Centre and West Bengal Government showed paradoxical unease in parting with the documents required by the Commission to get the basic inquiry started. There was no way Justice Mukherjee could have moved an inch without the aid of official papers on the mystery now that almost all the witnesses had departed. West Bengal Home Department became too possessive about certain Index Books concerned with Bose. The Union Ministry of Home Affairs was finding it impossible to trace even "the complete original records of the proceedings of Justice Khosla Commission of Inquiry, including the evidence recorded by and documents produced before the said commission."[6] The Ministry of External Affairs was clueless where in the world the records of the proceedings of Shah Nawaz Committee had disappeared. Both Intelligence Bureau and Research and Analysis Wing[7] were shying away from filing affidavits before JMCI over an issue that most journalists felt was dead as dodo.

When the information began to trickle in, stunning riders accompanied them. The PMO sent some "Top Secret/Secret" files to the Commission on 24 July 2000 with a request that the " information contained in the 'Top Secret' papers may be made use of by the Commission, in camera, since these are classified as 'Top Secret,' they may kindly consider not publishing the same."[8] The Commission gave it back to the PMO. What was there to fear? Why should they do so, they asked, when "the Commission is holding a public enquiry and its report will be a public document and the contents of those files may have an important bearing?"[9] At times it was impossible to even elicit a response. On 25 August 2000 the Government was told to furnish a copy of the report of a said inquiry into the Taipei crash by the Taiwan Government at the behest of Jawaharlal Nehru to Chiang Kai-shek. The same letter asked for a copy of the report dated 31 December 1945 of CSDIC sleuth BC Chakraborty countersigned by his boss Colonel Stevenson. The Government was reminded that this report was "referred to in the published report of the (Khosla) Commission,"[10] so it had to exist. No answers came; the Government just clammed up.

Some revelations by the PMO put a stamp on the conspiratorial angle to the mystery. At the Commission's instance, the office owned up that some very crucial files on the Bose mystery had been destroyed. So, on 25 August 2000, Justice Mukherjee instructed the PMO to "produce immediately Xerox copies of the orders of destruction of files/documents concerning Netaji Subhas Chandra Bose as also Xerox copies of the list of files/documents destroyed."[11] They wanted to know who had ordered the destruction of these files, why and under what rules. The reply from the PMO on 21 September stated that "no order as such regarding destruction of files/documents could be located." That is, several secret files on Bose — all originating in Nehru's times — had been destroyed in gross violation of rules. The Commission asked the Government to make available the "contemporary official documentary records" because of which Prime Minister Moraraji Desai had given in to Samar Guha in the Lok Sabha. The PMO's answer on 18 December 2001 was bewildering. "Due searches were made in this office to trace any 'contemporary official documentary records' based on which the then Prime Minister had made the statement on the floor of the Parliament on 28 August 1978," Joint Secretary Jarnail Singh stated. "But no such records could be found in this office." The (PMO) "is not in a position to provide any clarification/explanation regarding the circumstances under which Late Moraraji Desai, then Prime Minister, had made such statement on the floor of the Parliament."[12]

Well, no Prime Minister would ever make a statement in Parliament without due checks of official records. Desai was not being whimsical when he had referred to "contemporary official documentary records." These records existed, Justice Mukherjee later found out, but had vanished. Someone in the PMO, prior to Vajpayee's time, had obliterated the trail of an anti-national act.

The antics of the Ministry of Home Affairs, the repository of sensitive information, also gave rise to suspicions. The Director of Internal Security in the Ministry filed an affidavit on 20 June 2000 saying that the ministry had only two files on Bose and that "those files do not have any direct bearing on the on-going Inquiry." In private, the Commission's officials scoffed at this 'joke.' Just two files on an international controversy that had been boiling for over five decades! The Commission was disinclined to go by the Ministry's word, showing their distrust in the Government as regards Subhas Bose. Justice Mukherjee ordered the MHA to nevertheless "submit those files before the Commission immediately." What the ministry did then was unimaginable. They cited a number of laws to state that they couldn't comply with this order. Home Secretary Kamal Pande filed two affidavits claiming privilege under the Evidence Act and Article 74 (2) of the Constitution, which barred disclosure of any record containing advice rendered by Ministers to the President of India. In his supplementary affidavit of 27 April 2001, Pande stated he wouldn't "produce the said records or disclose their contents or give any evidence derived therefrom." A consummate and thorough "No!" The reasons lay in the contents of the listed documents of early 1990s comprising views of top bureaucrats and ministers on the controversy on Bose's death, Renkoji temple ashes and the decision to bestow Bharat Ratna on Bose. Kamal Pande made an enumeration of the rules that barred disclosure of the "Secret/Top Secret" files of such type. These "are unpublished official records relating to affairs of State, and contain communications made to public officers in official confidence. The disclosure of the records would cause injury to the public interest ... the records ordered to be produced also belong to the classes of documents which it is the practice to keep secret for ensuring the proper functioning of the public service."

But what was in these two files that needed to be kept secret in year 2000? It seems that Narasimha Rao Government had done some clandestine firefighting following the Bharat Ratna fiasco. In the process, the Ministry of Home Affairs, External Affairs and the Director of Intelligence Bureau, in early 1990s, prepared reports on Netaji death controversy and the ashes in Japan. In late 1993, Russian magazine *Asia and Africa Today* began carrying articles on Bose, and, despite their public posturing of disinterest, the Government was quick to take note of the news breaking in Russia. VK Jain, Special Secretary, MHA, wrote to Foreign Secretary K Srinivasan and the R&AW on 18 March 1994 "regarding disclosure made in a series of Articles based on classified KGB records." R&AW prepared a report (No. 11/1/94-IC-2829) on 25 March 1994, and, around a month later, Home Secretary NN Vohra (of "Mission Kashmir" fame) wrote to K Srinivasan. Simultaneously, Vohra wrote to AN Varma, Principal Secretary to the Prime Minister, ıegarding "controversy regarding Netaji's death and bringing his ashes to India from Japan."

By mid-May preparations had been made for the issue to be thrashed out by the Committee of Secretaries (COS), the apex bureaucratic body of India comprising the Secretaries of Defence, Foreign, Home and Finance. Eventually, Cabinet Secretary Zafar Saifullah took a meeting of COS on 11 July 1994 to consider "the Cabinet Note about controversy about Netaji's death." On 20 July there was another meeting, this time of the "Core Group," to brainstorm on the "COS Note on controversy about Netaji's death." Hadn't the top officials of India anything better to do than to discuss a 53-year-old accident? On 9 September new Home Secretary K Padmanabhaiah wrote to AN Varma and on 2 February 1995 a note had been prepared for the Cabinet over a "proposal to bring the mortal remains of Netaji from Japan."

By 14th "a contingency plan for proper upkeep of the mortal remains" at Renokji temple had been put in place. Was the Government expecting some crisis? DO letter No.67/3/1/95-Cab of 2 July 1996 from D Dasgupta, Additional Secretary in the Cabinet Secretariat, dwelled on "directions of the Cabinet on the question of bringing the mortal remains of Netaji from Japan". In November, S Prakash, Joint Secretary, MHA, wrote to PMO over "mithochondrial DNA analysis of the ashes presumed to be of Netaji." "Presumed"? This belied the prevalent feeling that the Government was not alive to the proposition of a DNA test. They applied their brains to the mithochondrial technique barely 3-4 years after it was adopted by America's Federal Bureau of Investigation (FBI). DO letter No.67/3/1/95-Cab dated 3 July 1997 detailed directions of the Cabinet on bringing the ashes to India. And finally, an undated communication from Home Minister SB Chavan to Prime Minister Rao, the man who wouldn't speak up, discussed the prospects of bringing the Renkoji temple ashes to India.

Home Secretary Kamal Pande had to know what this was all about. He browsed through the two files and possibly the documents connected with them, and spelt out the reason they could not be handed to the Commission which was inquiring into a matter of public importance.

"I have carefully examined the documents ... and I am bonafide satisfied that the disclosure of the documents would cause injury to the public interest and the public interest would suffer thereby. I believe that disclosure of the nature and contents of these documents would also hurt the sentiments of the people at large and may evoke wide-spread reactions as these documents if disclosed may lower the image of Netaji Subhas Chandra Bose. Diplomatic relations with friendly countries may also be adversely affected if the said documents are disclosed."

We at *Hindustan Times* came to know about these developments at a time we were veering around accepting the crash story. But what with all these details, missing files and excuses offered by MHA and PMO, in a separate affidavit, we began to smell a rat. True, these records had not hinted anything contrary to the crash theory, but the perplexity with which the Government had sat up to take note of some articles in Russia was very very fishy. In particular, the part about lowering Bose's image was off putting. Sitanshu Das summarised the propaganda unleashed against Bose and discounted any possibility of anything which could lower his image in the eyes of Indians. That there was something in those two files which would affect India's relations with friendly nations too would not make any sense to us. The article I quickly wrote afterwards on Pande's affidavit was product of a suspicious mind. In hindsight, I missed wood for trees.

The points where I think my thinking was right were: These two files were the tip of the iceberg the Government did not want to be exposed to the people. Had they made available these files to Commission, Justice Mukherjee could have called upon the civil servants and ministers mentioned therein and asked them disturbing questions. The prospect of people like Narasimha Rao being grilled would have electrified media and brought the much-needed attention to the Commission's proceedings. Second, the Commission would have certainly asked for the official inputs/documents on the basis of which the IB, R&AW, COS, MEA, MHA and PMO had thrashed out their strategies, as enumerated in the two files. Obviously nobody learnt about Netaji's disappearance as students.

We reeled under shock having found out that some of the most credible upholders of the Taipei crash theory were bluffing. (At this time I hadn't been informed by the ROC Government that this crash had never taken place.) Like all Indians, we had great regard for Sisir Bose, the most famous among Netaji's relatives. We discussed the whole gamut of issues with Dr Purabi Roy, but did not touch upon her charges on Dr Bose. In him we saw a link to Netaji and so he was above board. It all shattered when we discovered that Dr Bose was not willing to tell Mukherjee Commission on oath what he had been publicly saying. He had repeatedly said over the years, specially since 1985, that his uncle had died in Taipei crash and that his ashes must be brought to India. He had been dismissive of the new Commission and its work. His views were most respected. He was so dignified. He was not just a nephew of Netaji's, but also his biographer and a custodian of his legacy. Such a man would have known better.

Extremely strange then that Dr Bose did not put his money where his mouth was. It was expected of him to follow others and file an affidavit detailing the reason he had formed that view and help the Commission and the nation. When he did not, the Commission summoned him. He refused to appear. The nephew showed no inclination to cooperate with the inquiry into his uncle's fate. "Since the end of World War II in August 1945 till to day I have not received any direct information from him (Netaji) or about him," he instead cryptically wrote on 22 September 2000 to Pradyot Kumar Sengupta, Secretary to the Commission. "I have no personal knowledge as to the issues referred to the Commission. I am therefore not competent to depose in this matter."[13] He went on to add that "as an octogenarian with a serious heart ailment, such appearance may prove to be an uncalled for health hazard" for him.

Concerned as it was only with the legalities, the Commission decided that "no useful purpose will be served by examining him (Sisir)." Which meant that Sisir, on the basis of his own admission, was not to be taken seriously over the mystery. But to us this was not what we had expected from that man who had risked his neck for Netaji in 1941. If Sisir knew nothing concrete, why he kept on making statements in media that Taipei crash had taken place? His not hearing about or from his uncle since the end of the war did not necessarily mean he had died! We checked up old references and found out that unlike most of his relatives, who were not too happy at his stance, Sisir and his Netaji Research Bureau had been consistently countering any piece of information that went against the crash news.

Maybe Dr Purabi Roy was right! I was told that Sisir had visited Taiwan in 1960s and possibly found out what others did. But he did not depose before Khosla Commission. It was a common knowledge in the Bose family that Sisir's father and mother had died "waiting" for Netaji to return. Why and on what grounds did Sisir then perpetrate contradicting stories? The illness he had referred to in his letter was unfortunately there. But then, he could have given his views in writing or requested the Commission to organise a sitting at his residence. For issue as serious and historically important as this one, Samar Guha and Major E Bhaskaran requested Mukherjee Commission to examine them in their houses. Both were octogenarians and in the last legs of their lives. Inflicted by a grievous paralytic stroke, Guha was not in a position to walk when PK Sengupta saw him in Kolkata. A blind and bed-ridden Bhaskaran lay quietly when Sengupta called on him in his daughter's residence in Chennai.

Not only late Dr Sisir Bose, his wife Krishna Bose, a former Congress MP, and their pompous son, Professor Sugata Bose, engaged in activities that undermined the work of Mukherjee Commission. Sugata Bose made statements reflecting his dislike for Justice Mukherjee's inquiry. The Commission summoned him to appear before them on 28 March 2001 so that he could spell out his stand for the benefit of the nation. The professor was busy with his work in America, so the Commission requested him "to send an affidavit duly sworn by him in respect of his contention that there is strong evidence that Netaji Subhas Chandra Bose was tragically killed in the aircrash in Taipei on 18th August, 1945 and that there is absolutely no evidence that

Netaji was spotted in a variety of places subsequent to that day."

"He was further requested to furnish to the Commission Xerox copies of all evidence collected by Dr Sisir Kumar Bose as stated by him in his aforesaid letter dated 2.2.2001. He was also requested to keep the Commission informed of his programme of next visit to India well ahead so that he could be examined in India as a witness if the Commission thought it necessary. No response to the Commission's said letter dated 23.2.2001 has yet been received from Prof Bose," the Commission strongly stated in its Status Report dated 2 April 2001. Sugata did reply, but without detailing any "evidence" collected by his father. Both he and his mother never appeared before the Commission.

The next example in the league was of the person who symbolized the INA. Like Sisir Bose, Captain Lakshmi Sehgal too had been going all over making statements that Netaji had died in 1945. She had been quite clear about it and had not bothered to read what Suresh Bose had written in *Dissentient Report.* But despite her strong conviction, she had not felt the need to tell Shah Nawaz Khan and GD Khosla what all she knew. The earlier panels did not summon her, but Mukherjee Commission did. They noted her assertion that the Renkoji remains were of Bose's as was published in the *Ananda Bazar Patrika* of 4 December 2000. She was issued summons to appear before the Commission on 28 March 2001. Sehgal, who had made umpteen trips to Kolkata, refused to come. "I am not keeping good health .... I, therefore, request you to excuse me from travelling to Calcutta to appear before the Commission." She was steadfast in her view that Bose had died. "I firmly believe that Netaji Subhas Chandra Bose expired after 90 % burns which he incurred in the aircrash at Taihoku airport on 18th August, 1945." The Commission made things easier for the octogenarian icon by fixing a sitting at a venue near her residence. She couldn't refuse this time.

On 4 June 2001, in the Circuit House in Kanpur, Communist leader Lakshmi Sehgal took oath to "tell the truth, whole truth, nothing but truth, and not to conceal anything." Then she was resolute in boldly defending her conviction during the cross-examination by the Commission's Secretary PK Sengupta, a former judge, and some deponents. She came up with some nice sound bites: "We had no information then that he (Bose) would go to Manchuria." "The matter of his disappearance has now become a myth." "I do not think that this Commission will be able to come to any truth other than that of the earlier two commissions."

Comrade Sehgal's expressions changed when she saw All India Forward Bloc's VP Saini brandishing a tape. Saini had met her in her residence on 13 July 1992 and discussed the mystery for two hours. "Please tell us whether this is the video recording of the interview?" he asked her. Sehgal did not find it amusing that the tape be publicly played on a VCR brought at the venue. "Yes!" she said slowly even as her image appeared on the TV set. Saini asked Sehgal to verify if he had indeed sought her guidance "to unfold the mystery shrouding the disappearance of Netaji" and had suggested that "the reason for Netaji's not returning to India might be that he was under arrest in Russia."

"To that, you replied that there were some comrades of yours, specially Abid Hasan, who was personal secretary to Netaji, who had a feeling for a long time that Netaji had been arrested and he was in prison in Russia. Am I correct?"

Her memory jogged by the tape, Sehgal made a 180-degree turn from what she has been saying up to now. "Yes, this is correct. I said so during the interview." No slip of tongue. Throughout the interview Sehgal held on to the view that there was a good chance of Bose being alive after 1945. She even gave him what she described as "one lead." She recalled that at the end of the Second World War, she was examined by American intelligence personnel. "They told me that they followed a person whose physical description answered to that of Netaji up to the Russian border." In the tape Sehgal also sounded earful to the theories linking Nehru to Bose's disappearance. She referred to an alleged letter of Nehru to Mountbatten, saying that Bose "should not be allowed to return to India until the process of partition of the country was completed." She subscribed to Saini's view that "there was an international conspiracy to keep Netaji out of India," adding "India was a party to that conspiracy." And having said all that, she couldn't have but felt that "there should be further investigation to put a finality to the matter."[14]

Lakhsmi Sehgal's perjury remained unnoticed perhaps until *Hindustan Times.com* made it public. Unfortunately, no other media shared our concern that she owed some explanation to the country. In 2002 she ran for the Presidency. She did not face any health problem in touring the country. Not a day passed when her comrades did not highlight her importance as a former colleague of Bose's.

There was yet another witness that the Commission wasted its time on. As if shady examples involving a Bose kin and a former associate were not enough, we had one of our tribe having a share in the mess. Executive Director of *Ananda Bazar Patrika* and senior journalist Suman Chattopadhyay had penned a number of articles on the mystery. Chattopadhyay harboured strong feelings against those who rejected the crash theory. And he wrote as much in a number of his articles in the *ABP: Netaji bhaktader tandab — andha biswaser grase subhaddhi* (Vandalism by devotees of Netaji — good sense in grip of blind faith). *Netajir mrityu sandehateela-othibhaktader ke bojhbe* (Death of Netaji is beyond doubt, who would make super devotees understand it). Chattopadhyay even targetted Mukherjee Commission in one of his write-ups. "It will be a sheer idiocy to even say that the findings of the third commission of inquiry would be different of the earlier two commissions (sic) appointed to solve the mystery of disappearance of Netaji."

It was presumed that this senior journalist must have based his writings on something solid. But he began with thumbing his nose on the Commission. Summons were served on him by registered post, but he had no time to respond to the Commission's office situated in the heart of Kolkata. An angry Justice Mukherjee stated on 28 September 2000 that "Chattopadhyay has neither presented himself before the

Commission nor sent any communication explaining his failure to appear." Then he ordered to issue fresh summons against him and pressed that if he failed to appear "this time as well" without any justifiable reason, "appropriate legal action" would be taken against him. Chattopadhyay finally turned up on 23 November to take the Commission on an ego-trip:

"I have written a number of articles, including the present one on Netaji and on his death. I have written all those articles in my capacity as a student of history as well as a journalist. For the information of the Commission, I like to mention that I am the translator of Netaji's work from English to Bengali published by Ananda Publishers. Currently, I am the treasurer of the Netaji Research Bureau .... I had the privilege of travelling to various places including Tokyo, twice with the then Prime Minister (Narasimha Rao). During one of such visits, I took time off from my official assignment to visit the (Renkoji) temple to see for myself what was happening there ...."

Justice Mukherjee stopped Chattopadhyay's harangue and wondered if his faith in the crash story stemmed merely from the reports of Shah Nawaz and GD Khosla.

"As I told you, I am associated with the job for quite some time now. I tried to do my own research. It is a fact that I have not been able to get any fundamental evidence, but I have been trying to collate all the evidence that have been recorded already in the various forms."

Justice Mukherjee wanted substance, so he put to Chattopadhyay if he had "any documentary evidence" to back his case.

"I don't have," was the answer he got.

Commission's counsel Bhasker Sen drew Chattopadhyay's attention to one of his well-crafted articles where he had drummed up some trite reasons to prove the death story.

"You have written that John Figges who was the Head of the British Intelligence Agency at Mountbatten's Headquarters conducted an inquiry into the plane crash involving Netaji in

September, 1945 and came to the conclusion in his report that Netaji expired in that air crash. Do you have any copy of the said report?"

I don't have any copy of such report. I am told that the report is in the India Office Library in London and I think it is now available for anyone."

"Did you yourself see the report?"

"No."

"In the article you have mentioned that in 1945 the Government of India deputed two teams of representatives headed by Finney and Davies to Saigon and Taipei and they came back and submitted their reports. Do you have a copy of that report?"

"No. I don't have. These are available in the office of the Government of India."

"Have you seen the report?"

"(I) Have seen the gist of the report."

"Gist prepared by whom?"

"Prepared by biographers and scholars."

Perhaps Chattopadhyay meant researchers aligned with Netaji Research Bureau headed by former Congress MLA Sisir Bose. All this was not leading to anything worthwhile. A senior journalist had authoritatively tried to prove the Taipei crash in a top daily of India on the basis of evidence he had never seen. He did not sound like he knew the exact details of inquiries done by IB deputy directors Phillip Finney and WFW Davies. Counsel Sen felt irritated and took a pot shot at Chattopadhyay. "You have written the articles on the basis of this type of evidence?"

Shaken, Chattopadhyay soon divulged the moving force behind his belief. He had written that "in 1997 there was a meeting in the Indian embassy in Moscow ' ... e Russian historian, Mr Vergov, had stated that there was no question of Netaji going to Russia on the day which is being mentioned in many of the other articles." When questioned, Chattopadhyay could not furnish any details about this meeting, but he dropped the name of Ronen Sen, then Indian Ambassador in Moscow. Sen, he said, had "corroborated" the Russian's statement. This gentleman had turned a deaf ear to the Asiatic Society researchers when they had approached him with the evidence of Bose's presence in Siberia. In the light of Vergov's claim, Justice Mukherjee was tempted to again ask Chattophadhy if he had "any documentary evidence to prove the alleged plane crash or the alleged death of Netaji?" The reply was as before.

"No. I have no such documentary evidence."

Then came the best part. Chattophadhyay referred to some intriguing act of Pranab Mukherjee to jack up his case, but it only brought him and the former External Affairs Minister into disrepute. He said that "during the period when Narasimha Rao was the Prime Minister, Shri Pranab Mukherjee, the then Foreign Minister of the country, showed me a letter in Russian language in which it was stated that there was no document relating to Netaji after 1945 in the archives of Russia. Later it was corroborated by Mr Ronen Sen, the then Indian Ambassador to Russia."[15] If the Minister and the Ambassador had some trump card up their sleeves, should they not have shown to the people of India? And what about the Official Secrets Act that forbade them from disclosing official information in such a manner?

Many reasons piled up before the *HT* team concluded that there was little to go by the crash theory. Going public with the results of the public probe brought us feelings of triumph and sadness. A tragedy had been metamorphosed into a tale of horror. If there was no plane crash, where did Netaji vanish? Into the USSR most likely. And Stalin, Siberia, gulag conjured up a dreaded phantasmagoria. Four of us — Sitanshu Das, Shailesh Shekhar, Shali Ittaman & myself — were summoned by the Mukherjee Commission and we presented ourselves for examination in Delhi's Vigyan Bhavan on 15 October 2001. There were no media persons around but lo — Pranab *Babu* was there. He was examined before Shali. Justice Mukhejee sought a CD of the *HindustanTimes.com* probe and we were asked some simple questions. Facing a commission of inquiry on an issue like this was quite a perplexing experience for me. But what happened to Pranab Mukherjee? He stood in witness dais with his face flushed. Maybe he had apprehended that he would be grilled about his not too well-known misadventure. It had happened almost six years earlier when he was the External Affairs Minister. On 20 October 1995 at about 10.30pm an angry Emilie Schenkl rang up her grandnephew Surya Kumar Bose in Ausberg, Germany. Pranab Mukherjee was coming over on the next day "to convince her and Anita to give their approval for bringing the so-called 'ashes' of Netaji to India." Mukherjee "also wanted her to sign a document which he would take back to India as proof of her approval."

Surya Bose had heard it from his auntie many times that she believed Bose had made it to the USSR. That night she repeated that "she had never believed in the plane crash story." She said she "would neither sign any document nor agree in any way to bringing the 'ashes' to India or to anywhere else." The next day things came to a head. "Anita and her husband Dr Martin Pfaff had to take Mr Pranab Mukherjee out for lunch as auntie could not tolerate any discussion on the so-called 'ashes' in her presence. Auntie told Pranab Mukherjee quite clearly that she did not believe that Netaji had died in a plane crash in Taihoku and that those 'ashes' in the Renkoji temple had nothing to do with Subhas." The outcome of this meeting were astonishing. On 28 October an Indian daily carried a report in which Pranab Muklherjee was reported to have "stated that Mrs Emile Schenkl had given her approval to the Government of India's plans for bringing the 'ashes' to India, and that he had a document to prove it." Surya rang up his auntie the moment he came to know of this report. "She reiterated that she had signed no such document and had approved of nothing. Mr Pranab Mukherjee was propagating an untruth for reasons best known to him and the Government of India."[16] On 13 December 1995, MP Pasumpon Thakirttinan asked in the Rajya Sabha about the External Affair Minister's trip to Ausberg. Pranab Mukherjee's deputy RL Bhatia gave a misleading answer bereft of the ignominous details.

Luckily for Mukherjee, not many questions were put to him before the Commission on this episode. His cross-examination went more or less smoothly and there was a feeling among the Commission officials that the deponents' feeble querying had let him "go off the hook." The Congress Working Committee member was mostly on a strong wicket. Justice Mukherjee asked him about his role in bringing the ashes to India. He replied that "a proposal was mooted in the Ministry" as the Government had been requested by the Renkoji temple authorities. The receptiveness of the Government was indicative of their acceptance of the crash theory. "Does not that necessarily mean that you were in firm conviction that Netaji was dead?" Justice Mukherjee wondered. "At that time the position of the Government of India was that the ashes were of Netaji," the former minister replied.

"What is the basis of such conviction of the Government of India?"

"The basis was the earlier two reports of Shah Nawaz Committee and Khosla Commission."

Justice Mukherjee finished his questions by asking why "in spite of such conviction or basis ... the ashes were not brought from the Renkoji temple?"

"The controversy aroused about the decision of the Government of India to bring the ashes to India."

A deponent reminded Pranab Mukherjee that when his Government was planning to bring the ashes back, a PIL was being heard by the Supreme Court of India and Ministry of External Affairs was a party to the case.

"I do not exactly remember," was what erudite Mukhejee had to say about the well-known Bharat Ratna petition. He also could not properly recall the statement of the then Prime Minister Morarji Desai in the Lok Sabha about the reports on which he had put his faith. "I have read this in the newspapers that there was some debate in the Lok Sabha," he made light of the historic announcement. The former minister replied in negative to the question if he concurred with a former Prime Minister's statement in the Parliament. Of course he did not have reasons or facts to back up his stand. Mukhejee's answers gave the impression that Bose's death was a partisan issue. The Janata Government felt that the evidence did not prove the death, whereas the Congress party swore by the Taipei mishap. Anyhow, Mukherjee did not let his strange body language cast shadow on his balanced responses. The only time he betrayed his shakiness was when he was asked about the Cabinet's role in conferring Bharat Ratna on Bose. Once he said that the decision was of the Cabinet, and later on said it wasn't.

The appearance before the Commission marked end of the role of *HindustanTimes.com*. We thought we might get another chance when the Commission would release its findings. In the days to come, except me, everyone managed to free themselves of the sinking feeling about Netaji's fate. I got stuck as phones in the offices kept ringing with callers saying something or the other about the mystery. I again started making enquiries to bolster our claim or figure out the rest of the story. If Bose had fled to the USSR in 1945, it would have become known to Indians sooner or later. We were quite close to that country. If somebody like Babajan Guffarov could have revealed something to Ram Rahul, the chances of others doing following the suit were there. The clue about Netaji's fate had to be available in India and maybe with our intelligence agencies. He was our man and successive Indian Government must have made covert attempts to know about his fate.

My efforts were shots in the dark. The only time I got it right, if I could say so, was when I found out from a source why Home Secretary Kamal Pande had to take privilege on two early 1990s files on Netaji. What I was told was revolting. The source said that there was a report in the files, and it said that Netaji was a "traitor." I rechecked facts and was perhaps able to pinpoint the problem area. In December 1993, the Ministry of External Affairs spotted the article *Against whom Subhas Chandra Bose fought during the years of Second World War* published in the Russian journal *Asia and Africa Today*. Its writer, Victor Turadzhev, had assumed on the basis of his scant knowledge and one or two stray KGB reports that Subhas might have been a British agent who worked against the Axis. (Turadzhev later realized his error). Turadzhev's write-up was discussed by our ministers and bureaucrats when Narasimha Rao was Prime Minister. This possibly made Kamal Pande write in his affidavit before Mukherjee Commission that the disclosure of the contents of the files would "lower the image of Netaji" and "may evoke wide-spread reactions."

How I wish I could get some more help. Journalists, Government officers, politicians — for most there was no use raking up the issue even if Bose was alive after 1945. "What is the use of it now?" they asked. This feeling of ingratitude was hurtful. Those who saw otherwise said the matter was "top secret" and known to only a few. Just when I thought it was all over, one day, a phone rang in my office. The caller identified himself as a relative of a former Home Secretary. He said he had something very important to tell and wanted me to believe that what he was going to say was true even if it sounded otherwise. "Go ahead," I said. One should not reject any claim before hearing it out. The caller recalled his talks with his uncle on the death of Bose. He said he had been rebuffed by his uncle for saying that Netaji had died in 1945 in a plane crash. "Why would you be wishing he had died?" "He slipped into Russia!" The "uncle" spoke about the existence of number of some inaccessible Top Secret files in Governmental archives. He added the Shah Nawaz and Khosla's reports were eyewash. The 1990s files were nothing but red herrings. Thus far the caller's brief fell into a pattern, and then it drifted to the incredible. He said, as per his uncle the Government of India was "in touch with Netaji until 1985." "The whole issue is very complicated. It will not get into the heads of people. It should not be brought out. Many people will get into trouble. It will not benefit anybody. Let it remain where it is!" "What nonsense!" I told the caller. I mouthed an expletive and he hung up, and never called back. I couldn't care less.

At *HT* we had received many innovative letters, phone calls etc. One fellow had the ludicrous story of an abortive coup attempt in the Indian army after 1962 and the reason was Bose. "The Army officers were angry with Nehru's handling of the China war and one of them had come to know that Netaji was in India." The plot, he said, was, intercepted by the Intelligence Bureau and some generals were blown up in a chopper crash. He gave out names of the victims but couldn't be sure who was the one with "Netaji link." Daulat Singh, Bikram Singh, Pinto .... I had never heard of any such thing or about these generals. This "information" and the one coming from the "uncle" couldn't have stuck to my gullet for obvious reasons.

The terse message from Faizabad was different. The sender had identified himself. "I know that Netaji did not die in 1945 because he was with us until 1985," Dr Indroneel Banerjee wrote in his e-mail. Nineteen-eighty-five — a straight jump to our times. Rajiv Gandhi was the Prime Minister then. It sounded like an escapist offshoot of the myth and so I, out of curiosity, wrote back to Indroneel. This young man was a third generation homoeopath. He promptly replied to say he had written on behalf of his father Dr Priyabrat Banerjee. Theirs was a holy man theory, wholly farcical in nature. Since there was nothing else for me to do, I spoke to Dr Priyabrat Banerjee on phone. Suave as doctors are, he repeated, in English, that one swamiji who had lived near their home was indeed Bose. "This was reported in newspapers many times!" I had no such recollection. I asked him how could he say that swamiji was Bose. "He was he. Swamiji was a Bengali," Dr Banerjee said as if this was the best he could offer. "I don't presume you ever saw Netaji before he disappeared?" I expressed surprise. "No, I did not, but my parents did. They saw him again in 1979." I asked the Faizabad doctor if this swamji talked about any crash. "Not with me!" Dr Banerjee said. He added that he and others never felt the need to question him as he was right before their eyes. "I am not a historian. I did not know about the 1945 crash and I never asked him about that."

This was leading nowhere so I thought to give Dr Banerjee a little test which most of the Bose-baba theorists had flunked. I asked him to tell me the height and complexion of swamiji.

Going by Dr Banerjee's answer, his swamiji was similar to Bose in height and appearance. I tried to confuse the doctor by telling him that Bose was taller, so he couldn't have been his swamiji. He remained firm. The only impression I could form was that Dr Banerjee was speaking the truth as he knew it. He sounded reasonable, capable of admitting his mistakes in case facts were furnished. Which is what I had in mind: Clear the air about the nonsensical Bose-holy man phenomena. Dr Banerjee suggested that I get hold of some "inventory" of the items kept by swamiji. This brought me to Dr Alokesh Bagchi, the doctor I not long ago had refrained Shali from meeting. He had a similar story to tell and the very idea of Bose living in India as a holy man irked me no end. Now I was willing to meet him to understand the issue. Meeting the doctor was the turning point.

I found Dr Bagchi's assiduous interest in Bose mystery inspiring. This forty-something laproscopic surgeon had quite a successful career. He and his doctor wife ran one of biggest clinics in Gorakhpur and he could boast of a nice pedigree. He was grandson of a freedom fighter who had once hosted Bose. He felt quite strongly about Bose and had in fact successfully challenged the UP Government in court when he found a government publication declaring Bose to have died in 1945. Dr Baghchi had made on the spot inquiries about the Faizabad baba and that's where my interest lay. He showed me numerous old paper clippings of 1985 and 1986 vintage which speculated and even claimed that Faizabad's Gumnami Baba (the saint with lost name), the swamiji of Dr Banerjee, was Subhas Chandra Bose.

More pertinently, Bagchi gave me a voluminous file which was the inventory Dr Benerjee had told me about. The list contained details of over 2,500 items that had been recovered from Gumnami Baba's residence. "Has the Commission seen this?" I asked him? "Yes, I gave them a copy long back!" he replied with a sense of pride. I checked that up to see how the Commission taking it. Mukherjee Commission like Khosla Commission had been approached with claims linking Bose with some holy men. The tales of Shoulmari Baba, who had died in Dehradun in 1977, still reverberated and new babas had popped up in Madhya Pradesh and in Sitapur in UP, where Dr Bagchi used to frequent. But ... upon my word! The Commission was showing much interest in Gumnami Baba. This wasn't a scoop; I was a late entrant. They had already examined a few witnesses, including Dr Banerjee and his family. Save one or two people, everyone had claimed that Gumnami Baba was Netaji Subhas Chandra Bose. This had happened in August 2001 when Justice Mukherjee had deputed his Principal Private Secretary NK Panja, a retired judge, to take the witnesses' evidence. I discovered that what Justice Panja had returned with had impressed Justice Mukherjee, and the senior judge was now himself planning to go to Faizabad.

This was getting interesting. A former judge of the Supreme Court of India had set his mind on a wild story.

Notes:

1 Public appeal. *HindustanTimes.com* Netaji probe phase 1.

2 JMCI status report dated 22 March 2000.

3 JMCI proceedings dated 28 September 2000.

4 JMCI proceedings dated 13 June 2000.

5 JMCI proceedings dated 28 September 2000.

6 JMCI proceedings dated 31 August 2000. The Government is yet to release the exhibits and many other important papers related to Khosla Commission and Shah Nawaz Committee.

7 The IB eventually filed a "secret" affidavit, but not the R&AW.

8 JMCI proceedings dated 31 August 2000.

9 Ibid.

10 JMCI proceedings dated 28 September 2000.

11 JMCI status report dated 26 September 2000.

12 Affidavit dated 18 December 2001 filed before JMCI.

13 JMCI status report dated 26 September 2000.

14 JMCI proceedings. 4 June 2001.

15 JMCI proceedings dated 23 November 2000.

16 Surya Kumar Bose's affidavit dated 6 March 2000 before JMCI.

11

Man of Mystery

The investigations and piecing together of the exciting material, painstakingly collected, with enormous efforts night and day, led us to the inescapable belief that the man (Bhagwanji) ... was one of the greatest personalities India ever had.

Editorial in *Northern India Patrika* on 20 December 1985.

I searched and this is what I found: Gumnami Baba was Mahakal and Mahakal was Netaji. Now, it is up to the people, the Government and the judiciary of this country what they would like to record in history.

Ashok Tandon in *Ganga* magazine in February 1988.

We tremble even as we release the evidence ... but we do so in the belief that Indians have the maturity and the strength of mind to handle the truth, however stark it may be ....

Introductory editorial for *HindustanTimes.com* Netaji probe phase-2 which in April 2002 furbished the older claims of Bhagwanji to be Subhas Bose.

Fifty-six years after the vanishing act in Saigon, the trail left by Subhas Bose "appeared" in India. On 26 November 2001, the quest for truth unnoticeably took a paradigm shift as Faizabad, a laidback north Indian town, replaced the snowy expanse of Siberia as the end-point of the Subhas Bose mystery. His feet firmly on the ground, Justice MK Mukherjee knew precisely what he wanted from what appeared to be a back of the beyond place. Some formidable evidence to authenticate the testimonies of the biggest chunk of witnesses before the Commission he chaired. He proceeded in a white official Ambassador car to the centre of town straight to an unkempt, poorly-whitewashed 1950s structure. This was Faizabad district treasury building. The redeeming feature here was the crowd, the largest ever at any venue of the Commission's sitting. Unlike in Delhi and Kolkata, the enthusiasm of the people for Netaji in this far-flung land was bountiful. The elderly and the middle-aged — from Lucknow, Basti, Sitapur and Ayodhya — had gathered since early morning, impatiently waiting for what they thought was a prelude to India's moment of truth.

The stifling atmosphere of the dark makeshift courtroom inside failed to dampen the excitement hanging in the air. The source was a nearby dark cell, where some two dozen trunks had been lying locked and sealed for 15 years. They were to yield a treasure trove of information on Faizabad's mysterious saint who many believed was Subhas Bose in hiding.

This fantastic shift in the story came not in November 2001, but 16 years earlier. An inaccessible holy man who lived in a shanty attached to Gurubasant Singh's spacious house "Ram Bhawan" was reported dead on the evening of 16 September 1985 by his medico disciples Dr Raghunath Prasad Mishra and Dr Priyabrat Banerjee. The news devastated only a handful of people. After all, the saint was never seen. He was, even for most of his disciples, a great will-o'-the-wisp, just a resonant voice from the other side of a cinnamon curtain. He was said to be 90 years old and had been engaged in a spiritual quest that forbade his public appearance. He had never emerged from his room and, save a few, no one ever went inside. Addressed variously by honorifics such as Bhagwanji, Sriswami, Swamiji, Babaji, Sri Vijaya, he was Dashnami Sanyasi – a saint having ten names. In fact he had no proper name. Those not acquainted with him, called him either Gumnami Baba (saint with lost name) or Anam Sant (unnamed saint).

The legend of Bhagwanji would have remained a subdued local affair had it not been for the unusual incidents following the 16 September night. Gurubasant Singh was refrained by Bhagwanji's disciples from having a look at the body of his tenant. The disciples said that their guru's wishes were to be followed even after his death. Bhagwanji did not want to be seen and known that's how it was. For the next two days, the body remained in the room Bhagwanji had lived for two years under the constant guard of Dr Mishra, Dr Banerjee and Saraswati Devi Shukla, Bhagwanji's trusted attendant for three decades. The younger disciples were told that the wait was for some special Bengali followers of Bhagwanji. On 19 September a body wrapped in the Tricolour was swiftly moved out of Ram Bhawan under the cover of darkness. Within minutes a funeral pile was raised at specifically chosen, secluded Guptar Ghat on the banks of river Saryu. The last time similar rites were performed here was for Lord Ram. Leaping flames rapidly consumed the body and in the ensuing drizzle the disciples detected a divine empathy. They all were locals from Faizabad and Ayodhya, where Bhagwanji had lived earlier. Most were well-to-do; three of them were doctors. They all carried a resolve — To uphold the promise they had given to Bhagwanji that they would not reveal his identity to anyone. Up till now they had kept their word.

An emotional Panda Ram Kishore was the first to bewail. "We are only 13 here to see him off on his last journey. There should have been 13 lakhs." In 1977 when he had facilitated the shifting of Bhagwanji to Ayodhya, Ram Kishore had been given the idea who the man was. But he needed an emphatic confirmation to set to rest the doubts. Sometime later on the ageing saint's health break down again and came rushing Dr TC Banerjee. From day one, the homoeopath from Faizabad had been in an enviable position. One afternoon on 1975, Sarswati Devi had come to his clinic and begged him to visit a seriously ailing Bhagwanji. Banerjee left the clinic to his son Dr Priyabrat Banerjee[1] and headed to Ayodhya, a couple of kilometers away. When he returned, Dr TC Banerjee was flabbergasted. In his first visit, he had chanced to do what most could not even after years of devoutness. The doctor had to see his patient so he went to the other side of the curtain. He saw Bhagwanji and down went a chill. Flashback 1939, Lucknow: A young TC Banerjee standing attentively, beholding the Congress President.

Ram Kishore saw Dr Banerjee emerging from Bhagwanji's room. He walked up to him and inquired how the old man was. "He's stable as of now," Banerjee said. Slowly the doctor took a few steps before turning to Ram Kishore. Something had overcome him. He was not reneging his pledge, he was simply complimenting a man who had been looking after his swamiji. "You are blessed to be sparing some moments in the service of Subhas Babu."

Bhagwanji's disciples were wrecked by an emotional turmoil on the night of 19 September. With the each passing day they became more restless and outspoken. They had only their experiences and beliefs to tell. In that part of India, the identity of Bhagwanji had been a matter of speculation for long. Wherever Bhagwanji had lived, rumours of his being Subhas Bose gained currency. His remaining confined to a room was never of any help. Prodded by his schoolmates that the saint his maternal grandfather Mahadeo Prasad Misra and mother Saraswati Devi served was Netaji, young Rajkumar posed the question to Bhagwanji. "Look at my saffron clothes. Am I not a sadhu?" Bhagwanji convinced the boy with much ease. Grown up, Rajkumar heard his mother confirming the rumours with a warning that it be kept a secret. Then, one day, he himself saw Bhagwanji "admitting" to a pestering elderly disciple that he was Bose. The number of whisperers constantly increased. Since 1975, Bhagwanji was forced to change as many as six residences in dramatic ways. He did not find solace in the city of Ram. A local weekly on 3 July 1977 published a sensational story. "Who is it in the guise of a saint?" it asked. "People say that he is a great personality and if he emerges, there will be an earthquake in Indian politics."

Gurubux Singh Sodhi, for one, disliked his tenant. For first impression, he had "the invisible" saint moved in stealthily past midnight. Then the disciples tempered with the rented accommodation at the historic Brahamkund Gurudwara in Ayodhya. They erected fortification-like walls around the house already perched on a cliff facing Saryu river. Bhagwanji also rubbed Sodhi the wrong way by being nice to his estranged elder brother Mahant Narain Singh and his family. In between his long hours of prayers and meeting visitors, he found time to teach nuances of English to Harpreet Kaur, mahant's granddaughter. It was not long before Sodhi started making efforts to turn his tenant out. But to his surprise, the local administration resisted his moves. He went to the police and wrote to senior officials but ended up being ticked-off. Finally he was advised to slap a case against Bhagwanji. The idea of an appearance in a court was a complete no-no for the holy man, so he surreptitiously left the house on the night of 15 May 1978.

Sodhi knew that local hacks were curious about Bhagwanji. He found in Virendra Kumar Mishra, correspondent of Bombay-based *Current* magazine, a man who shared his obsession to "unmask" Bhagwanji. Mishra was more interested in currying favour with the authorities than dispatching stories to his editor. A 7-page dope landed on 19 February 1979 on the desk of Faizabad Superintendent of Police Jyaneshwar Jha. Detailing the antecedents of "Gurudev Swami alias Deshnami Sanyasi," it began with a note that Mishra was forwarding the information with the request that "Ayodhya police station is not involved in your investigation." The caution had stemmed from Sodhi's brush with them over Bhagwanji. Mishra listed out a number of reasons why he felt that there was "something suspicious about Gurudev Swami."

"Some people say Babaji is a CIA agent. He has a transmitter and he sends messages .... Someone said Babaji is Subhas Chandra Bose and wants to remain in hiding. Four years ago, when a local teacher had brought Babaji from Basti to Brahmkund, his attendants too had given similar impression .... This year on Ganesh Chaturthi, during night the interior of Babaji's house in Deokali was decorated and ... the birthday of Shri Subhas Chandra Bose was celebrated .... This date was near about 22-23 January .... The disciples who come from outside are not seen at the house of Babaji. For past three years, 5 Bengalis have been coming without their families to meet him at Brahmkund around Durga Puja. They stay with him for 3-4 days and on asking give vague answers .... That the disciples of Babaji are engaged in different occupations is also suspicious. Teacher, lawyer, doctor, artist, politician and well qualified woman are their types .... Babaji calls himself Dashnami Sanyasi but is in the bad habit of smoking .... At Shankar Niwas, Darshan Nagar (where he lived) Babaji had brandished a gun at people who had climbed on a tree to have a look at him .... The former Inspector of Ayodhya, Shri Zalim Singh, tried to investigate about Babaji. But due to efforts of Panda Ram Kishore, he later became his disciple."

Jha took Mishra's letter seriously. He sought to meet Bhagwanji, but was denied permission. When he pushed for it, he was transferred. The incident was a replay of events elsewhere. In the dead of night, cars of different makes would be seen stopping near Bhagwanji's residence in Faizabad, Ayodhya and Basti, where he had lived in 1960s in a run-down palatial house owned by a local king. This was the time when spotting a car in this part of India was a spectacle. Only at night, people in three-piece suits, allegedly Government officials, would descend to spend hours with Bhagwanji. Once Gurubasant Singh ran into an army colonel. "When he went in, his chest was puffed. He emerged staggered and said, 'he is a General – that man inside.'" Disciples later recalled what all the saint dwell on from the other side of the curtain. His sermons were mostly about national/international politics, the paranormal and were interspersed with quotes of Indian and Western thinkers. The lingua francas would be Hindi, Urdu, English, and sometimes a spattering of Sanskrit, German and other foreign languages. Before his most trusted disciples Bhagwanji spoke in his mother tongue – Bangla. The Calcacian accent was indicative of his having lived in Calcutta for considerable years.

Whimsically, Bhagwanji would pick up his thoughts scattered far and wide. From Indian freedom struggle to war in Vietnam and beyond. He would recall a time long ago when he had travelled for months under the seas in a submarine and, in the same breath, liked to discuss life on other planets. Stuttgart, Berlin, Siberia, Tokyo, London, Kabul, Saigon, Singapore and Calcutta were some of the places he had been to. Gandhi, Nehru, Jinnah, Azad were no historical characters for him; he spoke as if he knew them intimately. "Oh, you smoke!" a disciple saw Bhagwanji puffing a cigar. "Mussolini gave me this bad habit," the saint spoke *sotto voce*. His past, which was much too eventful, was made up of memories of wars and bitter wranglings. He remembered meeting "Chancellor Hitler." "America hasn't been able to win even a single war since the end of Second World War. Thingle! Do you know Churchill could not pronounce 'S'? I am alive to tell you this!" On German and Japanese soldiers, Bhagwanji lavished praises. Partition of India was a pain in his heart and independence of Bangladesh elated him. He spent hours explaining the manoeuvers the Mukti Bahini and the Indian Army made to drive out Yahya Khan's marauding army. He always spoke as if he were an authority, but without a hint of self-aggrandisement. He discouraged discussing himself and would refer to self only in passing and as a second person. "This body" was his pet phrase. "'This body' was closely associated with Kazi Nazrul Hasan," he once said of the Bengal singer, a friend of Bose.

Seldom came the occasion when Bhagwanji would step out late in the night and get into a curtained Ambassador car which would take him far away. His face was mostly covered, and when it was not, a closer look was forbidden. A strongman in Basti tried to come up close, but was scared stiff by a booming stentorian voice and a blinding torchlight. In 1964, Inspector Jitendra Bahadur Singh carried out a swoop on Bhagwanji's house at night. The information had been leaked; the cops found just the empty rooms. A little later Basti's District Magistrate TK Charlu initiated similar moves but could not proceed. Forward Bloc activists too tried to crack the riddle, but Bhagwanji thwarted their moves sitting in his room.

Stories such as these became talk of Faizabad when the news of Bhagwanji's death spread. There was no way the matter escaped the notice of the administration and intelligence agencies. Ram Bhawan was situated near the residence of the top official of the town. A body covered in the national flag had been cremated in a spot close to Army cantonment land without any intimation to and permission of the authorities. An FIR was lodged against all the 13 disciples for unlawful disposal of a body in a public place. Dr Mishra, a civil surgeon, was too well known, and Dr Priyabrat Banerjee had inherited the good name and profession of his father. He was on friendly terms with Ajai Raj Sharma, the DIG of Faizabad, and would-be Director-General of Border Security Force. The others, Dr BN Rai, Ravindra Shukla, Dr Mishra and his son Anupam never denied that they had cremated a body on Guptar Ghat. Most of the disciples publicly stated that the man was Netaji. Some even dared the authorities to take action against them. Despite all this, the police kept mum. Why? "Because they knew he was Netaji!" a follower contended. "If he weren't, they would have clobbered us and thrown us into jail. Don't you know how UP police works?"

After a month of doing nothing, the police took some overt action beginning with a goof-up. Sub Inspector Harish Chandra Singh took Saraswati Devi and Rajkumar to police station on 27 October 1985. Their "arrest" sparked anger among the disciples. The next day a local daily let the cat out of bag. Ashok Tandon, the editor of local daily *Naye Log*, had known some of Bhagwanji's disciples. His instincts beginning to tickle, Tandon asked reporters Chandresh Srivastava and Ramteerth Vikal to make inquires. The result was the breaking news on 28 October 1985. A six-column headline on top screamed – "FAIZABAD'S NETA SUBHAS CHANDRA BOSE PASSED AWAY?!" Along with it appeared an editorial by Tandon, calling for official probe into the issue. Saraswati Devi, who knew more about Bhagwaji than anyone else, also came out with her belief that the man she and her father had served was Bose. She told *Naye Log* that Bhagwanji blamed Nehru-Gandhi dynasty for his ordeal and claimed that Bhagwanji's identity was known to many VIPs.

The story sent ripples across the town. Tandon heard about the systematic attempts to suppress the circulation of *Naye Log*, but the news was too big to be contained. The administration reacted in a knee-jerk fashion. The same day the District Magistrate rubbished the attempts to link the reclusive hermit to the indomitable freedom fighter. He said the inquiry by the District Magistrate and the Superintendent of Police had revealed nothing of that sort. On 29 October Panda Ram Kishore, also a small time Congress leader, released some more information. He was given a patient hearing by Congress MP Nirmal Chand Khatri who said he would personally take up the issue in Delhi. Thereafter, Khatri disappeared. The day also marked the beginning of a series of meetings addressed by local politicos, many trying to make the best of the situation. An advocate petitioned the District Magistrate to do something about the property of Bhagwanji over which some wrangling had started. He proposed that the *Naye Log* editor should be arrested if he were found to be misleading people. The Senior Superintendent of Police of Faizabad on 30 October ordered for preparation of an inventory of the belongings of the dead man. In pursuance, Inspector Harish Chandra Singh and a cop reached Ram Bhawan. Also making to the spot were Ashok Tandon and his brother-in-law VN Arora, a correspondent of *Northern India Patrika*. For the first time the other side of the curtain was exposed to the outsiders. There were trunks and boxes lying everywhere. Some items, including a transmitter (or a ham radio), had allegedly gone missing. What had remained were books, so many that the room looked like a mini library. The cops' work was not approved by those present. General observation revealed that the items, specially the correspondence and pictures, related to Bose and people connected to him, yet the cops went about their work perfunctorily. The inventory that they prepared was devoid of vital details. They made a note of a letter written in broken English by one Durga Prasad Pandey of Basti to Bhagwanji but left out its contents. Pandey had hinted to Bhagwanji that he knew his identity and beseeched him for an access.

"An old and very religious ex-revenue officer Late Sri Jawala Misra Vakil Basti told me as to your identity while breathing his last keeping full confidence in me to maintain the secrecy of this vital secret. Truth can't be pressed in, it abruptly comes out.

You had been an ex-ICS officer ... January 23 was celebrated as your birthday here the most auspicious day of the country when the immortal words 'Jai Hind' resounded ...."

Also traced in the same room and left out of preview by cops was the rough draft of the answer Bhagwanji had sent to Pandey.

"Your two effusive communications have been received and, the tender solicitation contained therein have stirred in me mixed feelings of pleasant surprise .... I felt quite amused and, can well guess the persons who have gossiped with you .... Well dear, that only goes to prove how shallow, indiscriminate and immature they are to indulge in such unwarranted speculations .... I am a bonafide Dashnami Sanyasi and you well know that a man under the holy orders incurs death according to the civil laws. And a sanyasi is dead to his former life; it is in the keeping of divine mother Durga and father Lord Shiva .... In passing, you shall find cogent answers to all your hypotheses, queries, thoughts ... both as expressed in your letter, and which remain unexpressed in your heart. Peruse with your heart calmly, quietly, lovingly. Every word, phrase, sentence and their constructions are pointers for you, they are pregnant with possibilities. Seek and thou shall find."[2]

Naye Log in its 1 November 1985 edition reported that the house was yielding many evidence related to Subhas Bose. This was followed by a flurry of stories in vernacular *Swatantra Bharat, Dainik Jagran, Amrit Prabhat, Aaj, Dinman* and Calcutta-based *Jugantar.* Among English dailies only one, *Northern India Patrika* of *Amrita Bazar Patrika* group, thanks to Arora's inputs, covered the sensational event. Its 3 November issue posed the question everyone in Faizabad had on their lips. "Nameless saint was Netaji?" On 9 November it was the turn of the *Swatantra Bharat* to put the same poser. The press coverage fuelled the socio-political activity. In bigger demonstrations, politicians of all hues demanded inquiry by a Supreme Court judge. News filtering through official quarters suggested that the police were conducting some inquiry and the chances were that Intelligence Bureau would be asked to assist. Some officials began to say, albeit privately, that Bhagwanji was a political thinker and possibly an associate of Subhas Bose.

The confusion persisted the next week. On 15 November a representative of the Freedom Fighters' Association rebuffed the claims. *Maya* magazine of Allahabad carried a statement of the Uttar Pradesh Chief Secretary that Bhagwanji was not Bose. At best he was some associate of his and that could be looked into. The views of DIG Ajai Raj Sharma were at variance. He told *Naye Log* on 24 November that "there was something about Baba" as the whole episode threw up many questions. The man was a nationalist and politically savvy. "His handwriting should be matched with that of Netaji." He said that an inquiry was on and it was likely to last up to a month and a half. The cover story of *Saptahik Sahara,* 24-30 November edition, brought the issue upfront. The story began on a premise that Bhagwanji was no ordinary mendicant and ended with an averment that "it was more or less clear that Netaji Subhas Chandra Bose did not perish in Taihoku crash and had been living incognito in India. It is quite possible then that Gumnami Baba was Netaji." More pertinent was the side story that uncovered the perplexity in the official circles.

"Next to Ram Bhawan is Faizabad Commissioner Kamal Tawari's residence. For two days the dead body was kept in this posh area but no one reacted. It was not that the police and civil administration were not in the know of the incident. Even when the body was cremated, no one did anything. District Magistrate Indu Kumar Pande told this correspondent (Punit Tandon) that no permission for the cremation was given. But Pande's statements have not been consistent. When a local paper claimed that Bhagwanji was Netaji Subhas Chandra Bose, he brushed it aside without getting into any sort of investigation .... The administration's apathy led to anger in public and there were many demonstrations all over the town. It was heard that the administration agreed to make an inventory of Baba's belongings only after being informed by local intelligence unit that there was nothing suspicious in Ram Bhawan and there would be no harm if Baba's room was shown to people ....

After an inventory was drawn up by the police, series of secret meetings took place among senior officials of local civil administration, central intelligence agencies, senior state officials. Now the administration is keeping mum as they have received no instruction in this regard from the top."

In December some national publications jumped into the fray. Tabloid *Blitz* did a story on 7 December, and in its December 1985 issue *Dharamyug* mooted a test between Bose's and Bhagwanji's handwritings. The high point came on 20 December when *Northern India Patrika* (*NIP*) published from Lucknow, Allahabad and Kanpur began the "Man of Mystery" series. Concurrently, the Hindi version of the same series ran in sister publication *Amrit Prabhat*. The man behind it was NIP news editor Sayed Kauser Hussain. Hussain remained a ringsider in his Lucknow office until he had heard his colleague VN Arora. He sounded Tushar Kanti Ghosh, the chief editor of the group at Calcutta. After the suggestion was approved, a high-profile journalist was called from Delhi office to assist Hussain and Arora in making sense of it all. The Delhi journalist was internationally acclaimed Nirmal Nibedon,[3] an authority on the North-East.

The first instalment of their stories opened with a note that "this is in the series of our investigation reports about the nameless saint. Taking into account the gravity of the subject and the political sensitivity involvement, we have taken every care to record the results of our inquiries dispassionately and objectively, and will stand by our report before any ... forum or authority. We want our readers to judge it on merit and with an open mind." The trio lived up to the guidelines set up by them. The 17 instalments that they wrote infused the much needed sophistication to the drab tale so far: "His (Bhagwanji's) extraordinary deep voice, would send a wave of thundering vibrations all around the area, giving the impression to all who heard him, that the man had perceived pages that belonged to a foggy past, they all had forgotten in the tumult of the rush. All, whether it was the rustic few, or the materialistic doctors around him, all felt a sense of exhalation and lightness before his hidden presence. The feelings, strangely, were unanimous. We did not have to prompt any one of the few characters who were in the outer or inner perimeter of the man, to come to this conclusion, the only conclusion they had come to before and yet not revealing his identity."

To counter the attention *NIP* series was getting, a major Hindi daily from Lucknow came up with its confusing version of the story. It was claimed that some of Bhagwanji's disciples had had criminal past. A politico was quoted as saying that an intelligence officer would come from Lucknow to meet Bhagwanji. It was noted with revulsion that some local cops had formed the view that man was Bose himself. For good measure, the new Chief Minister of UP Vir Bahadur Singh was asked to comment upon. He reacted sharply to linking Bhagwanji to Bose and ruled out any inquiry. Rather unconvincingly and abruptly, the readers were told on 7 January 1986 that after "investigation" it had emerged that Bhagwanji was either some spy or a blind Bose follower or some misguided Anand Margi.

Unabatedly, the *NIP* team kept on building up their stories on the lines of *Naye Log*. The last one was published on Bose's 89th birth anniversary on 23 January 1986. It was titled "The Man was Netaji." "The footsteps have been traced, the landmarks loom large, the reign of mist has turned mellow and as if dictates of destiny are taking us to the destination where a hazy shadow between truth and suspicions will be mingled with the exact."

Faizabad was hit by another surge in emotions. Enraged by reports that the authorities were considering auctioning Bhagwanji's property, social activists Dr MA Haleem and Vishwa Bandhav Tewari approached District Magistrate Indu Kumar Pande on 30 January 1986. They handed him a letter, marked CC to the Foreign Secretary at Delhi and Chief Minister Narayan Dutt Tiwari in Lucknow. A case for further inquiry had been made:

"An important English daily of Uttar Pradesh, *Northern India Patrika*, has after months of inquiry and investigations come to the conclusion that the saint was none else than Subhas Chandra Bose .... The most important evidence which the paper has cited is based on the records, documents and materials found in his residence of which an inventory was prepared cursorily by a police officer of a lower rank .... You are on record to have said that if the property found in the house remained unclaimed for ninety days, it may be declared intestate ... (this) will amount to destruction of evidence which may prove to be of great value in identifying the saint .... We may further point out that in a recent writ petition filed in the Rajasthan High Court by one Mr Nand Lal Sharma,[4] orders have been passed recommending the Union Government 'to hold a fresh inquiry with an open mind' .... Thus the matter regarding Netaji Subhas Chandra Bose becomes sub-judice and the records and materials found in Ram Bhawan residence of the saint could be subject to scrutiny by any authority or forum appointed by the Government of India in pursuance of the High Court Order .... We, therefore, submit to you that the documents and other materials found in the said house should remain sealed and preserved for the purpose of inquiry, and the guards posted there should continue to remain there in the national interest. We would like to be informed of the steps you propose to take in the matter ...."

District Magistrate neither acted on the plea, nor bothered to inform the two of any actions taken. Even a niece of Subhas Bose's could not shake off his stupour as she wasted her time with him on 5 February 1986. Lalita Bose, daughter of Suresh Bose, then met Vir Bahadur Singh, the new Chief Minister of Uttar Pradesh. The CM went one better than the DM in cold-shouldering her. Lalita's request to have an inventory made of Bhagwanji's belongings by a senior police officer or advocate-commissioner was turned down. She returned to Faizabad and resumed her meeting with locals and Bhagwanji's followers. She inquired from Pushpa Banerjee, late Dr T Banerjee's wife, about the physical attributes and temperament of Bhagwanji. She was told about some Bengalis who would secretly visit Bhagwanji. Some of them indeed knew her uncle. Time came when Lalita began to break down intermittently. Her mind went back to days when her sophisticate father was often contacted by a rustic man from Basti. Asking Lalita to react on the indifferent attitude of Sisir Bose to Bhagwanji issue was to make her mad. She accused her cousin of toeing the government line for financial gains.

Lalita Bose did not remain quiet and so would not Ashok Tandon. On 10 February 1986 she moved High Court and in the same month Tandon released his hurriedly written mini book on Bhagwanji mystery. The joint petition of Lalita Bose, Mohammed Haleem and Vishwa Bandhav Tewari was a big success. The writ petition to the Lucknow Bench of the Allahabad High Court made the state of UP, Chief Minister, state Home Secretary and District Magistrate of Faizabad as opposing parties. It referred to the *N/P* inquiry as "a great national service" which was required "to be probed in by an authentic forum." The petitioners lamented that despite people's interest in the truth, nothing was done by District Magistrate, who had been "sitting tight over the matter." They stated how perfunctorily the police had made an inventory of the items left by Bhagwanji. The possible administrative act of auctioning the items was countered by the argument that "the petitioner No 1 (Lalita Bose) being the niece of Netaji Subhas Chandra Bose has a right to the property, if the nameless saint is found to be Netaji."

"The petitioners feel strongly that the whole matter is of national importance and if ... the property left over intestate it will cause immense national loss as the country will be devoid of material evidence regarding the age-old mystery about Netaji ... huge number of books and other literature along with the material objects will be of immense value which will be of worth preservation in the National Archives ...." The court's intervention was sought as there was "no other alternative remedy available" due to "the callous inaction of the opposite parties", including the Chief Minister, who had been "absolutely unreasonable" and "unfair."

The judiciary made up for the uninterested executive's inaction. Justices SS Ahmad and GB Singh announced an interim relief on the same day. The opposite parties were called upon to file a counter affidavit "within six weeks" so that the court could take up the petition in April 1986. The main request was agreed to. The DM of Faizabad was ordered to oversee the preparation of a comprehensive inventory, giving comprehensive details of and about the articles, letters etc that had been found from the room of Bhagwanji in Ram Bhawan. "After the inventory has been prepared, the articles shall be shifted from Ram Bhawan Faizabad to the treasury to be kept in safe custody under his (DM's) own lock and seal."

On 25 February 1985 the matter was raised in UP Legislative Assembly. Krishanpal Singh and Nityanand Swami (would be Chief Minister of Uttaranchal) asked about Bhagwanji and Jagdambika Pal of Congress, even though he saw no Bose link, spoke about the need for an extensive probe. Speaking for the government, Finance Minister Baldev Singh Arya stated that an inquiry had revealed that Bhagwanji was not Subhas Bose. The members wanted to see the inquiry report, but the minister refused to oblige.

The process of cataloguing Bhagwanji's belongings began on 23 March 1986 under the supervision of advocate commissioner Satyanarain Singh. Ashok Tandon, also a lawyer, found his way in as Singh's deputy and so did some of Bhagwanji's disciples and officials. Lalita Bose and her cousin Jitendra Nath Roy, Bose's sister's son, were also present in the initial stages of the process which continued till 23 April 1987 during which 2673 items were indexed and preserved. For Lalita the experience was traumatic. The first glimpse of Bhagwanji's room convinced her that he was a Bengali. Pictures of Goddess Kali, Ramkrishna Parmahans, Sarada Devi, Vivekanand lay among innumerable books in English and Bangla. There were familiar handwritings. Lalita Bose had a closer look; it was her uncle's. In one of the trunks were discovered the photographs Bhagwanji had never ever shown to anyone. Lalita Bose saw faces of her grandparents. From Calcutta many photographs had been sent to Bhagwanji. One accompanying note had said that they were of "revered father and mother." In 1980s, in the isolation of his room, an old man in Faizabad beheld the pictures of Janaki Nath and Prabhbati Bose and their family as if they were his own.

Someone had sent an old-fashioned umbrella from Calcutta with a note that it was of "father Janaki Nath Bose." Bhagwanji had been keeping this memento reverentially. There were group pictures showing Subhas Bose's near and dear ones: Dilip Kumar Roy, Bose's bosom friend, and Suresh Bose, whose picture Bhagwanji had safely kept wrapped in silk. Lalita Bose also came across notes written by her father Suresh Bose on certain papers concerning Khosla Commission. She did not know how to react when the summons sent by the same commission to her father in West Bengal was located in Ram Bhawan. Did her father know Bhagwanji? Media clippings and related papers were found in stacks. For years Bhagwanji had meticulously tracked reports about Bose, specially the death mystery, with the help of his followers in Calcutta. A Bangla letter dated 16 October 1980 stated: "We could about completely do the photocopy of all documents from museum and German archives of all intelligence reports. The reports from the British museum shall be published in January next .... Nanda Mukherjee[5] is doing the collection work. A person is being sent to Austria to collect the pictures and the stories." The same person wrote the following a year later: "During last Pooja time I had written to you about the British and German documents. The documents from the UK were published on 3rd October 1981 ... and I am sending you a copy of it. I solicit your blessings."

Bhagwanji carefully read everything passed on to him. Like the *Times of India* story on 26 October 1982 titled *Soviet Scholars revise opinion of Netaji.* The news report that drew his interest like no other was the late 1974 *Ananda Bazar Patrika* series by Barun Sen Gupta. *Was Taihoku plane crash planned?* was written soon after GD Khosla's report had been made public. Interestingly enough, there were write-ups reporting the odd behaviour of some of Bose's associates in 1960s. They would suddenly go missing and later found to have visited Neemsar, a place of pilgrimage, to meet a holy man they thought was Bose. Bhagwanji had lived in Neemsar before shifting to Basti.

The diction in letters written to Bhagwanji emphasized his immensely exalted persona in the eyes of the senders. "You have attained the position of Brahma Rishi for the good of the nation," said a letter from Surendra Chaudhury, the king of Etawah. One Gurucharan Singh Bedi of Dera Baba Nanak, Gurdaspur, who had sent a copy of Guru Granth Saheb to this Hindu holy man, wrote, "Crores of Indians have put their eyes upon you. One day the Lord will himself salvage the sorrow of the people, the evil will be destroyed and the God shall prevail. You are our God in human form." There was a letter from Calcutta which likened Bhagwanji to Bhisham Pitamah, the invincible grand old warrior of the Mahabharat lore. There were instances when he was linked to Subhas Bose. Abdul Hafiz wrote to "respected secret sadhu" that he prayed to the Almighty for fulfilment of Bhagwanji's desires. "I am fully aware of the vision for the country that has burnt and turned into coal. I understand who you are, who you were and why this happened to you? Please take your original form at the earliest!" Someone wrote that "the present national scene warrants a big change. We are waiting for the right time." While in a letter dated 21 January 1981, the writer lamented that "in this long wait sometimes I get anxious and at times I get desperate. Sri Sri Sita Ram Onkar Nath Thakur[6] has told me that many people say that he has connection with Netaji Subhas Chandra Bose." Another letter by Gurucharan Singh, in broken English this time, stated that "people say you (Bhagwanji) are mother India's best son Netajee himself. If it is true, then for this twist of fate tears of blood must be shed."

The metaphor was oft-repeated. "I am a son of the motherland," Bhagwanji described himself in an undelivered letter to the king of Kashi. Kaushal Kishore of Calcutta wrote on 2 March 1983 that "we pray to God that India gets the best place in the world. May *Maa Janani Janambhoomi* (motherland) make her son healthy as soon as possible." Similar sentiments were echoed in a Bangla letter written in January 1984 from Calcutta on the 87th birth anniversary of Bhagwanji. "I got to learn from uncle that you have seriously injured your knee .... Under the guidance of the great poet, in the language of patriotism - O greatest son of mother India, on the 23rd January, I offer you the following verse." Jagatjit Dasgupta wrote as he quoted Rabindranath Tagore. Troubled by Bhagwanji's failing health, another follower rued: "If I were near you, I would be pressing your feet .... He who endeavoured to bring a new era is now bed ridden and suffering in a desolate obscure place. Perhaps there is nobody to take care of him. And there is certainly no proper food or medicine. He on whose mere wish can have royal comforts at his feet is today suffering. This could be a topic of deliberation for the historians, but for me it is quite painful."

There were indications that Bhagwanji was in contact with several prominent personalities. A letter by none other than M Golwalkar showed that the head of RSS took orders from this nondescript saint. His 1972 letter to Vijayanand (Bhagwanji) was laden with honorifics. "I bow before you a hundred times" was Golwalkar's opening salutation. Numerous pictures of celebrations of Subhas Bose's birthday over the years said their own stories. People in Calcutta celebrated the birthdays, not anniversaries, and sent Bhagwanji the photographs. One picture showed some people playing band and the caption was, "Birthday of Netaji — 1973 band party." Another captured a battery of lamps lit to mark Bose's birthday. Coupled with the pictures was the belief that Bhagwanji was born in the same year, day and time as Bose. "I wait for this day — 23 January — the whole year. My holy *Mahamanav* (super man), I bow at your lotus feet," was the crux of a letter written to him. Another one, written on 23 January 1967 stated: "On your 70th birthday, I cannot express my feelings for you. I am speechless. With one bow I send my countless regards." Bhagwanji's local disciples vouched that days from 22 to 24 January each year were exclusively kept for followers from Calcutta to come and celebrate Bhagwanji's birthday.

What Bhagwanji thought of himself was expressed obliquely in his own handwriting. From his room Ashok Tandon found a 2-page undated and unsigned letter in English. It was about businessman cum social activist Manu Bhai Bhimani who had backed Bose during his Congress presidency days. The letter summarised Bhimani's claims to be of use to Subhas Bose, presumed to be alive. Before sending the letter to Bhagwanji, the mediator had crosschecked with Sisir Bose:

"He (Bhimani) came in contact through a common friend. He talks too much. He says that:

1) If Netaji is in India why does he not appear or broadcast? All the people will accept his leadership at once ...

3) He helped Shri Sarat Ch Bose all the time till he was alive.

4) He helped Netaji when he escaped from Calcutta to Kabul. Sisir and Manu Bhai went with him. He has a special white bag which he used when he accompanied Netaji.

I verified the points 3 and 4 from Sisir Bose. Point 3 is correct, and point 4 is not correct. (and you ... can say also) Bhimani also sent me a letter which has been sent for your kind perusal."

Bhagwanji did not approve of Bhimani's claims. "He has lied", he wrote against point 4. He even resented point 3 supposedly cleared by Sisir Bose. "False," Bhagwanji described Bhimani's claim that he had helped Sarat Bose until his death in 1950. He crossed out both points. "You don't know facts. *Mejda* helped him. Everyone knows this except you fool."

Mejda was the byname used by Subhas for Sarat Bose.

Rather enigmatic was the letter Bhagwanji wrote to Prasad of Calcutta in Roman Bangla and a smattering of English and Latin. In this he described himself *mritbhoot*, literally 'ghost of dead':

"Long time back ... the person that you knew so well, you used to watch and follow — just forget him ... he has been killed by his very own near and dear ones and the entire Bengal. He ... has turned into a ghost. Therefore, do not try to know this person .... You will end up completely misunderstanding him. In the past life, whatever spectacles were shown by 'others', it was an unforgettable lesson. As a result, after death he is *mritbhoot*. Strange, very strange are you and your government that they constitute 'loaded-dice-commissions' over and again just to know whether he is dead or not! You all are the reason behind this. *Populus Vult Decipt* - You All People Wish To Be Fooled. Anyway, all this talk is irrelevant. The truth is, - that the earlier 'he', - is no more. He is now transformed into *mritbhoot.* He is 'Inscrutable, Unfathomable, Beyond Everyone's Power, Through Right Or Wrong' ... his death is surrounded by impenetrable mystery."

The followers were quite clear what all this meant. Durga Prasad Pandey, who was around when inventory was being made, brought back the memory of the day he was allowed inside Bhagwanji's room in Shristha Kothi in Basti. Pandey had in 1939 seen Subhas Bose from a close angle for more than an hour. The moment he entered the room, the same visage reappeared. A fair oval face with sharp Mangoloid eyes behind round spectacles. The tummy had bulged, hairline receded further and a long moustache and beard had come about. Yet the face was the same. Older, shrivelled but with the characteristic gap in the upper teeth. Pandey caught his breath. "N-e-t-a-j-i!" he let it out. "You are talking about a dead man," Bhagwanji responded. "No, I am talking to the living Netaji," Pandey butted and held his ground until Bhagwanji gave up. In 1978 Banerjee family had a better experience. After her husband, Pushpa Banerjee endeared herself to Bhagwanji like a daughter and gained access into the room. Everyone wanted Bhagwanji to talk about his self. Cloaking her intentions, Pushpa once provoked him by speaking despondently about India. She knew how closely the holy man kept tab on national and international events. "You are not saying what's on your mind," Bhagwanji ticked her off. "You know well what is on my mind," she rejoined. Sitting on a bed, Bhagwanji pulled himself back. Touching his silver rimmed glasses he asked, "Do I look like Subhas?" "Who are we to say that. It is up to you." Pushpa wanted to hear from him only. Bhagwanji's head appeared to move subtly in a nod. "Hoon!" Yeah, he said. There were no expressions on his face for the Banerjees to read. Before they left, they were reminded that "whatever goes on here must not become known outside." "I know you have relatives in Calcutta;

don't tell anyone about me. It will not lead to anything good for the nation."

1987. Bhagwanji's belongings were placed in 23 boxes and sent to the District Treasury. With that the responsibility passed on to the authorities to clear the air. And that's where the story ended for them. Nobody contradicted Ashok Tandon when he returned with an incisive 19 part series in the widely circulated Hindi magazine *Ganga,* then edited by Kamaleshwar. "Who was he if he was not Netaji?" ended with an unqualified claim that Bhagwanji was Bose. The issue, Tandon wrote, resounded in the Rajya Sabha when a member sought clarification from the Rajiv Gandhi Government. The answer was that Bhagwanji was neither Bose nor a CIA agent. This put paid to that madcap theory about Bhagwanji. Not the one about his being Bose, though. The Government hadn't clarified who he actually was despite their claim to know that he wasn't Bose. Lalita Bose's reaction would have bordered on "elimination of possibilities" deduction. "Agreed, that Sant (Bhagwanji) ... was not Netaji, as Government holds, but then who was he? How come he possessed some personal articles of Netaji including some over-private letters? If the Government fails to prove the very identity of the Sant it *ipso facto* proves that he was Netaji," she had told the *Pioneer* on 31 March 1986. The UP government did not tell anything to the court for some unknown fear. They did not file the counter affidavit to Lalita Bose's petition as court had directed them. Years rolled by, but Lalita Bose kept on firing salvoes. On 23 October 1989 in Delhi in the presence of national media, she asked "why the Government was not serious to find out whether 'Gumnami Baba' of Faizabad was Netaji?" She said there was "considerable evidence to prove that Netaji did not die in an air crash." Bhagwanji, she said, "was of same age, size and colour of Netaji." The letters found in his room "suggested that he had direct links and close connections with India's top leaders."[7]

Lalita Bose gave up and Mohammad Haleem passed away, leaving Vishwa Bandhav Tewari to hold the fort. He wrote to Prime Minister, Home Minister, Speaker, UP Governor, Chief

Minister but in vain. In 1997, it transpired that the file of the Lalita Bose's petition had gone missing. The state government showed unexplainable aversion to furnish the inventory prepared at Ram Bhawan. Unyielding efforts by Tewari and others led to yet another judicial injunction in May 1998. Judge Brijesh Kumar of the UP High Court ordered the recreation of the file. Still nothing happened. Bose's admirer Dr Alokesh Bagchi began lobbying with the sympathetic Kalyan Singh government for the retrieval of a copy of the inventory which held the key to solving the mystery about Bhagwanji's identity. Bagchi found out that in the court records someone had fraudulently entered "case resolved" against Lalita Bose's petition. Bagchi succeeded at last. The inventory was traced and the Government of UP, as a result, filed a counter-affidavit 13 years after the court's order.

The affidavit dated 29 January 1999 was a spin by the babus. It had been filed on behalf of the State of UP, the state Home Secretary and the District Magistrate of Faizabad. An underhand case was made against the undefended petition of Lalita Bose. Most important aspects had been bypassed: The petitioners' arguments that "there has been lot of controversy and mystery shrouds about the death of Netaji" was met with brief statement that it needed "no comment." Lalita Bose's assertion that she was a niece of Bose and had "a right to the property, if the nameless saint is found to be Netaji" was rejected with an offending remark that this could not be believed in for "want of knowledge." Charges of governmental callousness were denied in absolute terms. The media was trashed. "No reliance can be placed on any news published in the newspaper without verifying the authenticity of the same."

The affidavit outlined a hollow case of government's verifications of the news reports. "All the three/four persons who were intimately concerned with the above 'Bhagwan Ji' have been closely examined by the police. None of them is able to give any solid evidence to suggest that this person was in fact 'Neta Ji.' None of them claimed to have seen the face of this person while he was alive. A police party was sent to Calcutta to talk to ... associates of 'Neta Ji' but none of them were able to give any information about this matter, and, in fact, they appeared to be reticent about providing any information to the police .... Even after the death of the nameless saint, all those persons who saw his face could not identify him to be 'NETAJI SUBHAS CHANDRA BOSE.' Some of them stated that the dead body of the nameless saint appeared to be similar to the look of a Buddhist Monk."

The police inquiry, which put the onus of resolving the case on Bhagwanji's followers, merely proved the urgent need for further investigations. That the followers in Calcutta were keeping things to their chest was suspicious. Many of them in UP were afraid to open their mouths. The 'solid evidence' could have been obtained by matching the handwriting of Bhagwanji with Bose as had been suggested by top cop Ajai Raj Sharma. Ram Bhawan could have been searched to lift fingerprints. The claims about Bhagwanji's looks were erroneous. Contrary to the police version, some followers had seen Bhagwanji and identified him to be looking exactly like Bose. The UP police did not need to take help from Scotland Yard to know that Netaji had the face of a Buddhist monk. Above all, the State and Central governments should have taken the matter further given the serious nature of press stories, which, among others, must have been seen by the Subsidiary Intelligence Bureau staff at Lucknow. But nothing was ever done for more than a decade. "The State Government has been informed of the preliminary inquiry conducted by the police in this matter and further instructions of the Government are awaited," the affidavit stated.

Justice Mukherjee briefed his staff in Faizabad treasury about the evidence he wanted to glean from Bhagwanji's belongings. He had carefully studied the inventory and made a shortlist of the items to be taken to the Commission's office in Kolkata for detailed examination. There was little evidentiary potential in Empire Corona typewriter or 16X56 German binoculars. Items such as these showed that Bhagwanji was an extraordinary saint, which Justice Mukherjee had already agreed to. His mind was set on getting handwriting specimens of Bhagwanji which could be scientifically examined, and, if possible, something that could yield DNA. "Smoking pipe. We are interested in his smoking pipe. If there is any remnant of saliva, DNA can be extricated. If there's a chance, we'll take it," a commission official echoed his view. Journalists were all over the place but few had the idea of the context in which the whole exercise was being undertaken. Justice Mukherjee ordered and one by one huge trunks containing Bhagwanji's belongings were brought in. The seals were broken and object wrapped in gunny bags were dusted out. Flutter was caused in the court when silver, round-rimmed old-fashioned spectacles were removed from a quaint case. It increased when Bhagwanji's watches began to appear. One was Rolex and the other — Omega gold. "Netaji's watch!" someone said. Bose had one Omega gold wrist watch, a prized possession, over which there had been much debate before Shah Nawaz and GD Khosla panels.

The Commission's staffers knew what they would find, but seeing was believing. When he was not meditating, the Gumnami Baba of Faizabad read *TIME, Reader's Digest,* The *Indian Express, Statesman, Pioneer, Times of India, Organiser, Dainik Jagran, Illustrated Weekly of India, Dharamyug, Hindustan Standard, Jugantar, Ananda Bazar Patrika, Amrita Bazar Patrika, Bartmaan* and many more publications. He savoured the best of the English literature. *A Tale of Two Cities, Great Expectations, Christmas Stories, American Notes For General Circulation, A Child's History of England, David Copperfield, The Old Curiosity Shop* ... there was not one Charles Dickens work that he had not lapped up. *The Works of Charles Dickens: The Authentic Edition* – 1 to 18 were all there in his small room in Ram Bhawan. *Richard II, Winter's Tale, The Tragedy of King Lear, Othello, Macbeth* — the Bard of Avon was also much in demand as was *PG Wodehouse* whose rib-ticking *Carry on Jeeves, Right Ho Jeeves, The Inimitable Jeeves* were found. "What sort of sadhu he was?" a scribe wondered. Religion was ingrained in Bhagwanji. Scores of complete unabridged treatises of Hinduism — in Sanskrit, Hindi, Bangla — were lying in one box packed in 1986-87. Almost all the works of Rabindranath Tagore and Sarat Chandra Chattopadhya were there too. Unusually for a Hindu saint, Bhagwanji read about Sikhism, Christianity, Judaism, and Islam. Justice NK Panja, who was culling out relevant items, got tired of flipping open so many books. *Gulliver's Travel* by Jonathan Swift, *The Odyssey* and *Iliad* by Homer, *The Bermuda Triangle* by Charles Berlitz, *Flying Saucers Farewell* by George Adamski, *Life Beyond Death* by Swami Abedanand, *Celebrated Crimes* translated by IG Burnham, *The Hunch Back of Notre Dame* by Victor Hugo, *Tropic of Cancer* by Henry Miller, *Alice in Wonderland* by Lewis Carroll, *The Sacred Rome, Rubaiyat* of Omar Khayyam, *Flying Saucers Have Landed* by Leslie and Adamski.

Justice Mukherjee eventually did find what he had been looking for. Non-fictional works which Bhagwanji had diligently pursued. In some cases, he hinted as if he had been a witness to them. Whenever he felt like reacting, he underlined the relevant parts or jotted down his comments on the margins. "Give that to me!" Mukherjee ordered the moment he saw the bulky copy of the scarcely available *International Military Tribunal for the Far East: Dissentient Judgment of Justice Radha Binode Pal.* Bhagwanji had underlined many of its paragraphs showing his approval of the courageous pro-Japan stand taken by Justice Pal. In *The Story of Civilization* by Will and Durant, Volumes 1 to 10, Bhagwanji had written many comments, criticising the Western historians for their lopsided views of the Orient. The comments on *Between the Lines* and *India Critical Years* by celebrated Kuldip Nayar, *Himalayan Blunder* by Brigadier John Dalvi and *India's China War* by Neville Maxwell were vitriolic on the whole. "A man always wrong," Bhagwanji thought of Morarji Desai and patted Brigadier Dalvi, who had been taken a PoW in 1962: "God bless you for your nobility and honesty. He saved you from death and brought you back to your people."

On a pamphlet eulogising Jagjivan Ram, Bhagwanji deplored in Hindustani that "this man did not pay his income tax for ten years." It was easy to see where Bhagwanji's special interest lay. *India Wins Freedom* by Maulana Azad, *The History of the Freedom Movement in India* Vol 1-3 by Dr RC Majumdar, *The Last Days of the British Raj* by Leonard Mosley, *Moscow's Hand in India* by Peter Sengar, *Moscow's Shadow over West Bengal* by Rajni Mukherjee, *Freedom and After* by Ravindra Nath, *Nehru's Fatal Friendship* by Sita Ram Goyal, *Charter of the United Nations* and *The Gulag Archipelago* by Aleksandr Solzhenitsyn. In all, there were many handwriting specimens for the Commission to take to Kolkata. Away from journalists' eyes, a tiny bundle was picked up and swiftly handed over to Justice Mukherjee. In it were two matchboxes, containing some teeth. This was the best find the Commission could hope for. Provided they were his, the decaying teeth were likely to contain Bhagwanji's DNA.

Representing *Hindustan Times*, I scurried through Faizabad and around with the help of Dr Alokesh Bagchi and "Bharat Ratna" lawyer Bijan Ghosh. I managed to meet bulk of people relevant to the Bhagwanji episode. Vishwa Bandhav Tewari, Dr P Banerjee, Dr BN Rai, Durga Prasad Pandey, Srikant Sharma, Ravindra Shukla, Gurubasant Singh and his son Shakti Singh all provided inputs. Nirmal Nibedon had died in a "suspicious" accident in Delhi, I was told, soon after "Man of mystery" series concluded. Both VN Arora and Kausar Hussain, whom I later met, deposed before the Mukherjee Commission and stood their ground. Ashok Tandon came as well and for good measure he extended to me his fullest help. I returned to Delhi with a heavy heart and a heavier bag stuffed with copies of several documents found at Ram Bhawan in 1985-87. The grey matter in me constantly told me that the Bhagwanji legend was a hoax. Netaji could not have lived in this pitiable manner for so long. Bhagwanji's runaway lifestyle was as far as one could get away from the daredevilry with which Netaji had led his. If he had wanted to be a holy man, he could have followed the footstep of Aurobindo. Anyhow, Netaji, to best of my belief, had made it to Russia in August 1945.

The second phase[8] of *HindutanTimes.com's* probe into Netaji mystery began with a view to exploring the Faizabad angle. I had with me a plethora of information about Bhagwanji, which "fitted" in the "1985 slot" provided by the anonymous caller. Shailesh, Shali and myself agreed that both these grounds, specially the wild input of an unidentified caller, were insufficient. There were only three ways to kick-start the probe. The DNA fingerprinting, a fingerprint test and a handwriting test. The first two were beyond us, but the third option was possible. Whether Bhagwanji was Bose or his impersonator would be seen through in his handwriting by an expert. Various investigative agencies, including the police and the Central Bureau of Investigation, utilised experts' opinions in cracking cases. Shali said we needed "India's top handwriting expert." Our requirement, apart from confidentiality, was a report with the commitment to defend it before the Commission if the need arose.

In B Lal Kapoor I found the man who fit the bill. Sources from the Special Branch and the CBI put him on the top both in terms of his expertise and integrity. He was retired but still flooded with cases by the government bodies for his expertise honed in over four decades in India, the US, the UK, West Germany and Switzerland. He had taken up countless sensitive cases referred by the CBI, Ministries and departments of Government, police courts and banks. Many of these cases he had handled in his capacity as Government Examiner of Questioned Documents (GEQD), which was the topmost post for a handwriting expert in India. He had also served as an Additional Director at the National Institute of Criminology and had been in the year 2000 awarded a lifetime achievement award at Indian Science Congress for his singular contribution in the field.

In our first meeting, Lal and I discussed certain basic questions which he later incorporated in his report. The job of a forensic document expert was vaguely understood. We at *HindustanTimes.com* heard some of our fellow journalists raising doubts about the legal validity of the opinion of a handwriting expert. Lal laughed away when I conveyed those to him. "If handwriting tests are not crucial, why are the governments world over wasting money on maintaining huge departments?" He roundly asserted that the forensic examination of questioned documents was a scientific process and handwritings could be positively identified. The opinion of experts was acceptable in courts world over. Seen with other evidence, the handwriting expert's opinion made up an irrefutable body of evidence. "Handwriting is an acquired trait. When fully developed, in the case of a matured writer, the habit becomes fixed in nature."

For a month after I gave him two sets of several documents containing mainly English handwriting samples of Subhas Chandra Bose taken from National Archives, Delhi, and those of Bhagwanji, Lal kept drowned in them. He refused to hint which way his examination was heading to. Finally he asked me to come over along with my boss Shailesh. We reached his modest office-cum residence to find him looking perplexed. He asked us to pull up chairs and began questioning me on various aspects of the story of Bhagwanji. And then he dropped it without any foreword. "He is the same man. The writer of documents brought from National Archives and the writer of Faizabad documents is same."

Our minds went numb for a while. "Are you sure, sir? Do you know what this would mean?!" Shailesh resumed the discussion. "My 44 years of experience tells me that all these are written by one person," Lal replied. We asked for reasons and Lal took his time explaining them. He was to jot down the following in his 19-page report which was given to Hindustan Times.com in March 2002: "The documents of this case have been carefully, thoroughly and scientifically examined ... there is gap of a few decades between the questioned and admitted handwritings .... A question arises whether there is an attempt to disguise? It may be stated that disguise is adopted in order to conceal the identity ... the writer has tried to hide his identity but had failed to do so. It is not possible for a writer to change his writings habit completely. Even in an effort to hide his identity, the writer is not able to leave his individual characteristics and other peculiarities found in his handwriting. There is such a faithful reproduction of some peculiarities that even a gap of time to the extent of decades cannot hide them.

"Similar habit of over writing the letters or lines or brackets — a sort of emphasis or trait to make the strokes more clear and more prominent to be seen are found both in questioned and admitted. Habit of underlining words is also found in both sets of writing that is questioned and admitted. Similar habit of making certain abbreviations and giving a mark over the figure representing year, is also found both in questioned and admitted .... In addition there are similarities in the manner of execution of various letters and their combinations and also the manner of execution of figures ... it has been found that there is no evidence to show ... that the questioned writing has been made by a writer other than Shri Subhas Chandra Bose by imitating/ copying the writing of Shri Subhas Chandra Bose ... it is found that there are characteristic similarities in general and individual writing habits, strongly suggesting common authorship of relevant questioned writings and admitted writings (of Shri Subhas Chandra Bose)."

Lal's report gave us the most urgent reason to try and bring together the different parts of jigsaw puzzle. Bhagwanji was beginning to throw up the image of a man missing for 57 years. I picked up the threads left by Nirmal Nibedon and Ashok Tandon. The other end was in Kolkata, the city of Netaji. I was to go out and look for some of Bhagwanji's surviving followers there. I had two prominent names to begin with. First was the man Bhagwanji called "Sukrit". His name was Sunil Krishna Gupta, Suresh Bose's confidant, the lawyer who had assisted Amar Prasad Chakravarty before Khosla Commission. Gupta was one of the "Bengalis" who would secretly visit Bhagwanji. When Khosla Commission was functioning, he would visit Basti to discuss the Commission's work. Many of his letters were found at Ram Bhawan. He had written one on 24 July 1973 after returning to India from Taiwan. "We got only 15 days in Taihoku .... Formosa's task is over. I cannot write everything in the letter. If you permit, I can come over for a week. The final argument (before Khosla Commission) has not yet begun. I would seek your blessings once it does."

The other man was prominent. Along with Gupta, he had also visited Taiwan to facilitate GD Khosla's work. Bhagwanji was the man on Samar Guha's mind when he had sworn in the name of God in the Parliament that Netaji Subhas Chandra Bose was alive.

Notes:

1 Dr TC Banerjee passed away in 1983. Dr Priyabrat Banerjee, his wife Rita Banerjee and her mother were examined by Mukherjee Commission.

2 Now an octogenarian, Pandey told Mukherjee Commission in 2001 that he eventually met Bhagwanji and identified him to be Bose. Since 1985 Pandey publicly stated his belief. He also wrote to Prime Minister Rajiv Gandhi in 1986.

3 Writer of acclaimed book *Nagaland: The night of the Guerillas*, Nirmal Nibedon was a contemporary of Shekhar Gupta, the Editor-in-Chief of the *Indian Express*.

4 The 18 January 1985 order by Justice SN Bhargava in the Nand Lal Sharma Vs Chief Secretary, State of Rajasthan case *inter alia* states: "This is a writ petition filed by Shri Nand Lal Sharma on a very important national issue asking this court to order for starting an open judicial enquiry on the international level to know about the whereabouts of Netaji Subhas Chandra Bose, a national hero, and further order to set him free, if he is still confined as a war criminal in any country .... The petitioner also filed an application giving the details of documents which he wanted to be summoned from the non-petitioner No 2, Secretary, Ministry of External Affairs, Union of India .... Notices were issued both to the State of Rajasthan and the Union of India, but it is very unfortunate that none of them have cared to file any reply of the writ petition and produce relevant material before this court to come to some definite conclusion .... In the facts and circumstances, I think it proper to issue a direction to the non-petitioner No 2 to look into the matter dispassionately and hear the petitioner in person patiently and examine the documents and the evidence that he wants to produce in support of his contention, and then come to a definite conclusion. In my opinion, six months, time will be sufficient for the Union of India to examine the whole matter afresh with open mind and if necessary, invite public in general to produce material whatever it wants in this connection before coming to a prima facie decision as to whether fresh Commission is necessary or not." The Government of India had no time to respond to the court's order.

5 Writer of *Netaji through German Lense*.

6 A well-known godman whose one famous disciple was Intelligence Bureau's BN Mullick. Thakur passed away in 1982, and saintly Mullick in 1984. Bhagwanji was in contact with Sita Ram Onkar Nath Thakur.

7 *Hindustan Times* report **Bose niece wants mystery solved.** 24 October 1989.

8 The findings of the phase 2 of *Hindustan Times.com*'s Netaji probe were more widely read than the earlier one. The stories were reported by the agencies like IANS and carried by well-known websites such as Sify and MSN. The articles in the *Hindustan* and *Hindustan Times* drew attention. On 15 May 2002, Karnendu Bhattacharjee of the Congress sought the reaction of the Government of India in the Rajya Sabha on "series of articles ... in the *Hindustan Times* ... giving a graphic description of the last days spent by Netaji Subhas Chandra Bose in Faizabad."

"It is a fact that Government does not want to re-open the case of Netaji's last days in the light of the facts mentioned in three articles for fear of public reaction in the country and rupture with friendly foreign countries," the member asked. The Government's brief answer, prepared by Ministry of Home Affairs, was evasive and did not touch this part. More questions were asked in Parliament about Bhagwanji, and the answers the Government gave were inadequate. Anyway, the *HindustanTimes.com* stories were neither contradicted nor challenged.

12

Living Dead

The country would burn if I opened my mouth.

INA secret service agent and Bhagwanji's operative Dr Pabitra Mohan Roy in September 1985.

(Bhagwanji) was not just a recluse, but an important political personality in the pages of Indian history, a history written more by foreigners than natives of the soil, a history that has undergone radical changes and corrections but now required a total overhaul.

***Northern India Patrika* in 1986.**

We shudder to draw a conclusion based on these facts .... we do not fear the inference that the hermit may be Netaji Subhas Bose, but we do gasp at the conclusion that will be drawn from the writings and letters that have survived this man. Taken on their face value, they have the potential to change Indian history the way we know it.

***HindustanTimes.com* in 2001.**

In the scantly attended public sittings of the Mukherjee Commission stood tall a 50-something Nandalal Chakravarty, conspicuous by his animated questioning of the witnesses. I thought he was a lawyer, but he turned out to be a deponent, a political science professor. Nandalal represented "Jyotish Chandra Bose and others". The name sounded like a big Bengali think tank, but, sadly, it wasn't. Netaji's fate ceased to torment the bulk of intellectuals in Bengal long ago. Either they were fed up, or they did not think much of Bose. There is a myth among rest of Indians that I must dispel. To say that Netaji Subhas Chandra Bose is adored by every Bengali is not true. The breed of the communists that is found in Bengal and surrounding areas, for instance, hated Netaji in pre-1945 period, and so one ideally should not expect their progenies to be loosing sleep over his disappearance. I would here share the mistrust of some researchers and politicians that one of the last things the Indian communists wish to know is what happened to Bose. An incident was narrated to me. Indrajit Gupta, when he was Home Minister, called some people and told them to forget about Bose mystery. The prospect of Bose's being incarcerated in their Utopia, the Stalinist USSR, has always been a scary thought for communists. This is the feeling I have got from All India Forward Bloc people who are otherwise part of communists and have been responsible for pushing the comrades to do some good deeds.

Returning to "Jyotish Chandra Bose and others," they were a motley group of middle class people who were spending much of their time and hard-earned money to assist Mukherjee Commission. They submitted an over 300-page bonded dossier, making the strongest ever case for Bose's not dying in 1945 and his having been declared a war criminal. The Commission took their arguments seriously, and, to tell you a secret, so did the Intelligence Bureau. It was in Faizabad treasury that I understood the *raison d'être* of "Jyotish Chandra Bose and others." "Nandalal, your letter!" a Commission official said in hushed tones as the process of sifting through Bhagwanji's belongings was on. An early 1980s letter written by Nandalal to Bhagwanji had been traced. Most unlikely that a 30-something Calcutta inhabitant could have contacted Bhagwanji on his own. Ditto for Nandalal's friends — Dr Madhusudan Pal, Jagatjit Dasgupta and Surojit Dasgupta — all part of Jyotish Chandra group. Dr Pal was in the apogee; he only knew of Bhagwanji's existence. Reserved brothers, Jagatjit and Surojit were much better placed. It was Jagatjit who had addressed Bhagwanji in one of his letters as the son of mother India. Surojit's most treasured memories were of catching a glimpse of Bhagwanji. Another friends of theirs,' Kaushal Kishore, deemed himself lucky to have paid one visit to Faizabad in 1983 to hear the sermons in Bangla and English. "Do you know the Russians invaded Afghanistan to preempt the Americans?" he was told. All friends were convinced that the saint was Subhas Bose.

One thing leads to another. The man who had made it possible for these friends to reach out to Bhagwanji was Das Guptas' reclusive maternal uncle Sunil Krishna Gupta. Gupta, in his late 70s, was running the show from behind for nonagenarian freedom fighter Jyotish Chandra Bose. It was Gupta who had pulled off a coup by helping obtain a favourable ruling by Calcutta High Court, which had made the Atal Bihari Vajpayee government constitute Mukherjee Commission. Gupta was the man I met the very day I landed in Kolkata. His rented dilapidated accommodation was the most unlikely place to get to the heart of the Bose mystery. An old-fashioned wooden door heralded me into his living room. It looked like a store full of books and papers on Subhas Bose. "This is my life. I live for him," Gupta, a former lawyer and trade unionist, did not hide "obsession." I gathered that the only journo who had been to Gupta's place prior to me was from *TIME*. Gupta was subsequently described in the magazine as "a devoted believer" who demanded "no recognition" and even refused "to be named." Genes, one might say, were responsible for this sort of dedication. Gupta and his 90-plus brother Atul Krishna Gupta, another Bose-Bhagwanji acolyte, shared a valiant martyr for a brother — Dinesh Gupta. A couple of kilometers away from Gupta's house was the famous BB Bagh where in 1930 the Bengali version of the Bhagat Singh-Rajguru-Sukhdev epic was enacted. Three teenagers — Dinesh Gupta, Sudhir Gupta and Binoy Krishna Basu — entered Writers' Building, the seat of the Bengal government, in broad daylight and shot dead the IG of Bengal Prisons. They had held the IG responsible for a grievous assault on Subhas Bose when he was a prisoner. Dinesh was caught and later executed. Binoy was killed on the spot, and Badal Das Gupta chose to end his life before the colonialists could lay their hands on him.

Sunil Krishna Gupta was not interested in talking about Bhagwanji. All followers of the Faizabad saint had been ordained to keep the secrets to themselves. That's why Samar Guha never mentioned Bhagwanji publicly much as he wanted to. Consequently, in all their representations before the High Court and Mukherjee Commission, Gupta and others had not touched Bhagwanji angle. This was strange. This was also one aspect that had made the Bhagwanji story stand out of other baba tales. While the other babas or their followers clamoured to establish that they were the real MacCoys, the "actual man" and his followers kept everything under wraps. Bhagwanji's orders for Sunil Krishna Gupta, Samar Guha and others were just to disapprove the Taipei plane crash. This was what they have been doing all the years.

Well, now Bhagwanji's story was out, and so I persuaded Gupta to talk. "How did you come to know that Bhagwanji was Netaji?" was the first question. "Suresh Bose," Gupta named his mentor, "told me in 1963 to go to Neemsar. He said Subhas could be there." Bhagwanji had lived in obscure Neemsar on Indo-Nepal border from 1958 to 1964. To find out how Suresh Bose came to know that "Subhas" was in Neemsar, I travelled to the outskirts of the city to meet the son of a historic figure whose name, I am ashamed to admit, I had never heard. There was something amiss in the history we had been taught in schools and colleges. "Leela Roy was one of the greatest freedom fighters of this country," stated former Vice President Krishna Kant in 1997 at a function to mark her birth centenary. Charismatic daughter of a "Rai Bahadur," Leela Roy (nee Nag) had refused to make ovation to the Lady Viceroy with bent knees. She did her MA in English from the University of Dhaka where no girl student was hitherto allowed. Philanthropy brought her nearer to her hunk classmate and revolutionary Anil Chandra Roy. She followed him to a path no girl of her stature had dared to tread. They became the leading light of Sree Sangha, one of the revolutionary groups whose motto was an eye for an eye. She participated in Civil Disobedience Movement and led a huge procession against killing of Jatin Das and attack on Subhas Bose at Octerloney monument in Calcutta. In December

1931 an attempt on the life of District Magistrate of Comilla was made. A few days later, firebrand Leela was arrested and not released until 1937.

Bose's kin vouched to me that Leela Roy was one of his closest associates. "She was looked upon by the family as an epitome of womanhood," a niece said. They knew each other in 1920s and with Bose becoming the uncrowned king of the revolutionaries, both she and Anil Roy, her future husband, closed their ranks with him. They joined the Forward Bloc and visited Bose just before he fled to Germany in 1941. He tipped them of what lay ahead and entrusted the couple with some responsibility of managing the Forward Bloc. Leela Roy became the second editor of the weekly *Forward Bloc* after Bose and also wielded her pen for other papers. A leading English daily of Calcutta began a vituperative attack on Bose in his absence. Bose was dubbed a "convinced pro-Fascist" and his execution was demanded. Leela Roy gave vent to people's anger in a series of articles captioned "We shall not stand it" in *Hindustan Standard.* She was arrested in 1942 and for eight months guards were posted outside her cell in jail because the British believed that Bose had sent her a letter about a revolutionary uprising. Later they picked up the intelligence that the INA wanted to contact her. Her cell would be searched twice a week but that could not stop her from springing one surprise. A tricolour was found fluttering on top of the jail on the morning of 26 January 1943.

Leela Roy was elected to the Constituent Assembly, but she resigned protesting the partition of India. During the riots she provided succour in Noakhali, which Gandhiji himself praised. She risked her life while personally rescuing many of her compatriots like Ashrafuddin Ahmed Chaudhury from the riot-torn areas. In post-1947 period Leela Roy was struck by tragedies. Anil Roy suddenly passed away; Forward Bloc[1] got divided and her health began to fail. Her public role greatly cut down, Leela Roy began to concentrate on *Jayshree,* the magazine she had founded in 1931 with the help of Rabindra Nath Tagore. This continued till January 1963 when a new chapter in her life began. In 2001, the person who could best tell me about her amazing tale was Bijoy Nag, Leela Roy's nephew and adopted son. Nag was part of the group of Bengalis who clandestinely visited Bhagwanji, mostly around 23 January and Durga Puja. They were the ones who helped him remain in hiding. They served him in absolute secrecy for decades with no benefit whatsoever ever accruing to them. Rather they suffered hardships and many compromised with their and their families' well-being. Why would they do that was sought to be explained by a dramatic sequence of events.

On 18th January 1963 Nag returned home after having failed to get through Army Short Service Commission. He expected his mother to comfort him, but in one swoop Leela Roy turned his dejection into astonishment. "Don't feel that way. You have lost one opportunity to serve the country, but by the grace of God another has come your way. Netaji is alive. He is back to serve the country. I have sent a communication to him and a dispatch will be made before 23rd." Nag listened stupefied as Leela Roy drew hazy contours of some recent mysterious events. In April 1962, Professor Atul Sen, an ex-MLA, and an old acquaintance of Bose, by chance, met *Parde wala baba*, the saint behind the curtain, which was how Bhagwanji was known in Neemsar. On his return to Calcutta, Sen rushed to some of his friends, like historian Dr RC Majumdar, to tell them that he had run into Subhas Bose. His friends were former revolutionaries of Anushilan Samity group. Then Sen made "a mistake." Defying Bhagwanji's instructions, he contacted the Government, the Prime Minister at that, and forfeited his chance to meet "Subhas" again.

The news spread like wild fire in the Anushilan Samity circles. Dr Pabitra Mohan Roy tracked down Sen, heard him and decided to check out for himself. Pabitra was a man of inspiring antecedents. A revolutionary to start with, he had fled to SE Asia and joined the INA as a dauntless agent of its secret service. In 1943, on Bose's orders, Pabitra, Amrik Singh Gill, T Mukherjee and Mahindra Singh were dropped at Puri coast by a Japanese submarine. Their mission was to contact the revolutionaries in

India and turn the heat against the Raj. They arrived in Calcutta to find that people were too scared to help them. But for the shelter given by Suresh Bose's daughter Amita Mitra,[2] her husband Haridas Mitra and Jyotish Chandra Bose, they would have fallen into counter-espionage network much earlier. End came when T Mukherjee betrayed them. Mohindra Singh was caught in Bombay and was severely tortured.[3] He blurted out whereabouts of the others. Amrik and Pabitra were arrested and guilt drove Mohindra to suicide. The trial under the Enemy Agents Ordinance against the two and Haridas Mitra commenced on May 21, 1945 and by June end they had been ordered to be hanged. "Thanks to the efforts of Mrs Mitra, who lobbied Mahatma Gandhi, who in turn interceded with Lord Wavell, the death sentence was commuted to transportation for life on 4 November 1945."[4] Amrik Singh never needed any reprieve though. He won his freedom, making good a heroic escape through the winding lanes of Calcutta with the handcuffs on.

After several days' search, Pabitra zeroed in on a ruined Shiv temple complex in Neemsar where Bhagwanji was lodged. He had to try for a month or so before Bhagwanji agreed to meet him. They discussed many things of the past and present. Bhagwanji's language was couched in mystic analogism. He related strange anecdotes. An incident had taken place few years back in a famous optician's shop in Lucknow. Bhagwanji had to venture out to get himself new eyeglasses. He did not want to be seen, so he travelled lying under the back seat of a car. The car waited with its engines running while Bhagwanji stepped into the shop. A variety of spectacles were placed before him. He chose a round one and looked at his face in the mirror. He removed his headgear. There was a hush in the shop. Some customers saw a famous face. "Netaji!" one said and down went two young men prostrating before Bhagwanji. He rushed out of the shop and fled in the car. "Now you know why I am keeping long moustache and beard," Bhagwanji summed up the moral of the story to Pabitra.

The meeting convinced Pabitra that Bhagwanji was Bose. He was to return again and again. Over the years he obeyed

Bhagwanji's instruction with such secrecy that his own children remained in dark why their father had to frequently visit a holy man in North India. "Wherever I got any type of information, I religiously forwarded it without any delay, bias or fear. This has been your 'standing order'," Pabitra wrote to Bhagwanji in 1979. Many of his family pictures were located in Ram Bhawan and on a copy of his 1980 Bangla book *Netajeer Secret Service* (Netaji's Secret Service) he wrote that he was dedicating it to his Sadguru (Bhagwanji). In Basti, Bhagwanji once said off-the-cuff that "he had sent Pabitra and others from SE Asia to India."[5] In late 1985 a police team visited Calcutta to query Pabitra over his association with Bhagwanji. Pabitra was uncooperative, he gave vague replies and concealed information.[6]

Back in 1962, Pabitra returned to Calcutta from Neemsar with a list of things Bhagwanji had instructed him to bring on his next visit. The items were not exactly what a hermit would badly want. "A powerful transistor-radio" for use in "the back of the beyond." A chronometer, a telescope, a "Fowler's (or Oxford) dictionary" and cigars. Bhagwanji said "he would have very intensely liked to have all the records of Pankaj and Ramprosad."[7] The most unusual demand was a "26 yards long and 48 inches wide shimmering white pure silk cloth, one piece mulmull of same quality and size, one 13 and 1/2 yards x 48 inches shimmering white markin or of similar quality cloth." What for? "During his (Bhagwanji's) stay in Berlin, a radar scientist had said a few things, thus, the need for such clothes."

A man of modest income with a big family to support, Pabitra failed to arrange all that Bhagwanji had asked him to procure as "do or die missionary work." He wanted to return but orders had to be complied first. The only way out was to take support of someone trustworthy. The choice had to be such that it wouldn't anger Bhagwanji. "Didi!" "The elder sister" of revolutionaries came to Pabitra's mind. Leela Roy had dealt with Subhas Bose on equal terms. Pabitra told Leela Roy on 7 January 1963 that he had met "Subhas Bose" in Neemsar. In turn, she let it be known to her relatives and Sree Sangha confidants: Sunil Das, Shaila Sen, Bijoy Nag, Ajit Nag, Helena

Dutta, Santosh Bhattacharya, Sagrika Ghosh, Basana Guha and Professor Samar Guha. They also held a detailed confabulation on the subject of "Leader." Just as the old days, the deliberations were kept secret and all were placed under oath. On 20th January Roy dispatched a consignment of items Bhagwanji had asked Pabitra to arrange. On 21 March the ailing lady accompanied by INA secret service's Anil Das, Shailo Sen and Samar Guha, set out for Neemsar. They reached on 23rd and lodged themselves in a dharamshala not knowing that some high-profile visitor had preceded them. A godwoman revered by Gandhi, Nehru, Bose and Hollywood stars had visited Neemsar to meet Bhagwanji. Anandamayee Ma willingly endured long wait to meet an unknown holy man. Similar trials were in store for Leela Roy.

The visitors from Calcutta offered a life-time opportunity to a local follower of Bhagwanji's who had been drawn to the saint due to his familiar voice and rumours that he was Bose. Two decades earlier, Srikant Sharma had seen Bose in the same area — in Sitapur, Biswan and Sidhauli — as the then Congress president toured then United Province. Getting to talk to Bhagwanji had been of little comfort to Sharma, but even a step beyond the door pane was strictly prohibited. On 25 March 1963 he crossed that barrier for the first time and he lived to the age of 92 to tell Mukherjee Commission that he saw "old Netaji" inside the room.

Leela Roy gave Saraswati Devi, Bhagwanji's attendant. two books as presents to be handed over to Bhagwanji. *The Last Days of British Raj* by Leonord Mosely and volume one of the *History of Freedom Movement* by Dr RC Majumdar. Bhagwanji returned the gesture by sending a cup and plate, wrapped in a saffron cloth. The communication began with Leela Roy sending Bhagwanji a note in Bangla, a torn part of which was traced in Ram Bhawan in 1986: "Please accept my respectful greetings. I arrived here on 23rd around 11.30 and it has not been possible to establish contact ever since. If credentials are necessary, they can be sent. The person who stayed here for two months earlier (Pabitra Mohan Roy) took a long time to inform me. Nothing specific could be gathered from that person. I was expecting that instructions for establishing contact would have been available. I cannot understand why this was done."

Emotions rose on both sides. The gap was intermittingly bridged by Srikant who shuttled to and fro from Bhagwanji to Leela Roy. Leela Roy asked if "he" (Bose) had received the consignment of the items. Bhagwanji told Srikant to "go tell her 'yes'." "To Leela Roy only and not to Samar Guha," he cautioned. "He was a child when I left India." She asked, "how do I know it for sure that it is 'he' who has received the items?" Bhagwanji lapsed into silence and then began to tell Srikant many of events from the life of Subhas Bose. He told him of the time when cholera was raging in Bengal and how Subhas Bose and Leela Roy, without informing their families, went about taking care of the patients. Bhagwanji also recalled some details of his 1941 escape and parts played by Amita Mitra and Leela Roy. Srikant was told to convey to Leela Roy that she should not take the pains to visit him again. "It won't do anyone any good if I emerged now." For Samar Guha, he had a warning: "Do not take interest in my being alive."

Leela Roy began to weep. Samar Guha flared up: "I'll go inside. Who will stop me from seeing him?" Srikant stood up in his way. "Over my dead body! Here, everyone follows Bhagwanji's orders!" After it had cooled down, Leela Roy expressed the desire to communicate with Bhagwanji. This was agreed to. On 26 March the three visitors sang devotional songs in Bengali, and inside the room Bhagwanji joined singing. Later on Leela Roy and Bhagwanji got to talk on one to one. Bhagwanji was firm that he would not come in front of her. "Lee[8], you have had two strokes. I do not want to endanger your life. You may not be able to withstand this sight of me." He gave her some instruction written by him in Bangla and asked her to make a note of it. He was not yet ready to let her take to Calcutta a specimen of his handwriting. "My hands trembling — had to write every (Bangla) letter remembering after two decades of lapse. Please transfer it to your own writing and, return the paper."

Leela Roy left Neemsar on 30 April and returned to Calcutta with no doubt that Bhagwanji was Subhas Bose. "He has done so much for the country. He is suffering even now. I want to give him some relief," she told her son. "There was no way Leela Roy could have made a mistake in identifying uncle. She knew him too well," a Bose kin told the writer. On 6 April 1963, Leela Roy, the city sophisticate, wrote a letter in English to villager Srikant, underlying the hopes her visit had given birth to. "We also earnestly pray that there might be cause for great joy & relief for us and for our dear mother country in the near future, in hope of that we live, work and strive." Samar Guha wrote on 28 April. He addressed Srikant as his brother-in-arms and apologised for his bad Hindi:

"I received your letter. But since I was away from Calcutta for party work, I could not answer earlier. Please forgive me. You may have received Didi's letter. On our return, we saw her so distraught and sad as we had never seen her before .... In India there is no disciple of Bhagwanji's like Didi ... God knows what is on Bhagwanji's mind. It is very important that Bhagwanji again meet Didi or anyone sent by her. How can I tell you about the importance of this? If there is any chance of Bhagwanji meeting with Didi or anyone sent by her, please do try facilitate the meeting. This is my request to you. This is all what we want. This is not for personal interest or any other reason. It is very important for a special reason. When we get a chance, we will ourselves discuss with Bhagwanji. On the 1st of May I will go to Delhi to take part in party's central committee meet. There is a chance that I will meet President Radhakrishnan. You please ask Bhagwanji if I should try to know what he (Radhakrishnan) thinks of this subject (of Bhagwanji's). If Bhagwanji wishes, I can come over there before I go to Delhi. Whatever be the case, reply me as soon as possible. The condition and place in which Bhagwanji is staying is a matter of great concern and pain for all of us. Ensuring his well-being is a duty of all of us."[9]

Some time after Leela Roy's departure, Pabitra returned to Neemsar along with former revolutionary Amal Roy.[10] The duo stayed in Neemsar, that jungle of a place, for two months. Then came Kamalakant Ghosh, an alternative medicine practitioner. His coming before others had to do with Leela Roy's worries about Bhagwanji's health. Further down, more emissaries from Leela Roy began to line up in Neemsar. Many of them were hard-core revolutionaries and Subhas Bose's followers of yesteryears. The person Leela Roy first told about Bhagwanji was a Pakistani. Trailokya Nath Chakravarty "Maharaj" had set a sort of record during the freedom struggle. Such was his nuisance value that the British kept him behind bars for unimaginable 30 years which included over a decade in Raj's concentration camp in Port Blair. Leela Roy asked her confidant Sailendra Roy to cross over to East Pakistan and tell Maharaj of Bose's being alive and in India. Roy handed over Maharaj her letter and returned with a letter for Leela Roy. Sailendra Roy lived to the age of 88 to tell his side of story to Mukherjee Commission. The Commission also came to know about a letter discovered in Ram Bhawan in 1986. It had been written in Bengali on 11 April 1963 from Calcutta. The sender was Trailokya Nath Chakravarty.

"After the country's partition, I decided I would not leave my country and stay in East Pakistan. Hence, I am staying in East Pakistan only. The person with whom I was lodged in Mandalay Jail ... we played tennis together, we participated in Durga Pooja together — I have not forgotten him — I'm still with him. In Delhi, in the year 1940, at Shankar Lal's residence I was accompanying him, I was by his side while we toured United Province — on a chilling winter night in the Agra ground, hundreds of people were waiting for him till nine at night. I'm eagerly waiting for the same person. The oppressed and tortured people of East Pakistan are waiting for him."

"Here Maharaj writes as if the letter is for Subhas," a Bose family member told the writer after carefully going through a copy of the letter. Shankar Lal was Forward Bloc's general secretary. It was with Subhas Bose that Trailokya Chakravarty had been bundled to dreaded Mandalay Jail.

Next in the line was perhaps Ashutosh Kali who had been tipped off by Pabitra. An Anushilan Samity veteran who was older than Bose, he too had been prevented by long years in prison from playing a bigger role in freedom struggle. Now in 1963 he offered himself at the service of Bhagwanji whom he unmistakably took to be Subhas Bose. He wrote to him on 9 May 1963: "I think I need to explain a bit why an old revolutionary like me wants to meet you now when you are in a state of turmoil. After having thoroughly ascertained your whereabouts, I and Hashimay Sen of Dhaka[11] are now preparing to visit you. It's been decided that for the next discussion we will include Dr Pabitra Roy. Dr Pabitra Roy is a co-worker from our team of revolutionaries, and is also loved and trusted by you. The decision may be taken by Dr Pabitra or we shall act as per your instructions .... The moment we received your instructions we started maintaining secrecy. Pabitra is familiar with military life, he has not undergone any training for diplomatic life .... I am determined not to allow any laxity on our part and ensure your safety, security and complete secrecy. Any danger to your existence is not just so for you but also for us all .... It can result in a great disaster as well as an immense damage to the nation."

Kali died in an accident in 1965 but before that he visited Bhagwanji. Another undated letter of his was discovered in Ram Bhawan.

"Last May, I had paid a visit ... to seek your advice regarding what all we should do in the present situation ... ever since we got news of you, we all, I mean the entire Anushilan group, have been yearning to gain from your guidance and work under your instructions .... You and Maharaj do know everything. He is in East Pakistan. Due to lack of much scope for work there and owing to his ailing health, he had agreed to come and stay here in India on our request. But after hearing of you he has completely given up on that ... he has now taken the difficult stance of staying back in Pakistan. Now he too is waiting for your call.

"I have crossed the age of seventy ... (but) ... the idealism that I imbibed from the valiant revolutionaries, the courage with which I fought ... everything is still burning bright within me. All we need is a leader and his guidance. If you exhort, even at this point of life I will not hesitate to join the movement .... I wanted to inform you that Basanti Debi is desperate to receive news of you. She has requested us to let her know about your whereabouts."

In last part of his letter, Kali referred to one Basanti Debi, who apparently was the wife of Bose's mentor Chittaranjan Das and a motherly figure to Bose. Basanti Devi had survived her husband and son into 1960s. No one could tell if Basanti Devi contacted Bhagwanji, but the information came through that Subhas's *sejda* took Bhagwanji to be his brother. Pabitra and Leela Roy informed Suresh Bose about Bhagwanji, and in late 1963 Suresh sent Sunil Gupta to Neemsar. Leela Roy also tried to inform some other members of the Bose family, but the outcome was unknown. She personally confided in the secret of "Bose" being alive to industrialist Ashutosh Ganguly, Swami Asimananda Saraswati, a holy man who knew Bose, and Bose's friend Ashraffuddin Ahmed Chaudhury. Unconfirmed input had it that on his birthdays Bhagwanji used to feast on delicacies prepared by a Bose family member. As Bhagwanji had apprehended, Leela Roy's health deteriorated after her return from Neemsar. On one such despondent day, she wrote to Subhas's bosom friend Dilip Kumar Roy, who had turned ascetic. Two messengers were rushed to Dilip with the letter he was to read and return. The letter dated 27 July 1963 informed Dilip that his friend was alive:

"I hope this finds you in good health. Cerebral stroke has made me immobile. That's the reason I cannot meet you — and I wanted to meet you for a purpose. Since my right hand is paralyzed, I have difficulty writing. Let it be. Anyway, this is not the reason for my writing to you. I wanted to tell you about your friend. I am not entitled to speak much, but I can only inform you that he is alive — in India. He has mentioned about your friendship with him many times. For example, 'It was Dilip who always wanted to make me mystic.' For this reason, this letter is important. After reading this, please return to Mrs Shailo

Sen who is carrying the letter. If you trust me, then it is 100 pc correct. No one else should know about it – this is the stern injunction on me."

In July 1964 Leela Roy sent Bhagwanji "the Credentials of Anil Das alias Renu." The former INA secret service agent had sought a meeting and as a prerequisite had jotted down in Bangla the reasons he should have been given the opportunity to serve "him" again. He wrote about his role in the freedom struggle that had began in 1930s and lasted beyond the disappearance of Bose in 1945. Leela Roy, who vetted his letter, vouched for Das with the comment that "he is a dedicated, honest, upright idealistic worker."

"With the commencement of the Second World War, I (Anil Das) rushed back to Bangkok and met Swami Satyanand. When Netaji came to Singapore, I also headed for the same place. It was in Singapore that I met Netaji. Myself and some other persons were trained for the reconstruction department work there only. Then we were sent to Rangoon. When war broke out I was sent to Azad Hind Dal's Moreh Camp. I became commander of a group. My group operated within Indian borders only. When the INA and Japanese Army started retreating, we too returned following orders. After a few days, following Netaji's orders, I went to Rangoon to take charge of SS Group's camp.

"On the night before he left Bangkok, Netaji took individual interviews of a number of people. I was one of them. When Netaji called me it was half past 2am. He told me about the post war work and cautioned me against getting arrested. Then he gave me a letter addressed to Hikari Kikan .... On receiving Netaji's letter, Hikari Kikan gave me a few revolvers but they did not have any money. I remained underground in Thailand with all this material .... Netaji said that wherever he may be, he would remain in contact with us via wireless.

"When I heard the news of the crash of Netaji's plane, I knew such a news would come and it would not be true. I waited for over a decade and in 1956 I visited India and told everything to *Pisima* (auntie — Leela Roy). In 1961 I left Bangkok for good and last year *Pisima* sent me to Neemsar and thereafter whatever small or big news I wanted to know I came to know from *Pisima*. Now I am waiting for your orders."

Anil Das got the clearance to visit Bhagwanji. In the meeting, Bhawanji corrected him on some of the points he had made in his letter. He said that his secret meeting with "him" in August 1945 was held not only at Bangkok but also at Singapore. He also asked Anil to tell him in detail what had happened thereafter and in particular he wanted to know what statements Debnath Das, the PGI minister, had given to the British. Anil gave a lengthy answer to Bhagwanji in writing. This was also traced in Ram Bhawan.

"I received 2 wireless sets and a few revolvers, pistols and stenguns from Hikari Kikan. They could not give me British currency. Keeping all this with me I went underground. Within 6-7 days the British Military reached Bangkok. In the meanwhile the news of the 'plane crash' also reached and the whole city was engulfed by gloom. There was a condolence ceremony but nothing substantial happened, people just cried. It was published regarding the accident news that Netaji was alone in the 'plane.' After 2 months, Debnath Das reached Bangkok and he informed that Netaji took only Habibur Rahman with him. Since the plane Netaji was travelling in had no more accommodation, the rest of the party followed minutes after in a 'second' plane. But that plane landed in Hanoi. Later it was told that Netaji's plane had crashed.

"... first Debnath Das surrendered before British military authority, and he was let off after his statement was taken .... An Indian captain, who was a nice man, took his statement. Debnath told him about me and he replied that no one would be arrested. A statement on our part would do, he was told. One day Debnath came to me along with this man and my statement was taken. I was asked how I reached there from India. Having heard that this person took out his file and told that I need not say anything more for whatever I had told him was true. His file had all the details about my moving from one place to another. The INA soldiers were confined to a camp after the British military reached Bangkok. Whoever was arrested had to give individual statement, so I would not know what statement were given by others."[12]

There was no count how many such freedom fighters contacted Bhagwanji who regularly destroyed sensitive correspondence. He would keep his local followers at an arm's length from visitors. One follower would be instructed to pick up the guests, the other arrange for their stay and another see them off. An inkling of what might have been the contents of the sensitive letters became known with the discovery in 1986-87 of a small note apparently signed by former West Bengal Chief Minister Prafulla Ghosh. Ghosh had lamented that "whatever happened after the Haripura session leading to the Wellington Square happenings — if they had not happened, then life would have taken a turn probably in a different direction." Haripura Congress session had elected Bose to Congress presidency, and, then he was sacked at the behest of Gandhi.

Letters from Sunil Das,[13] another fearless former revolutionary of Leela Roy's circle, were descriptive. Das lost his all three siblings, including kid sister, during the freedom struggle. His elder brother was beaten to death in Dacca jail and this act of barbarity was chided by British MPs in the House of Commons. An MA in physics who had published a paper in the *American Journal of Physics*, Sunil Das had a very bright future ahead when he decided to turn a freedom fighter. From 1963 onwards, this hard-core Subhas Bose loyalist kept his ears to the ground for Bhagwanji: "This morning (January 24, 1964) I had a chance meeting along with .... (Forward Bloc leader) Sri Hemanta Bose and others, with Sri Surendra Mohan Ghosh MP ... in the room of (West Bengal) Chief Minister Sri Prafulla Chandra Sen. He had been there to ascertain whether the government would lift the ban on processions and meetings for the observance of the birthday of Netaji on the 23rd January .... When the Chief Minister had left the room, we had a long talk with Sri Surendra Mohan Ghosh about Shoulmari Ashram and Netaji."

Till the time she slipped into coma in 1968, Leela Roy maintained regular link with the "Leader." She gave up in 1963 her public life and through *Jayshree* she began to voice her opinion disapproving Bose's death without ever referring to Bhagwanji. "We'll wait for India's new leadership, new directions and the new sunrise — the leader who has been deprived of his right to serve the country all these years through the deceitful declaration of his death."[14] She guided Samar Guha when he began his fight for Bose. "The portrait (of Bose) shall be placed only in the Central Hall (of the Parliament). The funds will be borne by us and no one else," she enjoined on him in 1967. Thanks to her and Pabitra Roy many got in contact with Bhagwanji. Late Santosh Bhattacharya and Dulal Nandi, who gave evidence to Mukherjee Commission, executed Bhagwanji's house moving manoeuvers with military precision. Bijoy Nag's first visit was in 1970 following his mother's death. Apurba Kumar Ghosh, who appeared before Mukherjee Commission at age 93, was sent by Leela Roy to Bhagwanji several times in the 1960s. He had been an attendant of Bose in pre-1945 days. When he visited Basti, Bhagwanji identified him and recalled a 1940 event that only Bose could have known.

The followers were usually disallowed to refer to Bose in their correspondence with Bhagwanji. But at times the reference became unavoidable. "Could I tell you why do I take you as my guru?" wrote revolutionary Vishwanath Roy in his 22 December 1964 letter. "In 1923, when I was 12 years old, yourself, Deshbandhu (Chattaranajn Das), Santosh Kumar came to the grounds close to my house. That day I was attracted towards you and I had vowed I would be like Subhas Chandra Bose."

Through his followers, Sunil Krishna Gupta and Samar Guha, Bhagwanji kept a watch on Khosla Commission's work. From the start, Bhagwanji doubted if the probe would be fair. "Khosla won't do justice. Khosla's pen is Indira's pen," he said on one night in late 1971. Crisis erupted when Samar Guha released a picture in 1979 and claimed that Bose was alive. Angry Bhagwanji severed links with all his followers in Bengal and decided to leave the place he was living in. For many months he was incommunicado. When Pabitra had mustered the courage to write to him, he tried to make amends by reaffirming his allegiance to Bhagwanji: "I wish to say something - your own words – 'You are my intelligence officer - without fear or favour must act'- Now allow me to begin in a similar way. Keeping in mind *Ma Kaali - Deshmata - Bangajanani - Bharatmata* (Mother India) and your feet, I tell you that just like the past, I still have the same unflinching faith, love, trust, unwavering obedience, total dedication and loyalty towards you ...."

In an another letter running into several pages, and discussing among others President Sanjiva Reddy, Pabitra gave a date-wise account of the 23 January 1979 episode from his side:

"In the end of January 1978, the letters (from Bhagwanji) stopped coming in the aftermath of the events perpetrated by these people. I have been feeling bad for not having been able to send you the full report. Earlier I could tell you things in brief. They played their dangerous game involving my Sadguru for a long time and in 1979 end on a holy day (23 January) and then came the result — court case and bad name.

"September 4 (1978): Sukrit came to meet for the first time after January. Among others, he said that he had got hold of a picture. The photo was of 'his.' In his words, a number of people had that photograph. Then he described the picture. It was taken in ancient temple in some dense jungle. 'He' is standing on the temple entrance. He described how he is standing, and what is the posture of hand. According to him, 'he' is wearing a thick woollen garment and has a muffler on. He said there would be no difficulty in identifying him even though age has brought changes.

"Sukrit also said 'he' himself gave that picture so that it may be published across India. 'He' would soon give green signal to do this and they were just waiting. He also said that he received this picture some 3-4 months earlier and they had been busy over this in Delhi. And this was the reason they could not meet me. Off and on again, he pressed that I too would soon receive a picture. He also said that some 150 copies were ready. A list was also prepared to whom they would be sent. Sukrit claimed that he had seen the list and that it contained mine and Sunil Das's name. A number of selected ministers, MPs and MLAs too were in this list. The list of newspapers too was ready.

"Sukrit said they had to wait for the green signal by him. He added that he was in constant touch and that three more pictures would come and they would be published one after another. Also, the photo would contain 'his' words at the bottom. Sukrit said there was some delay in obtaining those handwritten words and the moment it is received it would be copied and published along with the picture.

"January 23, 1979: All the newspapers in Calcutta covered the press conference. The photo and teacher's (Samar Guha) statement were also displayed prominently.

January 30, 1979: This day a statement of Congress leader Subrato Mukherjee was published. Along with were shown 2-3 pictures. He has tried to prove that the picture released by teacher was a fake. It was actually a work of superimposition. He said a picture of Netaji's brother Sarat Chandra Bose was used and its head was replaced with that of the Netaji."

Pabitra wrote that there had been a conspiracy to finish off Guha's political career. He had been given the fake picture by deceased INA Colonel Thakur Singh's wife and despite reservation he fell for it. Bhagwanji did not forgive Guha. Sunil Gupta clarified his stand and was pardoned. Excommunicated from Bhagwanji's circle, Guha for years suffered the tribulations. His desire to tell the truth was genuine, but he was helpless. "If he doesn't want to come out, what can I do," he was to bemoan. People pooh-poohed him until the end of his life without noting the hints given by those occupying the highest posts of the land. President Neelam Sanjiva Reddy released Guha's book on 8 March 1978 knowing well that it had the rider that Bose was alive at that time. "Let us see him (Bose) even for one day,"[15] the President of India wished 33 years after Bose "death" and remarked that "India would make another attempt to unravel the mystery of Netaji's death." "He urged the USSR to cooperate with the Government of India in ascertaining the truth about Netaji. He said ... (he) would coax the Soviet authorities to 'send Netaji back if he is there.'"[16] In 1979 Guha told President Reddy about Bhagwanji. In 1983, a better-informed Morarji Desai chaired a function to re-release *Netaji: Dead or Alive?* The former Prime Minister, who surely had seen the secret files under the control of the PMO, told the gathering that there was a "story that he (Bose) was alive and ... had taken *sanyas*."[17]

Some Bose kin too affirmed their belief in Bose's remaining alive decades after his "death." Suresh Bose said so during his deposition before Khosla Commission. Lest it be construed that a dying man was wishing that his kid brother had survived 25 years as a prisoner in Siberia, up came the cross-examination of Dwijendranath Bose. He was pointedly asked if he had tried to find out the identity of *Parda Baba*, i.e. Bhagwanji. Dwijendra's answer was that he was not his uncle. But then, Pabitra Mohan Roy, Sunil Das, Anil Das and Samar Guha had also deposed before this Commission and had said nothing of Bhagwanji. Bhagwanji did not want the people to know his identity and his followers took his commands as articles of faith. The relevant part of Dwijendra's testimony came later. He was asked if he had indeed made a statement on 6 March 1966 in Thiruvananthapuram, which had been published by *Amrita Bazar Patrika*. "Netaji is still alive, says nephew," was the headline. "Dwijendranath Bose reiterated here today that Netaji was still alive and was working in a place very near the borders of India."

"Yes I did say," Dwijendra affirmed. The report was further quoted to him: "I can tell you that last September, Netaji had an attack of pneumonia and was examined and treated by some very eminent doctors whom I know, but I won't name. Mr Bose told reporters."

"Yes, I did say that," Dwijen repeated.

The writer ascertained that Leela Roy had in 1966 sought the counsel of Dr SK Das, personal physician to President Rajendra Prasad, for ailing Bhagwanji.

The *Patrika* also quoted Dwijendra saying that one reporter had almost uncovered the truth about Bose. "A staff reporter of a Calcutta daily had gone to the place where Netaji was staying, and had returned convinced that he was alive. The reporter, of course, could not meet Netaji."

Asked why Netaji was still in hiding, Mr (Dwijendra) Bose replied that "it was not correct to say that he was in hiding. He is not hiding. He is still working for India. He will come out into the open and enter India at the appropriate time in such a way that he establish a new order in the country." When asked if he still stood by his 1966 statement, Dwijendra said, "Yes."

"Therefore, may I understand that your case is that though all these sadhus are not Netaji, but Netaji is still alive?"

"Yes."

"And it is within your knowledge."

"I do not get this information day to day, I mean, where he is. Not only me but there are others also, I would not name them, of course, who get information after he had left a place say months or one year after that Netaji was at such and such place."[18]

"You mentioned about the staff reporter of a Calcutta daily who had gone to the place where Netaji was staying and had returned without seeing him. Are you prepared to disclose that?"

"I am not prepared to disclose that. He did not meet Netaji but he was convinced."[19]

"He had gone to the place. You have also mentioned in the statement that he will come out in the open and enter India at the appropriate time in such a way that he can establish a new order in the country. This statement which you have made was conveyed to you by Netaji himself or you have just heard from somebody else?"

"Things come. That is all."

"You cannot say that Netaji had said ... nor you have seen him personally!"

"Neither I have received his writings personally nor I have seen him."

"In spite of all this, you still believe that he is alive?"

"I am convinced that he is alive."

"You will excuse me for putting an annoying question. Government is spending so much[20] upon this inquiry Commission and the subject matter of the inquiry is to disentangle the mystery about Netaji's disappearance. So ... is it not unfair to the people and the Government to allow this inquiry to go on when you have positive knowledge and you are not prepared to disclose?"

"If I give a clue in this Commission, that would be made public and the Government will know of it and that is dangerous to Netaji. It is for him (Netaji) to decide when that should be made public or when he should return to India."

Bhagwanji was supplied with copies of Dwijendra's statement along with other papers concerning Khosla Commission. The search of his belongings in 1985-86 also yielded group pictures showing some of those in contact with the saint. Suresh Bose and Dwijendra Bose figured therein.

There was clear evidence that Sunil Das was in contact with Bhagwanji and he took him to be Subhas Bose. Das was examined by Khosla Commission on 6 September 1972 and was asked by the counsels to reflect on the rumours of Bose being alive and of Leela Roy's views on the issue:

"The point that I want to ask from you (Das) is that you knew Netaji well intimately so as not to mistake his identity?"

"His identity? So far as I am concerned, good heavens, never. How can I mistake his identity. No Bengalee can mistake his identity, even a teenager cannot mistake his identity."

"Do you think that if Netaji is really alive there is something really insurmountable which would prevent him or would actually prevent him from coming into the arena when the country is in utter confusion and chaos?"

"Your question has two parts ... regarding the first part of the question my reply is, I believe that Netaji is alive. Regarding the second part I have no competence to go into it."[21]

"How many times you think Mrs Leela Roy met Sarat Babu? (Sarat Chandra Bose)."

"I think almost every day."

"Was there any discussion regarding Netaji's alleged plane crash?"

"As far as I remember, Sarat Babu never believed it ...."

"Did Didi ever write regarding the disappearance of Netaji ... in *Jayshree*?"

"There were occasions when this subject cropped up in editorials after 1963, I should say, we noticed a change in her — within herself. Although I happened to be her closest colleague and in many matters she shared counsel with me — as you know, we had been trained in the crucibles of secret revolutionary politics and we have developed a code and we maintain the code in this way — unless I am specifically told, if somebody in the hierarchy wants to keep something within himself or herself, we do not try to get it. That has been our training. Up till now I carry that thing with me .... After 1963 (the year Leela Roy met Bhagwanji) this subject came up in her writing and editorials repeatedly. I can show you some of her writings where she dwelt at length on this aspect of the matter. .... This is *Asaradia Sankhya* of *Jayshree*, 1372, equivalent to October number 1965. In the concluding part of this editorial she writes that the finding of Shah Nawaz Committee is thoroughly unreliable and has to be rejected and his so-called death in the plane crash does not bear scrutiny ...."

"Will you kindly try to refresh your memory and tell this commission whether any article of Dr Ramesh Chandra Majumdar, the eminent historian, was published in this paper, *Jayshree*, about Netaji?"

"Not only once but a number of articles were written by Dr Majumadar in *Jayshree* about Netaji. He is very close to us[22] and in the Netaji number of *Jayshree* which comes out every year, Dr Majumdar had written a number of articles .... I will draw attention of the commission to one or two aspects of the articles ... he says that one of his friends who was very intimately known to Netaji and who, of course, died recently — a former professor[23] — had told him that he had spoken with Netaji from behind a screen or behind a closed door, a person who was behind closed door. Then he says that although Netaji did not go out and did not appear before him he told him about many past episodes which were not likely to be known by others. That is how he has written. Then he says that this highly educated, respected gentleman really believed that the person with whom he had conversed was Netaji."

"Would you agree if I say that she (Leela Roy) had close connection with Netaji even after the alleged plane crash and Didi narrated those things to you?"

"We had discussions about these matters. We do not believe that Netaji is dead and she has pointedly put in certain editorials and she has increasingly become affirmative — more and more affirmative as days passed — and she has categorically stated that India will some day enjoy the benefit of his leadership."

"And so she was emphatic that Netaji did not die in the plane crash?"

"Yes, there is no doubt about it."

With answers like those it was but obvious that the counsels put straight questions to Sunil Das, who was bound by Bhagwanji to an oath of secrecy.

"Do you know if late Mrs Leela Roy of revered memory did have any special information about the fact of Netaji being alive and did she say anything to you to that effect?"

"I have already told you that I have been brought up amidst revolutionary politics. We have some code of conduct .... It was in the month of April 1965 when she called some of us and told us that something was likely to happen on the Indo-Pakistan border — border between India and East Pakistan. She told us that lakhs and lakhs of people, she told about 50 to 60 lakh, would come over. She also told us that it would be our duty ... to save the suffering people from an impending catastrophe and to organise those people .... In 1965, with that frail body ... he along with some ladies, young women and girls, accompanied us to the border .... That struck me very strange How could she think of it, what was the basis of her conjecture I do not know but it struck me very strange."[24]

"... my question has not been answered .... I am not asking you to disclose the source of Mrs Roy's knowledge .... Did she make any positive statement to you at any time prior to her death?"

"Yes, she made statements on many occasions that he is not dead and in all probability he would come — that was her assertion and she was very emphatic."

In the end of his examination, Sunil Das was probed about some queer write-ups about one Mahakal that had been frequently appearing in *Jayshree*. Das had taken over the editorship of *Jayshree* and allied publications following Leela Roy's illness.

"Can you kindly enlighten us about the identity of the writer who writes under the pen-name of 'Mahakal' in the publication of which you are associated?"

"At the moment the writer chooses to remain anonymous. Therefore, you cannot expect me to tell his name."

"The writings are startling and extraordinary and of such dimension which are rarely seen in the ordinary rung of writers. That is why I asked this question that if you are in a position to do so then disclose ....?"

"Readers are free to make their own conclusions from such writings."

Jayshree had published a number of Mahakal's write-ups that were later complied in a Bangla book titled after a Tagore song. *Oye Mahamanav Ashe*, or "A Superman Shall Come", was incidentally also recited in Parliament when a portrait of Subhas Bose was unveiled in the presence of President Reddy, Prime Minister Desai and Minister Vajpayee. But Mahakal was not the author of those write ups, he was the protagonist. *Oye Mahamanav Ashe* was mostly based on Mahakal's talks with his followers. The compiler was Charnik, a pseudonym for one or more of Bhagwanji's followers. Mahakal was one of Bhagwanji's many names.

Prima facie, *Oye Mahamanav Ashe* appeared a fictional, clumsily written narrative that randomly changed tack and referred to events, places and persons connected to Subhas

Bose. Like Beni Madhav Das and Hemanta, who were Subhas's childhood teacher and best friend. But peeping behind printing errors, and a charade of mysticism and semi-historical analogies, were the definite leads to crack the Bhagwanji-Bose mystery. Bhagwanji said he was "Dead man" because his name had been "crossed out of the human register." "I have cheated death so often. I have been cheating death in every day of my life." He often paraphrased a Rudyard Kipling quote which used to be on Bose's lips. "If Bengal lives who dies? And if Bengal dies ... who lives!"

Wrapped in strange and at times misleading musings, Bhagwanji left an account of his "known" and secret life. One needn't have known Bengali to get the gist. Some passages were in English. Thus spoke Mahakal on his younger days: "To understand a man you have to understand the bed-rock on which he stands and he works. My most and only beloved mother was a direct initiated disciple of Paramhansa Deva. By every suck of her breast, through every kiss of her, by the channels of her caresses, touches, tender looks and words, the *Tattwa-Shakties* (powers) of the Divine Mother flowed in and filled me. My father gave unto me thoroughness and strength in service to others and fighting activeness. My Governor, first tutor-guardian gave me missionary sacrificing zeal and all-fighting all-overcoming stamina .... I inherited Mysticism from Mother, Parmahansa and Vivekanada. Throughout I have been constant. Even during most hectic times the deepest hours of night afforded a bit of time for that."

"I heard them say that I was born in *Ajapa Yoga,* see consult my ... horoscope .... From my childhood I began hearing and perusing scriptures. As I grew up my mystic hunger also grew. I went through all scriptures and philosophosies again and again. In college and University years I used to seek out, hunt for the so-called — great seers and wise men of our days and questioned-questioned-questioned them on mysticism. None satisfied me, I even left everything (once) in search of true Mystic Satguru and searched far and wide in the country and high and low in the Himalayas. None could satisfy me. It was bitter winter. I remembered my own mother dear, darling adored mother and came back at her lap and feet."[25]

This was definitely an account of the "Indian Pilgrim"[26] Subhas Chandra Bose's early life. Even in the midst of war, Bose never let go of the saint in him. At Singapore he would drive incognito to the Ramakrishna Mission, and spent hours meditating. Mahakal described himself a "Yodha-Sanyasi" (warrior-saint), the one who regarded "ahimsa" (non-violence) as "bunkum." He gave indications of his having had some military experience:

"But always remember: whether war should be brutal, cathartic or a humane business is beside the point. Every one knows that no war can be conducted and fought with kid gloves. Modern war especially takes an appalling toll both on human life and property. No civilized nation risks it lightly but when it is forced on, it has to be waged in a manner that makes the opponent wince. This is done not in any vindictive spirit but in a cold-calculated manner to break the opponent's morale, so that he is forced to sue for peace. Abstract principles have nothing to do with waging of war."

Oye Mahamanav Ashe clearly referred to Gandhi, Congress, and the partition of India:

"I shall tell you two things more: he has no rancour for Bapu, though Bapu and Congress thought otherwise. Your Dead man has no rancour because Bapu at least turned a volte-face and preached fighting for freedom and honour .... He stoutly opposed partition and during the last fateful meeting he wept like a child before them .... Also it has been kept secret that your Dead man went with Bapu's full blessings and concurrence of the inner committee."

Well, my interest was in the disappearance. I queried Bhagwanji's followers, checked papers and *Oye Mahamanav Ashe.* Engrossing details came forth. What really happened on 18 August 1945? Going by Bhagwanji's account when "he" arrived in Saigon aerodrome on 17 August, he saw Chandra Mal, the IIL transport secretary. Since he suspected him to be a spy, he changed his plan. The "original plan" of Bose's escape,

Debnath Das had revealed in a 1953 letter to Leela Roy, was "to go to India and continue the country's liberation fight from some underground centre."

"Japan agreed to take Netaji from Bangkok to somewhere in Bengal and agreed to take responsibility so far as the necessary transport was concerned. All other paraphernalia were made by us from the middle of June 1945 .... On that understanding, Netaji emplanned for Saigon, as according to the Japanese, it could have been easier for him and his officers to go to India through Saigon, as there was less vigilance of the Allied Forces on that route .... After reaching Saigon only, the Japanese military authorities separated Netaji from the rest of us on the ground that there was no accommodation in the plane. Not only that, we were informed for the first time that he was to be taken towards Tokyo ...."

"Immediately I gave vent to my feelings that there should be no change in the plan and that Netaji must be taken to India — the only logical step for him. 'Even if we are captured,' I said, 'the people will come to know and help us.' ... General Isoda ... suggested that the Alternate Plan be taken up (The principle feature of the Plan was to keep Netaji safe somewhere in East Asia) and gave me an idea of bases and routes. General Isoda said, that there would be no difficulty and so long he lived, he would keep Netaji safe ...."

The plane that took off for Taihoku was a "dummy" flight. "He" was never meant to go there. The air crash was a "concoction." In Basti and elsewhere Bhagwanji made passing remarks about the air crash that never was. "Air crash did not take place there on that day — it is a fabricated story." He was beholden to the Japanese and said Tsunamasa Shidei was a "generous general."[27] In one meeting with the visitors from Calcutta, he suggested that Dr Satyanarayan Sinha should visit Taipei ahead of Khosla and gather evidence backing his claim. *Oye Mahamanav Ashe* recreated the scene at Saigon airport on the evening of 17 August as "Mahanayak" (read Subhas Bose) prepared to take leave of his staff, including his young "adjutant" (read Habibur Rahman who was 28 in 1945):

"Having completed all his work Mahanayak (the hero) came out of the house. Meanwhile, the Japanese generals desperately pressed that there should not be any delay. The hero proceeded towards his generals — everyone was eager to know who would have the opportunity to accompany him. Each of the generals thought he was the only deserving candidate. Expressing his deep attachment to each one of them, the hero said — 'I don't know whom to take along and whom to leave out! But my foreigner friends have agreed to only one person accompanying me. Therefore, I will take along my youngest general, my adjutant with me.' Saying so, he pulled along with his 'adjutant' on to the plane. Before anybody could realise what was going on, the plane took off."

The plane made an "unscheduled" stopover, perhaps in Tourane. Here Mahanayak took leave of his adjutant, who was ordered to proceed further:

"The plane landed at a place where it was supposed to halt. But suddenly something happened. There was a sudden development, some indication that some people were after Mahanayak. He could not afford to wait further. He bid adieu to his trusted adjutant. He told his adjutant — remember my instruction, I have no time to tell you everything in detail. I have told everything to my most trusted Japanese generals. Learn from them and do accordingly .... Thereafter, Mahanayak left for an unknown destination."

Oye Mahamanav Ashe said SA Ayer was in the know of the escape plan. He was to follow Mahanayak in an another plane along with the INA treasure. But he flew straight to Tokyo. The INA treasure did not get burnt or lost — it was looted, Bhagwanji charged. Others did too. The fingers were pointed out at SA Ayer, Ramamurti and Jawaharlal Nehru.

"I do not propose to say anything about the valuables or the INA treasures," Khosla wrote nonchalantly in his report. Witness J Murti, brother of Ramamurti, said little to negate the rumours that his brother had become a multimillionaire overnight in 1945 after SA Ayer met him in Tokyo. He disclosed that Ramamurti was not willing to appear before the Commission.

And, Coionel JG Figges of British Intelligence, who had given a positive report of Bose's death, was a pal of his brother's. Casting clear aspersions was a 1 November 1951 MEA report — "INA treasure and their handling by Messers Ayer and Ramamurti" — from RD Sathe, who rose to be a Cabinet Secretary, to Prime Minister Nehru.

"Mr Iyer (Ayer) recently visited Japan with the ostensible purpose of investigating the present position in regard to the treasure. Mr Iyer's activities in Japan have been rather suspicious .... Netaji had with him in Saigon substantial quantity of gold ornaments and precious stones .... There is a party here (in Tokyo) who has seen the boxes in Iyer's room and who was also to buy off the contents of these few boxes. What happened to these boxes subsequently is a mystery as all that we have got from Iyer is 300gm of gold and about 260 rupees worth of cash. You will, no doubt, draw your own conclusion from all this, but to me it would appear as if Iyer, apprehensive of the early conclusion of the Peace Treaty came to Tokyo to decide the loot and to solve his and Murthy's conscience by handing over a small quantity to Government in the hope that by doing so he would also succeed in drawing a red herring across the trail."

"Suspicion regarding the improper disposal of the treasure is thickened by the comparative affluence in 1946 of Mr Ramamurthy when all other Indian nationals in Tokyo were suffering the greatest hardships. Another fact which suggests that the treasures were improperly disposed off is a sudden blossoming out into an Oriental Cargo export of Col Figges, the Military Attaché of the British mission in Tokyo, and the reported invitation extended by the Colonel to Ramamurty to settle down in UK."

Mahanayak, in the meanwhile, remained in the vicinity of Saigon. In a small hotel there, he was accidentally seen by some Japanese and Allied personnel. To "adjutant" who "remained true to his words" all his life, Mahakal expressed gratitude: "My adjutant was a perfect human being. Perhaps that is the reason why he was not given shelter in independent India. I have not come across such an extraordinarily trustworthy and dedicated person — someone who could carry out the instructions with such devotion."

If Bhagwanji was to be believed, *Mahanayak's* "unknown destination" was Soviet Russia. A few days after "the crash" had taken place, he reached Diren, Manchuria, and from there he travelled in a jeep to enter the Russian-held territory. This line of story was "corroborated" by two independent sources. The first became notoriously well known the moment it was stated on oath by a witness before Khosla Commission. The witness Sham Lal Jain, who was a confidential stenographer of Asaf Ali, "alleged that Pandit Nehru had asked him to make typed copies of a hand-written note that said Bose had reached Russia via Diren. He also alleged that Pandit Nehru asked him to type a letter to British Prime Minister Attlee, that 'Bose, your war criminal, has been allowed to enter Russian territory by Stalin ....'"[28] The other source was the public statement of Dharmendra Gaur[29], who claimed that as an Intelligence Bureau officer, during 1950s he came to know something from the horse's mouth. Gaur also published his side of story in Hindi daily *Amar Ujala* on 4 April 1982. He alleged that during his private visit to India in October 1956, Clement Attlee, former British PM, was subjected to surveillance by the IB. In Lucknow, where Gaur was looking after foreigners and security branch of the bureau, the British Premier had a heart-to-heart talk with state Chief Minister Sampurnanand. This talk was bugged. Earl Attlee told the CM that Bose, helped by General Shidei, escaped to the USSR via Diren in a jeep.

Bhagwanji said, as Jain had imputed, that Stalin had indeed allowed "him" to enter the USSR. The escape plan was in the making for a long time and was eventually executed. "Does anyone know that prior to *Mahanayak's* last journey he had gone to the country of bears and established links with the country's leaders? He met the country's leaders and organised everything," read *Oye Mahamanav Ashe.* That Subhas Bose made a secret trip to Soviet Russia much before his disappearance was also the claim made by Suresh Bose, without citing any evidence, in his deposition before Khosla Commission. "Mr Bose admitted that Netaji had a plan to go to Russia via Manchuria in the event of Allied Forces winning the war. The plan was drawn up in early 1944 and it was accepted by the Japanese Government," said a *Times of India* report dated 6 November 1970. The *Hindustan Times* on 18 November 1970 had the rest of the story: "Maintaining that Netaji had a plan to go to Russia in the event of Japanese surrender to the Anglo-American allies, he (Suresh Bose) said in December 1944, when the Azad Hind Government was functioning and the INA was engaged in the battlefields, Netaji was absent from there for about fortnight. During this period, Netaji had been to Russia and had probably met Marshal Stalin, he said."

Suresh Bose's statement was supported by an intelligence paper in the file 249-INA-II (H) GHQ, which became available recently. The relevant portion reads: "SC Bose was preparing to leave for Moscow ... it was also said that Col SA Malik[30] would follow SC Bose to Moscow .... In December, 1944 Lt Sadhu Singh of HCI Divn, INA, who was acting as QM of the YE-U Rest Campt, informed ... that SC Bose had left for Moscow and was soon expected back in Tokyo."

Occasionally, Bhagwanji would describe his stay in Siberia. "Not one or two, there are 49 concentration camps there. There are teachers, doctors, writers, scientists — some 15 to 20 thousand people in each camp. And what are these people doing there? They're producing goods .... In that bitter winter, one has to do heavy work to keep one's back warm." The "memories" of the hardships lasted a lifetime. In 1983, after years of lobbying, a relative of Dr T Banerjee managed to gain access inside Bhagwanji's room. Dilip Mukherjee wept inconsolably as he saw "Netaji" face to face. Their discussion, in Hindi and Bangla, began on a nostalgic note but headed towards discussing politics. "What do you know about Communism?" the saint commented disapprovingly. "I have seen them from close. I have seen how a few luxuriate while the rest suffer. I have been to their grand palaces. 'This body' has also suffered torture in Siberia."

If only the saint had spoken of the exact place in Siberia where he said he was kept. He left a vague description. It was somewhere in between Baikul Lake and Ural Mountains. One could only hazard a guess thereof. Ardhendu Sarkar, the PSU official who deposed before Mukherjee Commission, recalled before the writer the words of engineer Zerobin about the location of the camp where he had met Bose: "It was beyond the end of trans Siberian Railways in Ural mountains. The place was not connected by road or railway and could only be approached by helicopter." During her Russian sojourn, Dr Purabi Roy was pressed by Professor V Kluev to consult "the prison papers of the city of Irkutsk." Irkutsk in Siberia, beyond the Urals, where long ago there was a gulag in the vicinity of Baikul Lake.

Notes:

1 Old timers blame the Communists of vivisecting Bose's party. They say that CPI's KN Joglekar and Soli Batliwala joined the Forward Bloc with this aim in mind. Sardul Singh Caveesher, Leela Roy, Anil Roy, RS Ruiker, HV Kamath, Sunil Das, Samar Guha, Dr Atindranath Bose etc parted way and formed the Subhasists Forward Bloc. Whereas the Marxists formed the present day All India Forward Bloc. It comprised Sheel Bhadra Yajee, N Joglekar and Hemanta Bose. A Subhasist Forward Bloc has survived in Tamil Nadu.

2 Mother of Amit Mitra, the general secretary of FICCI. Once Bhagwanji broke down remembering 'Bela' (Amita Mitra) who had passed away prematurely in 1952.

3 "The counter-measures of the Raj against the 'Secret Service' of the INA were cruelly successful. Most of the infiltrators were apprehended, tried under Enemy Agents Ordinance and executed." From: *Towards Freedom: documents on the movement for independence in India,* 1943-1944, Part III. ICHR. General Editor: Sarvepalli Gopal.

4 Ibid. Page 2801.

5 Durga Prasad Pandey's oral statement to the writer.

6 Police recorded cross-examination of PM Roy on a tape. Journalist Ashok Tandon chanced to hear it.

7 Bhagwanji's record collection included Nazrul Geet in the voice of Rabindra Nath Tagore, Bismillah Khan's shahnai, Ravi Shankar's ragas, songs of KL Saighal and speeches of Subhas Bose.

8 Subhas Bose addressed Leela Roy as "Mrs Roy." Bhagwanji coined nicknames for several of his followers.

9 Both these letters were produced by Srikant Sharma before Mukherjee Commission.

10 Like Samar Guha, Amal Roy had an urge to tell others about Bhagwanji. He even tried to take a picture once and had to face wrath of Bhagwanji.

11 Bhagwanji received many visitors and communications. What the writer knows is only a fraction.

12 Anil Das appeared before Shah Nawaz Committee and Khosla Commission. He narrated a similar account but did not tell Khosla Commission anything about Bhagwanji.

13 Sunil Das passed away in 1994. He was listed by Bose's American biographer Professor Leonord Gordon as one of the sources of information for his landmark book *Brothers against Raj.*

14 Quoted by Sunil Das in his examination before Khosla Commission.

15 The *Nagpur Times* report **Netaji is still alive: Prof Guha.** 13 March 1978.

On 23 January 1978 while looking at the portrait of Subhas Bose in the Central Hall of the Parliament, President Reddy had remarked: "Netaji has come back today, though not as expected."

16 The *Times of India* report **Reddy hints at another bid to unravel Netaji mystery.** 9 March 1978.

17 The *Indian Express.* 6 July 1983.

18 Leela Roy, and later, Pabitra Mohan Roy were nodal to contacting Bhagwanji. All correspondence and instructions were routed through them. They would keep the others informed and none was permitted to contact Bhagwanji on their own.

19 The reporter was possibly Barun Sen Gupta.

20 Government of India spent Rs 7,67,000 on Khosla Commission.

21 Sunil Das was forbidden by Bhagwanji to speak on this part.

22 Dr Majumdar deposed before Khosla Commission. He was emphatic that Bose could not have died in 1945. "There is absolutely no evidence of any person who saw his dead body." In August 1977, he, Sunil Das, Pabitra Mohan Roy, Amar Prasad Chakravarty, N Dutt-Majumdar and others wrote the following to Prime Minister Morarji Desai: "On all accounts the findings of both the Shah Nawaz Committee of 1956 and the Khosla Commission of 1970 ... were "command performances" .... Now that a new Government has been formed at the Centre free from the inhibitions of the Nehrus in regard to the distinguished role of Netaji ... in the struggle for the freedom ... we would request the Prime Minister ... to go into the question of the disappearance of Netaji ...."

23 Atul Sen

24 Bhagwanji kept close watch on situation in East Pakistan and then Bangladesh. An authentic copy of Bangladesh's constitution was found in Ram Bhawan.

25 Biographer Durlab Singh wrote in 1941: "Absorbed deeply in the ideas of eternal peace and salvation, in the winter days of 1914 he (Subhas Bose) decided once for all to forsake the pleasures of the world ... and ran away into the heart of a jungle amidst the valleys of Himalayas in search of some spiritual teacher .... He spent full six months there .... Scenes of his home return were most dramatic. Everybody was sitting in the drawing-room when he suddenly made his entry into it. He first of all proceeded to his mother ... and touched the dust of her feet ...."

26 Title of Subhas Chandra Bose's unfinished autobiography. It means *Bharat Pathik* in Bangla. In one letter Bhagwanji referred to him as "Pathik."

27 Thousands of Quantung army officials were captured by the Red Army. Samar Guha hinted that Shidei might have turned a monk after he helped Bose escape to Russia. Had Shidei survived the war, he would have been dubbed a war criminal and prosecuted.

28 **An Indian ambassador met Netaj in Moscow.** *Hindustan Times* Big Story. 4 March 2001. Justice MK Mukherjee was not given an access to the Attlee-Nehru correspondence for the relevant period during his London visit. He was told that the British Government will declassify some other papers on Bose " only after 2021 if the Indian Government so desired."

29 Gaur worked with Force-136, a British Special Operations Executive commando unit, which took part in the counter-offensive against the INA in Kohima and Burma. After his retirement from the Intelligence Bureau, which he had joined after Independence, he wrote extensively in newspapers and magazine and also published books. In 1990 Gaur provided the fullest account of Earl Attlee's revelations to Bose mystery researcher Ranjeet Panchalay, who reproduced much of it in his Hindi book *Bhumigat Subhas*. Gaur passed away in 1998. The writer spoke to his son and had the account confirmed. The writer did not come across any refutation of Gaur's public statements.

30 Captain Malik was in INA secret service. This particular document is in National Archives, Delhi.

13

Postlude

Even my enemies will not have the audacity to say that I can injure the interest of my country.

Netaji Subhas Chandra Bose.

He beamed when the Calcutta correspondent of the United Press of America walked into his room in his Woodburn Park residence. Sarat Chandra Bose, brother of Subhas, was dying. But this was not worrying him. He sorted out some papers and made a most significant announcement India was to forget. "My brother is alive," he contentedly said. But for further details, the correspondent could have taken Sarat to have been stuck in late 1945 or early 1946 when the talk of Bose being alive was commonplace. More than four years had elapsed since Subhas Bose had taken leave of his compatriots to cross over to the USSR. He had calculated that he might have to hide in the Soviet Union for ten years — by which time the cold war would have come to fore. "Bose was certain that once the Russians agreed to take him, they would give him all the necessary protection. He also thought that in the event of an Anglo-American split with Russia, which he definitely foresaw, he might be of some service to the Russians and thus further the cause of his own country."[1]

The opportunity knocked well earlier — this was the story from Bhagwanji's side. "Stalin did not treat me like an enemy," he said. In late 1949, at the onset of Cold War and end of war criminals' trials, "Dead man" left the Soviet Union for good with the best memory of having been feasted with choicest Indian cuisine in Kremlin. Time was not ripe to go to India. The Russians, "still looked upon India as a colony of Britain."[2] Those who had vowed to attain "Purna Swaraj," the complete independence, discarded their pledge when it came to crunch. "They got independence in begging bowl," Bhagwanji charged. Dominion status meant that the British rule "continued" in India after 1947. The British monarch remained the head of Indian state. King George VI signed the letters of credence and appointment of Indian ambassadors. The Indian Government was as hostile to Subhas as it was before 1947. The chiefs of the Indian Air Force and the Navy were British. The Army Headquarters in 1949 issued a circular against displaying pictures of Subhas Bose "at permanent places, in canteens, quarters etc."[3] No wonder, Winston Churchill, the rabidly anti-Indian, felt happy with the transfer of power arrangements. "The Union Jack did not disappear, don't forget," an equally satisfied Lord Mountabatten, opponent of Bose and independent India's first Governor-General, was to reflect about the Independence Day. "It was still used, on holidays and great days and even now, they very often fly the Union Jack,"[4] he said in 1975.

Life was infused one last time in the dying brother as he received a message. "Dead man" was welcomed into the newly created People's Republic of China (PRC). On 7 October 1949, the *Nation*, Sarat Bose's newspaper, ran as the main lead the story he had given to United Press of America scribe a day earlier. "Mr Sarat Chandra Bose said ... that the Government of India were in possession of definite information that Netaji Subhas Chandra Bose was in Red China of Mao Tse-Tung."[5] Mao did he say? Yes. All Indian leaders of those years thought well of the Chinese irrespective of their ideological affiliations. Sarat Bose himself revealed that Bose was pro-Chinese from the time he was Congress president. "He very often came in conflict with the then leaders of Japan over their external policy."[6] Debnath Das told Khosla Commission that one of escape plans Bose had toyed with was to go "to Yunan, the headquarters Mao Tse-Tung, who would help him to carry on his campaign against the British."

If Bose was in China, why was he not coming to India?" Sarat Bose was asked. "I don't think time is ripe for his coming back home,"[7] he replied.

The news flashed to the West. On 28 November 1949, *Interpress*, the German news agency, released story *Babu Bose: Mann Hinter Den Fronten* (Mr Bose: The Man Behind The Front).

"There has been a nuclear explosion by the side of India in October last, which is of a political nature .... It came to be known within a few days by a radio announcement that Subhas Chandra Bose, the lost Indian revolutionary, might deliver a speech over the Communist Radio of Peaking. Of course, nothing has been heard after this mysterious announcement ....

"Though in a broadcast from Tokyo, it had been announced that Bose was killed in an air-crash ... none in the world paid any heed to this news .... Subhas Chandra Bose ... was a man with good health, psychologically strong and a fore-seeing politician. Immediately after his joining with the Japanese he had a doubt as to the result on the joint expedition of the Japanese army and his army. It cannot be ignored that this strong and foreseeing man did not think for future. Was it now known to him how Moscow would utilise the renaissance of nationalism in Asia in the greater political game at present or in future?

"In 1945, when a chaos was prevailing over the whole of China on the victory of the Allied Powers, he could have easily entered into the Soviet border ....

"Mao Tse-Tung's victory in Red China may open opportunities for an unexpected victory of Subhas Chandra with the Kremlin's help ... (the) Buddha faced veteran yogi ... already occupies a position of highest estimation in the Indian mind .... Today, if he and Marshal Stalin reach an agreement, he may deliver speeches from Peaking Radio as he did from Berlin and Tokyo addressing his countrymen. But he has not done that yet .... If he remains alive ... the whole world one day will hear again his speech.'"[8]

The world did not, but one illustrious Indian proclaimed he not only heard Netaji, he also beheld him. Muthuramalingam Thevar had been a member of the 5-men "war council", comprising Sarat Bose, Srinivas Ayyangar, Shankar Lal and himself, formed by Subhas Bose during the Second World War. He was the man who was then laughed at, but his greatness, as a leader and social reformer, had to be recognised eventually — in our time. President Abdul Kalam and former Prime Minister Atal Bihari Vajapyee unveiled his statue in the Parliament House. Thevar went to China on Sarat Bose's instruction. He slipped out and came back without a passport. The Intelligence Bureau came to know of that. No one dared contradict Thevar or slap charges at him when he detailed before the media in Delhi, Calcutta and Madras the outcome of his "illegal" Chinese trip:

"Thevar said Netaji was at present the Indian representative on the Asian Liberation Force which had its headquarters at Sikiang district in China on the Assam-China border. Netaji regarded the present India as a 'Royal republic' and so he had not reappeared on the Indian scene. He had a 'mission' and he alone could decide when to return to India. Claiming that he had lived with Netaji for nine months from January 1950 to October 1950, Sri Thevar said that towards the end of 1949 when Sri Sarat Chandra Bose was ailing, he went down to Calcutta to meet Sri Bose. He saw Sri Bose on December 7 and stayed with him for ten days. They had consultations on the matter as Sri Bose apprehended that he was going to die.

After these talks, Sri Thevar said, he left India incognito on December 17. He crossed the Burma border and entered China where he stayed almost the whole of 1950. He met Netaji in January but where he would not divulge. He returned to India in October 1950. He said that the Government of India knew that he had visited China but if it doubted that, he could prove that he had been to China.

Sri Thevar said that the War Council had regular contacts with Netaji and of late he and others were keeping contacts with Netaji Bose. He had been maintaining contacts with Netaji since 1949. He had last contacted Netaji between December 1955 and February this year ...."

Thevar claimed that "Subhas Babu was taken to Manchuria by the Japanese because it is due to Subhas Babu that the neutrality pact between Russia and Japan was kept intact .... The surrender of Japan was an arranged affair, to avoid Anglo-American entry into Manchuria. The military might of Japan ... to a very great extent had been transferred to Manchuria long before the surrender .... War ended in September 1945. An Asiatic Liberation Army was formed by Netaji and the Japanese. Chinese (under the leadership of Mao Tse-Tung), Burmese, Indo-Chinese, Malaya, Indonesians, Philippines, Siamese had all joined this army with the assistance of the Russian Government."[9]

Bhagwanji reached from China to India or its borders around 1953. He came through Nepalgunj and with the help of Mahadeo Prasad Misra, he made it to adjoining Uttar Pradesh. Surendra Singh Chaudhury, former king of Itawah, became his first disciple. Then came Dr Sampurnanad, the UP Chief Minister from December 1954 to April 1957. Around 1955 Bhagwanji made a house in Darshan Nagar in Lucknow as his abode. Disciples say that another UP Chief Minister and would be Prime Minister, Chaudhury Charan Singh, often visited Bhagwanji. He was the Union Home Minister when Samar Guha announced in the Lok Sabha that Bose was alive. He deferentially listened to Guha and almost announced the formation of a new commission. Bhagwanji would shower praises on the Jat leader's agrarian policies.

But what did Bhagwanji do all those years? He did not remain locked up in a room all the time. In his words, he ventured out secretly: "You cannot comprehend, to what end your Dead man is working and with what powers. Your imagination will be awed, your brain will reel if, even by chance, you could come to know even a fractional part of his present activities .... It is not for nothing that an old man, in the course of recent months went out of India twice, braving all the fatal hazards to his life and frail body. The result is before you ... war is not an emotional business, it is a cold-calculated affair."

What did he mean? Where did he go? Vietnam was one country he named. Bhagwanji spoke of witnessing the war and being welcomed by Ho Chi Minh in a grand palace. Was it a flight of fancy, a piece of misinformation or some hidden truth? Some time before his disappearance, Subhas Bose had sent his emissary to Minh.

"His (Minh's) pride of nine generals and a shadow behind them," Bhagwanji resumed. Once, well before the Vietnam war ended, he issued a wanton challenge betting for the sure shot defeat of the United States. "This may sound laughable. I tell you a very interesting story in which Mahakal has a hand. In this war in Vietnam, on someone's advice, the very best quality of cocaine and opium was distributed free of cost in south Vietnam. The Americans have avidly consumed 1000 tonnes of it. America, the greatest might of the present world, can fight this war for one thousand years but it will never win north Vietnam." Bhagwanji took some prominent Americans' name. William Rogers, Secretary of State under Nixon, and Robert McNamara, Defence Secretary from 1961 to 1968. Bhagwanji remarked: "As long as McNamara was in a key government post, he kept mum. But after becoming IMF chief he said 'We have categorically different news regrding the publicised death story of so and so'." "'Mr so and so' was our way to address Netaji before Bhagwanji," disciple Ravindra Shukla chipped in with a reminiscence.

Corroboration (or the inspiration?) was traced in Ram Bhawan in 1986. It was a typed copy of a news item published in a daily in Kuala Lumpur in May 1970. On the sidelines of an international conference in Jakarta, McNamara's successor Clark Clifford had made a sensational disclosure. He said that in the army of Vietcong there was a division of Asian Liberation Army headed by some missing second world war generals. Which generals, he would not tell. Then something came up in mid 1990s. An Indian journalist visiting Vietnam was told about the existence of some files on Bose. A JNU professor, an expert on China, made a similar claim — about files in People's Republic of China. Some Vietnamese files were of post-1945 vintage and could only be disclosed if the Government of India properly approached their Vietnamese counterpart. " ... material on Netaji ... have been accessed by the government here (in Vietnam) while collecting archival material on both the World War II and the Vietnam War period."

"Ironically, the Indian government seems reluctant to pursue this lead, which is likely to ... unearth some exceedingly interesting material on Netaji's disappearance since it will reopen the entire issue,"[10] a "highly placed source" told Prabha Jagannathan, the Indian journalist, in Ho Chi Minh city.

He admired Chairman Mao, but "Dead man" never thought good of "Godless creed of communism." "It is God's truth, and take it from the horse's mouth. Communism shall die at the place of its birth. Even the Gods have not the power to nullify these solemn words .... This creed is carrying its death in its own cell," he prophesied. Eventually, he drifted away from the Soviets and the Chinese.

The mysterious stories went on and on. A scribble by Bhagwanji referred to a meeting between Ho Chi Minh and Chinese general Liu Po Cheng on 19 August 1945. "An American intelligence officer Alfred Wagg knew about it and he informed his government." One Alfred Wagg, a stringer with the *Chicago Tribune*, had indeed been active in SE Asia during the war. He came to India with some sensational news. He claimed he had made on the spot inquiries in Taipei when he had gone there with General MacArthur's forces. He met Nehru, Gandhi, Sarat and others and told them that he saw Subhas days after the crash in Saigon. Mountbatten's intelligence network picked up signs that Indian "political circles" were "greatly interested in the recent news item which alleged that Bose had been seen alive in Saigon after the air-crash accident."[11] Jitendranath Ghosh, former editor of the *Nation*, wrote a letter to Shah Nawaz Khan on 22 April 1956, requesting that he should lay his hands on Wagg's report. Neither Shah Nawaz nor GD Khosla did anything.

Wagg moved freely in the corridors of power. Niranjan Singh Talib, Punjab Congress chief and a state minister bumped into him at Defence Minister Baldev Singh's residence. Singh told Talib that there had been some "Top Secret" inquiry into Bose's death. Talib recalled all before Khosla and so did another Congressman. Jagdish Kodesia said he had visited Saigon in 1961. "There we were taken to a summer resort known as Dalat where we were specially invited to an exhibition held by a Girls' School." This was the place from where Field Marshal Count Terauchi had supervised Bose's escape. Kudesia further narrated that a "bishop asked me whether I believe that Netaji Subhas Chandra Bose is alive or dead. I told him that I am sure that he never died in that accident. He patted me on the back and said, 'Young man, I can tell you this much, that on the day BBC announced the death of Netaji, he was in Dalat and I was staying with him at that time.'" Kudesia, former Delhi Congress chief and confidant of Prime Minister Lal Bahadur Sahstri, had more things to tell.

"From the records of Parliament it was seen that always a stereotyped reply was coming when questions were put about Netaji. The feeling among the various Congress leaders was that Panditji had an aversion for Netaji .... I may say that Shastriji was one person who did not believe that report of Shah Nawaz Khan ... when he became Home Minister ... he was quite interested and he wanted to know the truth whether Subhas Bose was alive or not. In the whole Cabinet he was the only man who was very much interested ... (as Prime Minister) Shastriji ... showed it by impressions and expressions ... that Netaji was living ... (he) definitely wanted that there should be another inquiry commission. If he would have lived longer, he must have seen to that."[12]

One-eyed Liu Po Cheng rose to become a famous Chinese marshal. In 1956 Shivprasad Nag[13] of Calcutta wrote a booklet in which he theorized that Cheng was none but Bose himself. Shivprasad was in contact with Bhagwanji, who did not back Shivprasad's claim. His statement was that one "General Death" or "General Shiva", who had helped the Dalai Lama in the 1950s, was his *nom de guerre*. BN Mullick was asked before GD Khosla if he knew about General Shiva or had read the book

The Dalai Lama by famous American adventurer Lowell Thomas Jr. "No", he said. Thomas, in his 1961 book, was unclear. He described one "General Siva" as someone whose "identity has never been revealed."[14] "A total mystery to me," Thomas, a former Lt Governor of Alaska, wrote to the writer when asked to reveal the identity of "General Siva" or "General Death."

It was not that Bhagwanji upheld all strange stories making up the mystery. He shot down the claims about certain "post-death" pictures showing Subhas Bose in China and India. "You cannot take pictures of a ghost," he said in a lighter vein. The man on Nehru's funeral bier, they said, was Bose. They who? The propagators that Shoulmari Baba was Bose. The man was clearly visible in a documentary made on the last days of the late Prime Minister. Good God! The one next to his body did look like older Bose. Even Bhagwanji got foxed. The picture created a flutter when the documentary was shown. Emotions ran high forcing the Government to censor it. Prime Minister Shastri feigned ignorance about it in the Parliament on 29 March 1965. "If I see it, then alone I shall be able to say (whether he is Bose or not). He never cleared the air. BN Mullick in his testimony before GD Khosla tried to muddy the water. "I was most of the time with the dead body of Pt Nehru and I do not remember that sadhu or his photograph. Many tricks are possible in photography."

The photograph was there and the man in the reel was for real. He was Vira Dharmawara Mahathera[15], a revered Cambodian monk and a friend of Nehru's. Shorter, but Bose-like from an angle. Shastri had himself received Dharmawara at Teen Murti in May 1964. But why did the chief of Indian intelligence lie about the existence of a picture, movie reel, the whole India knew about? Bhagwanji charged that there had been a conspiracy to confuse the people with the Shoulmari Baba and such like stories. It was the "parallel bluff", staged to ward off "a political earthquake." It was set up by the "combine," said Bhagwanji. They knew he was in India and were looking for him.

Bhagwanji's disciple and former revolutionary Vishwanath Roy wrote in 1964: "Ashok Sen (a former Union Law Minister) asked me: 'Well, does your gurudev live in India? Was Shoulmari sadhu Netaji himself?' I replied, 'I have heard ... that this sadhu was not Netaji.' I avoided the first question and slunk out. I doubt these people know something. You (Bhagwanji) should be vigilant." Dwijendra Nath Bose openly alleged before Khosla Commission that one SC Mukherjee of Intelligence Bureau was running the Shoulmari machination as the ashram's administrator. During his cross-examination, BN Mullick was forced to admit that "there was probably one SC Mukherjee, DCIO (Deputy Central Intelligence Officer) at Shoulamri sometimes in the early 1960s." Shoulmari Baba's longest lasting follower Suresh Padhaye told the *Indian Express* on 1 July 2003 that long after the controversy had died out, Shoulmari Baba was on the run from the IB sleuths. "Whatever be the conspiracy," said Bhagwanji, "Mother India will save her son."

Subhas Bose was indeed looked for. Barun Sengupta told Khosla Commission that "whenever there is a rumour or a story, the Central Intelligence people and the state Intelligence people go and investigate into it. They also come to us (journalists) for further enlightenment and to know whether we have any information. Not only they but even foreigners like Americans, Britishers and Russians go there and investigate into these things ... they have the largest source of intelligence throughout the world .... If they are sure that Netaji had died in the plane crash, why shall the Americans, Russians and Britishers and central people go there to chase this wild story?"

Gobinda Mukhoty disclosed during the argument before Khosla Commission in 1974 that "a political correspondent of a Calcutta English daily" was accosted by IB personnel who "sought to know from him on November 6, 1970 on Netaji's disappearance." " If the Government is certain about Netaji's death, what is the purpose of the IB asking the correspondent about Netaji?"

In early 1980s the CIA declassified a document. Two decades after his death, in the thin and thick of the Cold War, Subhas Bose was still raising eyebrows in the agency which, on the face of it, should have had millions of relevant things to do. The document was heavily sanitised before being declassified. Many of its vital parts, like the names of the sender and receiver, were completely blackened. It was a memorandum dated 27 February 1964 for some "Chief (Censored)" and it had originated from "Deputy Director of Security (Censored)." Subject was censored too, but in the ink was written "Subhas Chandra Bose." The information had come from a man who had been a British counterintelligence officer during World War years. A request had been made by the higher ups to interview this man in Washington DC and the contents of the document were based on his observation:

"On 26 Feb at approximately 13:45 hours (censored) related a story concerning the possible return of one Subas or (Subhas) Chandra Bose. This individual is a former disposed president of the Indian National Congress, 1938-39, and is believed to have died in an airplane crash after the War. However, there now exists a strong possibility that BOSE is leading the rebellious group undermining the current Nehru Government."[16]

The US administration proved to be of little help when Mukherjee Commission sought help through the diplomatic channels. The answer they received did not take them anywhere. The US authorities said that in their embassy and consulates in India there was no document on Bose. The Embassy and consulates? Why would they be keeping such records there? Shouldn't they had better searched the records of ... say, the State Department? Were it not the Americans who had first interrogated Habibur Rahman? Was it not them who had reached Taiwan in September 1945? Was not the US intelligence keeping track of Bose's activities? Mukherjee Commission was told to consult the declassified documents available in American archives. And the secret ones? The Commission was free to approach the US Government under the Freedom of Information Act (FOIA). They don't call America the land of the free for nothing. The US Government wouldn't have disappointed them had the Indian Embassy made more efforts. The Embassy said FOIA entailed tedious process. Apparently, they had many better things to do, like help organise dance shows, than to worry about the fate of Netaji.

The followers did ask Bhagwanji why was he hiding away from his own people. One brief reason the saint gave was exactly what Muthuramlingam Thevar and Suresh Bose had claimed. "I have been declared an international war criminal." Atul Sen was given some elaboration in 1962. Perhaps Dead man's "post-1945 activities" had something to do with it. Sen got so disturbed that he felt compelled to write to Nehru.

"I take the liberty of addressing these few lines to you in the matter of the widely prevalent belief that Netaji Subhas Chandra Bose is not dead. Mine is not mere belief but actual knowledge that Netaji is alive and is engaged in spiritual practice somewhere in India. Not the Sadhu of Shoulmari, Cooch-Behar, in West Bengal about whom some Calcutta politicians are making a fuss at this movment. I deliberately make the location a little vague because from the talks I had with him for months together not very long ago I could understand that he is yet regarded as Enemy No 1 of the Allied Powers and that there is a secret protocol that binds the Government of India to deliver him to Allied 'justice' if found alive. If you can persuade yourself to assure me that his information is not correct or even if it is correct your Government shall resist any action by any of the said powers against the Great Patriot I may try to persuade him to return to open life."[17]

Nehru should have rebuked Sen for his temerity to insinuate such a ghoulish story to the Prime Minister of India. But all he did was to deny the charge against the Government without trashing the thrust of Sen's letter that Bose was alive and in India.

"I have never heard of any secret protocol about Netaji Subhas Chandra Bose. Certainly the Government of India have not bound themselves to any such thing. Even if any country asks the Government of India to hand him over, it is not going to be agreed to."[18]

That Bose was going to be treated as a "war criminal" had become clear way back at the end of Second World War. Suresh Bose wrote in *Dissentient Report* that he as "a British Indian subject" had "waged war against his King and Emperor." Bose was "a top-ranking 'International War Criminal', against which persons, after the last war, the maximum penalty was generally inflicted." Bose had "collaborated" with the Axis countries whose leaders, like Japanese Premier Hideki Tojo, were hanged following the war crimes trials.

After the War the Government of India classified several of the INA soliders as "war criminals." One list that the writer saw had the names of Mohan Singh, MZ Kiani, AC Chatterjee, SC Alagappan, Mahboob Ahmed, GR Nagar, Gulzara Singh and Gurbaksh Singh Dhillon. The charges against them were evidently trumped up with the assistance of the likes of Captain Hari Singh Badhwar of 3rd Cavalry who was a British intelligence mole. Badhwar rose to be a general in free India, while most INA veterans lived lives of sufferings and humiliations.

There was no reason why the British shouldn't have clubbed Bose in the same league as his men. Even his doctor was categorized as a "war criminal", and Dr Taneyoshi Yoshimi, who had treated "Bose" in Taipei, was interrogated by War Crimes Section in 1946. Propaganda had it that Bose's men had tortured Allied military personnel and that they had extracted money from Indian expatriates. Alfred Wagg stated in a press meet on 29 August 1945 that Bose "should be treated as a war criminal because his men fought and killed many Americans ...."[19]

Certainly, both the Japanese and Bose knew what lay ahead after the end of the War. Colonel Muraji Yano, chief of the India section, Southern Army HQ, was interrogated by the British on 6 March 1946. He spoke of "general opinion ... in favour of withdrawing Subhas Chandra Bose from the Southern regions" at the close of the war. Because of "admiration of his integrity" and the realisation among the Japanese that Bose "would be more harshly treated than anyone else if he fell into Allied hands."[20] Dr S Vasava Menon, Bose's doctor, told Khosla Commission that one of the points discussed in Bangkok on 17 August 1945 by Bose and others was that "the Japanese did not want him (Bose) to be caught as a war criminal." Lt Colonel Morio Takakura who in 1945 was posted at Imperial General HQ in Tokyo, testified that he had known of an Allied decision to arrest Bose had he landed in Tokyo. Which was precisely what the Britishers had been thinking in July 1945. "We should be thinking what to do with SC Bose," wondered Viceroy Wavell. "If the Japanese surrendered, we should presumably require him to be handed over to us." The views of his Private Secretary EM Jenkins were that "Bose ... is one of the bigger war criminals and has offended against His Majesty's Government quite as much as against India."[21]

In August, it was communicated that "His Excellency (Wavell) understands that a 'surrender list' of traitors whom we wish to be handed over to us has been prepared in the Home Department .... His Excellency ... is not at all sure that Bose and his immediate associates should be returned to India .... It might be better to have them dealt with as war criminals outside India."[22]

On 23 August 1945 it was stated that as reagrds Bose's case the "full backing" of His Majesty's Government was essential as dubbing Bose a war criminal was tricky as he was "clearly not one in the ordinary sense of that word" and "nor does he appear to come within the extended definition which has now been adopted by the United Nations." Keeping in mind the situation the Home Department "short listed a number of ways to deal with Bose." The first option was to "bring him back to India and try him either for waging war or under the enemy agents ordinance." The matter also came up for discussion in the British Cabinet on 25 October 1945: "It was generally agreed that the only civilian renegade of importance was Subhas Chandra Bose."[23] It was stated that the "Indian renegades rounded up outside India" should be tried in India as this was the accepted way to deal with war criminals.

The foggy Raj-era view was not considered by the Calcutta High Court in 1998, when the formation of a new commission was ordered. Chief Justice Prabha Shankar Mishra and Justice B Bhattacharya asked: "Who ... will call Netaji a war criminal? Any Indian public except a traitor, a person who does not have the defence and love for the country and its heroes alone can do so. We do not have any hesitation in concluding that the statements in documents which are lying in archives which are to the effect that Netaji is a war criminal and all persons who have been saying such a thing are relic of the British raj .... The people of India, and the GOI since it is the Government of the people of India, can ever in dreams would think of Netaji as a war criminal ...."

During the *HindustanTimes.com* probe, I heard over and again, from the United States to Uttar Pradesh, about the war criminal theory. Background information and commonsense prevented me from lending ear before I realised how strong were the suspicions. Mukherjee Commission had raised questions and even a historian of the stature of VN Datta had expressed doubts. "Had he (Bose) been alive, the British would have been compelled to declare him a war criminal."[24] The controversy erupted off and on again since 1950s. Muthuramalingam Thevar was of course the first to lock horns with the Government. Shah Nawaz Khan told him that the "Government of India is not in possession of any information on this point." Thevar countered that by asking why it was so when a person of Bose's eminence was involved. "This information lies with the UK and USA," Shah Nawaz answered. Thevar proposed that Government of India, in that case, should publicly disassociate itself from "the declaration made by the Allies in regard to war criminals," which Shah Nawaz disposed off. Thevar then went public with his demand: "It is necessary on the part of the Government to make it known categorically to the public whether Netaji's name is still in the list of war criminals and if not, when was it removed and how?"[25] A little later Suresh Bose took up the matter with Prime Minister Nehru who recorded that India would not take up the issue with the UK, the US or any other foreign country.

In their answers in the Parliament on some occasions, some ministers of the Government stated that to the best of their knowledge Bose's name was not borne on any list of war criminals. The British High Commission in Delhi too came out with a qualified statement in 1961 that Bose's name did not appear in any "British list" of war criminals. Was there ever a "British list" of war criminals? In a parliamentary debate on 22 August 1963, participated by Jawaharlal Nehru and Atal Bihari Vajpayee, BD Khobaragade said, "It is generally believed that

Netaji Subhas Chandra Bose is still alive but that he is not coming out of hiding because if he comes out, perhaps he may be treated as a war criminal." AM Tariq queried if "confirmation has been taken from the American Government and the German Government that he is not in the American Government's list of war criminals." Dinesh Singh, Deputy Minister for External Affairs, replied "No." "... so far as ascertaining it from the American Government is concerned, this question has never arisen because they have never said that there is any list in which he figures." I guess the onus was clearly on India. The Government was to request the United States over the lists of war criminals, kept classified until recently.

Home Minister Lal Bahadur Shastri stated in a September 1962 letter that "Bose's name was not included in list of war criminals drawn up by the United Nations War Crimes Commission." He had also been asked how the Government was going to treat Bose in case he made an appearance. Shastri did not respond to this aspect and it seemed to have caused concern. Jagdish Kodesia told Khosla commission that later he had "argued" with Shastri at length. "Why doesn't the Government make a statement?" he asked. Shastri, Kodesia said, told him to go and make a "statement on his behalf that if Netaji arrives in this country, he will be the first man to garland him as the Prime Minister."

"I told him that it would be much better if he could himself make the statement, that we could call a meeting on some birthday of Netaji and he could make the statement. Again, the same thing happened. On the next birthday of Netaji, when he was the Prime Minister, he could not come. He only sent us greetings for that." Kodesia recalled. He was further cross-examined over his talks with Shastri.

Q: You raised question about Netaji being a war criminal.

A: I did raise this.

Q: You raised this question of war criminal and that Government of India should make some announcement whether he is international war criminal or not.

A: Yes.

Q: Did Government of India of Shastriji make any direct statement that Netaji Bose was not an international war criminal?

A: He did not say that there was anything to say that he was war criminal or not. He never disclosed anything to me. He said, if Netaji is alive he would be the first person to garland him.

Q: Categorically, no statement was made by Shastri or Government of India that he was not an international war criminal.

A: No statement has so far been made.

If Sunil Das's input to Bhagwanji was to be believed, the Government took the war criminal angle rather seriously even in 1960s. Das passed on to Bhagwanji some information he had collected from MP Surendra Mohan Ghosh whom Das had met in Bengal Chief Minister's office in the presence of Hemanta Basu, the AIFB leader.

"Sri Ghosh had been to Shoulmari Ashram and had long talks with Sardanandji of Shoulmari .... Before he went to Shoulmari he had talks with Sri Jawaharlal Nehru, Dr Rajendra Prasad and Sri Moraraji Desai .... During the course of his recital ... he suddenly opined that he knew the real reason for Netaji's non-appearance .... Then he went on to say the Allied Powers (this is government opinion) have by common consent ... struck off the name of Netaji from the list of war criminals because they have officially ... concluded that Netaji was dead. Now, if Netaji reappeared he would immediately be declared an 'imposter' by the Allied powers."

"Reading between the lines, one could see that he was giving ... the mind of the Government of India and not of the Allied powers," Das disapprovingly wrote in his letter dated 24 January 1964. He also described Ghosh as "an agent of Sri Jawaharlal Nehru" who was trying to "trace his (Netaji's) whereabouts."

In 1997 Air Vice Marshal Surenji Goyal (Retd) passionately appealed to UN Secretary General Kofi Annan to strike off Bose's name from war criminals' list. In reply, written by Shashi Tharoor on behalf of Annan, it was stated that Annan was "powerless to undo any reference that may have been made in the past." Oslo-based NRI economist Amalendu Guha wrote to British Prime Minister Tony Blair and was advised in December 1999 to refer to the correspondence published in Transfer of Power series which was indicative that the Government of British India, legally the same as Government of India, viewed Bose as a "war criminal." In 1998, responding to a PIL filed by former MP Shyam Sunder Mohapatra, the Orissa High Court directed the Centre to take up the matter with the UK Government so as "to remove the name of Netaji Subhas Chandra Bose from the list of war criminals." New Delhi communicated with London and the answer received was reported to be on the same lines as before. Mukherjee Commission was forwarded a similar reply.

Of all the instances, Khosla Commission provided the best platform to debate the issue. The Bose family led the contention and GD Khosla behaved as if he were the Government's spokesperson. He took no note of Satyanarayan Sinha's claim that certain "military mission papers" would show that the British asked the USSR to hand over "war criminal" Subhas Bose to them. Jan Sangh MP and former IFS officer ML Sondhi crossed swords with Khosla who said "there was no question of Mr Subhas Chandra Bose being treated as war criminal if he appeared in any part of the world .... (Khosla) remarked that he was authorised to state that Netaji's name had never figured in any war criminals' list. When Mr Khosla was pressed (by Sondhi) to reveal the source of his information, he said, 'I am making the statement on my own authority.'"[26]

Similar treatment was meted out to the counsel for the Bose family, who argued that the "Government of India has deliberately suppressed or destroyed evidence which would have proved that Bose's name was included in the list of war criminals."[27] In his rebuttal, Khosla noted that he had put the following to the Ministry of Home Affairs:

"1. Was Netaji's name borne on the list of war criminals prepared at the conclusion of World War II?

2. If so, is there such a list which is still in force, and is Netaji Bose's name on that list?

3. Should Netaji Bose be proved to be alive, is the Government of India under any obligation to hand him over to an international body for being tried upon charges of committing war crimes?

4. What will be the Government's attitude towards the freedom of Netaji Bose, should he be found and appear in person?

5. Was any list of war criminals maintained apart from the list which was placed before the international court which held its sittings in Japan?"[28]

Khosla then outlined the outcome in his report:

"A reply was received to this letter ... in which it was stated that the Home Ministry has consulted the Ministry of External Affairs, the Ministry of Information and Broadcasting and the Ministry of Defence, and all three Ministries had stated that no such information was available with them. This reply, however, did not deal with the five questions which I had referred to the Ministry, and so a fresh reference was made.

"A more detailed reply was ... received ... and in this reply it was stated that enquiries made from the Indian Missions in The Hague, New York and Tokyo had revealed that the name of Netaji was never borne on any list of war criminals, and therefore, questions (3) and (4) which I had posed in my first letter did not arise.

"Despite this ... Mr Majumdar (counsel for Bose family) again raised the issue .... His argument was to the effect that ... the Government was not willing to assist the Commission .... He made a prayer that the Minister of External Affairs, Shri Swaran Singh, should be summoned as a witness, and indeed the Prime Minister should also be called to make a statement on this matter.

"There was, however, no positive affirmation by Shri Majumdar to the effect that Netaji was accused of war crimes, and that this was the most important, if not the only reason, for his remaining incognito. I reiterated my belief in the correctness of the information given to me by the Ministry of Home Affairs ... but Mr Majumdar continued to persist in a demand for more evidence and denounced the Government ...."[29]

A postmortem by the writer revealed that there were quite a few catches in Khosla's assertions. The information from the three ministries — MEA, I&B, and MoD — had simply stated that they knew nothing. Or that they were not in a position to confirm anything this way or that way. The Ministry of Home Affairs, repository of vital information, hadn't made it clear whether they had responded on the basis of "zero information" provided by the three ministries or the knowledge of the Government of India. Points 3 and 4 were not answered because, Khosla wrote, enquiries made in The Hague, New York and Tokyo yielded negative responses to points 1 and 2. This was a misleading observation as the earlier enquiries made in these places in 1967 were inconclusive.

In Japan, the matter was taken up by a First Secretary in the Indian embassy. JN Dixit wrote back home on 5 May 1967, giving a short "interim reply" that as per "some preliminary inquiries with the Japanese Foreign Office and academic circles here" there was a "tentative confirmation that Netaji Subhas Chandra Bose was not declared a war criminal." The response from the Hague on 8 May was that of ignorance. "As Netaji Subhas Chandra Bose is stated to have been tried by UN War Commission in Tokyo and not by the International Court of Justice, The Hague, the required information is likely to be available either at New York or at Tokyo. However, discreet enquires were made at our end, but no information on the subject is available here."

The Ministry of External Affairs sent Note Verbale No 534 CDA/67 on 16 October 1967 to the Japanese Foreign Office. The MEA asked the Japanese if the records of the International Military Tribunal for the Far East contained evidence "supporting the alleged arrest, prosecution or conviction" of Bose as a POW/ war criminal. The misconceived MEA note carried a wrong address. Bose was never arrested and tried before the IMTFE. And the complete records of the IMTFE, the whole world knew, were in Washington, DC.

The Japanese reply, Note Verbale No 136/ASW dated 20 December 1967, was on the anticipated lines. Informal and unsigned as note verbales are, it merely repeated the old line. "According to various information .... Mr Bose was killed in an aircraft accident on August 18, 1945 upon his departure from the Taipei Airport .... As far as the records of the International Military Tribunal for the Far East (including indictments, writs of judgment, etc) are concerned, no evidence is found supporting the alleged arrest, prosecution or conviction as a 'war criminal' of late Mr Subhas Chandra Bose by the said Tribunal. Nor exists any evidence supporting the pronouncement by the Tribunal of late Mr Subhas Chandra Bose as 'Prisoner of war'."

The reply from the Permanent Mission of India to the United Nations in New York on August 10 elucidated on the issue with greater details. The Mission told the External Affairs Ministry that they were in no position to confirm anything. This was entirely different from what Khosla had attributed to them in his report.

"Please refer to your letter No. UII/151(27)67 dated 4th July 1967 concerning Netaji Subhas Chandra Bose. The United Nations War Commission mentioned in your letter was an inter-allied body, set up by a diplomatic conference at the Foreign Office, in London, in October 1943 before the present United Nations Organisation was born. It would appear that this Commission was set up primarily to investigate and record the evidence of war crimes identifying, if possible, the individuals responsible .... As regards the Far East ... it had a Sub-Commission at Chungking to investigate the war crimes committed by the Japanese against the Chinese ... the files and records of this Commission and its Sub-Commission at Chungking are hardly available now with the present United Nations Organisation and without an access to such files and records it would be difficult to say whether the name of Netaji Subhas Chandra Bose ever figured in the considerations of the body."

I made more enquiries. Some records of the Nuremberg War Crimes Trials showed that Netaji's name came up during the Ministries Case before the US Military Tribunal IV in 1948-49. The twenty-one defendants, including three Reich ministers, were charged with committing various crimes of war and crimes against humanity.

The reference to Netaji appeared to be in passing while dealing with Wilhelm Keppler of the German Foreign Office. Keppler was the State Secretary in charge of Indian affairs. "The only activity that Keppler carried out within the framework of the Foreign Office was the care of the Indian, Subhas Chandra Bose. Even this task was at (Foreign Minister Joachim) von Ribbentrop's order; it was not based on Kepplers' initiative .... The Indian Legion in Germany, composed of volunteer Indians, reached at most the strength of a regiment and was not used as a combat unit. About twelve volunteer Indians were trained in the Security Police Service. No violation of the Hague Rules of Land Warfare is apparent here."

In the footnote, Netaji was described as "an Indian Nationalist, opposing Ghandi (Mahatma Gandhi), who had declared his sympathy for Germany, where he founded the so-called Indian Legion to fight against Great Britain."

Phillip Stonehouse, Director of india and South Asia section in the Australian Foreign Ministry suggested that I consult the staff of Australian National Archives. They were most kind, as were the NARA (National Archives and Records Administration) staff in the US. The NARA informed me that in the declassified minutes and lists of war criminals concerning Chungking Sub-Commission, there was no mention of Subhas Bose. The Australian Archives in Melbourne and Canberra hinted at the same. But there was a piece of advice from a considerate reference officer. "While it is possible that we may hold the information that you are seeking, it is not our policy to conduct detailed searches for specific documents on behalf of researchers.

Unfortunately your topic is such that would require extensive research."

Given this background, the last word on the war criminal angle to Bose mystery cannot be claimed to have been pronounced. Hence it would be imperative that Mukherjee Commission in the course of its inquisitions, cleared three lingering postulations:

1. Khosla refused to ask the Government of India to state why on 12 January 1971 they had signed the "Convention on the Non-Applicability of Statutory Limitations to War Crimes and Crimes Against Humanity". This treaty, adopted by the United Nations on 26 November 1968, was "intended to ensure that persons responsible for war crimes and crimes against humanity will not escape prosecution merely because no legal case is brought against them within a specified period after the commission of the crime." The parties to the convention undertook "to adopt domestic measure for the extradition of persons responsible for these crimes."

   Bhagwanji's followers and others asked the reasons for India, an Allied nation, to ratify this treaty related to "war criminals" of WW II. They read in Government's ratifying the treaty their tacit admission that certain "war criminals" could still be at large in India decades after the war ended.

2. Khosla also refused to direct the Government of India to request the USA, the UK, the then USSR and France, all friendly to India, to state their knowledge/position on the issue.

3. Most importantly, Khosla rejected a request made on behalf of Bose family that the Prime Minister of India should personally confirm before the Commission that Netaji Subhas Chandra Bose's name was not included in any lists of war criminals.

No matter what we make of all this, most people would feel outraged by the whole debate. From the start, I had been incensed by the anti-climax Bhagwanji's followers were peddling for a man I knew had the heart of a lion and nerves of steel. There were several instances. Somewhere under the seas in 1941, 'Herr' Bose crouched in a U-2 submarine. He vented his anger before his attendant for the time he wasted with the Nazis even as the tide of war turned against his plans to free India. "Subhas just felt short of killing Hitler ... had he been allowed to stay longer in Germany he would surely have done so," Dr Welter Norden, his attendant, recalled years later. "See his courage, he was telling me, a Nazi, that he wanted to kill Hitler."[30]

Rangoon, 18 October 1944: Bullets rained down from sky. An enemy aircraft attacked Mingaladon parade ground and closed in where Bose conspicuously stood on a platform. Officers asked him to run for cover. He "stood at his post firm and determined." Then he came down slowly with a fearless poise. "I had made up my mind that if I had to die, I would rather like to die in this position than be caught while trying to take shelter,"[31] he told them.

"And you people have the temerity to suggest that he had turned into a paranoiac fugitive!" I asked Bhagwanji's followers. Why? For fear that he might be caught and deported as a war criminal?

"Oh, you've got it all wrong," I was told. Bhagwanji wasn't afraid for himself. He wasn't afraid of anything. He cared for India. He felt that his appearance would unleash havoc in the country. His people would have suffered. His emergence at any point of time would have put India into a spot. The new world order that had been in place since the end of the World War had no place for a relic of the Axis bloc. World powers would have sought action against him, which Indians would have never allowed. The world powers would still have pushed for it in their interests.

Until the last, Bhagwanji held on to the decision he had conveyed to a weeping Leela Roy in March 1963: "My coming out will not benefit anyone — the country, the people and myself. India is at a stage of infancy; she would not be able to stand the pressure of the world powers. Do not disclose my whereabouts to anyone, or else the nation will suffer. My coming out is not in India's interests." Mahakal put it more philosophically. "Dead man took nothing from you."

"He wanted nothing for himself ... he gave himself to India and he effaced himself away."

Notes:

1 No 1300/SE, CSDIC, Red Fort, Delhi 21 March 1946. Re-interrogatation of Major JK Bhonsle on "Last Plans of SC Bose."

2 *Reminiscences Discreet and Indiscreet* by TN Kaul. Page 150. Kaul was a former Foreign Secretary and Indian Ambassador to the USSR and United States.

3 File No C 551/4/64-JB-Misc.

4 From *Freedom at midnight* by Larry Collins and Dominique Lapiere. The book, possibly the best in its genre, was largely based on lengthy first-time interviews given by Lord Mountabtten to the authors.

5 **Netaji in Red China.** The *Nation.* 7 October 1949.

6 Ibid.

7 **Netaji in Red China.** The *Nation.* 7 October 1949.

8 Mukherjee Commission is said to have verified from *interpress* that this news was indeed flashed.

9 Extract of *Hindustan Standard* report **Story of meeting Netaji last February** dated 9 April 1956.

10 **Vietnam archives hold key to Netaji flight** by Prabha Jagannathan. The *Telegraph.* 26 September 1994.

11 No 1005/3/GSI(b). 14 September 1945. South East Asia Command and India Command Fortnightly Security Intelligence summary No 3. Transfer of Power, Volume VI.

12 Extracted from the record of Jagdish Kodesia's cross-examination before Khosla Commission on 1 March 1971.

13 Shivprasad Nag has passed away, but his son deposed before Mukherjee Commission.

14 *The Dalai Lama* by Lowell Thomas Jr. Page 83.

15 Dharmawara died at age 110 in California in 1999.

16 Copy of an OSS/CIA dossier on Subhas Bose was sent by Friends of India Society International, California chapter, to Indian newspapers in 1994.

17 PM File No. 2(64) 56-66 PM Volume II. Page-89/A. "Letter dated 28-8-62 from Prof Atul Sen to Shri Nehru saying that NETAJI is alive and war criminal."

18 PM File No. 2(64) 56-66 PM Volume II. Page-90/A. "Reply of Shri Nehru to Prof Atul Sen." No. 1446-PMH/62. August 31, 1962.

19 *Hindustan Standard* report **Subhas said to be alive.** 30 August 1945.

20 SACSEA report dated 7 March 1946 on the Interrogation of Colonel Yano Muraji.

21 Extracted from Volume V of the *Transfer of Power.* Page 1297.

22 *Transfer of Power.* Volume VI. Page 47.

23 Ibid. Page 405.

24 The *Tribune* article **Did Netaji actually die in 1945?** by VN Datta. 19 August 2001.

25 Extract of *Hindustan Standard* report **Story of meeting Netaji last** February dated 9 April 1956.

26 The *Times of India* report **Netaji not war criminal, says Khosla.** 25 December 1970.

27 Netaji Inquiry Commission Report. Page 56.

28 Ibid. Page 57.

29 Ibid. Pages 57, 58.

30 UNI story **Netaji wanted to kill Hitler, says ex-Nazi.** 17 February 2002.

31 *India's Struggle for Freedom* by Major General AC Chatterji. Page 241.

Index